QUEEN OF THE EXILED

By G. L. Preston

Queen of the Exiled: Book 2 in the Stag & Hollow chronicles by G.L Preston

Disclaimer: This is a work of fiction. Names, characters, business', events and incidents are the products of the author's imagination. Any resemblance to actual persons, living or dead, or actual events is purely coincidental.

Permission requests can be sent to gemlpreston@gmail.com.
Editing by Emma O'Connell
https://www.emmasedit.com
Book cover by G.L.Preston
Paperback: 978-1-3999-2849-6
ASIN: B0C9N591FM

Author Note

Queen of the Exiled is an epic romantic fantasy. Whilst enjoyable, the story does include some elements that might not be suitable for some readers. Mentioned death/illness of a parent/child, *reference* to homophobic/transphobic/racist views, sexual scenes, alcohol use, animal deaths, discussion of SA, dismemberment, war and murder are present in this novel. Readers who may be sensitive to these elements, please take note.

Pronunciation Guide

CHARACTERS

Eltanin: El-ta-NIN
Althea: Al-thee-AH
Dracho: Dr-AY-co
Antares: An-TA-rez
Jeshwa: Jeh-SH-wuh
Thuban: Th-OO-ban
Bastion: Bas-tea-UN
Vyn: V-IN
Eliana: Eh-lee-ah-NUH
Morgwn: Mor-GUN
Connaught: Con-UH
Teyrnon: TEY-air-nun
Roux: R-OO
Sizwe: Siz-WAY
Bisa: Bee-SAH
Azande: Ah-ZAN-day
Kanu: CAN-oo
Jareth: JAH-reth
Jakard: Jah-CARD
Engel: ENG-el
Cubra: COO-bra
Cirdan: Sir-DAN
Jandar: YAN-dar

PLACES

Tenebris: Ten-eh-BRIS
Mythbrook: Myth-BROOK
Chaepstow: CHEP-stow
Laugharne: LAF-arn
Meridium: Meh-rid-EE-um
Stillmere: Still-MEER
Aion: Eye-ON
Volente: Vol-en-TAY
Cefidan: KEH-fi-dan
Coed: C-OID

OTHER

Edjer: ED-jah
Pistwyll: Pis-TUL
Gwdhŵ: Good-WHO
Purdue: Per-DOO
Notherworld: Nuh-THUH-world
Ryu: RI-yoo

RUVALON
THE SCIRES
CRYSTALWOOD
LALOW OCEAN
LAUGHARNE
THE SILENT ROAD
STILLMERE
TOUFORT
MADAIN
N
S
W
E

S
ADREF
MYTHBROOK
CHAEPSTOW
ORCROFT
CEFIDAN
COED
ASAPH
SOLVA BAY
VILDSPIRE DUNES
TEMPLE OF THE HOLLOW
THE STILL SEA
UM
RHUTHUN
VILDSPIRE DUNES
FALLSTONE
CAREW
VOLENTE
THE MARSHES
FARCROSS
AION
AKRAYA
ESHMNOR

To all the incredible women I've met, and the ones I haven't.

The survivors and the fighters who are afraid to go after what they want, and do so anyway.

To those who do not break.

Prince of the Ancients:

A summary

Dragon shifter Dracho Celesta's home is in danger from the one place he should never go - the mortal realm.

Draconi have not ventured there since the ending of the war – the Tain - twelve years prior. It surprises the young prince when his father, the Emperor of Tenebris, allows him to travel south to find answers about devastation that is plaguing the continent and drawing nearer to his home. It is vital he hides his identity, keeping to his human form as he and his fierce companion, Antares, flee the sheltered confines of palace life and navigate through the mortal lands.

They meet a trio of humans whose interests align with their own, deciding to share information and travel together to find answers. Eli is the brazen but loyal woman who leads the group, and she introduces Dracho and Antares to some of the towns of the continent. They soon discover a survivor of a recent attack, who informs them of some magical element to the chaos, leading the crew to believe mages may be involved.

Knowing of a mage that resides within Eli's home city - Meridium – they arrive there, and Dracho soon discovers that Eli is royalty. A princess who lives with troubled memories that made her flee her palace and comfortable existence. Dracho meets her father, King Cervidae, and is unnerved at rumours which have suggested his own kind are the cause of the attacks throughout the land.

They venture to the woman's homeland, Aion, meeting Chief Bisa and her fascinating daughters, Roux and Azande. They discover that the cause of the escalating destruction is an ancient entity that has risen – the Hollow. After learning from the mages about a temple which holds knowledge of such a creature, they are horrified when they come up against the Hollow themselves.

Arrogant in his own abilities, Dracho attempts to fight the Hollow, but is thwarted. Eliana saves his life, and the creature takes out his wrath upon Aion, where Azande is killed. Roux succumbs to her grief and desperation for revenge at her sister's death, her own magic corrupting her and creating a new threat to the land. Dracho and Eliana help her through a confrontation with her spiritual ancestors, where they aid her to overcome her grief, and deem her worthy of greater powers. Powers that will help this newfound family on their journey.

They discover Roux's uncle may be involved, and plan to attend a ball in the kingdom of Stillmere where the mage will be. On the way there, Eliana's life is suddenly at stake and Drachos only option to save her is to reveal his dragon form before her, and his identity as the prince of Tenebris. After the initial shock, Eliana takes it surprisingly well, and Dracho believes it has to do with secrets she is keeping herself.

They do not find any trace of the Hollow surrounding Roux's uncle, and so the only option they have left is to discuss the magic with Dracho's father – Emperor of Tenebris.

Through their journey their relationship has developed, and Eliana and Dracho become intimate before they cross the boundary of Dracho's land.

Once the group arrive in Tenebris, they rush to the palace, where they find his father impaled in his own throne, by the very weapon the Hollow defeated Dracho with. Not only that, but the sigil of Eliana's father, King Cervidae, is pinned to his chest.

In his grief, Dracho's inner beast takes over, demanding Eliana and her crew be seized. Without evidence, he later decides to free them, banishing from them from Tenebris – but not before Eliana threatens revenge if he returns to the mortal realm.

Drachos coronation as new emperor arrives, and so with it the merging of him and his dragon. During the ceremony, the combination of his grief and an influx of new magic changes him forever, and to the gathered crowds he swears to return south, to see Eliana again and seek retribution against those who murdered his father.

Now their story continues...

Chapter 1

His expression was contorted into one of unrelenting pain, eyes rolled back as his mouth opened wide in a silent scream.

My breath caught as I blinked... and his face returned to normal.

He laughed, the sound bright and playful. "Come on, Eliana! You can do better than that!"

My face was red from the effort of gripping the handle of the short sword, refusing to let it drop. It was a difficult feat for my young, untrained arms, and my scrawny muscles screamed in protest.

"I am trying!" I insisted, refusing to let fall the tears that pricked at the corner of my eyes.

The edges of his mouth kicked up in an amused smirk; the gravel crunched under his feet as he stepped closer to me, swiping hair out of his eyes. "You're clearly not trying hard enough, little doe."

With heavy arms, I swung the sword out in front of me, groaning as he jumped out of the way, laughing once more.

"It's a good thing that's blunt, or you would have torn my shirt!"

"You don't fight fair!" I bared my teeth at him.

He pointed his sword at me with one hand, making it look as easy as holding a twig. "Ah-ah. Stop that."

My jaw clenched shut. I pouted.

Bright green eyes scanned the arena, checking if anyone was nearby. "An enemy would not fight fair, little sister, so you must not fight fair. You must look for any opportunity, or moment of distraction, to strike. Remember, little doe... you do not break."

I nodded as my hands dropped, the relief in my arms instant. I dumped the training sword by my feet, huffing out my frustration. "Isn't there something else I can try? Like a dagger?" His own ornate dagger, strapped to his thigh, drew my eyes.

He stabbed the end of his blade into the soft ground then knelt beside me, reaching to tuck a strand of hair behind my ear with a smile. "Once you learn to master a sword, I'll teach you how to use a dagger in close combat."

My lips stretched into a grin. "You promise?"

He nodded. "Maybe Father will let me get you a blade of your own."

I jumped up and down on the spot before throwing my arms around his neck. "You're the best brother ever! Thanks, Morgwn!"

His laugh tickled my shoulder. "No worries, little doe. Now, go clean up before dinner. Or Mother will have both our heads."

I kissed his rough cheek quickly before running back to the palace, ducking under a maid's arms as she exited with the freshly cleaned laundry. Excitement swelled in my chest as I ran to my room. I couldn't wait to fight with a dagger just like my brother's.

I entered my room, the door slamming shut behind me, and my smile fell. There was someone in here.

A foul smell reached my nostrils. I spun around, and someone knocked me from my feet. My back hit the floor, winding me.

Not someone. Two strange men.

Suddenly their hands were on my legs, pulling me towards them. The spark of fear in my belly turned into bursts of adrenaline as I kicked out. But the room began to shrink, the walls closing in as the cream-painted walls turned to grey stone—into a cramped, cold, windowless cell where just the men and I remained.

The man pulling at me unsheathed a short, claw-shaped knife from his jacket, before dragging it along my thigh. I kicked out, aiming for his face, as a searing pain shot up my leg. Before I blacked out, I swore I could see a pair of icy blue eyes staring at me from the shadows.

I groaned as I came to. My face was clammy.

The heat of the dream stuck to my skin, sticky with the sweat and tears that my nightmares regularly brought me. Nightmares that had been happening more frequently over the past several months. There was no light when my eyes opened, no glimmer of morning coming from behind my curtains.

My mouth curled in disgust as I wiped a hand across my brow. Keeping perfectly still for a moment, I steadied my heavy breaths. My eyes skipped around my room, ensuring I was alone.

The sound of a secret door creaking on the far wall pulled my gaze towards it.

I exhaled shakily. "You can come in, Bas."

His cheeks reddened as his sheepish face appeared from the hidden passage behind the floor-length mirror. "Heh, sorry, E. Old habits die hard."

I gave him a small smile. Now we were back in Meridium, it seemed redundant for anyone to call me Eli; there was no one to hide my identity from.

"Did I wake you?" My stomach clenched as the guilt ate away at me.

Bas shook his head, making his way over to climb into the bed next to me. Settling down, he held open his arms.

Scooting over, I melted into them, enjoying the slight coolness to his skin. Bas had been sleeping in my brother's old room for years now. It didn't matter that he denied it—I knew it was for my benefit that he stayed. He might have been the joker of the group, and forever inappropriate, but his saving grace had always been his caring nature... along with his large arms and broad chest, which made for the best hugs.

Even if my body told me the arms were all wrong. That it was the wrong person embracing me.

"Do you wanna talk about it?" His soft tone wrenched me from my thoughts, his concern washing over me like a soothing wave.

I didn't.

But I would. I had learned a long time ago that bottling up my nightmares made them worse. My tongue darted out to moisten my lips, and I took a deep breath.

"It's mostly the same as it's always been. They get into my room..."

His brow furrowed but he stayed silent.

"Only now, I'm not in my room. It turns into a cold cell, a dungeon with no way out. And no secret doors where someone can save me."

Bas's jaw clenched, his gaze turning away from me as he swallowed the vitriol he no doubt wanted to spill about the person who was responsible for how my nightmares had changed. I kept reminding myself that it was completely irrational, that we had only been in those cells for a few hours... but apparently, that hadn't mattered to my subconscious. Now it deemed it appropriate to torment me by combining my past traumas with my fears and recent memories.

Not long after we had returned from Tenebris, I'd told Vyn and Bas that I no longer wanted to hear *his* name. We were not to speak of him. As far as I was concerned, he was gone. It was to be like he had never existed...

But sometimes my mind wandered, and my body remembered the feeling of him.

Bas cleared his throat. "They're happening more often now, huh?"

I chewed my cheek. "Do you keep an eye on me every night?"

His tone was serious. "Most nights." His arms tightened around me.

A guilty huff escaped my lips. "You don't have to do that, Bas."

"Yes I do, E."

I pulled away to look at him.

A half-smile tugged at his lips as he tucked a strand of hair behind my ear. "You're not the only one who dreams of what happened."

He didn't have to say anything else. Bas had witnessed what had happened all those years ago, when those men broke into my room. He had saved my life by taking another's—the first life he had ever taken. It had been a long time before he'd come to terms with the blood he saw on his hands, even if his actions had been justified.

Humming contentedly, I settled back in his arms and hoped sleep might visit us both soon. I let out a long sigh. "I'm not looking forward to the ball."

Bas's arms tightened around me. "I know."

The upcoming event was to celebrate the anniversary of the end of the Tain—a brutal war that had waged across the continent. It was also the anniversary of my mother's and brother's deaths.

The ball alternated every year between Meridium and Stillmere. I had been away for the previous two due to my... *escapades* with Bas and Vyn, and I couldn't say I had missed it. But this year... Meridium would have the honour of hosting.

And the sinking feeling I had in my gut told me something terrible was going to happen.

My father was a pragmatic, likeable man. He had a friendly nature that pulled everybody in; even if he was the King of Meridium, he was still approachable. It was one of the reasons my mother had fallen in love with him.

Before the war, I used to curl up on one of the chairs in the dining hall after dinner, where Morgwn and I would watch as he swung Mother around in a dance without music. We all revelled in the smile that used to brighten her face at his teasing.

Mother would laugh before dancing with Morgwn, whilst I danced with Father—and I always respected him for spending time with his family to put a smile on our faces. For how he was strong and kind, someone who knew when to put duty and work aside.

There had been no silent dances since they had passed. And even though he still smiled at guests and his kind nature remained, despite his grief, his eyes no longer creased in the corners as much as they used to. Now he was quieter, more thoughtful.

Now, it was difficult to *know* him.

I knew that was because of me. My absence over the past couple of years had pushed us further apart. Even though I had been home since returning from Tenebris, that rift remained, making it difficult for me to show even a glimpse of openness. It was why I had never shared what happened in Tenebris. I'd told Father about our journey and the Hollow, but I hadn't divulged everything... especially not about *him*. Only Vyn and Bas knew about that.

But I had a funny feeling it was going to come up at some point, and soon.

"Can't we say no to hosting it this year?" I knew I sounded like a petulant child, but I couldn't face the disgusting display of niceties anymore. Not after what had happened six months ago. Seeing King Jareth Proditor's son, Jak, would also be an inconvenience—especially if he came with his fiancé, Illyra.

A moment of silence passed.

"You know it's our turn, Eliana."

I crossed my arms. "You'd think they would realise it's not exactly a *celebratory* event for us."

Father's gaze was piercing, making me look away. He knew it also reminded me of what had happened the night before the Tain's ending, when those men had broken in and taken away all my peace.

My eyes found the sword that hung upon the wall behind his desk. A hilt wrapped in extravagant, smooth, jade-green leather held the long blade made of silver steel with thin sparkling lines. The blade had a broad, curled cross-guard, adding just enough weight to make sure it sat firmly in the owner's hand and offered protection. A shining emerald, just like the one in my dagger, was embedded in the hilt's top. The sword of Meridium, Antur.

The king's sword. My father's sword.

It would be mine, one day.

Chair legs scuffed on the floor as he pushed himself to his feet, making his way over to me to gently grip my arms. "My Eliana, to us it will always be a time of great loss. But remember, to the people, it's a day to remember *everyone*, and celebrate the end of that awful war. When I'm gone it'll be up to you to continue the tradition."

Chastened, I nodded begrudgingly, tipping my head forward to rest upon his chest as his arms wrapped around me. It still felt odd to me to have him so close by all the time. But since returning to Meridium, I had found no reason to leave. After the emperor's death in Tenebris and the attack on Cefidan, no one had seen or heard from the Hollow. No further attacks had happened, and no more towns had been ravaged.

It was as if the Hollow had just disappeared. While it was a relief that no other citizens of Ruvalon had lost their lives to its destruction, I couldn't help but feel uneasily that it wasn't over.

My being back in Meridium made Father happy. He thought it meant I would not be running into danger, and despite the ache I felt at returning with no answers and no culprit, I wouldn't go vanishing again to find a ghost. Perhaps my father felt that I had grown more comfortable here now. That the memories of the past had abated. But he didn't know about the new dreams that tormented me, and I was determined to keep it that way.

I coughed lightly, clearing my throat. "At the very least, can we forget to invite Illyra?" The request was not even remotely a joke.

I felt the vibration of Father's throat as he laughed. "You'll be glad to know she won't be attending. She and Jakard are doing an engagement tour amongst the Southern lords and ladies that aren't coming to the ball."

"Oh, thank the Goddess. I mean..." I shrugged within the safety of my father's arms, suddenly grateful they had left their tour so late. "Shame."

Father moved, holding me at arm's length, a knowing smile on his face. "I know you dislike them, but I've commissioned you a new dress. Just... *try* to enjoy yourself. Everything will be fine."

After our talk, I wandered down to the crypt below my mother's statue, seeking counsel I knew I could never receive. I placed a hand beside the urn that contained her life dust, the ledge of her plinth raised slightly higher than the others around.

"I miss you," I whispered.

Every day in the palace was a reminder she wasn't there. Seeing her portraits—lifeless, albeit beautiful—reminded me I would never look upon her true smile again. Would never feel the touch of her soft fingers as she stroked my hair as I tried to fall asleep. How I wished we had a monument to celebrate my brother, Morgwn. There was a stone memorial in the palace's private gardens, a small tribute for him, but not his remains. His body had never been found or returned to Meridium, having been lost in the blast of magick during the Tain. An empty urn sat in Morgwn's tomb. It was where my father would go when he died—and so would I.

When I'd been younger, not long after the Tain, I used to pray to the Goddess that Morgwn's body would be found. My prayers were never answered; after all, our Goddess was a mere legend at this point—one without any tangible following anymore. A being whose tales had been lost to time. The oldest legend said that she had been mortal and had lovingly sacrificed her life during a time of great peril to protect Ruvalon. It had earned her a place amongst the Gods of old, and in the hearts of many—showing that even those without great power can do great things.

When I'd started my journey to find answers surrounding the Hollow—long before I met our guests from Tenebris—I had felt a kinship with the Goddess's story. Despite the fear that coursed through my veins at the thought of ruling one day, I would never flee in the face of saving my people. My father knew that, which was why he had banned me from going... until I'd taken matters into my own hands and fled the city.

I could never prevent the grin that rose on my face when I thought of that night. I had purposely chosen a night that Connaught had off, knowing that if he had caught me—had gotten wind of my plan—he would have locked me up in my room and guarded it day and night. I remembered how Bas and Vyn had known without needing to be told that we were leaving, and how ready they'd been to accompany me to Laugharne—mostly so they could grab a pint at the Griffin, of course.

Realising that night had been over two years ago was a sobering thought. It made me wonder how much more could change over another couple of years.

Chapter 2

I knew it was going to be a bad day if I felt like stabbing someone first thing in the morning. Today that honour went to my best friends. They had clearly never realised how much of a difference their presence made to my mood. They usually always tried to do more for me, despite my protests—which was why I felt so put out this morning when they refused.

"Are you *sure* you don't want to come?" I whined.

Vyn snorted, giving me a long look from his sharp, hooded eyes. "I'm *absolutely* sure. Besides, Bas has invited me to his parents' house for his little brother's birthday."

I spun to face Bas, glaring at him in mock betrayal. He paused in the middle of chewing some bacon.

We sat at one of the long tables in the belly of the palace's kitchens as staff strolled about behind us. It was the warmest and most welcoming room in the entire castle, and I always savoured the aromas that floated about, the piles of fresh breads tempting me from across the room. A large stove was housed in an alcove on the back wall, the top covered in pans of various sizes and shapes. Bas was lucky it had been Marie he'd encountered when he strolled in, hoping for a plate stacked with breakfast. Eiram would have never allowed him in.

Eiram and Marie, nymph twins born under a full moon, ran the kitchens, and considering that they were almost mirrors of each other, they couldn't have been more different. If I wanted to sneak a few fresh cakes before lunch, I could always rely on Marie to fill my arms before giving me a squeeze of my cheek. Eiram would never allow me to take food from the kitchen before it was served—but if I sneaked down at night for hot cocoa, he would make it for me, regaling me with tales of their younger days cooking with their mother.

The kitchen was even busier than normal. Mountains of fresh fruit, vegetables and meats had arrived at the palace kitchens early, and a multitude of staff had descended upon it, preparing it for the evening. The weeks leading up to the ball had been full of such preparation; every room in the guest wing had been cleaned thoroughly, and the stables prepared for the inundation of horses we'd receive from the arriving carriages.

My job was simply to be ready and look pretty. And behave accordingly—something I had been avoiding most vigorously since my maid Beatrice had come looking for me. I'd sneaked out the passage between Bas's room and mine before she could notice I was there.

"What?" Bas asked. "I knew there was no point in asking you. Daddy Cervidae would never let you miss the ball."

"But you two can?" I stole a slice of the crisp bacon from his plate.

"Hey!" Bas swallowed, rubbing the back of his head. The braided rows of dark hair he used to have were now gone, replaced by waves. "You know it's killing me not being there to support you. Vyn too. But it's Jonah's thirteenth birthday. The King allowed my dad to skip it 'cause he can officially start training with the guards now. It's a big thing."

I nodded. When boys of Meridium turned thirteen, they were permitted to start training with the guards in the palace arena. It didn't matter their station; anyone was given the opportunity to better themselves and protect their city. There weren't as many girls who opted in, but once they were fifteen, they could also join if they chose to. Only a small group had, but they were some of the fiercest soldiers Meridium had ever seen. Having trained with the royal guards and some of the soldiers from the city's army, I knew how disciplined and loyal our men and women were. Many considered it the biggest possible honour to represent the city.

I pouted at Vyn, and he shook his head as he pointed his fork at me. "No. No, don't give me those doe eyes. I am not going. You know I can't stand all the pomp and circumstance. The *elites,* looking down their noses at me."

As half-djinn, Vyn had always been looked down upon by some in noble society. Only a minority, but it was enough to leave its mark.

I leaned my elbow on the table, resting my head on my fist as I chewed my bacon. "I know. I just..."

He looked sympathetically at me and I turned away, watching as Bas continued to shovel food into his mouth.

Vyn put his hand on mine. "I *know,* Eliana. But it's one night. One night of pretending to be the spoiled princess, and then you can go back to kicking our arses in training."

I looked up, appreciated the small smile he sent my way, and smiled back. As if he could tell what else anxiously swirled in my gut, his eyes narrowed. "Is there something else bothering you?"

Bas stopped chewing at that, looking at us both in confusion.

Vyn had always been the more empathetic one. Despite Bas's more teddy-bear qualities, Vyn somehow always noticed when something was wrong. It was one of the reasons we had become so close to begin with. After the war had ended, I would escape the confines of my palace walls by exploring the city. Connaught used to spend hours looking for me, feeling more like my babysitter instead of one of the royal guards. It had annoyed my father more than worried him; he was never very concerned over me dressing as a commoner and wandering the city streets, but ever since the attack on me in the palace, the streets had felt a little more dangerous.

One day, when I was wandering past one of the temples to the Goddess, I'd spotted a brilliant blonde head of hair being pushed around by a few boys larger than him. When I'd physically 'reprimanded' them and dragged the boy away, his yellow eyes had stared at me in awe.

I'd seen immediately that we had a kinship, something in common. *Loneliness.*

Unable to truly understand it, back then, but feeling how my heart squeezed at seeing my own pain reflected in his eyes, I'd held out my hand... and he had taken it with no hesitation.

Father had been most surprised when I had appeared in his study and demanded Vyn be given a room. Nevertheless, he'd allowed Vyn to stay with us—and he'd never left.

Over the years, he'd grown close to Bas and me. Trained with us, as he learned to hone his wind-like powers. Worked hard on not resenting them once he had learned of his heritage.

He'd wandered with me through the streets, trained with Sizwe, and got to know the people. He'd watched how I grew to love them—seen that despite all my loss, I gave my all into getting to know my people. Those I would rule in the future, even if the idea of ruling terrified me.

It wasn't intentional; it was never a goal I made, to put myself out there. Quite simply, it helped me avoid memories—both bad and good—inside the palace.

Vyn watched me grow, watched me navigate a relationship when a young Stillmerean Prince attempted to sweep me off my feet, and held my hand after I had made my first kill. Not in combat or revenge, but to give mercy to a young man who had been gravely injured by a cart at one of Meridium's crowded gates. His sandy-brown hair had been caked with blood; his leg broken from where the cart had fallen. A wooden shaft of the cart had snapped and impaled him through his chest. His mother had arrived in time, but he had been in so much pain, and the woman had begged for someone to ease his suffering.

His name had been Luka.

It always amazed me to remember how some of the mercenaries around that day had simply watched. I would never forget the woman's deep blue eyes as she caught mine in the crowd and mouthed the word, *please*.

There had been no hesitation in my decision as I stepped forward, despite Vyn's concern. And when my dagger had eased the poor man's pain, his mother had taken my hand, shaking it repeatedly in both of hers as she cried her thank yous.

That's when I began to take a true interest in what would be my kingdom. After several meetings with Father and Connaught, a major renovation took place around the rise of the city. Several gates were added, and the city was segregated, each area focusing on one purpose. The crowds entering the castle eased, with only the trading gate busy during the day. It made the city more functional and ensured no more accidents like that happened again.

Vyn and Bas had been there through it all, and it was something I would always be grateful for.

Shaking my head, I pulled my hand free of Vyn's to pat him softly. "No, not at all... I'm just not looking forward to the pomp. Like you said."

He hummed but nodded, and Bas returned to his meal.

Swallowing hard, I stood. "Well. I guess I'll see you guys tomorrow?"

Bas nodded. "You can fill us in on how *fun* your night was."

Vyn grinned; I rolled my eyes. "Oh, please. I'm sure there'll be nothing to tell." I smiled at one of the wood nymph members of staff, Kael, as I left, noting a blush rise on his cheeks.

I would usually visit Sizwe in the library, but she was away visiting Aion. It had been thirteen years since Sizwe had last seen her homeland, having chosen to stay in Meridium with me and my father after my mother had died. It had been a bit of a shock, finding out the year prior that she was none other than a sister to the Chief Mage of Aion—the mages' homeland. Had it not been essential to our journey to find out, I didn't believe she ever would have told me, opting to spend the rest of her days keeping a vow made to my mother: to help raise and train me.

I couldn't imagine the weight of the sacrifice that Sizwe had made to leave Home Tree, but I was glad that she was starting to visit. It was for that reason that she and her sister, Chief Mage of Aion, Bisa, would not attend the ball, choosing instead to honour the loss of their fellow mages in a ceremony upon the beaches of Aion. Having been welcomed into their community many months ago, I knew it would be a beautiful experience for them all. A ball of emotion tightened my throat as I thought over the experiences I had there... of the Hollow's attack that had torn through the Aioni, and those we had laid to rest after. Of Azande, youngest daughter of the chief mage, who had unfortunately fallen victim to the Hollow. That sweet young girl who had so quickly infiltrated all our hearts with her happy nature and curiosity.

Whose life had been taken far too early.

I could only think of those days for a few short moments before panic gripped my chest, a physical reminder of the guilt I held deep down for the attack on Aion. Our actions the day before, when *he* had fought the Hollow and I'd tried to stop him, may have enticed the Hollow to attack Azande's home.

My mind went to Roux, her older sister, and stuttered. She had accompanied us on our journey; we had been through so much together, and I hadn't seen her since she had decided to stay in Tenebris. I had no idea where she was—whether she had returned to Aion, or if she was still with...

I pushed away the painful thoughts from my head as I reached my bedchamber. Beatrice stood just beyond the door, a stern look on her face.

"And *where* exactly have you been, young lady?" she demanded, and I gave my first genuine smile of the day.

Early that evening, my eyes found Beatrice in the mirror, humming a tune to herself as she braided my hair. Beatrice had been my mother's maid when she was alive. Now she was mine. She was the only person I allowed to touch my face and hair—besides her daughter, Milly. They were the most loyal staff we had at the palace, and I trusted them with my life.

She had twisted most of my hair into a bun, pinning it at the back of my neck, before bringing my two signature braids from the front and wrapping them around the side of my head, securing them tightly around the bun.

Taking a deep breath, I examined my reflection. The midnight chiffon dress fell in delicate waves; I'd requested one alteration—a slit running up my unmarked thigh on the one side. Out of habit and comfort, I'd strapped my dagger to my leg; enough layers would shift to hide it from view unless I moved around too much.

Anyway, I had no intention of joining the dancing that was in full swing by the time I descended the steps and entered the ballroom.

I had already warned my father that I would be very cross if he or Connaught should bully me into a dance. It was bad enough that, out of respect, I would have to with any lords who asked—which was precisely why I was hovering around the outskirts of the room.

It looked beautiful. Thick emerald drapes hung over the windows, and tiered crystal chandeliers glittered in the soft, warm light. Golden bubbles rose in the flutes of expensive champagne being served; guests floated about in pleasant conversation with one another. Round dining tables were pushed back towards the walls, leaving a large enough space through the length of the room for dancing as a quartet played a variety of music from the far end, near my father's noble throne made of silver. It was currently empty.

Connaught spotted me from the other side of the room, where he was conversing with one of the guards. He did a double take, his eyes widening slightly, before raising his hand in a hesitant wave. Allowing my eyes to roam over him and the tailored fit of his full captain's dress uniform, I raised a thumb to acknowledge that I approved. He pursed his lips, evidently not amused.

I glided through the guests, looking for my father, and moving in the opposite direction when I spotted King Proditor and his entourage of guards. The man's face looked severe as his narrowed eyes scanned the dance floor. A rush of relief ran through me; Jak and Illyra were not in attendance.

That relief guttered when I remembered that Demetria, Lady of Laugharne and one of my dearest friends, was unable to attend due to a large shipment of tradable goods coming into her port the next morning. The imports had been arranged by her and my father to bring in aid for the northern towns who had suffered from the Hollow's attacks. Its devastation of key farming villages had caused the supply of crops to dwindle, so Father had called in favours elsewhere. Being liked and respected had its perks; many had come to our aid to supply the towns. With the shipment, escorted by some of Laugharne's finest, there would be plenty of grain for all.

Despite her good reason for being absent, I missed Demer greatly, and wouldn't likely see her for another few weeks until my birthday. I'd have to settle for Connaught and my father instead.

I tipped my head in welcome to those who offered their greetings, engaging in small talk but not lingering long enough to have a deep conversation. Outfits in various colour were scattered around the room, cutting across my view of the dancing as partners moved together gracefully to an uplifting song. It was certainly a joyous occasion, laughter ringing out amongst the guests as champagne flowed. A sharp contrast to the grief that was a heavy burden on my shoulders.

And I couldn't shake the tense feeling that had settled within my gut. Perhaps it was just the punch of sorrow I had felt since this morning, the bitterness that tinged my veins at everyone dancing merrily as I grieved. Still grieved, so many years later. But there was something else... I could feel it in my spine—that something was on the verge of happening.

My feet carried me forward to another spot on the edge of the dancefloor. It was a pull, as if some invisible rope had wrapped around my chest and yanked me in a different direction. I couldn't explain it. Closing my eyes and honing in on my senses, I focused on the sounds around me, trying to decipher if anything was amiss. That was when a familiar charge shot through my body, brushing over my skin like a loving whisper.

One I had not felt for months.

My eyes snapped open, glaring furiously around the ballroom, through the moving throng of dancers on the main floor. *Nothing*.

A couple twirled from their position into the next rise of the music. Icy blue eyes met mine.

My breath hitched as I moved my head to the side, trying to catch them again around the dancers. But they had disappeared, and my relief was palpable. *Wrong hair, anyway*.

Still, my senses were now on high alert, instinct telling me my mind wasn't playing tricks on me. I set off to find that gaze. Moving around the edge of the dance floor, politely declining the hands of lords asking to dance, I followed that pull to the dim, empty hallway that led down to the kitchens.

My heels clicked loudly on the floor as the noise from the main hall faded.

The hall was empty, low lighting flickering in the sconces between each darkened alcove. I still couldn't shake the uneasiness in my gut—but it now manifested into another unsettling feeling.

I am being watched.

A small breeze raised goosebumps on my skin, and I felt the presence behind me more than heard it as it sneaked up on me. Before they could touch me I had unsheathed my dagger from my thigh, twisting to shove the person into the nearest alcove. An almost forgotten sensation ran through my arm as I pressed it against a hard chest.

My breath stuttered as I became aware of the height of the person under my blade, as I felt the pressure on the balls of my feet from having to tip myself upwards, even in my heels. The scent of citrus and something akin to a campfire surrounded me as I looked up—past the edge of my blade that pressed against his throat, and into the silver-lined blue eyes that had invaded my dreams.

A plethora of emotions assaulted me as his name finally slipped past my lips. "*Dracho.*"

I swallowed as the silver in his eyes seemed to glow. His full lips turned up into a triumphant smirk.

"Hello, Princess."

Chapter 3

I released the shaky breath I'd been holding. My eyes travelled over him, noting the changes, but in denial that he was here. In the flesh, under my blade—after I'd promised him I would make him suffer if he ever stepped south again! I resisted the urge to run my hands over him and determine if he was an apparition. The arm holding my dagger tensed.

He arched one perfect brow as if sensing where my thoughts had gone. "Ah, ah, Princess. You might want to hold off from harming me."

Words still failed me. My chest constricted as I took in his painfully beautiful face, wondering how the angles of his jaw appeared sharper than when I'd last seen him. The passage of time since I had last seen him had only ensured my memories and nightmares did his appearance no justice.

Now, he was *more*. Any boyish features that had been present before were long gone. Now he was graced with a frustratingly, perfectly straight nose, the rise of sculpted cheekbones, and full lips. Lips that had once infuriated me with his cocky words... that had caressed and travelled their way over my body.

My face heated at the thought, until I realised those lips were still grinning at me. My nostrils flared at the audacity of the man before me, but I was caught off guard when a strand of hair fell across his eyes, the end resting softly against his cheek.

I was aware that I was staring at him, but the lack of silver shocked me. His hair was now black, although flecked with silver so that it looked like a canvas of the night sky.

His bright eyes lowered playfully as he caught mine. Shaking myself from my stupor, I pressed closer to him, digging the blade deeper against the flesh of his throat. If he had been a mortal man, the blade would have cut his skin by now.

"What the fuck are *you* doing here?" I spoke between my teeth, hearing a chill in my voice I hadn't thought I was capable of.

My pulse quickened as his grin grew wider, and his eyes twinkled. "Exchanging filthy words already, Princess? You know how that excites me."

I blinked a few times at the blatant meaning behind his words, hot rage coursing through my veins at him calling me that. The worst thing was, he knew he was making me angrier. Something else that had changed—his arrogance had increased. Before, he had been cheeky; now he was bold. And the tenor of his voice was deeper, smokier.

"Don't make me ask again," I told him, a bead of sweat trailing down the back of my neck.

"On the contrary, what are *you* doing here?" His hand plucked at a shorter strand of my hair that had come free, twirling it between his thumb and forefinger. I noticed the ring he was wearing: a silver signet ring with a black stone, a symbol of a dragon embossed onto it—his royal sigil. "Not that I'm complaining..." His eyes slowly travelled over me, pausing at the expanse of skin that showed above my cleavage, and I sucked in a breath. "But we both know this 'pampered princess' look isn't you."

"You don't know me," I spat at him.

The look he gave me made my spine straighten, painfully so.

"We both know that's not true, don't we?" He leaned forward, pressing his neck against my blade, his eyes sparkling with mischief. "In fact, I think I *know* you rather well." His smile flashed as he bit down on his bottom lip.

Twisting the blade, I pressed the sharp tip of it hard into the skin of his throat, drawing a single drop of blood and eliciting a hiss from between his perfectly white teeth. His eyes closed. When they opened to show pure silver, the vertical slits of his dragon took me in with a hint of confusion, which changed to cold fury. I hadn't realised how silver could look like a raging fire until then. The dangerous look in his eyes almost made me look away.

"You know that tiny blade won't do much..."

It was true; the tiny cut healed almost instantly. I was surprised I had marked him at all.

"But I shouldn't have to remind you that attempting to murder the emperor would be classed as treason." His eyes narrowed, his head tipping forward as his voice dropped to a whisper. "But maybe it runs in the family?"

My hand twitched as dread landed in my stomach, almost making my knees buckle. In my shock at seeing him, I had forgotten, just for one moment.

He had taken the crown... and he was now *emperor*, meaning that he had merged with his dragon. The man before me was no longer the Dracho I had known, but someone else entirely. I swallowed thickly, ridding myself of that sliver of fear that lurked in my veins, as his infuriating mouth turned up at the edges. My anger rose.

"It's not murder if I gave you forewarning."

His brow arched in amusement. "What is it, then?"

My teeth clenched at his mirth. I was a joke to him. Someone he would always underestimate. My hand tightened on the blade. "A promise kept," I hissed.

He grinned cruelly, contempt visible in his dragon eyes.

"You've changed." The words slipped out of my mouth.

I could have sworn the silver of his eyes flashed blue as his eyes widened slightly. He schooled his expression, sarcastic retorts written all over his face.

"You were never this man," I went on. Too late to stem my words now.

"Man?" his chuckle was dark. "Sorry, Princess, I killed the man." His face drifted closer; my stomach clenched as he leaned down, his mouth inches from mine. "Now all that's left is the *monster*."

I bit my tongue, stopping the automatic response from leaving my mouth. I wanted to tell him that the man *I* knew hadn't been a monster. But I didn't want to give him the satisfaction—so I didn't react as the dragon's words sank in.

"So fearless." His eyes scanned the length of me before returning to mine. "Are you sure you don't have a bit of dragon in you?"

"I'm sure." My response was dry.

His eyes were hooded as his tongue darted out to moisten his lips. "Would you like some?"

I scoffed in disgust as I shoved off him, putting some distance between us and feeling the connection break as my skin tingled. It took everything in me to stay still as we stood, watching each other.

Now we had some distance between us, I took a second to look at the rest of him. He was dressed in the finest black jacket I had ever seen, even finer than the one Yenn had crafted for him back in Stillmere. His white button-down had the top couple of buttons undone, revealing the smooth skin at the top of his chest. He was broader now; the cut of his jacket tightened around his muscular arms as he placed his hands into the pockets of his trousers.

"What *are* you?" His words were an astonished whisper that shook me from my staring. He took a step closer and my hand darted out to keep him away, flattening against his chest.

My pulse increased, my chest heaving with the breaths I took. "I'm nothing."

"I don't believe that for a second. There's not even a scent of fear around you."

"Why would I fear *you*? And *why* are you here, Dracho?" I repeated.

I could have sworn I saw his face soften as I spoke his name again, but the cavalier smugness returned too quickly for me to be certain. He sucked his teeth. "I'm just here for the party. It is for everyone to celebrate the anniversary of the Tain's ending, isn't it?"

I threw his own words back at him. "Now, why don't I believe that for one second?"

He smiled widely, making my stomach dip. "Come now, Eliana." Surprise shot through me at the use of my name, my heart skipping a beat. He stepped closer, bending down to whisper against my ear. Goosebumps rose upon my neck. "Don't distract me from my fun."

My breath hitched before I stepped away, trying to rid myself of his intoxicating scent. Closing my eyes, I took a deep breath before surveying him again. His eyes had returned to their unusual blue. They held a conflicted sadness; his mouth turned down in a frown as he seemed to fight with some inner turmoil. I studied him cautiously as he took a step forward.

"Eli." I jerked at that name and shook my head, halting him in his tracks. He spoke softly. "I know this day means more to you than most. More than just the end of the war."

My back stiffened, surprised by the sudden change of topic. Of course, he remembered that this day meant the anniversary of not only my brother's death, but also my mother's. Emotion I couldn't decipher swelled in my chest. I didn't know whether to be touched or offended that he'd mentioned it. He was the only person, besides my father, to have brought it up directly to me, on this day. I knew he too had experienced such loss. He was one of very few people I had ever spoken to about such things.

Before he betrayed me.

Swallowing the knot in my throat, I turned my eyes away from his concerned gaze. *I can't do this.* "I can't..."

His brow furrowed and he reached out to me, but I took a step back. I couldn't stand the concern written on his face.

"You know what I told you would happen if you returned." My voice was ice as my body fought over what I felt was right and what I *wanted*, somewhere deep down in the recesses of my memory, to do. The raw emotions made me feel horribly vulnerable.

"Eliana—"

"No," I interrupted him, lifting my chin as my arms dropped to my side. "You are not welcome here. Not after what you did. You had me thrown into a dungeon."

"That's not—"

"And you know what?" The rant that had played over and over in my brain for months spewed out before I could stop it. "As soon as I saw that pin, I knew I'd be a suspect. But I could handle your guards' and councils' stares, the distrust in *their* eyes as they looked down upon me. I've been used to that my whole life, surrounded by bureaucrats as the female heir to Meridium. I could deal with that because I didn't know them. And they didn't *know* me.

"But *you*. You knew better. Yet in a split second everything changed, and you couldn't even give me the benefit of the doubt. You wouldn't even give me the decency of hearing me before a *trial*. I treated Derwin, in that shabby little rundown inn back in Morcroft, better than you treated me!" I squared my shoulders. "No one should be treated that way."

His eyes were sad for a moment as he took that in, but then his gaze turned icy, a careful mask slipping back into place. A shiver ran up my spine as his jaw tightened, the hue of his eyes chilling. The air between us seemed to charge.

"And what of the betrayal *I* suffered?" he asked, his tone low.

"You don't know that my father—"

He snarled as he stepped, blindingly fast, into my space, but not before I raised my dagger. I felt the resistance as it pushed back towards me and heard the sharp hiss as his teeth snapped together. He froze inches before me, his eyes remaining closed for a moment.

I swallowed hard, not daring to move as I stared at the hilt of my dagger, flush against his left shoulder. *That was... relatively easy.* The shock I'd felt at his speed was nothing compared to my astonishment that my blade had pierced through fabric and skin and was now embedded in his shoulder. Inches from his heart.

I suddenly felt sick at the thought.

His eyes blazed open, looking down at me with a terrifying ferocity in his silver eyes I had never seen. He hissed as he ripped himself back off my blade. The rage in his eyes disappeared for a moment, a sad, stunned look passing over his features, but I saw him push away whatever thoughts he had from his mind. He looked down at the hole the knife had left in his suit.

"Hmm. Well, that's rather interesting." His eyes scanned my dagger, still held in mid-air, before returning to my face. "You're right. I *don't* know. But neither do you."

Eyes wide, I lowered my blade, wondering how he could know that I hadn't asked my father about the assassination. I pressed my lips together, hoping he couldn't read in my face the reason I had tried to bury since Tenebris. My fear that perhaps my father *had* been involved in the emperor's assassination. Perhaps he did have a link to the Hollow.

"All I know," Dracho continued, "is that your father questioned me about rumours of Tenebris's involvement in the Hollow's attacks... and that was when he *didn't* know who I was."

My spine stiffened. "What do you mean, didn't?"

He brushed the lapels of his suit, giving me a smouldering smile before he leaned down to whisper. "Enjoy the party, Princess."

He stepped around me as I released a breath. I turned to ask him again what he'd meant, but he had already disappeared.

My nerves were on edge, feeling like an exposed wound as I sheathed my slightly bloody dagger at my thigh, hiding it beneath my skirts. I strode swiftly back into the ballroom, trying to catch sight of my raven-haired ghost, my blade the only thing keeping me from thinking I had made it all up in my head. Connaught caught my wrist as I tried to storm past. Father stood close by, speaking to a guest.

"Eliana, have you seen... What's wrong?" His brow creased in concern as he noted the look of panic in my eyes. I swallowed hard, and Connaught's hand hovered over his sword as questions swam in his eyes. "Eliana—why is your leg bleeding?"

I glanced down, realising a sliver of my skin was showing and Dracho's blood was slowly dripping from my sheath. "It's not mine," I began, but the sound of tinkling glass rang through the hall, silencing the crowd. My head snapped round, looking for the cause of the commotion; I moved around Connaught to move through the crowd.

That's when I saw them.

Dracho had ascended the main staircase, stopping halfway to face the throng of guests below. My eyes widened in shock as I recognised the stern face of Antares, watching the crowd from the bottom step; the blonde female I remembered as Althea stood on the other side, preventing anyone from getting near. Dread consumed my stomach as I considered them, full leathers visible, weapons strapped to their bodies. *How were they able to enter the castle?* Lords and ladies muttered confused whispers to each other as Dracho waited for their silence, a smile playing on his lips.

"Good evening, everyone," he said. "I apologise for the interruption. I promise not to keep you for too long from your entertaining night."

My father and Connaught passed easily through the crowd, stopping at my side.

"Where have you been? You didn't tell me Dracho was coming." Father looked at me pointedly, a grin on his face.

"I didn't know," I muttered. "Wait—did you know he was here?"

He arched a brow. "Yes, I met him and his entourage earlier."

My breath hitched in horror. Dracho had already spent time around my father?

"But what's going on?" Father asked, his gaze turning back to the staircase.

I licked my lips, preparing myself to launch into an explanation before Dracho could publicise his accusations, but he was already speaking.

"Firstly, I must give a hand to both King Proditor and King Cervidae for their generosity tonight." He clapped his hands.

The guests joined in eagerly, not noticing the slight lengthening of the nails that protruded from each of his fingertips now, the ends turning black. The only hint at the fury that simmered beneath the surface. The display of his shifter nature caught me by surprise, and my chest heaved as I stepped slightly closer. Antares's eye caught mine in the crowd, a slight turning up at the corner of his mouth as he watched the guests.

I spotted movement from a darkened alcove to my right and baulked at the familiar eyes staring at me from the shadows there. Holding my gaze, Roux shook her head ever so slightly. *Don't,* she mouthed in my direction. I hesitated, not wanting to make things worse.

"Now, I know no expense has been spared for tonight's feasting... so, on my way here, I took it upon myself to provide the struggling villages and farmsteads with rations and resources for you."

I inhaled sharply as an uncomfortable silence blanketed the hall, everyone thinking over his words again as if they had misheard him the first time.

The King of Stillmere, Jareth, stepped forward, brushing a guest aside as he emerged from the centre of the crowd. Several of his royal guards followed closely. "Who are you, boy?"

I winced and held my breath as Dracho's eyes bored a hole into Jareth's skull. He flashed a perfectly white smile. "Ah yes. How rude of me. I didn't introduce myself the last time we met, King Proditor."

"We've met?" The king had a disgusted sneer on his pale face.

Dracho's smile spread further. "Why, yes, I attended a ball at your palace with the beloved Princess of Ruvalon. Where is she?" His eyes searched the faces amongst the crowd. "Ah, there she is." He nodded in my direction.

"I remember you now," Jareth drawled, as if he hadn't been worth remembering—just a common face in the crowd. Dracho smirked, probably at having been underestimated so badly. "Your hair was different."

"Well, I'll forgive your lapse in memory," Dracho said. He played with an errant strand of midnight hair, twirling it between the ends of his fingers. "After all, I do look different after my transition."

Realisation settled in the pit of my stomach: he was here to reveal his identity. I took a step forward, then stopped when I caught Antares's hand tightening on the hilt of his short sword.

"Transition?" my father called out.

"Yes." Dracho's eyes darkened. "As I was saying... Allow me to introduce myself."

I opened my mouth to stop him, but the warning growl from Althea shut me up. I shot her a glare which she returned tenfold; her blue eyes boring into mine. This time when I tried to move closer, my father grabbed my arm.

"What's going on?" he demanded.

Dracho's eyes skipped to me for a second, his lips turning up at the edges before speaking. "My name is Dracho Celesta."

I felt Father freeze at my side as muttered conversation resumed through the hall. A few gasps broke out amongst a couple of the elder guests—those that remembered the old names.

“For those,” he spoke louder, “who were familiar with my father, Emperor Eltanin...”

The noise was much louder now, as incredulity spread throughout those in attendance. Disbelief, anger and shock rolled off the guests, some evidently believing it was a joke in poor taste. Connaught stepped closer to where my father and I stood. Lucky I had my dagger—even if fighting in this damn dress would be more difficult.

“You’ll be most distressed to learn of his passing,” Dracho concluded. His jaw clenched as my father’s breath hitched beside me.

A beat of silence followed his announcement.

“Do you think such tales are funny, young man?” Jareth called.

I felt my father tug on my arm slightly, pulling me closer to him as we watched Dracho’s eyes lower to meet the southern king.

“Of course not, Your Majesty. My father’s murder is a great cause of pain for me, and for all Tenebris. In fact, that’s why I’m here.”

Everyone held still, eyes flitting around nervously. We were all still wondering if this was really happening.

“You see,” Dracho added, his voice deep and ominous, “I’m hoping you’ll help me find his killer.”

Great black wings ripped from his back as he smiled down upon the crowd, two razor-sharp fangs protruding from under his upper lip.

Chapter 4

Chaos erupted.

Lords and ladies scrambled backwards, falling over themselves and scrambling up, desperate to leave the palace. Stillmerean guards pushed guests aside to form a tight circle around Jareth, pointing their swords towards the three from Tenebris, as our own guards on the outskirts of the room unsheathed their weapons, standing to attention until they received their orders from Connaught. He had come to my father's side to pull him to safety, but the king was refusing to leave without me.

I wrenched myself forward, grunting as someone barged past me. I had hesitated in my moment of shock, but now I recovered, pulling my dagger free and facing down the winged beast that now stood before us on *my* staircase.

Althea's gaze honed in on the red-coated blade. She twisted to stare at Dracho's suit before glaring back at me with shock in her eyes, her lips shaking with her barely contained growl.

I halted for a moment; my gaze pulled to the silver talons that tipped the bony fingers of Dracho's wings. The obsidian skin and scales that stretched over those bones. The tendrils of silver that ran through the membrane, thin enough that they looked transparent as the flickering candlelight caught them.

"What do you want?" I called out over the thunderous noise of guests fleeing behind me, wrenching my gaze to his eyes. The black vertical slits of the dragon were visible.

He couldn't have looked more amused if he'd tried. "I told you. I want help to find my father's killer."

"This is hardly the best way to ask for help, is it?"

"Would you have met with me if I had asked?"

No. I didn't say it out loud.

His eyelids lowered as a half-smile pulled his lips. "I want to call a meeting of the rulers."

"What is the meaning of this? Who do you think you are?!" Jareth called out from behind his wall of steel.

Draco bared his fangs at him. His wings flared out, showing their full size, and the Stillmerean guards tightened their formation, looking as though they were about to shit themselves. "I am Emperor and one of the rulers of Ruvalon. The treaty no longer stands—not until one is made with the *new* emperor."

Jareth was silent.

"Then you shall have your meeting." My father's voice rang out as he stepped forward, coming to my side, his hand pushing mine down to lower my dagger. I stood straighter, strapping it back into its sheath.

"Father, are you sure?"

He nodded. "Of course. Dracho is now a ruler of Ruvalon. And he is right. The treaty no longer stands. A new one must be forged."

"It's not just you who can make that decision, Teyrnon!" Jareth yelled, barely visible behind his guards.

"Do you then suggest we ignore the special bond between our lands?" Father countered, receiving silence in return. He went on. "Two weeks." Antares's eyes narrowed; Dracho stared at Father. "Eliana's birthday is in two weeks."

Dracho's brows rose.

"We are having a ball. Come. We shall have our meeting in the days that follow it. It will give Chief Bisa time to reach Meridium—if she accepts the invitation."

"She will." Roux stepped out from her alcove.

My father's eyes snapped to her and widened in surprise. He shook it off and nodded. "Very well. We shall discuss these matters further then and, with your permission, we can work together to investigate this injustice. Until then, for the sake of Ruvalon, can we make a rulers' agreement that peace will be maintained?"

"Agreed," Dracho replied immediately. Jareth grumbled his acquiescence.

Father sighed in relief. "Dracho, Your Excellency—you shall stay here until that time in our guest wing. If, of course, that is all right with you, Jareth?"

Jareth scoffed. "If you want to house the beasts—"

A rumble sounded from Antares's chest; his amber eyes were furious. Jareth's mouth snapped shut.

I placed a gentle hand on my father's arm. "Fath—"

"Your guard is also welcome, if you have any concerns for your safety. But my home is yours. Jareth, I assume we shall see you at this meeting?"

A grunted affirmation came from the southern king before he shuffled back within the circle of his guards, turning to leave the hall in haste.

Father waited for him to disappear before continuing. "Well, I must check on my guests... I shall bid you all good evening, and see you in the morning when we break our fast. Eliana, wait for me in my study. Connaught, see them to their residences."

He didn't give Dracho a chance to respond, and his tone left no room for arguing. My skirt flared around my ankles as I turned, taking one last cautious glance at our new guests. I saw Roux's small smile and Dracho's intense gaze before I left reluctantly, unsure about leaving Connaught and the four royal guards alone with them.

I made my way to the king's study, throwing myself down into a chair. Father would no doubt spend plenty of time checking on the guests caught up in the commotion, using every bit of his charm to smooth things over.

After what felt like an age, he joined me. His shoulders were visibly stiff with anger as he entered the room, closing the door behind him.

"So, I feel that there are certain things you need to tell me?" His voice was shaky, and I could sense the simmering anger underneath his seemingly calm words.

I breathed out slowly. "I found out a few weeks before I came home."

"You *knew* that he was the prince and heir of Tenebris and didn't tell me?!"

I flinched at the volume. "Our departure wasn't exactly friendly. I just wanted to—"

"Why?" Father interrupted.

"What?"

"Why wasn't it friendly?"

"Be-because of his father's death. When we found the emperor—"

He lifted a hand. "Wait. *Found* him... Did—did *you* go to Tenebris?"

I swallowed thickly, nodding.

Father blew out a long breath. He poured himself a glass of whiskey before dropping into the chair opposite me and loosening his ascot. There was a weight to his expression that I hadn't seen in a long time.

"Maybe I should start at the beginning?" I offered.

"Probably best," he said dryly.

So I told him everything. Well... almost everything. From the moment I'd found out who Dracho was, to finding the emperor with the Hollow's spear embedded into his chest, and my time spent locked up in Tenebris—my subsequent banishment and the pin found on the emperor's body. By the time I had finished my father's eyes were glassy, staring at me in astonishment.

He cleared his throat. "Why didn't you come to me with this? You realise the danger you put us in? The danger you put *Meridium* in?"

I swallowed uncomfortably. "I... it got personal," I confessed, and his eyes narrowed. "But I left Tenebris under the impression that Dracho believed we had nothing to do with his father's death. That he would stay put and announce the change in ruler in his own time."

But he saw through me—saw the concern that pricked at my subconscious mind. His eyes softened. "Eliana... I did not organise Elta—the emperor's assassination."

"I know." It rushed out. "I think maybe my emotions got the better of me. A bit of doubt creeping in."

He reached out, taking my hand. "I understand; we hadn't seen each other for two years. But my pin was misplaced. I thought I'd lost it during my trip home from Stillmere, but it appeared back in my drawer not long afterwards."

My cheeks darkened. "That would have been me. I, um, sneaked into your room to see if it was missing and ended up putting it back."

His mouth parted before closing with a small smile. His hand squeezed mine reassuringly. "Darling, I don't ever want you to feel like you can't talk to me. I'm your father. Even if we don't agree all the time, I am *always* on your side. All right?"

I nodded, swallowing the ball of emotion in my throat.

"We'll get to the bottom of this. And the emperor's death. Maybe Dracho can help with that?"

I snorted, wondering how I could explain that the Dracho I'd once known was completely different to the Dracho we'd just met.

"He may surprise you, Eliana. I think the treaty was just an excuse to return here."

"Why would you believe that?"

My father downed his remaining whiskey. "Intuition. I can't be certain, but I'm sure we will find out. In the meantime, I want you to be careful."

I nodded, watching as his gaze dropped to his desk, a sorrow glazing his eyes that I hadn't seen in years.

He poured himself another drink, and I contemplated his words. If Dracho wasn't just here to find his father's killer and sign a new treaty, what other motives did he have?

Chapter 5

Bright stars shone overhead as I waited on the guest I had invited to the privacy of my room. Connaught had not been happy about it, especially unchaperoned, but I had insisted.

A gentle knock sounded on my bedroom door, and one of the guards closed the door behind my guest, throwing me a warning glance as he left. But I felt completely safe. Roux wouldn't hurt me.

Intentionally, of course.

My eyes studied her beautiful face as an awkward silence hung between us. Her hands clasped in front of her, she played with her fingers. My mind drifted back to a time when her fingertips had been blackened by corrupt magick. When her grief and anger had almost overwhelmed her, threatening to render her with madness.

The Roux before me was not like that, but not much else had changed. Her golden-brown eyes shone brilliantly, her once voluminous coils were now braided in rows, and her bright aura reminded me of when we'd first met.

"How are you?" My words rang out, breaking the silence.

Her hands stopped moving, and she smiled—a small, genuine smile—as she looked at me. "I'm good."

Baffled, I stared at her. Was that all I was going to get? She must have known that whatever had happened between us all, I cared about her well-being. That I was asking about her progression with her new powers.

She huffed a laugh. "*Really*. I'm well." She stretched out her hand, letting a brilliant orb of black and gold manifest there, the light shining in her eyes.

I shivered all the way to my toes, feeling the energy in the air between us.

Her other hand reached up, the orb splitting into two until she was holding one in each hand. I could see the reflection of light flickering in her eyes, and I was glad for her. Peace resonated from her.

"I've practically mastered my magick now. I learned a lot of new things along the way. And I only get headaches randomly, or if I use a huge amount of power." She closed each hand into a fist, putting out the flames.

Relief flooded me, tinged with a hint of sadness. I felt disappointed and somewhat guilty that I hadn't been there to help her through it. When Roux had been gifted more power by the mages, she had been in a vulnerable state, and I had seen the worry in her eyes as she navigated her new powers. In Stillmere, when she had eradicated the bodies of the men who had tried to murder her, I'd seen how much of a burden it had put on her shoulders.

This Roux who stood in front of me now was more confident, like the one I'd first met.

I swallowed, bile rising in my throat at the jealousy that hit me. Roux and Dracho seemed to have moved on, made peace with themselves—become closer. I felt like I had been left behind... left to deal with my demons.

I hesitated to ask my next question, but the need to know was overriding everything else. "Did you stay in Tenebris when we left?"

Her smile fell, and she nodded silently. My teeth found the inside of my cheek, and I nodded in return.

She took a step forward. "Dracho helped me with my powers, as he was doing before. With his own new abilities as Emper—" She stopped, her lips thinning into a chagrined smile.

I shook my head. "It's all right. I want to know everything."

"You do?"

I walked over to one of the armchairs and sat, indicating for her to take the other one. "I do."

I genuinely did. Despite how much it hurt, every bit of information I could get would be helpful.

"I... missed you," I told her.

Her face crumpled. "I missed you too."

I hoped she could sense everything I wasn't saying. I knew deep down that I didn't blame her for staying with Dracho. I couldn't imagine the pain from the ordeals she had gone through. Finding Azande on the beach of Aion after the Hollow's attack, and then her trial in Volente with the ancestors. She had been through more than most, and Dracho had been helping her. I'd seen how close they had grown during our time together, and I couldn't resent her for choosing to stay with him and master her new abilities.

She exhaled deeply, coming to sit in the chair by mine. "Well. Tenebris has this huge library, filled with texts on the first mages and the powers they possessed. I've learned ways to harness my flames that mages haven't known for centuries. I've almost fully mastered them now."

A smile split my face. "I'm so happy for you, Roux. You sound so much more confident. It's genuinely lovely to see."

Her own smile widened.

"Did you find out anything about the Hollow?"

The smile was extinguished. "No. There was nothing in the library. And since the attacks stopped, we haven't found out anything new."

I nodded, deciding to change the topic. "So, what type of powers?"

Roux smiled slyly, glancing at the door as if she was about to let me in on a secret. She leaned in. "I can stop a draconi from transforming."

My mouth parted in astonishment, but I didn't let my gratitude show, though I felt incredibly touched to be trusted with this information. When I'd seen her at the ball, I'd had the awful feeling that we were now enemies. That she had picked a side in whatever this current situation was. *Dracho's* side.

I couldn't help the feeling of betrayal that had hit me—a feeling I had grown too accustomed to. This moment gave me hope for our relationship.

"*Completely* stop them?" I asked.

She nodded. "Dracho let me try it on him and, well, he's the most powerful draconi there is. I mean it takes a lot of energy, but yes... it's been fun."

I wasn't surprised Dracho would allow her to practice on him. He had always dived head-first into his quest to help Roux with her powers. To help anyone. I was glad that trait had stayed with him after his merge.

"So..." I swallowed hard. "Are you and him...?"

For a moment she looked confused, but then her eyes blew wide with understanding. "Me and Dracho? Spirits, no!" She laughed, shaking her head. "Just—no. More like a brother."

I breathed out, pushing down the relief I felt until I could not sense it. "What... what happened to him, Roux?"

Her face fell, her hands once again fidgeting in her lap. "You know what happened to him." Her words were quiet, sad. "You were there. He lost his father. The only parent he had left. I believe that his grief was so potent at that moment, the beast was able to take over. Because of that, he lost you both."

I turned away, staring at the closed bedroom door instead.

"Now, he carries more grief and anger than any army could bear. He doesn't know the difference between pleasure and pain anymore. I've felt it during our exercises. He only knows his mission now. To find out who did it."

I said nothing as she exhaled sorrowfully. "The last time I saw peace in his eyes... was when he looked at you."

White-hot anger shot a path through my veins. "Whatever was going on between us—it meant nothing. *He* means nothing."

Roux chuckled darkly. "I think we both know that's not true."

My head snapped towards her. "That's the man who put me in a *cage*. Who took my worst nightmare and used it against me." I spat out the words, not giving myself a chance to censor them. Roux's eyes filled with pity, and I had to look away once again.

"I'm sorry. I won't defend him. His actions can only be explained by him. He was wrong, Eliana... but put yourself in his shoes."

I laughed. "In his shoes, I would have given the person I cared for, I would have given my—my friend—a chance. A chance to speak, at least."

She spoke softly. "You don't know until you're in that situation. He had just lost the only parent he had left. Realised he was all alone." I opened my mouth, but she held a hand up. "I see both points of view. Dracho had another being within that he was fighting with for his emotions. He wasn't completely in control at that moment. But that's no excuse."

I knew that. I remembered his eyes changing, showing the vertical slits of his silver dragon's eyes as he told his guards to seize us. But his dragon was a part of him, and it was hard for me to separate the two. Especially since he had now merged.

It would not be a simple thing to forgive, if I could ever forgive him at all.

"Eli... I want to say I'm sorry. I wasn't there for you after—"

"It's fine. Honestly. I don't blame you. I think you were meant to stay with him." I truly believed it.

She looked at me quizzically.

"You had both been through something similar. Something awful. I think you were the best person for each other to find comfort. To move forward."

Roux smiled, unshed tears in her eyes. A beat of silence passed between us; she took a deep breath. "So, are you excited for your birthday?"

"Um." I pinched the bridge of my nose, closing my eyes. "I hadn't really been thinking about it, to be honest."

It was just another day. Since my mother's and brother's deaths, I hadn't really celebrated birthdays, despite my father's efforts. A ball was being thrown in my honour this year, because he insisted he had to make up for the previous two he had missed.

"Well, I'm sure it's going to be amazing!"

I forced a smile at her enthusiasm, suppressing a groan as I realised I would have to survive the next couple of weeks in Dracho's presence first.

Chapter 6

I still felt utterly exhausted from the events of the night before, but I hurried to bathe and dress so I could get to breakfast, eager to present a united front with my father. I quashed the dread that settled queasily in my gut, determined to show Dracho that his presence here was nothing more than a nuisance.

My father had arranged for breakfast to be set on the upper level. Bright sunlight flooded the room through the stained-glass windows. The ornate silver dining table in the centre of the open area was laid with our best crockery and silverware. Every comfort was put in place for us all to endure the meal.

Our guests were the last to arrive.

Connaught stood guard closely behind my father, other fully armed guards stationed around the outside of the room, whilst Bas and Vyn sat on either side of me. Bas was visibly shaking with rage. I knew it was going to be hard to rein him in—Bas, who was usually so laid back. It was clear from his agitated demeanour that it didn't matter whether Dracho was stronger than him, or that he was an emperor. No—whatever thoughts were running through Bas's mind were purely vengeful. And I certainly didn't have it in me to stop whatever he had planned.

Two members of staff opened the heavy doors, and my breath hitched in my chest. Dracho strolled in as if he owned the place, Althea and Antares trailing closely behind. I was so busy studying the changes in Dracho that it took me a second to realise that his steps had faltered a few feet from the table, confusion settling upon his brow.

I turned to Vyn, whose hands were outstretched. He was holding Dracho in place with an invisible rope made of wind. I could tell from the vein in his neck that it was taking everything to hold it for as long as he had.

Bas surged from his seat and swung a fist towards the emperor's outraged face.

A snarl erupted through the hall; a flash of blonde rushed forward, too fast for any of us to see clearly. Althea met Bas's fist with her hand a breath's distance before it hit Dracho's face. Her teeth were bared. A muscle twitched in Bas's temple.

Father wrenched himself to his feet. "Bastion Ekker! You will sit this second, and if you dare presume to harm my guests again, I shall have you removed from the castle."

I caught sight of Connaught's lips turning up in a smug grin. Bas didn't respond, merely turned to stare at Althea. She growled quietly in her throat before releasing his hand.

Bas stood straighter, his eyes jumping back to Dracho. "That would have been the least you deserved."

Antares stepped forward, murder written in his frightening molten eyes. Dracho's hand shot out to the side, preventing him from moving further.

His voice was soft smoke, the promise of violence if he wasn't obeyed. "You can release me now, Vyn."

Antares looked at Vyn as the wind dissipated. The half-djinn turned away from his gaze as Bastion returned to his seat beside me.

Father exhaled deeply. He indicated to the chairs opposite. "I apologise, Your Excellency. Please, sit."

My lip curled in disgust at the title, but I knew Father was trying to be diplomatic. Dracho took a seat opposite me, Antares and Althea beside him.

Father continued. "I'd like to thank you all for coming, and for agreeing to reach an understanding."

The doors opened once more, and I could have sworn I heard a choked noise escape Bas's throat. Roux walked in, her braids bouncing as she walked forward and sat at the end of the table: a living, breathing metaphor of her being caught in the middle of everyone.

"I apologise for my lateness, Your Majesty. I, um, got distracted in the library." She addressed my father with a bow and lowered eyes before glancing at Vyn and Bas, offering them a small smile, which they returned.

My father laughed. "Just like your Aunt Sizwe." Roux's cheeks darkened as he took his seat. The staff proceeded to serve breakfast. "Now. Dracho, I understand this will be a difficult discussion... but I must admit that I had no idea of what had occurred since your last visit to Meridium until last night. Eliana had *not* told me of the events of Tenebris. Much to my dismay."

He looked at me pointedly, and I huffed. I could feel Dracho's gaze burning into my face.

"And did she tell you what was found on my father's body?" he asked without removing his eyes from me.

Father winced but nodded gravely. "I can assure you I will do *everything* in my power to help you find out how that happened."

Draco's eyes narrowed.

"Please know that I... I am so sorry for your loss, Dra—"

"You can say it." Dracho's false smile was tight-lipped.

"Say what?" Father asked hesitantly.

"He's dead," Dracho said, and my father flinched. "I have not *lost* him. He died. He was stolen from me. State the bluntness of the situation, Your Majesty. It helps me to be reminded of the truth. It gives me focus."

I saw the fury in the lines of his face and knew what Roux had said last night to be true. All he knew now was his determination to find his father's killer. Nothing would stop him from hunting this world to find them.

Father took a deep breath, ever determined to be an empathetic diplomat. "I know it must have come as a shock to find that on him, Dracho. Especially after forming a friendship with Eliana—"

"Oh, I think we had formed more than that; don't you, Princess?" Dracho drawled, grinning as his head tilted in my direction. My fingers clenched around the arm of my chair. He leaned back, sitting completely at ease with a glint of challenge in his eyes.

Antares grumbled beside him, crossing his arms and muttering something which sounded like *do we have to*. Althea looked like she'd rather be anywhere else. Bas stiffened; Vyn sucked in a breath and Father's brow furrowed, a beat of silence filling the room uncomfortably. Connaught looked between me and Dracho with an unreadable expression as Roux sat looking awkward.

My cheeks heated, my nostrils flaring with rage. With a flick of my wrist, I picked up and threw my butter knife at him. Expecting to hear his grunt of pain as it hit him where I'd aimed, between the eyes, I pressed my lips together when Dracho's hand shot up so quickly it blurred and grabbed the knife in mid-air. My stomach dipped in fear as I saw him return it, my back suddenly vibrating with the impact as I turned, seeing the blade embedded into the back of the chair, inches away from my head.

Turning back to him, I bared my teeth, resisting that deep pull within me to succumb to the rage. "You're a fucking prick—do you know that?!"

"Careful, *Princess*. You could be one insult away from starting a war."

He's bluffing, the wicked part of me whispered, daring me to challenge him further. My clenched teeth started to ache. "Don't you have a city to rule over? People to boss around?"

"Boone and my uncle have taken over that duty for me, but thanks for asking." He smirked.

"How fortunate for us."

"I think that's quite enough, don't you, Eliana?" My father's words rang out impatiently.

A small grin pulled at Antares's mouth. I crossed my arms, shuffling down into my chair as I stared back at the draconi opposite me, the vertical pupils of his dragon visible. I held his gaze, refusing to be the one to look away first.

Father took a sip of his water before speaking. "Dracho, I swear upon my royal crown. I swear upon my daughter's *life*. I played no part in your father's death."

Dracho said nothing, only looked at my father.

"But I also swear to help you find whoever ordered the Hollow to kill him. Finding the Hollow and those behind these attacks will benefit us all, so it's in my interests to assist you to the best of my ability."

We all waited for a moment with bated breath.

"Very well. What do you suggest?"

My heart jumped with relief as a rough exhalation left my father. But underneath that came a wariness I had never felt. There was no way Dracho would ever let my father off that easily. What were his true motives?

Father cleared his throat. "I believe it would be best to discuss these matters in full once we convene again with King Proditor. It will help build relations between us all as we discuss the new treaty. You are more than welcome to reside here for the duration of your stay in Ruvalon, Your Excellency. I would advise staying in Meridium. Word of your... arrival will no doubt spread throughout the city, and I believe in the interests of *everyone's* safety, remaining here would be best."

Dracho's teeth flashed in a sly grin. "I don't think we need to worry about *my* safety, Your Majesty."

My hand moved to hover over my dagger at my thigh. Antares spotted the movement and raised a brow. Althea cleared her throat harshly, pulling Dracho's attention, and mine, to her. They shared an intense look for a moment, and I knew they were conversing as draconi did. Using their strange mind ability to talk together privately.

An ability I was most definitely envious of.

My father looked at them, his brows furrowed. I let out an impatient breath. "They can converse through their minds, Father."

Father looked at them; Althea looked put out. Draco's head swung round to me, his expression satisfied.

"A power, I'm guessing, that has increased since my coronation," he said. "I can, of course, communicate with anyone who has celestral magick. But since I was able to converse with Eliana in my dragon form before my merging, I wonder if I can speak to any mortal—"

Using my mind in my mortal form.

My gasp was audible. I felt a gentle caress against my mind like soft fingers—and his voice had sounded in my head.

Bas swung round to watch me. "What is it?"

Draco looked at him, silent for a moment, but a strange look passed over his features as Bas didn't acknowledge him. His gaze caught mine again in apparent wonder. "Interesting."

A small cough sounded from the end of the table.

"Actually, your Majesty"—Roux's voice rang out like a bell—"I was going to travel to Aion to personally invite my mother to the meeting. And was hoping Dracho would come with me. I know he would like to visit Aion again." She looked to Dracho, and I saw a softness enter his eyes as they seemed to communicate silently.

Father hummed, glancing between me and Dracho. "Well, I obviously will not stop you. I can only advise. We shall hold Eliana's ball in a fortnight. Eliana, perhaps you would go with them—you can travel back with Sizwe then?"

I didn't bother to hide the surprise or fury on my face. My father stared back at me, tilting his head forward a little. It wasn't a request. My father and king was giving me an order.

I spoke through gritted teeth. "Of course, Father. It would honour me to escort our guests."

Dracho's grin was positively feline.

"You may leave someone behind if you wish, Dracho."

I understood what my father was saying. If Dracho was concerned over my father's actions or of him betraying them whilst we were gone. Dracho understood too.

"No thank you, Your Majesty. I'm sure all will remain as it is whilst we are gone. Whilst the princess is with us."

I suppressed the need to roll my eyes. Father wouldn't dare do anything rash while I was with Dracho. Still, I wasn't frightened in the least—only angered by the implication. How dare he try to use me to control my father?

Father ignored the jab, refusing to rise to the bait. He clapped his hands together. "All right. Now—"

The doors were flung open. One of the guards rushed in, his face covered in black soot. Connaught jerked forward as the soldier stumbled, falling to his knees. I was out of my chair before anyone else, kneeling beside him, my hand on his shoulder.

"Tomas, what is it?"

Tomas was one of Connaught's most trusted men. He had been on rotation to the northern towns and hadn't been due back for a few days. His breath came fast, as if he had run all the way here without stopping.

"Forgive me, Your Highness, Your Majesty. It's... it's Morcroft."

I caught Connaught's eye, frowning. Morcroft was a small town to the north-east, less than a full day's journey from here on foot. Dracho had been there with us before. It was where we had found Derwin and finally obtained some valuable information about the Hollow.

Connaught came to help, pulling Tomas up to sit as he handed him a cup of water. Everyone around the table had stood, all eyes upon the soldier.

"What has happened, Tomas?" Connaught's voice was stern but calm.

Tomas's face was filthy. He drank the water greedily, drops splashing down his chin and onto his armour. He gasped once he had drained the entire cup. "It's gone."

"Gone? What do you mean, *gone*?" Father exclaimed.

Tomas exhaled heavily. "We were heading back from our watch in the early hours when we noticed smoke on the horizon. Too much for any campfire. The whole town was burning. Attacked by wyverns."

Roux gasped. My eyes narrowed in on Dracho, finding him looking at me as if I'd called out his name.

"Did you see anything suspicious on your journey?" I asked him.

"We were there," Dracho stated, his eyes hard like steel.

"In Morcroft?"

He nodded. "I didn't lie when I said we delivered resources to the towns on our way here. We were in Morcroft the night before last. There was no sign of an attack."

"Don't you think it's a bit of a coincidence that the day you return, Morcroft is attacked? When there have been none in the last six months?" Vyn fired at him.

"Vyn. Be mindful of what you accuse people of," Father commanded.

Dracho just smiled. "Whilst I can say without a doubt that we had no part in this, as someone once told me, I don't believe in coincidences." His eyes flashed silver.

"What happened once you came upon Morcroft, Tomas?" I asked.

He looked at the floor. "We tried to help. We entered their homes, tried to pull them out. But the fire was unlike any I've ever seen. It was like it acted with its own mind. Morphing and changing its path to consume all."

Roux looked at Dracho, worry etched on her brow.

"That was all we tried to do... until—" A beat of silence passed as Tomas tried to find the words. "Gregori is dead, Captain."

Connaught's head reeled back; my chest tightened. Gregori was Connaught's oldest friend. They had trained together in the royal guards since they were young. Connaught's mouth hung partly open, speechless.

"How did it happen?" Antares's deep voice asked as he stepped forward, eager for information.

Tomas sniffed, sparing only a second to glance over our guests. "It came out of nowhere. We were busy dealing with the fire and hadn't seen any wyverns. But something jumped out from an alley, and before we could do anything it had its jaws around Gregori's throat. It must have been a straggler left behind. One second Gregori was standing there, the next..."

His head bowed in sorrow as Connaught grasped his shoulder tightly.

Dracho stood. "Did you see anyone else? Any mortal-looking being?"

Tomas looked confused, shaking his head.

Father's throat cleared. "What happened to the creature?"

"That's the thing, Your Majesty—"

The main doors opened. The rest of the company filed in, the six men struggling to carry a wide wooden pallet between them, covered by a large canvas. Assuming it was Gregori's body, I stood, giving them room to place it upon the ground.

Althea gasped when they removed the cover, revealing one of the creatures that had decimated the town.

The shape of the wyvern's body was deformed, stretching its skin so thin that you could see the veins beneath it, beyond the leftover patches of fur. Its long, bat-like ears were chewed and mottled by dark spots; a stump sat above its hind legs where a beautiful tail once would have been. Its neck had been nearly cut from its body with an axe, by the looks of it. The edges of the wound were congealed with dried blood.

Althea stepped closer, studying it. "It's a loscura," she said to Dracho.

She wasn't wrong. It had clearly once been a loscura, a beautiful hound-like creature, before this strange magick had corrupted it. Its body was twice the size of a normal one, but the features were still there. Antares stared at the creature, unmoving, his eyes unusually emotive.

"What could do this?" Althea asked the room at large.

"Magick," Roux said, kneeling next to the creature. Her hand reached out, hovering an inch above its skin, a faint glow lighting up her palm. "Corrupt magick. Can you see that?"

Squinting, I leaned in. Under its skin, illuminated by Roux's magick, were thin, black, vein-like tendrils... moving as if alive. Like worms, they slithered throughout the creature's body, as if fighting for a way out. I noticed they followed the path of Roux's hand, as if they wanted to reach out for it.

"What *is* that?" I asked.

Antares gasped roughly, his face paling as he turned to Dracho, who looked like he was going to be sick.

"I've seen this before," he whispered, seemingly more to himself than to anyone in the room. Antares's hand reached out as if to comfort Dracho, then dropped back to his side.

"Dracho." His fully silver eyes snapped to my face once I spoke his name, his brow crumpling. "What is it?"

He swallowed, before turning and storming out of the room. Antares went to follow, but Dracho held up a hand. I pushed myself to my feet, ignoring Connaught's shout for me.

"Deal with that," I told him, pointing behind me to the dead creature upon the floor.

If Dracho knew something, I had to know. The dead loscura was a vital find, but if Dracho had more information on the magick that flowed through its body, it could help us solve everything.

The draconi ran down the empty hallway ahead of me until he halted abruptly, leaning against the wall for support. Panic laced through me as I jogged to catch up, slowing beside him. His breath came in harsh pants.

"Dracho?"

He held a finger up. Annoyance flashed through me, but he clearly needed a moment. He breathed deeply in through his nose, released it, then stood straight, collecting himself.

"What is it?" I asked.

"It doesn't matter." The mask was back in place, a coldness in his voice that hadn't been there before.

My brow arched. "Doesn't look like it."

A muscle in his jaw ticked. "Leave it, Eliana."

My chest jumped at his use of my full name, but I ignored it. "If it's something that's going to help, then I think I should know, Dra—"

"My mother." It burst from his lips. "Those veins, beneath its skin... my mother had those before she died."

My brain stuttered for a moment. I took in the sorrow in his eyes, silence falling between us.

"I thought your mother fell ill," I said at last.

He nodded. "With an illness we couldn't identify. But she had those markings under her skin. And I didn't make the connection until now, but my father had veins like that around the wound in his chest."

I swallowed thickly. "And your father's mage never realised?"

Dracho shook his head. "Boone had never seen it before. It was like nothing he had ever seen before."

I nodded. "How—how would your mother's magick have been corrupted? What does this mean?"

He closed his eyes and blew out a breath. "It means... I'm now looking for my mother's killer, too."

He turned, leaving me in the emptiness of the hallway, processing the enormity of what we had learned.

Chapter 7

"I'm not sure I follow." Bas wiped the sheen from his brow with a tattoo-covered arm, a look of confusion on his face.

"That's not surprising, Bas," Vyn quipped, earning himself a rude gesture.

I shrugged as I jumped from one foot to the other, raising my fists in front of my face. "It's like I said. Dracho has seen those marks before, when his mother died."

Bas and I stood in the pit of the training arena. The events of the past two days had messed with my head, so I'd asked him. He'd accepted, of course, even though he would get his arse kicked.

Vyn sat on the sidelines, cutting an apple with a small blade. "You know, somehow this has all got to be connected. The same markings appear on *both* his mother and father, all these years apart? Does that mean the Hollow has been around for that long?" he said as Bas sauntered towards me, throwing a jab at my face.

I moved to the side, brushing him away with one arm and smacking him upside the head with the other. He jerked, glaring at me before backing up.

"Four-nothing to me." I nodded at him before turning back to Vyn. "I'm not sure. Dracho's mother died almost thirteen years ago."

I sidestepped as Bas ran forward, his arms thrown out to grab me around my middle. Swinging a leg out behind me, I caught his foot. He crashed to the arena floor, dust flying up.

"And we haven't seen anything like this before, so why now?" I added. "Why wait all these years before killing his father?"

Bas pushed himself to his feet, spitting out a mouthful of dirt and wiping his mouth with the back of his hand. I peered at him, satisfied with the fine layer of dust that now covered his training gear.

"It's obviously linked to Dracho somehow. But I'm not even sure *he* knows why," he commented with a heavy sigh.

"You'd be correct in that assumption, Bastion."

I bristled as the deep voice called out from the platform above the pit. All three guests from Tenebris stood there in gear suitable for training. The tight leather vest fitted Dracho's muscular chest perfectly, and I couldn't help but swallow as he walked down the steps into the pit. His biceps flexed as he gripped the wooden handrail.

"You can leave. You won't have an interested audience this time around," I told him, referring to the way Vyn used to watch Dracho and Ant train. My hands found my hips as I shifted to face him fully. Despite myself, it was nice to see him in better spirits than the previous morning.

He threw his arms out. "I think there's plenty of room for all of us." He turned to face Althea and Antares. "Don't you? Perhaps a match together, Princess?"

The movement caught my eye; lines of smooth black crept around the back of his bicep. Dracho had a tattoo. I swallowed the question that rose on my tongue, my curious nature wanting to see more.

I hated the flash of envy that lanced through me when I glanced to Althea. Her hair was a tumble of blonde that rested over her slender shoulders. It was completely obvious that she was comfortable in her own skin by the way she carried herself. The only flaw in her elegant appearance was the permanent scowl on her face, pulling her full lips down at the corners and bringing a dullness to her brilliant blue eyes. She consistently looked bored.

She flexed her neck, looking at me with no emotion, whilst Antares glanced at Vyn, who was doing his very best to ignore the draconi. Antares—whose sleeves were rolled up to the elbow, revealing new ink of his own. My eyes roamed over the lines, making shapes of the different shades of grey and black.

Two intense eyes stared out from one forearm, set into the slender face of a black feline. A white spot in the shape of an eight-pointed star was inked onto its chest. It was drawn so well that it looked real. Swirls of black almost like shadows waved below it, wrapping over his wrist and touching the pale skin on the top of his hand.

The tattoo on his other arm made my throat close. It looked as if the flesh had been stripped from his fingers, leaving only shadows and bones; an intricate snake coiled between the knuckles and onto his hand. The scaled body of the snake wrapped around his arm, the tail ending before the crook of his elbow.

Studying the expression on his face, my eyes travelled between him and Dracho, wondering how Antares would react if I knocked Dracho on his arse.

"This isn't a good idea," I said, suddenly feeling warm.

Dracho took measured steps down into the pit. "Come on, Eliana. We're all adults here. Unless you're scared?"

I didn't dignify him with a response, despite the ground underneath my feet suddenly feeling unsteady. Because I *was* scared.

But not of him beating me.

Dracho didn't even blink. His eyes swept across us until they landed on Bas, and his face fell. He stepped closer. Clasping his hands together behind his back, he rocked on his heels gently.

"Bastion... I owe you an apology."

Vyn's blade froze on his next cut of his apple, his yellow eyes flashing as his harsh gaze lifted to watch. My gut hollowed as I looked at Bas.

Dracho exhaled. "The last time we were all together, I—I was dealing with a lot of pain. I took that out on you. I should never have put my hands on you or scared you. For that, I am deeply sorry."

A silence so awkward it was almost hilarious, rang out for a couple of moments. Bas flushed. Vyn's mouth fell open.

Eventually Bas shook himself out of his stupor. "Tch. Wasn't like I was really, *really* scared or anything," he muttered. Dracho smiled.

Bas took a step forward. Then he held out his hand. "I understand it was a bit of an awkward situation for you, and I can't say I've forgiven you yet..." His tone was wary. "But *we're* kind of cool. That doesn't mean you don't have more making up to do."

Dracho's expression was a mixture of relief and surprise. He took Bas's hand and shook it.

Anger and disbelief started to boil within me, heating my cheeks and forcing my heart to beat furiously against my ribs, and I tried to prevent it from bursting out. True, Dracho's physical assault on Bastion during our time in Tenebris had been a shock, but if I'd ever believed he would apologise for anything... well, the obvious infraction was throwing us into a dungeon and keeping us prisoner.

Bas was so easy-going and hated holding a grudge; he could usually move on as soon as he received an apology. I felt a bit of gratitude for what he'd said to Dracho, knowing all those nights of watching my nightmares would be playing on his mind.

But at least *he'd* got an apology.

Vyn started, "What about—"

I held up a hand, silencing him. "Don't. You know what, I *do* think I could use a new training partner."

Vyn thinned his lips to hide his grin.

Dracho's smile was positively cunning. "Excellent." He started to remove his weapons; I coughed loudly. His eyes met mine in curiosity.

"You can bring the dagger."

His head tilted, eyes wide with surprise. Antares stepped forward on the platform above, gripping the wooden railing.

"Are you sure? I wouldn't want to cut you, Princess." His tone was a deep timbre that I felt creep along my skin.

My teeth ground out my frustration. "Bring the fucking dagger."

He took his time removing the rest of his weapons, and I grabbed my emerald dagger from one of the benches lining the outside of the pit. I didn't want to hurt him but knew I would get some satisfaction from sparring with him, proving that he had not left me broken by his actions. Only a tiny amount of trepidation ran through me when I saw the excited look upon his face, as if he could sense the rage I felt within.

Althea and Antares came down to watch, sitting on one of the benches. They exchanged a quick glance, and I wondered if they were conversing privately.

Dracho stepped further into the pit, holding his dagger by his side. He smirked, the epitome of arrogance.

Bastard.

"Watch you don't carve up my pretty face, *Princess.*"

Bas leaned over to Vyn. "I wonder what will get him killed first—his cockiness or calling her that all the time."

Vyn snorted. "Definitely the nickname."

Dracho crouched, using one hand to rest his blade on his other arm, pointing it in my direction. "You know I'll win." His eyes gleamed like gems, gaze unwavering.

I relished the rough handle of my dagger as I twirled it along my palm, whipping my arm out to hold it away from my body. "But you won't win easily."

He smiled before launching forward at human speed, his dagger held out. A split second before he reached me, I ducked, landed a swift punch up into his stomach, and pulled away to stand, facing him once more.

His surprised look almost offended me. I hadn't even made that much effort to land a blow...

He was holding back.

I clenched my jaw as his gaze lingered, travelling up my body. He wanted to make me angrier; angry enough to make mistakes. I couldn't let that happen. Time to use his own game against him.

"Careful. The last person who looked at me that way ended up in my bed for hours."

His head jerked to meet my gaze as his cheeks flamed. I darted forward, kicking a leg out and tripping him. Dust floated in the air as he landed on his back, a shocked grunt escaping him.

Bas's laugh boomed from the edge of the arena.

"Sorry," I exclaimed, my voice dripping false concern, "are you all right?"

"All right." He got to his feet. His face was still red, but he was chuckling. His head angled towards Antares for a second before facing me. "Again."

The sound of our daggers clashing rang through the pit as we exchanged blows with no clear winner for some time, the strikes shooting up my arms and my palm becoming sore. My white shirt stuck to my back; sweat trailed along my skin.

Dracho paused to remove his own leather vest and short-sleeved shirt. A sharp inhalation caught in my throat, causing me to choke. I coughed harshly as I looked up again at the broad muscles of his back, the tattoo there moving with every flex of his shoulders.

Bas whistled. "Nice ink, man."

It was.

In similar shades of grey and black to Antares's ink, was a dark but intricate illustration of wings. Dragon wings. They travelled across the width of his back and onto his arms, so that if he were to lift them, it would look like a real pair.

Dracho glanced over his shoulder, catching my eye. I shook my head.

"Have you stopped showing off now? Can we continue?"

Althea's amused snort surprised me, but when I glanced at her, she'd already looked away.

Dracho huffed. "Hand to hand all right?"

I nodded, and we dropped our daggers.

Hand to hand meant I might get to punch that smug look off his face—but it also meant being closer, something I regretted once we started circling and my eyes kept dropping to the glistening drops of sweat travelling down his stomach.

He noticed.

"You know, there are other ways we could work up a sweat?" He wiggled his eyebrows.

I bared my teeth at him. He chuckled darkly and lunged forward, throwing the first punch. Protecting my face, I ducked it, slipping under his outstretched arm and throwing one of my own. It caught him in his exposed ribs with a satisfying crunch. He grunted. *Oops, might have put a bit too much force behind that one.* As we stepped back to our starting positions, I caught Vyn's pointed gaze, warning me to keep calm.

Dracho seemed elated. "What, not so talkative today? That's unlike you. Usually—"

"I'm going to break your teeth if you keep talking," I spat at him.

Bastion laughed from his seat, but Vyn, beside him, looked concerned. Antares's scorching eyes watched us, no doubt analysing every one of our moves. Althea still looked bored, gazing at her fingernails instead.

Dracho tilted his head to the side. "What's wrong, *Eliana?*" He drew out my name. "You seem... tense?"

My jaw was clenching so hard from my anger that my teeth could have chewed through rocks. I paced back and forth, looking for an opening. Vicious anger clawed at my mind. "Can you just fuck off already?"

"Eli," Vyn warned.

Dracho feigned shock. "I don't think I've ever heard her curse so much. Ant, did she ever curse *this* much?"

Antares's expression was studious. He shrugged. "It's obviously a testament to your conversational skills, brother... or your fighting skill. Take your pick."

I huffed as Dracho's eyes narrowed at his friend.

"I think Eliana would agree my *oral* skills are better than average, thank you," he announced.

Bas sucked in an awkward breath as my heart pounded, my anger rising. How dare he try to humiliate me this way?

"I've forgotten. So obviously it wasn't that memorable," I aimed at him.

He threw his head back, laughing, and I took the chance to strike. Right foot forward, I propelled myself high into the air to bring my elbow down upon him.

His eyes flashed to me, the vertical slits of his dragon appearing, and my breath hitched. He had tricked me into reacting too eagerly. Quick as a snake, his hands shot out to grab my ankle and forearm, turning to throw me the ground, the impact winding me slightly.

Dracho was on top of me a second later. His weight held me down as he straddled my waist, his hands firm but gentle as he held my arms down on either side of my head. I tried to buck him off, but his grip was too strong. My mind emptied as I became extremely aware of every place our bodies touched. But there was another sensation creeping through my veins—a dread that had my eyes closing as I tried to calm myself.

He leaned down to hover inches from my face. "As I was saying... you know I can always help if you need a little distraction." His seductive whisper sent shivers across my neck and along my exposed skin.

"Fuck you."

"Gladly." His eyes shone mischievously. I looked at his nose instead, avoiding eye contact. "You think I can't tell how tightly wound you are? That I don't feel the same?"

My eyes shot back up, warmth pooling in my stomach. He brushed his nose along the length of my neck up to my ear lobe, and I froze, wariness settling in my chest. "How many times have you touched yourself since that night, trying to find adequate release?"

I would never admit it to him. The nights I'd woken up, this time not plagued by my nightmares, my hands dipping between my thighs in hopes of ridding myself of my frustrations. They never matched the tingling sensations he had been able to elicit from my traitorous skin all those months ago. In some ways, those dreams were worse than my nightmares, my own body betraying the hurt I wanted to feel.

Making me feel emotions that I didn't want. And making me despise him more.

Dracho took a deep breath through his nose, a low rumble emitting from his chest. His pupils expanded so his eyes looked almost entirely black, displaying his hunger.

"Get off of me," I snarled at him.

"Are you sure?" His eyebrow shot up in challenge.

Panic rose in my chest. I *knew* this was Dracho, but my mind… it drifted to a darkened bedroom, where strange men held me down. My voice cracked as I whispered it. "*Please.*"

Dracho's eyes melted to a shade of icy blue as the heat there vanished and horror appeared. The look on his face was one I hadn't seen since we first met. Since that night he had first witnessed one of my nightmares.

He relented, releasing my wrists and helping me to my feet. Anger filled me as I turned away from him, tears in my eyes. I brushed myself off before walking towards the platform. I didn't look at my friends, knowing what they would see in my face. But my eyes caught Antares's furious expression—aimed at Dracho—and Althea's frozen form as I neared the steps. She was no longer staring at her perfect nails but contemplating me thoughtfully.

"Need a cold shower, E?" Bastion teased after me, egregiously misreading the mood. I could feel Dracho's eyes burning into my back.

I could feel it in my bones. He knew he had pushed me too far.

Chapter 8

Dracho

She was afraid of me. I didn't blame her; I'd become afraid of myself too.

I thought I had grown used to the new me over the past several months—a self that no longer felt the entity of a dragon within but had become the dragon. I had led my city and people from a place of darkness and grief, suppressing my own so deeply that at times I felt like an automaton, focused solely on finding those responsible for my father's death.

I'd led Tenebris from a danger I could see so clearly. I'd strengthened our borders, enhanced our magickal protections… I had pushed myself to the brink of exhaustion every single day, just to ensure my people felt safer, ignoring that pull in my chest that I knew led to her.

And my people had thrived, whilst I'd diminished.

But something had changed since I returned to Meridium. I had put off the trip for a long time, brushing aside my uncle's urgings to question King Cervidae until I couldn't any longer.

Seeing her again…

That fire of defiance, that light—it had awakened a glowing spark in my chest that felt right. It eased that restless discomfort just by being closer to her.

I had made mistakes when it came to her. I had hurt her. Betrayed her. But if we could work together to help Ruvalon, perhaps the rift between us could heal. Perhaps she could tame the beast I had become.

The spark in my chest swelled at the thought. I didn't know what it meant, but I decided to stop fighting it.

Chapter 9

Eliana

I had just settled into the armchair by my chamber window, the bath I'd just had doing very little to soothe my aching muscles, when Milly knocked on the door with an unexpected guest.

Althea had changed out of her training leathers. A white shirt now flowed off her slender shoulders, the hem tucked into a pair of leather trousers. I watched as she strolled in.

"I'll fetch a guard," Milly said.

"Not necessary, thank you Milly." I smiled politely at Milly as she closed the door behind her.

Althea's eyes travelled around the room, taking in the floor-length mirror and the small cream wardrobe against the wall beside my bed. Her lips seemed to pucker in surprise, but she strolled over and threw herself down into the armchair opposite me. Crossing one leg over the other, she hummed loudly.

A muscle ticked in my jaw. "I'm sorry, can I help you?"

Althea rolled her eyes. "I thought it was about time we got to know each other."

"And *why* would I want to get to know you?"

It was a bluff. The first time I had seen Althea and observed Dracho's interaction with her, I had been eager to find out more about her—and the extent of her and Dracho's relationship.

A smile pulled at her lips. "I can see why he likes you."

I stiffened. "I don't know what you're talking about."

"You know, when Ant told me Dracho had developed feelings for a princess of Ruvalon, I definitely didn't expect you."

I didn't bother arguing. "What did you expect? Some spoiled, naive girl that did as she was told?"

"Yes."

At least she was honest. "And?"

"And what?"

"Do I disappoint?" I asked, rolling my eyes.

She laughed, the sound like a harmony of tinkling bells. "You know, we're very alike."

"I highly doubt that." I knew I was being harsh. But after the morning training I was in no mood for niceties.

The sharpness of her bright blue eyes softened. "People like us. *Women* like us—it takes a lot to break through our walls, but not so much to build them higher."

I held my breath, not liking where the conversation was heading.

"I could tell from the way your hands trembled once Dracho knocked you down."

I swallowed hard.

"How old were you?" she asked, no hint of malice in her voice.

I chewed my cheek for a second, shocked at her candid way of asking such a question. It spilled from my mouth anyway. "It's not what you think. Not exactly, anyway. But—twelve."

I wasn't sure why it had come out. But her relaxed aura made me feel somewhat comfortable around her.

She nodded, a small smile on her lips. "I wasn't too much older." She looked away, playing with the sleeve of her shirt. "My mother died in childbirth, you see. She was a mortal and didn't have the draconi's ability of healing."

Of course they had the ability to heal quickly. I couldn't believe I'd let that slip my notice, but I supposed I'd been preoccupied with other things after Dracho had fought the Hollow.

"My father believed it to be my fault, of course. But, for the first formative years of my childhood, he generally left me alone, whilst his love for ale grew deeper than his love for his only child."

My breathing sped up as I listened, unable to look away.

"It wasn't until my early teenage years that the real beatings began. Ant and

Dracho would always question why my body ached so much in training. My father never touched my face, you see. The emperor would have taken his head if he had known."

"How did... how did it stop?" From the way she talked about it—like it had happened to someone else—I gathered that it wasn't a current experience.

A cruel smile lit up her face. "I'm not sure if I should tell you this, but... what has Dracho told you about me?"

My thoughts ran back over our time together. To the time outside the gates of Meridium. "He said he used to help you with panic attacks."

She hummed, nodding. "That was after. I imagine he didn't tell you much more?"

I shook my head.

"Dracho and Ant became suspicious after spotting bruises on my arm. It's not easy for us to bruise at all. One night, my father was feeling particularly vicious. Had me begging on the floor whilst he beat me over and over. Slashed at my arms and legs with his claws... that night, I truly learned about monsters."

I swallowed the emotion that was clogging my throat.

"Eventually I just lay there, believing I was going to die."

I stared at her, knowing exactly what she meant.

She exhaled deeply. "Let's just say I was lucky Dracho and Ant made it there just in time." She pushed herself to her feet, heading back to the door.

"And your father?"

She smirked, and even in its cruelty there was beauty. "Dead."

"How?"

Her smile fell. "Now, *that*... that's not my story to tell." She assessed my confusion. "It's Ant's."

"Why tell me all this?" I asked as she moved to open the door.

She halted, her hand resting on the handle.

"Trauma changes us all. And not often for the better. It makes us hold onto our anger for longer; push those away who may be good for us. I'm ashamed to say that I was once that person. We may not see eye to eye on *all* things, Eliana, and may be on differing sides of this. But at the end of the day, whether dragon or mortal, us women have to stick together." She turned, sending me a wink, and I couldn't help but give a small smile back.

It was only hours later that I realised she hadn't asked for my own story.

It was surreal, feeling that I had to watch every step within the walls of my own home, worrying that I might accidentally bump into one of our guests. I still didn't expect to find someone waiting outside my door when I opened it, planning to sneak down to the kitchens for some of Eiram's hot cocoa.

"Goddess, Connaught!" My hand flew to my thigh automatically, but I'd left my dagger on my nightstand. It unnerved me that in my anxiety, I'd forgotten it.

"I'm sorry. I didn't mean to startle you, Eliana." He stepped away from his position leaning against the wall.

I blew out a breath. "No, it's fine. What are you doing here?"

His cheeks reddened, matching his hair as he rubbed the back of his neck. "I, um, I was guarding your room."

My eyes rolled. "Shouldn't you be guarding Father, if anyone?"

"He has four guards outside his door. My shift finished two hours ago."

"Finished? Connaught, *what* are you doing?"

Connaught had joined the army of Meridium straight from the same orphanage where I had found Vyn. He had risen through the ranks at unprecedented speed, becoming the youngest ever promoted to the royal guard. I'd used to hate him, thanks to a particularly embarrassing sparring session when I had sneaked into the training arena. But after that, and after he had saved my life that awful night during the Tain, my father had promoted him to be my personal guard and escort. His loyalty to the crown was second to none, and it wasn't long before he'd become one of my closest companions. When Bas's father had retired, he'd been made captain of the royal guard. His skills and authority were questioned by no one, and he was widely respected by all. It didn't shock me that he would exhaust himself to watch over me.

He took a step closer, picking up my hand delicately and holding it within his. "I will not rest whilst a threat remains within these very walls. To you or your father."

I smiled, used to his comforting affection. "Connaught, Dracho wouldn't hurt me." It was a lie. He absolutely would hurt me again, if given the chance. Why else would he be here? "Not here, of all places."

Connaught's thumb rubbed a soothing, familiar circle on my hand. He had always been one of my closest friends, next to Vyn and Bas, though he was always careful to remain professional around everyone else—many would have deemed it inappropriate for a captain and a princess to be so familiar.

Dracho's visit must really have him rattled if he felt the need to comfort me.

"I know he would not physically harm you, Eliana. But I fear from what I've seen that he could hurt you in other ways."

I froze. "You don't know what you're talking about."

"No?"

He stepped closer, letting go of my hand to hold my arms gently. He was so close I could feel the heat of his body. He studied my face.

"I know you, Eliana. Sometimes I know your feelings better than you do."

His brow arched as I turned away. Calloused fingertips gripped my chin ever so gently, turning it back to face him.

Inhaling deeply, I gave him a small smile. "I'm fine."

"I believe you will be. But... if, at any moment, you feel like you did when—"

He paused. Steps sounded at the end of the hallway.

We turned to look, but I already knew who stood there. His electric aura pulsed out from him.

His eyes narrowed at Connaught's hand on my face before pinning me with their intense gaze. My body felt on fire under that blazing look, and I stepped out of Connaught's arms. He swallowed and stood to attention, bowing from the waist as Dracho walked towards us.

"Your Excellency," Connaught said, only a hint of disdain audible.

Dracho said nothing, staring at the top of Connaught's lowered head, but I noticed that the line of silver around his pupil had widened.

"What are you doing here, Dracho?" I asked impatiently as Connaught straightened.

Dracho's eyes snapped to me, and I tried to ignore the little bolt of electricity that ran up my spine. I wasn't sure what Dracho was looking for as his eyes travelled over my face, but he seemed satisfied by what he found. "I was going to ask you if you'd accompany me for a walk. I don't think Red here would like it if I suggested we talk in your room."

Connaught stiffened next to me; Dracho's lips curled at the edges.

"I don't think that's necessary. There'll be plenty of time to talk on our way to Aion," I told him, taking a step back towards my room.

Dracho stepped forward, his hand reaching out. "Please, Eliana. I'm sorry—"

The apology on his lips stunned me for a moment, but steel rang out as Connaught pulled his sword halfway out of its sheath, moving to stand in front of me.

"My lady declined, Your Excellency. I think it would be prudent if you returned to your chambers."

Dracho's pupils lengthened and thinned, and I anxiously watched the silver dragon's eyes as he considered Connaught. Dracho may have been slightly shorter, but it was obvious who held the power in this dynamic.

All I knew was that if I didn't do something, whatever weird energy was flowing between them would blow out of proportion. Moving out of Connaught's shadow, I took a few steps to stand before Dracho.

"Not tonight, Dracho."

His eyes fell to my face, a splash of blue lightening them.

"I'm going to fetch Engel tomorrow after Father's announcement. You may accompany me if you wish."

Dracho nodded without a word. Eyeing Connaught once more, he retreated.

I rubbed a hand over my tired face and opened the door to my room, my quest for hot cocoa forgotten.

"Good thing I was standing guard after all," Connaught called, his tone amused.

I laughed. "Connaught, shut the fuck up."

Chapter 10

"Don't cry, little doe." Mother's hand smoothed comfortingly over my loose hair. She had silently removed the pins whilst I cried into my arms on the bed, and now that my tears had subsided, she was ever my kind, doting Mammy—trying to ease a small girl's worries.

"It's not fair!" I whined, raising my eyes to meet hers.

She smiled softly. "How old are you, Eliana?"

"Eleven," I muttered.

"Most girls do not join in with training until fifteen," she pointed out.

"I just wanted to be like Morgwn!"

"We gathered that, from the way you had dressed as a boy," she laughed. "You're lucky Morgwn noticed you before young Connaught could have done any damage, or revealed who you were in the middle of the training arena."

I scoffed, sitting up. "I could have taken him."

Even I knew I couldn't. Morgwn's older friend had knocked me on my backside twice, causing tears to spring to my eyes and his own to narrow with suspicion.

A knock sounded at the door, and my mother brushed my hair over my shoulders before granting permission to enter. It was Connaught, escorted by the master of the staff, Farley. The boy—five years older than me—gulped when he saw my mother by my side, and tipped forward in a bow so low I thought he would fall over.

"Your Majesty, Your Highness. I have come to apologise for my actions in the arena. I had no idea the person I was fighting was the princess. I would never harm her—"

"That's quite all right, Connaught," my mammy interrupted. "Eliana now knows how foolish it was to conceal her identity. Don't you, dear?"

I nodded, unable to wipe the scowl off my face. Connaught looked relieved, and he gave a boyish smile when he spotted my expression. He bowed once more.

"Thank you, Your Majesty."

He turned to leave, Farley holding the door for him, but his steps faltered. He looked over his shoulder at me.

"You fought well, Your Highness. I look forward to the day I witness you beat your brother in the training ring."

My face flamed as he left, and I looked to my mammy with a satisfied grin. She rolled her eyes, but she was smiling.

"As it so happens," she said, once the door closed, "your father and I have agreed that you may start training with Morgwn. Private *lessons," she emphasised when I started bouncing on the balls of my feet excitedly. "We don't want any accidents, now, do we?"*

"No, Mammy."

"Good." She tucked my hair behind my ear. "Now, get dressed; dinner will be served soon. I'll let you tell Morgwn the good news." She laughed as she walked to my wardrobe.

I bounced after her, eager to see the look on Morgwn's face once he learned he'd be training me.

I blinked, rubbing my hazy eyes as I stirred from the dream—a nice one, for a change. I smiled as I thought back on the memory. Morgwn had been speechless once I had told him, before asking Father if it was true. He had been thrilled at the opportunity to train me. Unlike other older siblings, Morgwn never complained about escorting me or entertaining me.

He'd been my best friend, despite our age difference. Now I was older and he was gone, I sometimes wondered if I had taken him for granted. Expected him to always be there.

Beatrice left my room begrudgingly when I informed her that I would prepare my own clothes for the day. Her pursed lips and narrowed brown eyes made me chuckle. Even before I'd left Meridium, I had always enjoyed the independence of getting ready for the day on my own. I didn't want to be a burden, and I certainly didn't expect assistance off anyone. But Beatrice had always loved helping me, and before that my mother. Most of the time, I would entertain her wishes.

Connaught wasn't outside my door when I left, but one of the guards, a large mountain troll named Marcus, awaited to escort me to Father's study.

"This isn't necessary," I told him.

He smirked. "Sorry, Your Highness—cap'ns orders."

"Of course it is." I rolled my eyes.

"Morning," Father grumbled as I entered the room. Marcus pulled the door closed, giving me a mocking bow in response to my vulgar hand gesture.

"Eliana," Father scolded. "Sometimes I fear you are *too* familiar with our guards."

"Nonsense." I smiled. "I knock them on their arses every other week. It would be impossible for me *not* to be familiar."

He sighed. "Whatever you say, dear."

"You wanted to see me?" I asked, stepping towards the large desk and noting a scattering of papers and letters.

"Yes... I wanted to talk to you about your journey to Aion."

"Go on."

"There have been several bandit attacks in the south—something I intend to talk to Jareth about, since it is his territory to manage. But be on the lookout. The last thing we need is an altercation with dragons, causing mass panic."

"At least people already know they're here."

He nodded. He'd given a proclamation in the palace courtyard, with Dracho and most of Meridium's citizens in attendance. Father, with Dracho's amused agreement, had presented it as a diplomatic visit by the new emperor.

The revelation of the dragons' ability to change into a mortal form was a shocking one to everyone except me, Bas and Vyn. Milly told me that, fortunately, most saw it as proof they weren't uncontrollable beasts. Others saw it as confirmation that gods walked among us, and that their time to rule over us again was nearing. No matter what the person's belief, all had bowed in respect when Father had announced Dracho to the city.

"I know you'll be safe together," Father said, "but don't stray from your path on the way."

"I know."

"Nor on the way back."

"Yes, Father." I couldn't help smiling at the worry so clearly etched upon my father's face.

He walked around his desk, clasping my shoulders gently. "I can't help my concern, dear daughter. I'm glad that you have Roux, as well as our guests from Tenebris."

I huffed impatiently. "Anyone would think you doubted my own capabilities."

His lips thinned as he suppressed a grin. "Not at all. But as your father, I would prefer it if you didn't have to put yourself at risk."

"I'd be a pretty bad monarch if that were the case."

He huffed out a laugh before sighing deeply. "There was one other thing I wanted to talk to you about, Eliana."

His hands fell from my arms and he took a step back, as if knowing I would want personal space for this conversation. Feeling the cold absence of his warmth, I wrapped my own arms around myself.

"Eliana..."

My gut sank. This wasn't going to be pleasant.

"Did—did anything ever happen between you and Dracho?"

There it was. It had been pointless hoping that Father had ignored or not realised the implication behind Dracho's words at breakfast the other morning. If there was ever a conversation I didn't want to be having with my parent, it was this one.

"I won't lie. We became... close."

"Before or after you found out his identity?"

I paused for a moment, wondering how he would take the truth. "After."

Father inhaled deeply through his nose, nodding slightly. I couldn't decipher the emotions crossing his face. "And now?"

"Now?" I asked incredulously.

"Well, my dear daughter, I cannot deny what is clearly in front of me."

"Why is everyone so determined to insist that we have feelings for each other?" I demanded, exasperated.

"Do you?" he asked bluntly.

"Yes. Of disdain... and annoyance."

Father grinned, looking at me as only a father could. "I can't tell you what to do, Eliana. You are no longer a child, and you must find your own way in this world. But what I *can* tell you is to be careful. Your heart is the most valuable thing you own; when you give it to someone, you give them the power to hurt you. I think you've had enough experience of that."

I had. My relationship with Jakard all those years ago had been public news. Although it had not been announced that we were officially courting, it was obvious how serious our relationship was; we'd attended functions together, and spent two summers *together* in Meridium.

I myself had been expecting an official announcement—so it had devastated me when Jareth declared that Jak had started courting Illyra instead. Father and Connaught had had to stop me from riding to Stillmere myself to get some answers. Jak and Illyra had barely interacted during our time together; none of it made sense. The only answer I ever got from him was a short, cold letter.

I'm sorry. I've moved on.

It was shortly after that I had run away with Bas and Vyn, the memories of all the good and the bad that had happened in the palace twisting my emotions until I was in turmoil.

"I understand." I didn't want to let Father know that I had already given that power to Dracho, and been burned for it.

"I won't apologise for being overbearing. I know you'll be safe with Dracho; I don't believe he will allow you to come to any harm. But I want you to be happy, as well as safe."

I smiled. "I know."

"I must admit I'm excited to see the great beast again."

Dracho walked several feet behind me on the shore of Solva Bay. Our trek down to the waters seemed to have emboldened him; he was acting like we were old friends.

"Eliana, I want to apologise."

I almost stopped in surprise, but I swallowed hard, saying nothing.

"I shouldn't have embarrassed you at breakfast the other morning in front of everyone."

That was what he was apologising for?

There was a moment of before he spoke again. "I also want to apologise for scaring you during our sparring session. That was never my intention, and I felt—"

I stopped then, turning to look at him, noting the colour that bloomed high on his cheeks. "You didn't scare me."

"I—oh... I didn't?" He looked confused, brushing his hair—I still wasn't used to it being dark—out of his face as I shook my head. "Then why did you react the way you did? I thought you were having a panic attack."

My spine stiffened almost painfully as I straightened. That was a part of it. But there was no way I would ever tell him that it was because of how my body had reacted to him. How in that moment my body and heart had been at war with one another, and it had taken everything to shove down that rebellious part of me and refrain from pulling him to my lips.

Because he could give every apology in the world for that moment, or the one at breakfast, but they weren't the right ones.

So I just shrugged, continuing my path down to the water. I waited, my chest tightening, to see if he said anything else. Any more apologies.

But there was nothing.

"Thank you for your apologies," I said at last. "It wasn't the most pleasant experience having to divulge my sexual exploits to my father." I almost grinned at the choking noise that sounded out behind me.

"Your father knows?" Dracho caught up to my side, his gaze piercing my profile.

"You weren't exactly subtle with what you were implying."

I saw him wince from the corner of my eye. "Well... again, I apologise."

For some reason I believed him. "Thanks."

The rest of our walk was silent, which I appreciated, a little unnerved by our relatively pleasant conversation. My thoughts drifted to the night before, going over his and Connaught's interaction repeatedly. I knew Connaught would always protect me to his last breath—even up against a draconi... but there were some things I was unwilling to admit when it came to how far he would go for me. The motivations behind those actions. Not wanting to confront those thoughts, I had interceded to end the tense moment. It was why I had given in and invited Dracho to come with me to fetch Engel.

A granite-grey sky rolled above us, only small fissures of sunlight breaking through the heavy clouds threatening rain. The cold water bit at my calves as I ventured in, reminding myself to focus. Bringing my fingers to my lips, I whistled the high tone I used to call Engel. It had been days since I had last seen him.

Dracho started to speak. "What do you think—"

The wind picked up, blocking out his words. A swirling circle of water appeared in the bay, gathering speed. Unease rose in my gut. Was something wrong? I couldn't see Engel, and I had never seen such a thing appear in the bay.

The splash from the water sounded like thunder as the beast in question burst upwards with shocking speed, turning to run across the surface towards us in a full gallop. His luminous mane rose from his body, the hairs along my arms echoing it. My heart skipped. His aura was as furious as the water he had sprung from, and I wondered what was wrong. He didn't look hurt. He also didn't look like he was planning to stop.

I took a step back onto the sand, turning to look at Dracho. His hand was held out, concern on his face. "Princess, I think—"

An ear-piercing squeal sounded from Engel as he galloped toward us. Dracho's head tilted; realisation seemed to strike him. He took a step back, holding his hands steady by his sides.

"What's—?" I started to ask.

With a final burst of speed, Engel jumped the final distance to the shore, skidding to a halt directly in front of Dracho.

The water horse tipped his head down so that Dracho was staring at his muzzle. Dracho kept still, a small smile at the corner of his lips. To my surprise, he didn't attempt to touch or stroke Engel, but allowed him this demonstration of dominance.

After a tense moment, Engel turned, his mane returning to its usual colour as he looked at me for the first time. He walked over to nibble on the end of my hair, before trotting away in the direction of the stables.

"What was that?" I demanded.

Dracho huffed, seemingly amused. "*That* was a warning."

I nodded as if in understanding, but I had no idea what had just happened. How could Engel tell that something had changed between me and Dracho?

The creature had paused and was looking at me expectantly. I suppressed a laugh at the glance he gave Dracho over my shoulder, and I stroked his side affectionately.

"Good boy," I whispered, smiling to myself.

Chapter 11

Hindsight was a wonderful thing, but I had discovered that *foresight* was much preferable—and it was something I should have had regarding my journey.

It should have been obvious how irritating Dracho was going to be. From verbally and telepathically sending me inappropriate words to calling me *Princess* every time he spoke... had I thought about it, I probably would have ordered Connaught to go in my stead. There was no rush to get to Aion, but the more he tried to converse with me, the more I found myself urging Engel to gallop onwards.

On day three, we stopped by a bubbling stream on Bas's suggestion. Allowing the horses to graze nearby as we refilled our canteens and stretched our legs after hours of riding was a nice reprieve; the soreness in my thighs and calves was worsening the longer we rode. Engel snorted in excitement as Vyn offered him an apple, moving on to the other horses.

Beside us was a small forest of trees so thick and dense, I could barely see into the shadows as I quietly walked the border. My pulse quickened looking upon it, a shiver crawling along my spine. It felt like being watched. The others had set up camp by the tinkling sound of the water, but I started to concentrate on the silence of the woods, wondering if something would creep out of the dark.

"So, Princess..."

I threw my head back in exasperation as Dracho approached, holding his extended glaive close to his side.

His grin grew into a wide smile. "Have you visited Aion since we parted ways?"

Hating the casual way he described our separation, I shook my head and took a step out of the shade of the trees.

"So what have you been doing all this time?" Dracho turned, his eyes narrowing on the forest before returning to me. I noticed Antares crouching further along the treeline, seemingly listening to something. He nodded at Dracho.

I studied the latter's face, wondering why he was asking. "Helping my father, training. Just normal—"

"Princess stuff?" He tilted his head enough for me to see his smirk.

"*Yes*, all right. I was completing my duties as—"

A whistle sounded through the trees. Dracho's free hand shot up inhumanly fast in front of my face. My eyes crossed as they focused, spotting the metal arrowhead an inch from my left eye.

How did I miss that?

"Here they come," Antares hissed.

I squinted, spotting the bow man. He had stepped out from behind the cover of a large tree and was nocking another arrow.

Almost as fast as he had caught it, Dracho threw the arrow towards him with extraordinary strength. The bolt tore through the bowman's head, cracking bone and splitting tissue. The sight was so graphic, so sudden, I almost didn't hear the deep cries that sounded out as dozens of men and women started running from in between the trees, weapons raised.

Dracho gave a devilishly handsome smile. "Let's have some fun."

He tore off, almost too fast to follow as he ripped through the first few men with his glaive. I pulled my dagger from its sheath to meet the man who would reach me first, but he went down several feet ahead of me, an arrow sticking out of his eye. I caught Antares's cold smile as he tipped his head towards me, lifting his bow again as he entered the trees.

Meanwhile, Althea sat on a boulder by the water, crossing one leg over the other, as if the fight wasn't worth her time—which it probably wasn't, judging by the speed with which Dracho and Antares dispatched the bandits.

"Your idea of fun and mine are vastly different," Antares called after Dracho, jogging between the tree trunks, firing each arrow with alarming accuracy.

“Weren’t gonna leave us out, were you?” Bas yelled, running up, Vyn close behind.

“These must be the men your father warned us about,” Vyn panted.

I only nodded as I followed Dracho into the forest, angry tension flowing through me. He spun to knock an axe from the hand of a nearby bandit and plunge his glaive into his gut. The fleshy rip of his skin made my lip curl in disgust.

“Shall we just leave him to it?” Bas asked from behind me, nodding towards Dracho as he took out another bandit, not even a speck of blood on him.

I huffed, pointing to the left. “I think you have your chance to join in, Bas.”

A man the size of a boulder was running towards us, a long knife held above his head. Bas’s smile promised blood; his hands twisted on the leather handle of his battle axe.

But the man erupted into golden-edged black flames, his final scream cutting through the air as he fell into a pile of ash.

Bas pouted. “No fair, little mage.”

Roux came to stand beside him, patting his arm soothingly. “All’s fair in blood and war, big man.”

“I’m pretty sure that’s not how the saying goes,” Vyn pointed out. Roux shrugged.

“Well,” I said, strolling further into the woods, “considering my head was nearly impaled by one of these bastards, I’d like to get a shot in before those two finish them.”

We spread out, eliminating the bandits one by one as they approached. Only a few remained of the group, weaving in and out of the trees. Some, realising how preternaturally fast and skilled both Dracho and Antares were, had turned tail to flee, but the dragons gave chase and turned them down.

Two women had—either stupidly or bravely; I hadn’t decided yet—tried to entrap Roux between them, their yellowing teeth bared at her. Roux’s hands unfurled, her fingers looking like the hooked claws of a jungle cat, waiting. They went for her at the same time.

All she did was flex her fingers, and they were swallowed by black flames. Their screams only lasted for a second before Roux clenched her fists again, and it was ash that fell to the floor, not bodies.

“Goddess above,” I whispered as Roux wiped her brow, but someone was creeping up on me from behind.

Raising my dagger and whirling round, I faltered once I truly looked at her.

Greasy, dark blonde hair fell over her eyes, a survivor's ferocity shining there. She crouched slightly, growling at me through cracked lips. My anger guttered as realisation struck me like a battering ram. These people were likely starving. Despite their methods, they were in need.

I held my hands up, and her eyes narrowed.

"I'm not going to hurt you. If—"

She swiped her blade in front of her. I jerked back slightly to avoid it, shaking my head impatiently. "If it's food you want, we can give you some. There's no need—"

She screeched, her eyes wild as she made a run for me.

Dodging to the side, I thrust my blade at her, embedding it into her chest. She grunted; blood pooled at the corner of her mouth. When I ripped my bloodied blade free, she fell face-down in the dirt.

Wiping my dagger clean with her shirt, I sheathed it. My hands felt clammy as I ran them over my face and growled loudly.

Steps approached, but I didn't need to turn. His formidable aura brushed against my back like a cool breeze.

"You all right?" Dracho nudged my arm from behind.

"Yes... No. It's fucking frustrating!" I ranted.

He was studying me like I'd gone mad.

"I gave her a chance. I offered her an alternative other than *robbing* us. I straight up offered her food! There was no need for her to die." I threw my arm out in her direction.

Dracho shrugged, not smiling for once. "You can't save them all."

I stepped back in surprise. The response was so different from the Dracho I'd known. "Wow. That's a rather strange point of view for a ruler."

His laugh was dark. "I'd rather be pragmatic than a bleeding heart."

"Says the person who provided aid to towns on his way here."

He growled, taking a step towards me. "Being a realist doesn't make me a bad ruler. You could have offered them the moon and stars and they wouldn't have stopped their attack. I could have captured the lot of them and taken them back to Meridium. Rehabilitated them within the city. But the result would have still been the same—except in that case, it would have been more lives lost after they ripped through the people of *your* city."

I jerked back at his assumptions. "You don't know that. How can you be so casual about their deaths?"

Dracho stepped into my personal space, lowering his head so I couldn't see beyond the intense look in his still-silver eyes. The vertical pupils made him more animal than man.

"Because, Eliana, they made their decision when they fired a steel bolt directly at your head. Even if you had spared the woman, all their fates were sealed the moment her companion went for *you*."

"You knew they were there, didn't you," I whispered.

His eyes confirmed it. "Antares sensed them a while before they attacked. We were waiting to see what they would do."

Bas and Vyn were heading towards us. "Then why—"

"No amount of negotiation would have prevented that altercation, Eliana. Some people choose violence. Some are too far gone."

"But..." I faltered when he held out his hand, offering it to me.

He growled when I didn't immediately take it. "Come on. I need to show you something."

I arched a brow, but he just waited. Against all my better judgement, I laid my hand in his, my teeth clenching at the charge that tingled up my arm. He clasped it, pulling me further into the trees.

"Should we be worried?" I heard Bas ask Vyn.

Vyn shrugged. "Nah. If he pisses her off she'll stab him."

Dracho scoffed, but otherwise didn't react as he led me through the trees. A pungent smell started to reach my nose. It was about five minutes before we stopped before a large ditch.

"There." His tone was resigned as he released my hand, pointing towards the hole. My stomach lurched; I covered my nose. "I didn't want you seeing this, but maybe now you'll understand."

Bile crept into my mouth, and I tried to push it down. The crudely dug hole was half full of *people*. Their clothes had been stripped from them, along with any belongings, showing pale skin and mouths open in horror. Some had already started to decompose; others were more... fresh. And all of them had had chunks of flesh torn from them.

I gagged. *We can't leave them like this.*

"Ant could smell it from outside the forest," Dracho said.

"Then why didn't you say anything?" I turned my back on the horror.

"We were going to deal with them tonight, had they not attacked first."

"You need to tell me about these things!" I spun to look up at him.

The silver of his eyes brightened. "If there is ever a time I can protect you from burdening yourself, then I will."

There wasn't a single part of me that could deny the sincerity of his words. It was promised in the smoke of his voice and the shining of his eyes. I swallowed, walking back towards the group. "That's not your place."

"Perhaps not, but it's the truth nevertheless."

I didn't deny it, not daring to say anything further on the matter.

"You all right, E?" Bas called out once we came into view.

"Yes." My voice was shaky; I was incredibly aware of Dracho beside me, his gaze never leaving my face. He smelled like fresh citrus and smoke. "Coming."

I'd only taken a few paces before my feet stopped of their own accord, words bubbling up in my chest.

"It's just annoying..." I didn't turn, didn't look at him. "That I couldn't make a difference for her."

Dracho's voice was soft, reminding me of before. "You can't make a difference to them all. But you *can* make a difference one at a time."

"Hmm." I walked past Antares, who looked at me pointedly.

"You can't save people from themselves. You can only try to wake them up," he offered.

A humourless laugh escaped my throat, my mind flashing back to a throne room filled with guards as I was dragged away to a dungeon.

"You've got that right," I muttered. "Bas... you know you love me?"

He sighed. "Who do you want dead this time?"

Behind us, Antares murmured, "This time?"

I smiled. "Inside the forest—you'll know when you find it. Set a small fire."

He looked concerned, but nodded and headed past us to put those poor souls to rest.

Two days later, we found ourselves in Aion half a day earlier than we had anticipated. The tall forest surrounding Home Tree was a beautiful sight to behold; I stood alone outside our tents, breathing in deeply, feeling its magick. It was nothing like the forest we'd left behind, now likely a smouldering pile of twigs, thanks to Bas.

"I said a small fire!" I'd scolded him, looking behind us to find billowing smoke and flames of red rising from the forest.

"Clearly a miscommunication somewhere," he had replied, causing Althea to bark out a surprised laugh.

Now, different hues of red, orange and yellow streaked across the blue dawn sky in what promised to be a cloudless day. The peace and magic of the Aioni soil must have had some calming effect on me, as no nightmare had plagued me the night before—for which I was grateful. Having some nosy dragon waking to any mumbled outbursts would only increase the awkwardness I felt by having them nearby.

As if summoned by my thoughts, a draconi emerged to stand beside me. Just not the one I would have expected.

"Happy to be back?" Antares asked in a low voice that sounded like thunder. There was no trace of anger in his question—just a hint of hesitation.

For a moment I was at a loss for words. Antares had never spoken to me one-on-one before my stay in Tenebris, and I couldn't say he was someone I would go to first for a casual conversation. Not because I didn't want to know more, but... the aura surrounding Antares was like no other I had ever felt.

I couldn't deny that my eyes hadn't appreciated his form once or twice—he was incredibly attractive. I had used to think that if Dracho was the dawn, with his silver hair and blue eyes, then Antares was midnight. The waves of his dark hair fell to his shoulders when he wore it loose, a streak of white contrasting harshly with the darkness. The sharp contours of his cheekbones could have been chiselled by a master sculptor. Even when talking quietly, his sonorous, rumbling voice could fill a room, quiet the loudest occupants.

But it was his eyes that gripped you. As bright and spellbinding as molten gold, they looked like they had been enamelled by the sun itself. But not in a way that made him approachable—no. They flashed fire in the way a wild animal's colouring could warn you away. It was a strange paradox: that Dracho's once-silver hair and icy blue eyes would make you feel warm, whilst Antares's honey eyes and dark hair could be so cold.

Before Dracho's transformation. Now, if it wasn't for the differing eye colour, you would have thought the two were brothers.

Before the events of Tenebris I'd used to ponder how the two were friends. Dracho was—had been—so personable and outgoing. Everything opposite to what Antares had shown. In fact, on a few occasions I'd had the distinct impression Antares didn't like being around too many people at all. Which I'd kind of empathised with... But there was still this feeling I always had around him, almost as if he wasn't very fond of me, or that he could turn on me at any moment.

Not that he had ever *verbally* expressed such disdain. Except for the time he'd implied Dracho should have allowed me to die before revealing his identity. Oh, and placing a blade to my throat.

Antares had always been quiet; never said anything in a conversation unless he absolutely had to. Yet I was acutely aware of one thing—Antares noticed *everything*. From the moment I'd first seen him, the vicious awareness and dangerous energy that rolled off him had kept me on my toes. Now that he was speaking to me, it made me feel more on edge.

It wasn't that he couldn't be kind; I had seen him show Vyn and Roux gentleness on occasion. But I'd never thought that would be extended to me. It made me question his motives, just like I constantly did with Dracho. I stared at him, wondering.

His eyes narrowed, and I realised I hadn't answered him. "Um, yes. It will be nice to see everyone again... You?"

He hummed, the sound low in his throat. Where Dracho's voice was like smoke, Antares's was like smooth liquor, rather pleasant to listen to. "Now that I know what to expect from the area, I must admit... I feel more comfortable here."

"Expect from the area?"

He nodded. "We can feel the celestral energy in the air. It feels different."

My eyes widened. I remembered Antares being even more unsociable during our time in Aion—spending more time with Roux's spirit guide, Cubra, than with anyone else. The two were rather similar, like quiet predators, so it hadn't been a surprise they got along.

"Oh." I wasn't sure what to say to that. "And you don't mind the company you're keeping?"

He glanced around at the group, before fixing me with a hard stare that was difficult to withstand. "It's not so bad. Speak later, Princess."

I swallowed hard as he returned to the tents, where the others had woken up and were gathering. When Dracho called me by my title, as annoying as it was, it was teasing and almost a term of endearment. When Antares used it, it sounded like a veiled threat.

But the exchange had been surprisingly pleasant, and even inspired a sliver of confidence in me that we were on better terms than before. A shock, considering he believed my father to be a suspect in the murder of Dracho's father.

On second thought, perhaps our conversation made me more nervous...

I caught Althea's gaze. She smirked and winked at me, but my attention was pulled elsewhere by a break in the medley of birdsong from the canopy overhead. Something was coming. Dracho and Antares reacted too, though from their expressions, it was friendly.

Roux dashed from her tent, beaming, as a great violet beast burst from the bush, his feathered tail floating along behind him. Roux laughed as she fell to her knees before Cubra, allowing the feline to bowl her backwards. He rubbed his nose against her face affectionately.

"Well, I would say someone has missed you, *ma chemiel*," a strong voice said. Bisa Xolani exited the shade of the trees and walked towards us.

Roux's eyes brightened as she looked up at her mother, getting to her feet and entering her open arms. Cubra strolled past them, wandering to Antares's side. The draconi reached a hand down to smooth the feline's head.

Roux and Bisa shared a quiet, sweet reunion, and then the chief mage's thoughtful eyes found me. She didn't have to offer an embrace; I was already there, enjoying the warmth of her strong arms as they encompassed me.

The corners of her eyes creased when she released me, holding me at arm's length. She studied my face, running a smooth finger along the skin underneath my eye. Her lips pursed, and her head turned to Dracho.

He smiled as she came towards him—and slapped him upside the head.

He jerked away, flushing pink, and rubbed his head. Antares was too busy giving Cubra a fuss to really pay attention, but Althea's head tilted as she watched the exchange with an intense curiosity.

"Bisa! What was that for?" Dracho exclaimed.

"*Inyoka*, didn't you listen to any of my warnings?" She looked close to smacking him again.

"*Inyoka*?" Vyn asked.

"It means dragon in Aioni," Antares told him.

Dracho scoffed. "You have no idea what—"

Bisa stepped closer, pointing a finger in his face. "Don't tell me what I don't know, boy."

Dracho had the sense to look chagrined. He nodded silently.

"How do you even know—" Bas started to ask.

"I am Chief Mage of Aion. I see all, Bastion Ekker." Bisa pointed to her eyes and then to the group; Bas visibly swallowed.

I suppressed a laugh. I wouldn't mention that I had written Bisa a letter upon our return to Meridium, updating her on some of what had occurred and Roux's new location. While I hadn't updated her on every detail, I'd given her more information than I had shared with my father.

"Now, come on. Sizwe is awaiting your arrival."

Dracho gulped at that, and this time my chuckle was out loud. One Xolani sister was bad enough—now he'd have to face two. He glared at me.

Antares and Althea offered to remain to help pack up camp. It amused me to leave them with Bas and Vyn, but an awkwardness settled over us as Dracho, Roux and I left with Bisa.

Fortunately, Dracho remained pleasantly silent during our walk through the woods, and I relished the pursed lips and petulant expression he wore. Roux jogged ahead of the group, swinging her arms out; she laughed freely, Cubra running by the side. I realised I had never asked if she had returned home at all during those months we had been separated. It seemed that she hadn't.

I couldn't help but feel her giddiness as the magick of the forest accompanied us on our path. The beams of sunlight that broke through the canopy and freckled my skin felt like bursts of serenity as the entire forest seemed to welcome us back.

Bisa laughed lightly, walking forward to link arms with her daughter, and I smiled, taking a moment to look back at Dracho.

His solemn expression almost made me stop. I remembered.

The last time we had entered Aion together, the ground was covered in chaos and blood. Mindless destruction and grief. The horror we'd seen that day would never leave his memory—I knew, because it had never left mine. But for one brief moment, jubilant in the feeling of the forest surrounding us, I'd forgotten.

This was the first time Roux had returned home.

I forced down the guilt and bile that had risen in my throat, watching the light dance in Roux's eyes as we approached the great tree, Draco's soft steps falling behind me. Cheers sounded out as Bisa and her daughter passed under the large entrance to the tree.

My brain fogged over as we followed, walking onto the main pathway up Home Tree. I tried to focus on my steps, to remove the flashes of images that invaded my senses. The bright red blood spilled over the ground, the acrid smell of corrupt magick in the air... a wet head of hair, strewn across the sand.

My fault.

I may not have provoked the Hollow myself that evening before Aion's destruction, but I'd made no attempt to stop it or to help Dracho. I may not have known its intentions, but I would still carry some of the burden for the chaos that had ensued.

The Aioni waved and greeted us warmly as we walked up the winding path. All I wanted to do was find a dark corner that I could curl up in—hide from my shame. My shoulder bumped into Dracho's, and I apologised, finding my emotions echoed on his face. It made me wish I had the ability to project my thoughts into his mind.

We halted at the top outside Bisa's home. Roux turned as Bisa went in, the edges of her smile falling once she noticed our faces. She gracefully danced over to us, and I jerked in shock as she wrapped a warm arm around each of us, pulling us closer.

I clasped my lips together in a bid to stem the wave of emotion as I placed my hand against her back. Dracho tipped his head forward, touching his forehead to hers. She pulled away after a moment.

"My friends. Do not be sad. Azande is with us. Can't you feel her?" she said quietly.

A lone tear broke free, trailing its way down my cheek. I sniffed.

"They are all with us." Roux turned from me to Dracho. "They are within us. Always."

Roux's beaming smile dazzled me. All I could feel was awe at her strength. I had always wanted to be strong. I'd constantly been told I was, but never believed it. Never felt it. Because of that, I rarely leaned on anyone for help unless I absolutely had to. But in this moment, I leaned on her.

For her strength. Her grace. Her ability to stay inspired when burdened by such tragic memories.

I found that after all the three of us had gone through—Aion, Volente, Tenebris—there was no anger here. No bitterness. Just a deep, powerful feeling of gratitude. I pulled her close, my eyes clenching shut as I embraced her as much as I could with her other arm wrapped around Dracho.

"Eliana?" a voice called, and I looked over Roux's shoulder.

"Sizwe." I smiled, rushing forward to greet the mage who had watched over me for so many years.

"I missed you, child." She released me from her arms, holding my face in both hands before kissing the top of my head.

"It's only been a month," I laughed, swiping at the errant tear on my face, annoyed that I was displaying such emotion so publicly.

"Hush, girl." A wave of blue light from her hands held open the curtain for us, her free arm wrapping around my shoulders. "Well, are you coming?"

she asked Dracho and Roux. They walked forward, arm in arm. Dracho's eyes still shone with the torment he was clearly feeling.

"It is so good to see you all again," Bisa said inside, taking a seat in the chair by her desk. Her brow creased. "Although I sense there is more to be discussed than a welcome home?"

"The attacks have started again, Bisa," I told her.

Sizwe's eyes crumpled with uncertainty.

"The Hollow destroyed Morcroft. It's gone," Dracho added.

Sizwe shook her head. "What are we to do, Bisa?"

The flecks in Bisa's eyes glowed, her face serious. "There is nothing we can do."

"But—"

"Until we have more information, there isn't much the mages can do. It ripped through our people, and it took every elder to make it flee. There was no beating it that day. Not with our magick. There is something deeper afoot, and until we find out what, we'd just be wasting lives trying to stem it."

"But Roux managed to knock it back that day she saved me from it," Dracho protested.

"That was a surprise attack, Dracho," Roux said. "We have no idea if my powers would truly *hurt* it."

"If you can stop me transforming, surely you'd be able to kill the Hollow?" he insisted. Bisa and Sizwe exchanged a surprised look as Roux shook her head.

"Our magick is compatible. I don't actually stop you transforming. I just... stall your magick for a few moments—and that's not without tremendous effort or discomfort. The Hollow is made from corrupt celestral magick. I would likely do more damage to myself before truly harming it. On my own, anyway."

Dracho brushed his fingers against her hand. "All right. We won't risk you. Not until we find out more and know you can beat it."

Roux looked at me, and I nodded.

"You can stop a draconi from transforming?" Sizwe asked.

Roux gave her aunt a small smile. "I learned more about my celestral magick whilst in Tenebris; Dracho helped me hone my powers."

Bisa smiled, but I tensed. Would those events be discussed now? Sizwe's eyes were on Dracho, but there was no animosity there.

"I'm glad you are mastering your new powers, *ma chemiel*. I can only hope this fight against the Hollow won't take its toll on your magick. Eliana, it is your birthday soon. I assume after your father's party you'll be resuming the hunt?" Bisa asked.

I nodded, though I hadn't discussed it with my father. "We have yet to investigate the temple you spoke of before. I'm not sure how much it will reveal, but it's our best way forward."

Bisa stood. "I agree. But for tonight, we are together once more. We shall celebrate. You are *all* welcome to stay." She gave Dracho a pointed look.

"I'll go and meet the others," he offered, leaving.

"So," Sizwe drawled once he had gone, "I must say I was surprised to see you back in *his* company. How did Dracho come to return to Ruvalon, and how have you left him alive?" Roux's tinkling laugh joined hers as she lowered herself to sit on the colourful rug.

I looked to the ceiling. I was about to be ambushed by all three of the Xolani women... and I kind of adored it.

"It feels so good to be back," Roux sighed, catching up with me and swinging her arms by her sides as we travelled back down the main pathway through Home Tree. Despite the lingering memories of tragedy, her joy was infectious.

"It really does," I agreed, nodding in greeting to the warmly smiling Aioni we passed.

"I am glad you decided to come with us."

"Decided?" I echoed pointedly.

"You know what I mean." Her teeth flashed in a wide smile. "It means a lot to my people to see you again."

My gaze dropped to my feet. The tips of her soft fingers brushed my hand, entwining with my own.

"Are you all right?" Roux asked.

A simple question. A loaded question—one which many people didn't ask often enough. But Roux did. She always noticed when people were in pain, when they needed help. She always saw the good in people, and when surrounded by their darkness, helped to create it within them. Her bright, playful aura was what had drawn me to her to begin with.

It had been so easy to fall into a friendship with her. To feel her pain when she suffered the loss of her sister; when she had to suffer the desolate atmosphere of Volente during her trial, risking her own life to overcome her grief and magickal corruption. Had she failed, she could have become so like the very thing we were trying to destroy.

In some ways, I wished I was more like her. That there was some way to turn around such grief and loss, to prevent it from making me ugly inside. Now, as I held her warm hand in mine, walking united through her home, the fragile hope in that thought grew stronger. In everything that was happening, she gave me hope.

A tiny clearing of her throat brought me from my idle thoughts and I nodded, avoiding her knowing gaze.

"He finds it hard to be here." She spoke quietly.

I made myself meet her eyes without flinching, knowing that he felt the same guilt as I did.

"Sometimes I fear he feels too deeply since his merging. That there are too many unresolved emotions he has to live with."

"He knows Aion was not his fault." My fingers curled tightly enough in my free hand that my nails would surely leave marks.

"I'm not just talking about that."

I pressed my lips together. *For Goddess's fucking sake.*

"I can't give him the forgiveness he seeks. The forgiveness you seek for him," I told her through gritted teeth. My pride held me back from demanding an apology from him, determined not to let her see how badly I was hurt by the lack of one.

"I don't expect you to," she said calmly.

I knew that, which made my insides twist. In some ways I wished Roux was less kind. Would give me an excuse to bite by demanding it of me. It was easier than her grace.

She sighed. "I just wanted you to know that his bravado is a mask."

I knew that too. Dracho was easier to read than I let on.

"He may have led many in Tenebris to believe his motives for coming here lay solely with finding his father's killer, but I think we both know why he was really drawn back here."

I said nothing. Mostly I wanted to deny what she claimed, but Dracho's emotions often broke through his facade, showing clearly on his face. The new, cold tension of his expression never lasted... especially not when I was looking at him. I would never acknowledge it, not whilst my heart was still heavy from his betrayal. But I still saw it.

I still didn't owe anyone absolution for their own actions.

Chapter 12

My eyes strayed to the sinking gold of the sun. The sound of small waves kissing the shore, the sweet whispers of the tall grass swaying in the breeze, soothed my heart, which was aching. I wrapped my cloak tighter around me in the chill of the early spring air.

It was such an intense feeling, sitting on this beach once again, staring out into the very waters where Azande's Uhane ceremony had taken place. Where all the mages slain in the Hollow's attack had been put to rest.

I held my hand out, staring at my palm and remembering.

That day, the celestral ancestors had accepted my plea and allowed the Aioni to move on. When I closed my eyes, it was as if I could feel their spirit-like presence around me, dancing across my fingertips. I could have never brought them back, but even if the toll had been almost too much for my body, I was glad I had been able to offer them some comfort in their grief.

A sound beside me made me open my eyes.

"It's beautiful," Althea whispered, staring out at the pink and orange sky.

I hummed in agreement.

She looked down at her clasped hands. "Dracho told me. What happened here... and how you helped."

I chewed the inside of my cheek, my lips pursing.

"So, with no magick of your own, you just decided to put yourself at risk to save their souls?" There was no malice in her question. She truly seemed to want to understand my motives.

"Maybe I like to find out for myself what I can't do, instead of being told. Anyway, it was worth it. To help them, it was always worth it."

She huffed. "You and Dracho are so alike."

I sighed, tucking my fingers into the fabric of my cloak to warm them. "How?"

"You both care about fairness."

A laugh burst from my throat, and Althea's sharp, feline eyes narrowed.

"If that were true, Dracho would never have had me thrown into a dungeon. He would have listened."

"Yes, well, we all make mistakes in the heat of the moment, and you were there less than a day."

I glared at her.

"You never know how you would have reacted—"

"*I* wouldn't have done it," I promised.

"You don't know that."

"I do." My resolve was as immovable as the Ballaraan mountains themselves. "If the roles had been switched, if it had been him, with all that had happened between us... I wouldn't have done it."

I had to turn from the way her eyes softened. It was part of what was drawing me to Althea. She was viciously blunt—honest, some would call it—but I was becoming certain that she also had a tremendous capability for kindness.

"What *did* happen between you? Before Tenebris."

My cheeks heated, and her slender eyebrows rose in realisation.

"Oh."

"He never told you?"

Althea shook her head. "We hardly spoke about you after his coronation. I think he kept himself so busy to avoid wallowing in his grief... to avoid thinking of you."

I clicked my tongue over my teeth. "Roux said something similar. Oh well, maybe he should have stayed in Tenebris—avoided me altogether."

Althea leaned back on her elbows in the sand, crossing one ankle over the other. "He couldn't put the trip off anymore. His uncle has been demanding he find the emperor's murderer ever since you left. Believe me when I say that our arrival was a lot more peaceful than what Thuban wanted."

I cringed, images of mighty dragons thundering over the mountains flashing through my mind. She was right—there were worse ways they could have arrived. "I understand why his uncle—why *he*—is angry. I really do. But my father didn't arrange it."

Althea chuckled. "Oh. He knows."

A brief silence wrapped around me like a cold wind. I stared at her. "What do you mean, he knows?"

"Dracho could tell your father hadn't done it the other morning at breakfast. His heart was unwavering as he spoke the truth."

"Then why didn't he say anything?" My voice rose an octave.

Althea shrugged. "Maybe he just wanted to let him sweat a little." I growled softly, and she laughed. "I think deep down, Dracho is still eager to find out more about the Hollow. It's why he came here in the first place. It all seems linked, so it won't just end at finding the person who ordered his father's death. It will be *done* for him when the creature is dead and buried."

"I understand that," I whispered.

"I can see this is painful for you, Eliana."

Perhaps I was more predictable than I'd thought. My head ached. This situation was so much more complex than just giving into my baser feelings. My traitorous body wanted Dracho unlike anything else—remembered the way he'd made me feel. But though I could see traces of the Dracho I'd known before in his new persona, I couldn't forgive the decisions and actions he had made in the past. Decisions which had deeply hurt me, and actions which he hadn't even acknowledged. I couldn't trust him not to hurt me again; it felt like all that was left of the man I'd known was a shadow.

I sniffed. "It doesn't matter. Coming here has reminded me that, despite our differences, we are together for one reason. The Hollow. That is all that matters. That is where my priorities lie. Not building bridges. Not making friends."

She laughed again, harder.

"What?" I asked, my teeth gritted in irritation.

"He said something similar before we left. I wonder how long you two will keep trying to tell yourselves that."

The Aioni offered us some empty huts in the Home Trees branches to sleep in, but the evening would be spent upon the beach. After the sun had set, the bonfires began. The Aioni people laughed and sang around theirs, but the atmosphere of those around our own was morose. Only Althea seemed at peace, her eyes closed as she swayed her body gently to the melodies.

That peace had been taken from me when the Hollow attacked this spiritual place. I could feel the energies brushing over me, as if the very celestral ancestors themselves were trying to lift my mood. A vision of memories flashed across my mind, causing my head to thrum. Of getting to know Roux, of Bas swinging Azande around whilst she laughed freely.

She would never laugh again.

So much loss, so much pain. My eyes watched over the people enjoying themselves, and I wondered how they were able to face happiness and the future in the face of it. An image of my mother and Morgwn came to the forefront of my mind, and I brushed the painful image away. I had faced my fair share of loss, but I couldn't imagine suffering as the Aioni had—first with Volente and the Tain, and then with the Hollows attack—it made me more determined to stop its wrath. To find out who was behind it all and bring them to their end.

I looked up across the flames, finding Dracho's face. His eyes met mine, widening slightly. After a brief glance around, he tilted his head.

Are you all right?

I managed to prevent my gasp at the caress of his words against my mind, and I nodded minutely, so as not to attract attention. Then I tilted my head forward, without breaking eye contact.

He gave a small, amused smile that didn't reach his eyes. *I am fine.*

I raised a brow, and he rolled his eyes.

All right, Princess. This is... difficult.

I nodded slightly again, dropping my gaze.

Azande should be here. His voice was a chord of sorrow and longing.

I said nothing, staring at the sand before my feet as I hugged my knees closer to my chest.

We'll get to the bottom of this. No more children will die at its hands.

I swallowed the hard lump in my throat, but dared to meet his eyes once more. I didn't need to nod this time.

Vyn tapped my arm. I took the cup of liquor he offered—an Aioni creation made from the cariper berries from the forest nearby—and took a swig. The sweet taste was delicious, despite the burning sensation that accompanied it.

"When shall we return to Meridium?" Vyn asked quietly, leaning over to rest his head on my shoulder.

Roux and I had extended Bisa a formal invitation to my birthday ball, and the chief had graciously accepted. A long sigh left me.

"Tomorrow," I whispered. "We need to make sure we're back for the ball. We have a few days spare, and I thought... I thought coming here would be a nice break, but I can't stay here. It's..." *Too painful.*

Vyn rubbed my arm softly. "I know."

A few Aioni rushing up from their bonfire further down the beach caught my eye, and I frowned. Antares's head shot up from where it had been resting on his arms, and he listened intently. My eyes narrowed as Dracho's gaze flicked to him, the two sharing some secret conversation. From two bonfires away, Bisa jumped to her feet, pointing to something in the sky. I tried to follow her line of sight but was blocked by the canopy of the trees.

Dracho stood quickly and headed further down the beach, Antares following a split second later. I didn't understand what they were staring at until I ran after them and looked up into the night sky.

It was on fire. Beyond Home Tree and the woods of Aion, flame and smoke rose somewhere in the distance.

Antares nodded at Dracho before taking off in the direction of the pathway. Further down the beach, Roux spoke hurriedly with her mother, then rushed after him. Bas and Vyn had come to stand by me, muttering to each other as they glanced towards the flame-kissed sky. The smell of salt and smoke, kept at bay for a while by the sea breeze, had started to drift over the beach.

"It's towards Carew!" someone shouted.

My blood ran cold. Carew was the nearest village to Aion, just a few hours ride to the northeast.

Not again.

"Vyn, Bas! Fetch your weapons and meet us at the entrance. We'll go check it out," Dracho called. I felt his gaze on me.

Bas eyed me for a moment, but nodded. Vyn turned with him, running for the hut where our weapons lay.

An isolating cocoon seemed to wrap itself around my lungs, squeezing painfully as my brain became overwhelmed. I could feel the tremble in my hands but had neither the motivation nor knowledge to stop it at that moment. All I knew was the rising panic that fogged my vision, making the edges of Dracho's form look blurred as my gaze darted up to him. I raised a hand to clasp my throat.

This can't be happening again. Not another attack. Not this close to Aion.

My legs buckled. Hands gripped my arms firmly, helping me to my knees upon the sand.

Eliana. The voice whispered against the fog in my mind.

I glanced up, seeing his mouth form words I couldn't hear. Those warm hands released me and I whimpered, but they cupped my face. The electric charge that jolted through me cleared the fog enough for him to speak.

"Eliana. Look at me. That's it. Focus on my voice. On my touch."

I stared into the icy blue.

"That's it. Remember what we did before, yes?" His voice was panicked, breathless. "I want you to tell me two things you can feel, with your hands."

I blinked slowly, my mind taking its time to grasp his words; my heart thundered in my ears. My hands dropped to my sides, the tips of my fingers brushing against the coarse sand. I sluggishly picked some up, rubbing it between my fingers. "Sand."

"Good, that's good. Something else."

There was nothing. Oh Goddess, there was nothing else around. The panic rose again, my hands scrambling in front of me to do as he said. My hand hit his chest.

That's it.

His breath hitched, but I laid my hand flat against his hard chest, searching. *There.*

His heartbeat was racing—too fast—against my palm, and I closed my eyes it as I counted its beats. I inhaled deeply as I counted, and felt as it slowed beneath my palm.

"G-good. Well done, Eliana." His voice pierced the veil across my mind. The panic was easing.

"Princess," he rasped, "three things you can see."

My eyes opened, darting to the water I knew flowed close beside me. "The water." He nodded. I looked over his shoulder. "The trees."

From the corner of my eye, I saw a small smile rise on his lips. I met the churning, silver-lined blue pools of his eyes.

"You," I whispered. My pulse raced, but no longer from the panic attack.

His hands picked up mine. "*Breathe*, Eliana."

I sucked in a breath as his hands tightened. His scent of smoke and citrus filled me.

He blew out a breath himself. "Better?"

Swallowing hard, I blinked a few times, getting my bearing, then pulled my hands from his.

"I'm all right," I said hoarsely.

Dracho stayed kneeling on the sand, awaiting my next move—giving me the space to ground myself. I stood on shaky legs, appreciating that he held his hands out as if to steady me, but did not touch me again without permission.

"I must go. If it's too much, stay here," he said, his brow creased in concern.

"I'm all right," I told him again.

And truthfully, I was. It had been a minor flashback that caused my reaction, and I was glad no one else was around to have witnessed it. I appreciated his offer to stay behind, but it meant more that he wasn't trying to stop me from going with them.

He simply nodded, taking a step back. I brushed past him, running to the main entrance to Aion. Bisa and the others were already there.

"I cannot ask my people to risk themselves. Not after the Hollow's last attack," Bisa stressed.

I clasped her hand. "I completely understand. We'll check it out."

Vyn stepped forward silently, offering me my dagger. The weapon was cold in my hands. He nodded at me once, quietly asking if I was all right. I just gave him a small smile, tying the sheath around my thigh.

"The fire is coming from the direction of Carew to the northeast. We'll take the horses," Roux called.

We rushed to where we'd tied our steeds and Engel, who had been roaming free, came to my side. I mounted him, glancing around and catching the concerned faces of the Aioni who watched our departure. Bisa stood close to the Home Tree entrance, ever the graceful and calm leader in troubled times. Sizwe stood beside her; she nodded when I caught her eye.

Bisa stepped forward, clasping Roux's hand for a moment. "Be careful. Take care of each other."

"We will, Mamona."

"Dracho," Sizwe called out, and he turned. "Look after my girls."

I swallowed a knot of emotion that almost choked me as Dracho nodded.

"Let's go!" Antares shouted, pulling off into the forest trail, Althea close behind. I took one last look at the Aioni before tapping Engel's neck, the beast turning to leave—hopefully, towards less destruction than what we had experienced here before.

Chapter 13

The flames grew brighter as we galloped towards them. As we drew closer, we realised the fire wasn't coming from near the village of Carew. It *was* the village. No one spoke as the flames licked the sky ahead in leaps of heat, as the smoke grew thick, coating us with a thin layer of ash and making my eyes painfully dry.

The fire was so intense it outshone the stars. Its raw energy roared across the land and sky. Dracho pulled ahead of us at the entrance to the village. As if alive with a will of its own, a flame reared back, coiling like a snake about to strike.

"Dracho!" Althea cried.

The fire whipped forward, bringing a burst of heat that made us all pull our mounts to a stop. I gasped as it struck at the neck of Dracho's steed; the horse reared violently, throwing him from its back. My stomach plummeted for the seconds it took for him to crash to the ground, the horse turning and fleeing into the night.

"Dracho?" Roux asked warily, squinting against the brightness of the flames.

My eyes were trained on Dracho's form as he lay flat on his front, but he groaned and moved. My shoulders sagged with relief as Antares dismounted, rushing over to drag him away and help him up. His hand clasped the back of Dracho's neck.

"You all right?" he asked, brows high on his forehead. It was touching to see Antares so concerned, though I knew that fall wouldn't have hurt Dracho much at all. Dracho confirmed he was, before nodding at Althea, who had joined the duo. Their eyes turned to the flames as the rest of us dismounted.

This was no ordinary fire.

"Be careful. The guard in Meridium said one of the Hollow's beasts attacked from the darkness," Antares warned. Dracho unsheathed his glaive, lowering into a slightly defensive stance as he extended the weapon.

Bas's grip tightened on the leather handle of his axe. "There's no way we'll be able to search for survivors if we can't get near the village to begin with."

An idea hit me. "Vyn!" I shouted.

"I'm on it!" He took a few steps forward, circling his hands gracefully around each other. A strong wind started to build between them. The muscles in his arms strained as he continued to build momentum, the gust now growing into a small whirlwind of power. Roux gasped at the swirling vortex; Antares flashed Vyn a look that was shockingly impressed. Vyn's arms stretched wider as it grew, and he grunted with the effort. When I thought he wouldn't be able to hold it any longer, he sent it forward with a shout, the cyclone stretching towards the sky as it headed towards the flames.

Come on! I rocked back and forth on the balls of my feet as it sped towards the flames. The mass of swirling air fought to smother them, pressing down on them—until it exploded outwards, whipping harshly at our faces. When I opened my eyes, I could still see the flames.

"No!" Bas exclaimed, as Vyn panted.

"Those flames are created with corrupt celestral magick. They won't be put out easily!" Antares called to us as he stepped forward, placing a hand on Vyn's shoulder to check he was all right.

Roux muttered something under her breath, before running forward to stand next to Dracho. He turned, catching her gaze, and she nodded. His expression became concerned, but he stepped back.

Roux's shoulders dropped; she took a deep breath. Her fists clenched tightly, then opened, embers sparking within them as her fingers flexed. Her chest heaved as those embers turned to flame, licking up the skin of her arms until they were wholly encased in fire. Her arms spread out as her head was thrown back, a visceral scream of power and pain bursting from her mouth. Bas jerked in surprise. My thoughts swirled as tears sprang to my eyes, trying to combat the dryness of the fire.

A shadow of black and gold flames burst from her chest, flying out and spreading over the village like a swarm of locusts. Roux gritted her teeth, her eyes closed tightly as the swarm of black and gold descended like a blanket, suppressing and suffocating the flames until there was nothing but smouldering buildings and broken fires scattered about, no bigger than a campfire.

Roux relaxed, her arms falling and legs giving way. Bas launched forward to catch her. She leaned against his side, smiling lazily up at him. "Good, right?"

He flashed her a grin. "Amazing."

Vyn's face bore nothing but grief as he looked at the remains of the village. It was obvious from the devastation and burnt-out buildings that no one could have possibly survived those magickal flames. A moment of silence fell amongst our group.

Until my ears twitched at a sound that reached out from the shadows—a clicking sound.

Antares pushed closer, taking a step in front of me as he looked in the same direction as me. There was something there. A shadow, in the wreckage.

"Show yourself!" Dracho yelled.

The clicking noise grew louder, igniting a spark of fear in my belly as I recognized it.

From the darkness of the main path through the village, a tall figure appeared. The armour was almost white, standing out amongst the destruction around it. Unlike before, there was no weakness present in the being. The creature walked confidently, taking silent, measured steps as its slitted helmet faced us.

The Hollow.

There was no spear now; the Hollow had left its blade in Emperor Eltanin's chest. Instead, the creature held a long silver sword that looked like it could cleave a man in two, a green stone shimmering at the end of the hilt. Amongst the smouldering flames that remained and the devastation it had caused, it looked like some god of death. It stopped about a hundred feet away, staring.

Snarls broke through the air, and deformed wyverns of all shapes and sizes appeared behind the Hollow.

They were creatures that usually dwelled in darkness, in scary stories—wendigos with their drooling maws and vicious claws, vernis with their dark scales and forked tongues. There were more loscura too, only twice their usual size, their fur matted and torn from their bodies.

It was a horrifying sight. *But why isn't it attacking?*

Roux pushed herself off Bas, grunting as she took a step forward. Dracho was too busy glaring at the creature to notice. His body shook with rage. His name froze in my throat as black claws ripped their way from his hands and his wings emerged from his back, tearing holes in the fabric of his leathers as a growl built louder and louder in this throat. He raised one sharp finger to the Hollow. No words were necessary; the threat was obvious.

But the Hollow just tilted its head.

Roux uncurled her hands as she took another determined step forward, and my heart dropped. We wouldn't win a fight. Not right now. Not whilst it had an army at its back. We didn't know its full capability.

Before I could reach out, Althea and Antares appeared before them in a blur of speed.

"No. Roux, you are too weak! Dracho—think wisely, brother. We don't know if our abilities will harm it. We *cannot* do this now!" One hand on Dracho's shoulder, Antares turned, taking in the image of the vile creature again for an instant. I saw a sliver of fear in Althea's blue eyes as they ran over the deformed creatures. "We need to be smart about this. Do this together. Please, *see reason*." I had never heard Antares sound so rattled, which only heightened the fear building in my chest.

Dracho's shoulders were still shaking. Having the thing responsible for losing his only living parent so close and being unable to enact the revenge he had surely dreamed of must have been torture.

I knew that thirst for revenge—how it tasted on my tongue. I had felt the same way that night I had been attacked as a girl, even though they had been killed straight away. The pain, the questions, the need to understand why... they could eat you alive.

I stepped forward to help Antares, slipping my hand into Dracho's, moving carefully around his claws. His warm hand engulfed mine and squeezed tightly. The grumbling in his throat ceased almost immediately as his surprised eyes cut to mine, a beautiful moonlit silver, the vertical slits of his dragon as black as the night sky above us. His eyes crumpled, his lashes touching his cheek as he blinked, letting me witness the pain there.

My throat tightened at the desolation I saw. Swallowing hard, I squeezed his hand back, shaking my head without breaking eye contact. "No, Dracho. It's not time."

His eyes closed, a shuddering breath leaving his mouth. Antares looked between us and the Hollow, tension lining his body, but the creature was still as stone, watching us. Roux had already backed off, staring at the ground.

Dracho's eyes shot open, causing my breath to jump in my throat. His icy blue gaze considered me, no longer the dragon's. His nostrils flared slightly as he took one deep breath, but the corners of his lips turned up, ever so slightly, and he tipped his head forward in a nod.

All right. His voice brushed against my mind.

My gaze turned back to the Hollow, my feet moving apart to ground myself, ready for whatever it brought our way. But when I looked at where its face should have been visible, my back stiffened, the hairs on my neck standing on end.

It was looking directly at me.

I wasn't sure how I knew it, but I could feel it in every fibre of my being. Something whispered in the recesses of my mind as I stared at the faceless monster. Almost against my will, my foot moved one step forward.

The Hollow stiffened—and took one step *back*.

Bas was suddenly behind me. "E, don't."

I shook my head. "I just…"

Like a moth to a flame, that something deep within me pulled me forward another step, but Dracho's hand was still holding mine, and he held fast. "Princess."

I glanced at him, breaking the creature's gaze and the strange feeling. But I hadn't been moving forward to fight it. I… I didn't understand.

Vyn sucked in a breath, and I looked back as the Hollow started to move. *Away from us.*

No one moved as it retreated, holding my gaze until the last possible second, before turning to leave, the wyverns following.

"What do we do? Do we follow it?" Bas's voice rose with his confusion as the last wyvern disappeared from view. Everyone was tense, uncertain. Antares paced, running a hand through his hair.

"No," I said. "We return to Meridium."

"Are we supposed to just let it go round destroying everything in its wake whilst we attend *balls*?" Roux asked loudly, frustration marring her face. Bas reached out to place a hand on her shoulder, but she shrugged him off, turning to walk away from our group.

Dracho exhaled deeply. "She's just—"

"Right. She's right," I told him—then almost jerked my hand away when

I realised it was still holding Dracho's. I pulled away as he and Antares turned to look at me, apparently shocked at my conclusion.

I understood. Holding balls and treaty meetings—and engagement tours—whilst all this was happening was the most ridiculous thing. We couldn't allow the creature to rain fire across the country, murdering everyone in its way. But I hoped Roux also understood my desire to learn more about it.

"We aren't doing enough. We don't have all the information, and despite our differences, I'm not willing to risk *any* of your lives." My arms crossed across my chest.

"Well, that's a good thing," Althea said, raising a brow at me.

"We need answers, but we don't have time to go to the temple now," I told them. "We *need* to attend the treaty meeting. The best way forward—despite our grievances—is to fight this as allies. And to do that we need all the rulers on the same page." I turned, following Roux. "Then we can stop this son of a bitch."

Chapter 14

Back in Aion, we informed Bisa and Sizwe of the loss of Carew. The Aioni held a vigil on the beach for the people lost, and we joined before silently retreating for the night. It was probably only thanks to the comfort of the magick that surrounded me that I had no nightmares that night. The ancestors must have answered my silent plea, ensuring a peaceful night for once.

Bisa, Roux and Sizwe said their goodbyes to the Aioni people before we left. Bisa was travelling with us, accepting my father's invitation to the ball before the meeting of the rulers—a huge honour. The chief mage had not attended any events since the first treaty had been signed after the Tain, when the Aioni people had retreated to Home Tree, cutting themselves off from the rest of Ruvalon.

I was glad for the Xolani sisters as we made our way back to Meridium. Cubra stayed by Roux's side and kept guard; Bisa and Sizwe spent the nights healing her aching muscles with their magick. Roux's body had taken a physical toll for the magick she had exerted in Carew. She described the throbbing pressure she felt in her head as the kind of pain that stole all your focus, making it difficult to function. Dracho rode with her since losing his horse, allowing her to sleep against his chest. I still watched her cautiously as we rode, noting when she'd had enough by the subtle tremble in her fingers and immediately calling a halt.

For this reason the journey back was longer, the atmosphere morose each day as we pushed the horses probably harder than we should have. Every time we set up camp, I made sure to treat each of them to some of the sweet feed and apples I carried.

After a couple of days, Roux looked almost back to her usual self. But I was certain of one thing. She may have mastered her powers exponentially since we had been in Volente, but she was nowhere near the power needed to defeat the Hollow. The effort could kill her. And she wasn't a sacrifice I was willing to make, whether she wanted it or not. I hope the temple of the Hollow would give us answers, meaning we wouldn't have to rely on Roux so much.

There were other gifted mages in Aion, of course, but not even Bisa's powers were a match for Roux's. Since the end of the Tain, the Aioni had shut themselves off from the rest of the world, refusing to involve themselves in outside matters. But if the Hollow's attacks continued to spread, I worried they would find themselves without a choice.

As we neared the large gates of Meridium, a sense of relief made its way through my body, taking me completely by surprise. Meridium hadn't truly felt like home for a long time. The palace, which had once been my sanctuary, had for years felt more like a cell—trapping me with the memories that haunted my sleep.

But it was familiar, and there were good memories; training with my big brother, breakfasts with him, Mam and Dad, and exploring the city with Vyn and Bas. I knew it was my burden to overcome, and it seemed like it was getting easier.

"What can we expect from your birthday ball, Princess?" Dracho asked as Roux snored lightly against him, his steed catching up to trot alongside Engel, who huffed.

"Hmm. Expensive champagne, too much dancing—and, oh yes, elitist pricks from out of town," I told him sweetly, fluttering my lashes.

He smirked, knowing I included him that group. It was nice to see his mood improve. "Dancing, huh? Well, we haven't done *that* for a while."

I pulled Engel to a stop, causing Dracho to rein his horse to a halt a couple feet away, his hand coming up to hold Roux steady. I looked at him steadily. "I shall *not* be dancing with you."

Dracho laughed darkly. "Now, now, Eliana. Don't be disrespectful. We are both royalty of Ruvalon. It would be *rude* to deny me."

"And I would pour a bottle of the cheapest champagne over you in front of the whole continent to show you a sliver of how rude I can be! You're lucky

I haven't impaled you on my blade."

"You technically did that already," he pointed out. "What would Daddy think?"

My teeth clenched. "I am not my father."

His eyes travelled across me, leaving a burning sensation in their wake. "No, you are definitely not. So who are you?"

I exhaled deeply. "None of your concern, that's who."

With a click of the tongue, I encouraged Engel into a canter, taking me away from Dracho's irritating presence.

When Engel and the other horses were stabled, I was grateful to stretch my legs, walking the rest of the way. Word had reached Father of our arrival, and he met us at the palace courtyard. He embraced me tightly, taking in my small disingenuous smile with mild curiosity before his gaze landed on Bisa.

Their reunion was sweet—I couldn't imagine going so many years without seeing Vyn or Bas—but as I looked at the two of them, laughing and smiling as if no time had passed at all, I saw beneath it. Behind the smiles, I saw the tenseness in the wrinkles at the corners of their eyes, the fingers that twitched. I saw the shared grief, the shared burden of leadership. I knew that would be my mantle one day, and mourned the sacrifices they had made.

"Are you all right?" Vyn asked as I watched Father, Bisa and Sizwe ascend the steps into the palace. Connaught, who had been standing guard, followed them, but not without a nod of greeting for me.

"I think so," I whispered.

The crease between Vyn's eyes deepened. He glanced at Bas, whose head tilted before his eyes widened in realisation. He nodded once, then jogged in the direction of the palace. I turned to ask Vyn what was going on, but he took my hand and tugged me forward.

"C'mon." He smiled, leading me out of the courtyard; I looked over my shoulder, catching Dracho's eye.

Vyn's hand was like a cool breeze against my own as he pulled me back through the main streets of the city. My lips quirked when I realised where he was taking me. We approached the white marble of my mother's statue, and Vyn blew her visage a kiss before jumping up onto the circular edge, crossing his legs under him. I pulled myself up to sit beside him, swinging my legs.

We remained in comfortable silence until Bas came running towards us, a brown paper bag in his hands. He swallowed whatever mouthful of food he had before grinning and holding out the bag.

I inhaled deeply as I opened it, already salivating at the fresh blueberry muffins Bas had clearly obtained from Marie in the kitchen. I laughed as I took one out, handing it to Vyn before grabbing my own, pleased that they both remembered this tradition.

Bas dropped down roughly onto the ground in front of us, stretching his legs out as he scoffed the remaining bites of his muffin. I picked at the blueberries visible on top of mine, bringing them to my mouth and relishing the burst of sweetness.

Ever since we were younger, if we ever needed time to talk or just relax and be ourselves, we'd always found ourselves here. Or rather, they had always found me here and started to join me, usually with spoils grabbed from the kitchen. They never pressed, never intruded with anything more than their presence—and that was exactly what I needed. Just their presence. It had become a bond between the three of us.

I guessed that after the memory of Aion and what had happened in Carew, before the attention of my birthday and everything that would happen afterwards, they knew I needed a moment to just be me. Just Eli, as I had been when we had travelled together, just the three of us.

Right now, it was just the three of us again.

Chapter 15

Trepidation rolled over me in waves as I stared at the gossamer gown in the mirror: a deep-forest-green creation, the neckline dipping low between my breasts and ending just above my navel. Tiny goosebumps erupted on my skin as the air brushed my exposed back. It was possibly one of the finest dresses I had ever worn; the capped sleeves had tassels made of lengths of dark emerald-green crystals which caught the light at every turn. I could hardly feel the fabric as it clung to me like a second skin, accentuating all my curves in all the right places.

And I had never felt more stunned as I looked at my reflection. I hardly recognised my own face, the rouge upon my cheeks and lips making them stand out. I wasn't usually a fancy-gown-and-make-up kind of woman, but I couldn't deny how beautiful I felt.

Walking to my dresser, I spied the gift on top that my father had given me that morning and smiled. A stunning brush made from a solid silver that never tarnished. It had been my mother's. I had vivid memories of her brushing my hair with it as a child, and its delivery had threatened to spill the tears I had felt building since waking.

A sharp knock at the door brought me from my thoughts. "Come in."

The door opened. The man behind it stopped in his tracks once his eyes met mine, shock freezing me in place.

"*Jak*? What are you doing here?"

He remained silent as his eyes perused my dress.

"Are you going to just stand there and gawk?" I snapped, perhaps a bit too harshly. His presence unnerved me, worsening how I already felt about the ball if he and Illyra were in attendance. The last time I had seen him, we hadn't parted on good terms. His judgemental tone and insinuations about my relationship with Dracho had actually driven me into Dracho's arms for the night.

"Yes—I, um, mean no." Jak shook his head and closed the door behind him.

"What are you doing here?" I repeated. "I thought you were on your engagement tour?"

He winced, pulling at the front of his jacket in clear discomfort. "I cut it short."

I raised a brow.

He laughed awkwardly. "I couldn't miss your birthday. Especially after missing the last two."

"Is she here?" He knew who I meant.

"Yes," he said awkwardly, running a hand through his crimson hair. "She, um... wasn't too happy about us attending."

"And I assume you've sneaked off to visit me in my *chamber*?"

A blush rose on his cheeks. "I did. I didn't think it best to tell Illyra where I was going."

I cringed, but knew that Milly wouldn't tell a soul—which was likely why Jak had asked her.

"No, I imagine not. Your father either?"

"No, he wasn't best pleased when we showed up..."

An awkward beat of silence fell between us, and when I caught his eyes back on my dress, my arms wrapped around my middle.

"Don't," Jak said firmly, striding over to stand before me.

I looked at him incredulously as he removed my arms gently from around my waist, placing them at my sides. His navy-blue eyes captured mine, his gaze intense.

"Don't," he repeated, moving his hands slowly up my arms.

I tensed under them, but he gently turned me to look back into the mirror. My heart raced with nerves as I watched him in the reflection.

"You *never* hide. You are magnificent. You always have been... and you are a future queen."

My chest tightened. "Jak," I sighed, my gaze dropping.

He held a hand up to stop me. "You walk out there as though every one of them is beneath you. None of them know how strong you are. I know grand balls aren't the environment you typically feel comfortable in." A light smile touched my lips. "But... it suits you. You look beautiful."

I felt the blush spread up my neck and over my cheeks, both grateful for his words and infuriated that I still blushed like an infatuated girl at the slightest compliment. I became extremely aware of his hands, still on my arms. He noticed me looking at them in the mirror and dropped them to his side.

"I have a gift for you." He cleared his throat loudly, striding to open the door; Milly entered, holding an extravagant wooden box decorated with engraved peonies. Jak removed it from her hands and dismissed her politely. She eyed him with veiled disdain, but left.

My mouth parted. "There really is no need."

He waved his hand, placing the box on the side table next to the mirror. "It's your birthday. I never forgot, and I owe you for the ones missed." He gave me a pointed look.

All I could do was nod as my heart pounded in my chest. Whatever it was, I would deny it. It felt wrong to be receiving a gift from him. We hadn't seen each other or spoken easily in a few years... and a gift could never erase what he had done.

He flipped the catch on the box, opening it to reveal an elaborate tiara. It was similar to my first crown, gifted by my mother and father. It looked as though it was made from hundreds of small silver horns overlapping, rising to a peak at the front. Evenly spaced out along the front were small emeralds and sapphires.

My fingers brushed over the beautiful piece gently, feeling the cold metal. *It's too much.*

I looked up at him. "Jak, I can't accept this."

"I insist. It would suit no other; it was made to be yours."

"Where did you get it?" It was clearly not an item that could have been crafted last-minute.

Jak's eyes dropped to the box sheepishly. "I, uh—had it made years ago. It would have been a gift. An *engagement* gift." I almost swallowed my tongue at that, but refused to give him the satisfaction of my questions. "I held onto it. I couldn't bear to part with it."

My stomach churned; I stared at him silently, unsure what to say. He gave me a dazzling smile.

There *had* been rumours years ago that he was close to a proposal. The staff of both Stillmere and Meridium had been alive with gossip and excitement about it. But he'd only been home for a few weeks after a visit to Meridium when news reached me of Jak's link to Illyra instead.

Despite the heartbreak and betrayal I'd felt at not hearing about it from Jak himself, I'd realised months later that a prominent emotion was relief. I had never felt truly comfortable in Stillmere, feeling the judgemental eyes of the people and king on me. It would never have been a place I could truly relax, could truly be me.

"Okay," I whispered.

"May I?" Jak indicated to the tiara.

I nodded and turned as he removed it from the box to gently place it on my head, securing it in place. He rested his hands on my shoulders. I admired the tiara in the mirror as it sat between my braids, my long hair flowing in waves down my back. It was astonishingly beautiful.

"It's perfect," he breathed. "Like it always belonged there."

"Thank you." I reached up to touch it lightly. "It's stunning—and too much."

Jak's mirrored face was conflicted. He lifted a hand to grasp a loose curl, tucking it back into the braid by my ear. Turning, I grabbed his wrist to halt the movement, a nervous breath leaving my lips. His eyes were a conflicted storm of blue, clouded with a familiar emotion.

I froze as he leaned forward, glance flashing down to my open lips and back up to my eyes. I couldn't move as he closed in those final few inches, my heart twisting. His lips were soft against the skin of my cheek—familiar. The pads of his fingers brushed against my neck, his woodsy scent softly brushing my nose.

Autumnal—not citrus. Dark blue eyes, not the hue of silver blue I always saw in my dreams. *All wrong,* my brain yelled at me as his lips neared mine.

I lightly pushed him away.

"That was... wrong." My stomach dropped at the devastated look that passed over Jak's face, the resigned sorrow. "*So* wrong. You're *engaged*."

"Eliana, you know that's an agreement. I could never lo—"

"Stop. Don't say it." I tried to calm my breathing. "It doesn't matter, Jak. Our paths took us in different directions. This was *wrong*. This makes me as bad as her. It won't happen again."

The heartbreak in his eyes irritated me slightly. Jak couldn't have his fiancée *and* me on the side. I was worth more than that, and after his betrayal, he didn't deserve me anyway. I understood that his relationship with Illyra was likely down to his father. But I had been hurt by it, and Jak had never really acknowledged that.

I rarely gave second chances, and when I did, they had to be earned. This *thing* with Jak and Illyra would only lead to trouble.

I thought he would argue, but he nodded before backing up a step. "I'm sorry, Eliana. I'll leave you be."

He left me with the shame that settled within my gut. *How could I be so stupid?* The worst part was that his fiancée wasn't even the first thing on my mind. This guilt that coursed through my veins was about *him*.

It was easy to be around Jak, despite our past. He had been one of my closest friends; I used to tell him everything—almost everything. So it had felt easy, falling into that comfort with him. But those feelings I used to have had gone. Now, I wondered if my feelings had even been that strong to begin with. Jak reminded me of times when I felt comforted, wanted and safe. That was why I had almost allowed him to kiss me, but I had moved on. I could only hope that one day Jak would find his happiness, as I had to find my own.

"Hmm. Shall we get this party started, then?" I asked the empty room, before heading to the door and what lay beyond.

"Fabe!" I exclaimed joyfully as I approached the captain of the Laugharne guards. I had just finished dancing with Bas when I'd spotted Fabian standing over by a table.

He pulled me into a tight, one-armed embrace, and the scent of liquor reached my nose.

"Starting early, are we?" I asked as I pulled myself free.

He scoffed, tucking his dark, shaggy brown hair behind an ear. "Ay, lass, don' ruin me fun. You know I can' stand bein' sober round these elite bastards."

I laughed, hushing him. "It's not that bad, surprisingly," I told him as I looked around the room, glad I hadn't been swept up into too many political conversations so far. My slight concern that there was no sign of Dracho was almost suppressed by the relief that I hadn't had the misfortune of bumping into Illyra either. "Has Demer arrived yet?"

"Ay, she was saying 'ello to your da. Eh." Fabe took a step closer, lowering his head so the scar across his face was more visible in the candlelight. "Is it true wha' they're sayin'? That lad with you back in Laugharne is from Tenebris in a mortal form? He's the emperor's son?"

My lips thinned, but I nodded. Fabe whistled as he stood straighter. "Well, tha's a surprise. Seemed the cocky sort when we met, but di'n't peg him for a dragon, of all things."

"He's the emperor now, Fabe."

His eyes widened. "Did ye know?"

"In Laugharne? Goddess, no. I didn't find out for a while."

"Bi' of a shock, eh?"

The huff I let out was humourless. "You could say that."

"Does him being 'ere now mean trouble?" Fabian asked.

I didn't answer for a moment, trading my empty glass for a full one from one of the staff. A familiar figure was heading towards me with all the airs and graces you'd expect from a lady of the land. I exhaled deeply.

"For me, definitely. For Ruvalon, I'm not sure," I rushed out, forcing a smile.

Lys pulled me in, planting a kiss on each cheek. I reciprocated the gesture before she pulled away to do the same to Fabian. Lys was my father's oldest friend and advisor; her town, Asaph, lay to the east, and was a crucial ally to the kingdom of Meridium.

"Well, nice to be seein' ya, ladies," Fabian said. "I'll be off. There was a wee beauty of a blonde round 'ere somewhere."

I rolled my eyes, wondering what woman had the misfortune of Fabe's attention for the evening. Although he was easy enough on the eyes, I had never fallen for his charm, having heard about his bedroom conquests long before I'd ever arrived in Laugharne. Fabe was an exceptionally good man, just not great with commitment—a fact he let all his ladies know.

"Go on, you scoundrel," Lys laughed, pushing at his arm.

"Only ever for you, Lys," he teased with a wink before leaving.

Lys turned to me. "Happy birthday, darling."

"Thank you, Aunt Lys." I smiled tightly, my eyes darting around the room in case our draconi friends had made an entrance.

"I must admit, after thinking they'd miss it due to their tour, I was dismayed to see Illyra here," she said dryly. I winced. "But even more surprised to hear it was the Proditor prince who had decided to postpone it. I wonder why?" Her eyes sparkled with amusement.

"I played no part in that," I insisted. "I had no idea he was attending until he came to my room." Her eyes blew wide, and I cursed myself for the slip-up. "He was presenting me with a gift, that's all!"

She hummed. "If I were you, *I'd* gift him with a swift kick to his nether regions."

I laughed. "Aunt Lys, you are terrible."

"Well," she drawled, waving a hand in the air, "I do try."

Shifting closer, she tucked her arm through the crook of my elbow, leaning in to talk quietly. "So, rumours tell me that the young man who enjoyed your *company* that night on the balcony in Stillmere is none other than the son of Eltanin the Wise?"

Her tone was playful, but I stiffened, my eyes slowly creeping to the sly grin on her face. I remembered the night clearly. The night she had caught me and a certain emperor a little too close for propriety on the balcony of the Stillmerean palace.

"Aunt Lys, it's not—"

"Hush, child. It's no skin off my nose." Her eyes twinkled. "He is a rather impressive specimen."

"Aunt Lys!"

She smiled coyly, and I laughed despite myself.

The sound of tinkling glasses reached our ears, and we looked to the grand staircase, where my father stood proudly. The sound of the chatter diminished as we all turned to face him. His dark green suit fit him perfectly, his crown sparkling upon his greying hair. He couldn't have looked happier as his eyes travelled over the guests.

"Dear friends and family, I'd like to thank you all today for attending this celebration." His voice rang out loud and clear. "A wise man I once knew said that friendship is one of the best measures of our worth. Well, looking out at many of the old faces I've had the pleasure of knowing all these years, *and* new faces I haven't known very long, makes me feel like the richest man alive."

Roux, Bisa and Sizwe smiled at Father from just in front of the stairs. Roux looked ethereal in a gown of black and gold that hung off her shoulders, the low back baring her smooth brown skin. Cubra was nowhere to be seen; I imagined the crowd's reaction to that feline if he had been in the room and grinned. On the other side of the room, in a shadowed area against the far wall, I noted a stern-faced Jareth, a few guards close by whilst Jak and Illyra stood dutifully beside him.

Connaught stood at attention at the bottom of the stairs, ever the fierce captain of the guard. Bas stood beside Vyn, stuffing his face, the waiter on his other side looking disconcerted. I stifled a laugh as my eyes darted around quickly, but I still couldn't spot the three from Tenebris anywhere.

"Eliana and I are so lucky to have so many that we consider friends—and family." He tipped his flute of champagne to the Aioni women, who returned the gesture. "We hope you have a wonderful evening. And my darling Eliana, no father could be prouder than I am of you. I know your mother and brother would feel the same. Happy birthday, my little doe."

Tears sprang to my eyes. I mentally vowed to kill him for making me emotional in front of all our guests.

He raised his flute into the air, the guests following his lead as *happy birthday!* was called out in unison. I nodded in thanks, cheeks flaming at the attention.

With a wave to the band from my father, the music started, lightening the emotional tension. I blew out a breath, looking once more to Lys, who laughed at my flushed cheeks. Vyn was strolling over to us.

"Get used to it, dearie. You'll be a queen one day," my aunt said.

"Thanks for reminding me," I muttered, taking another mouthful of champagne.

"Just think," Vyn leaned in conspiratorially, lowering his voice, "when you're queen, you can ban any events and live forever *alone* in your throne room."

I shoved him, albeit gently, as Lys snickered.

A masculine voice interrupted our conversation. "Princess Eliana."

Aunt Lys pursed her lips as the speaker made his way closer, and Vyn arched a brow at me. This public address looked bold to my closest friends who knew of our story, but hadn't heard the private sequel of earlier.

"Be nice," I hissed to Lys. She tutted in a disapproving way, giving me the side-eye. "Prince Proditor. I hope you are enjoying yourself this evening?"

Glancing over his shoulder, I winced at a furious Illyra, glaring at his back. I'd put our earlier interaction to the back of my mind, but Jak found it harder, judging by the blush that rose on his cheeks.

He coughed. "Yes, ah... as a fellow future ruler of Ruvalon, I was wondering if I could have this dance?"

My eyes widened, Lys's hand tightening on my arm. The wording of the request put me in a difficult spot. Technically, I couldn't refuse—not respectfully, anyway—but after what had happened earlier…

I laughed awkwardly. "I don't think—"

"Just one dance? Please."

I grumbled internally at the puppy-like eyes he gave me. "Fine. Just one."

Lys almost refused to release my arm. Amused, I gave her a pointed look before making my way to the centre of the dancefloor, hand in Jak's. As a new song started playing, his hand was a gentle weight upon my waist, and I rested my own on his shoulder.

The dance was… surprisingly pleasant. Jak was careful not to hold me too close, or make it look like anything other than two future rulers dancing appropriately at a ball. I could feel Illyra's eyes burning a hole through me, but I knew the only reason Jareth would allow this was to keep up appearances of friendship between the kingdoms. Illyra's protestations would only sow discord.

I would never give anyone the satisfaction of asking Jak why he had left me for her… or why his father obviously preferred her. I didn't know what Jareth was getting out of the alliance, but it was clearly not a love match. Once that would have given me vindictive pleasure. Now I just felt sad for Jak.

"I want to… apologise for earlier." He spoke quietly.

"Jak, it's over. We don't have to talk about—"

"I do, Eliana. I took advantage and almost kissed you and I shouldn't have."

I shushed him, feeling uncomfortable, but he kept going. "It's just—"

But I didn't get to hear what it was. At that precise moment, the large doors to the side of the room opened, and my feet stalled. In strolled Antares—and Althea sauntered up from wherever she'd been hiding in the crowd to link her arm with his. Fabian caught my eye from the edge of the dancefloor, his eyes never leaving the woman. *Well, now I know which blonde he was chasing.*

My breath was almost stolen from me at the sight of the two draconi. Their beauty was unmatched by anyone else in the room. It was rather frustrating that I didn't dislike Althea, because she was a goddess incarnate: long blonde hair fell in luxurious waves down to her waist, and a pastel-pink gown that highlighted the blue of her eyes clung to every inch of her. The eyes of the lords—and even some of the ladies—followed her every step, as if they were about to throw themselves before her and pray for her favour.

I swallowed tightly as my eyes passed over her and stopped on Antares.

Anyone who hadn't met him would never know how uncomfortable he obviously was, with his black suit tailored to perfection, walking confidently with a beauty on his arm. But I could tell. His clenched knuckles were white, and the intense stare he gave everyone from under his long lashes was a predator's warning to stay away.

Dracho was nowhere to be seen. I ignored the sliver of disappointment I felt at that.

As if he could feel my gaze, Antares's eyes snapped up to mine. He leaned over, whispering something in Althea's ear. She nodded with a smile and released him, turning to walk around the outskirts of the room. My back stiffened as Antares stalked like a feline to the dancefloor, the people parting as if he would snap at their ankles.

A few feet before he reached us, his molten eyes landed on Jak. The prince's hand tightened on my waist, and Antares bared his teeth slightly. A growl—quiet enough for only the three of us to hear—rumbled through his throat.

Jak's hand snapped back to his side. "I shall excuse myself for this dance. Happy birthday, Eliana." He bowed to me, nodded swiftly to Antares, and walked away from the dancefloor.

I narrowed my eyes at Antares, unsure whether I was grateful or nervous for the interruption. My teeth ached as I clenched them; he took a step closer, tipping his head forward. "May I?"

I could only imagine the look on my face as I stared down at his hand. Why would he, of all people, want to dance with *me*?

His amber eyes were aflame, his lips turned up at the edges. I cleared my throat, slipping my hand into his warm grasp. I shivered as his other hand found my waist and I clutched his shoulder a bit too tightly, my whole body on edge as something tugged at my chest.

He smiled lightly once more; we turned into a slow dance, following the same circular pattern as other guests on the floor.

"That was a bit rude, wasn't it?" I murmured.

His eyes flashed. "I rather enjoy making princes feel inadequate."

I rolled my eyes. "Does that include your friend?"

"Of course." He lowered his voice, hand tightening on my waist. "But he is an emperor now."

My eyes found Connaught on the edge of the dancefloor, his eyes the epitome of concern. "How could I forget?"

Antares didn't miss my sarcasm, and his sly grin made me feel unnerved.

He was exceptionally observant, and having him so close made me feel exposed, as if he would unravel all my secrets at any moment. My shoulders were tense, my neck stiff from looking up at him.

"Don't worry. I won't tell him about Jak," he said quietly.

Wait, what? He heard us talking? I had no idea how, given that he hadn't been in the room at the time, unless...

Althea.

"It was nothing, Anta—"

"None of my business," he informed me, looking bored. My shoulders relaxed. "So, are you enjoying your party?"

I watched him glance around the ballroom. "It's all right."

His eyes swung to me, and my breath hitched.

"I must admit," I went on, "I'm surprised you asked me to dance."

"I must admit that I'm surprised myself." His brows creased.

"Why *did* you ask me to dance, Antares?"

"Well, I couldn't really ask Vyn without causing a stir, could I?"

A laugh bubbled up through my throat, the unexpected remark catching me off guard. "Did—did you just make a joke?"

His teeth flashed. "Believe it or not, Princess, I *am* capable of it."

I snorted unattractively, and his brow raised as I felt my cheeks heat. Whilst Vyn's preference for male lovers didn't cause a stir in Meridium, other, less *accepting* members of Ruvalon—particularly from the south and Stillmere—would have been scandalised at the image of two men dancing so closely together. I didn't tell Antares that Vyn would likely relish the idea.

"Maybe. But I can't say your jokes were ever something I thought I'd be privy to."

"Well, since we are your guests and you're the object of my emperor's... interests... I thought it best to get to know you more."

I choked on air before allowing myself a humourless laugh. "If I'm a testament to how he treats those within his *interests*, then I'd hate to see how he treats his enemies."

Antares's eyes darkened, his eyes flashing. "You would."

I couldn't look away. I had learned that Antares didn't need to make empty threats.

Before I could reply, the dance slowed, and a charge that felt like electricity ran up my spine as a small cough sounded behind me.

"Princess Eliana, if you would give me the pleasure of this next dance?"

Chapter 16

I turned.

His tone, the bow, his frustrating smile: all of it made my blood boil. His portrayal to the guests that he was all pomp and propriety. He had left me no choice, asking me so publicly. I shot Antares one last glance; a satisfied grin played on his lips as he bowed.

"Happy birthday, Eliana." He left the dancefloor.

Traitor. His entire motive had clearly been to distract me, allowing Dracho to get close enough without me fleeing.

Fighting the urge to slap it away, I grudgingly took Dracho's hand. He turned, offering me a small bow as the music started, which I returned.

The delicious scent of him assaulted my senses as he stepped closer and took hold of me. It was exactly what my previous two dance partners had done, but this felt entirely different. My skin was on fire where his hand rested—and I hated it. Hated that he made me feel like this. Hated the onslaught of memories this position brought me, of when we'd danced in Stillmere.

Stupid body.

"I know you'd rather be anywhere else right now, but if this whole spectacle of civility is going to work, you're going to have to loosen up a bit," he complained. "You're too stiff—it's like dancing with someone in chain mail."

"I'd rather be in chain mail," I muttered.

"Now, why doesn't that surprise me?" He half chuckled and looked at me for the first time since the dance started, his hand moving to guide my hip as we swayed around the dance floor. My stomach clenched. His stare became intense, aflame with some unspoken emotion I couldn't decipher.

"Stop that," I told him.

"Stop what?"

"Staring at me."

"Would you rather I stared at your feet?"

I rolled my eyes, straightening my shoulders. He glanced over them for a second, then grinned. Butterflies erupted in my gut as his warm hand suddenly moved, pressing flatly against the small of my back to bring me impossibly flush against him. I let out a small gasp, but cleared my throat as I looked away.

We danced for some moments before I decided to at least try and offer an olive branch. That was the whole point of this, after all. "I never thanked you... for helping the villages on your way here. It was—very gracious of you." I didn't mention the dig he had made that night when he had announced his actions.

"I didn't do it for you." My hand on his shoulder twitched, and he gave me a sharp-toothed grin. "We still need to find answers about the Hollow. This whole situation affects my people too... and I *did* become emperor recently—or have you forgotten?" His tone became bitter, as if he resented that I didn't expect such kind behaviour from him.

I gritted my teeth, then leaned in, daring to softly stroke the hairs at the nape of his neck. His breath hitched.

"And here's me thinking you were solely here for revenge. But now you mention your... *promotion,*" his nostrils flared, "it's not something one would forget when they were dragged from a throne room by several guards. Maybe I should return the favour?" I mused.

He pulled back a bit, appraising me. "Oh, you could certainly try, but I don't think your men would be up to the challenge. Do you?" His brilliant eyes flashed dangerously, specks of silver moonlight bleeding through the icy blue as a sly smile played on his lips. His tongue dashed out across them and my eyes betrayed me, dropping to watch. His resulting grin was almost feline as my heart hammered.

"You could always try yourself," he suggested. "I dare say any excuse would do to put your hands on me further. Maybe a repeat of our past nightly activities?"

I reared back, not realising I had subconsciously leaned forward, but fuming that he could sense what my traitorous body revealed. "You assume many things, *Your Excellency*. But I'd rather spend the rest of my days in the dungeons of Tenebris than suffer *your* touch any longer."

I knew the words to be a lie as soon as they escaped my lips, an intense panic settling in my gut at the thought—and that my body was still betraying me. I pulled out of his arms, the weight of his hands dropping, leaving my body colder. I fled, making for one of the side rooms off the ballroom, ignoring the looks from guests on the dance floor.

Hot rage sliced through me, riling me up—hurting me. How was it that he could boil my blood so easily? My skin felt like it had been peeled back and all my layers exposed for the world to see. Layers I never wanted *anyone* to see. No matter how much I tried to give as good as I got, I couldn't shake the way his casual dismissal of our intimacy sliced me open. I had let him in, let him see everything I tried so hard to hide from everyone else—my scars, both mental and physical; my true self, barriers down. I'd allowed myself to be vulnerable with him, had trusted him, and this was how he repaid me? By mocking me about my attraction to him in a public place? By laughing about the humiliation I'd endured at his hands in Tenebris? I couldn't stand it.

My heels clicked on the hard floor as I stormed into the room, but another set of footsteps was hard on my heels. I spun to face him, gasping when his fingers reached for mine.

All my hurt, the anger and frustration built to a precipice until I couldn't withhold it anymore. Before he could open his mouth, I had wrenched my hand from his, raised it and—

The resounding smack echoed in the empty room.

His face hadn't moved an inch from the contact, though my hand stung; his eyes were like ice, only a sliver of blue visible now as they met my wide ones.

"I would advise you not to do that again." He spoke calmly, but a thrum of power vibrated under his skin, washing over me like a warm bath.

The veiled threat didn't stop me from raising my hand in defiance.

As I swung for his face again, his hand shot up to grab my wrist in a blur of movement too fast for me to see. His hold was gentle enough that I could remove my arm if I chose to, but his chest was heaving, fury etched into his expression.

His stormy eyes closed tightly as he took a deep breath, his nostrils flaring, his knitted brow easing slightly. When they opened, the vertical slits of his dragon shone back.

"I warned you." He smirked, his thumb smoothing the inside of my wrist.

My nerves were on fire. I bared my teeth at him. "Fuck you!"

His grin turned sly, and he leaned in to whisper. "Right here? Or shall we find somewhere more private?"

His draconi voice was a seductive tickle on my neck and I couldn't help the shiver that ran across my skin; I bit my lip to stop any noise escaping. Dracho pulled back slightly, staring at me in confusion as my breathing quickened. Something flashed across his eyes, softening them, and I took the opportunity to shake his grip from my hand. I threw my head forward, a satisfying crunch reaching my ears as my forehead connected with his nose.

He rubbed his nose. His breath came heavily, and a low, deep growl sounded from his throat, the sharp edge of his fangs visible. My petty attempt at hurting him had just pissed him off even more.

His eyes opened, and I bit my lip again at the intensity I saw there. His gaze fell to my mouth, and I cursed the throb I felt below my navel. My stomach tightened in knots as memories flashed to the forefront of my mind. Desperate, hot kisses. Hands gripping my thighs. I might despise him, but my body remembered how he had made me feel.

His hand lifted again, a trickle of uncertainty swirling in my gut as it travelled up slowly to rest against the skin of my throat—not tight enough to take my breath, but firmly enough to raise my chin with his thumb, forcing me to look him directly in the eyes.

Some part of me wanted him to leave. Another part of me—the wild, wicked part of me—wanted him. He must have sensed the change; there were now only inches between us, and I could feel the heat radiating from him. I worried my lip nervously, and his pupils dilated.

"If you bite your lip one more time, I'm going to do it for you," he threatened.

All thoughts left me. Lips parting, I let out a breath. Dracho groaned deeply, as if in pain, and tilted my chin up.

"Fuck this." He pressed his lips hard against mine.

I grunted as my back hit the wall behind me. It only took a few seconds for my mind to catch up with my body.

Both my hands found purchase in his hair—tingles running through them at the softness of it—gripping him to me as he wrapped his arms around my waist. His hot tongue brushed my lower lip, begging for entry. Despite my subconscious screaming at me, my lips parted once more, opening completely to him. A small growl vibrated through his chest as he pressed closer.

This felt better than my memories. The sensations he wrought from my body were unlike anything I had ever experienced. My hands moved of their own accord down his muscled body and—before I could fathom what I was doing or talk myself out of it—ripped his tucked shirt out from his trousers, slipping under it across the tight muscles of his abdomen and up his chest.

A rough groan escaped his lips against mine. His hand lit a fire across my skin as it moved down from the small of my back, travelling over my arse and around to my thigh. He pulled it up over his hip; I felt the air kiss my exposed leg as the slit in my gown moved. My whole body tingled, heat building at the apex of my thighs as my need for friction grew. The sensation of his hand resting high up on the underneath of my thigh had me burning. It would only take a small movement to reach where my body wanted it most.

My mind was a hazy frenzy between what my body craved from the man touching me, and what my heart felt for how he had treated me. I knew I should stop this. But Goddess, ever since he'd returned, I couldn't deny that my body had longed for his touch.

He pulled away to trail blazing hot kisses down my neck... and stilled. Like prey held by a predator's gaze, I remained completely frozen as his nose grazed along the skin of my neck, inhaling my scent deeply. I stood there, panting embarrassingly loudly, before he pulled back, unbridled fury in his dragon's gaze.

"The Stillmerean touched you?"

His voice was a whisper, and that was far worse. It was a threatening tone that made my insides cold. I didn't know what to say that wouldn't make him angrier.

A muscle in his jaw clenched. He gripped my face, looking me straight in the eye. By the cold silver eyes that watched me, I knew it was the dragon speaking. "He is *never* to touch you again. Do you understand? If he does, I will take pleasure in breaking every bone in his hands, before I remove them entirely."

I could see that he meant it.

He bared his teeth at me, bringing my face closer, so close that our noses touched. "I will erase *every* memory you have of his touch. I will burn my claim onto your very soul, so that no other man would dare touch you."

Before I could object—tell him I wasn't his—he scraped his fangs over my neck, the action firing a bolt of pleasure through my entire body. My gasp was loud in the silent room. My back arched toward him, my core heating as he pressed against me, the hardened length of him giving me much-needed friction. He made a quiet, animalistic sound deep in his throat.

"Dracho," I gasped, immediately regretting it.

"That's right, *mia estra*. It's my name you call out to the darkness," Dracho whispered against my neck in a voice that was not his.

I heard a thud from the other side of the room.

"Oh shit! I'll—I'll just leave you to it."

Dracho snarled, and I stilled as we both looked to the door—to see the back of Roux's head as she made a quick exit, using her magick to close the door behind her.

I threw my head back against the wall, trying to calm my breathing. In that moment I both hated and blessed Roux's timing.

Dracho untangled himself from me and stepped away slightly, his breathing heavy. I could already feel the absence of him, cold air brushing my exposed leg. His silver eyes stared at me intently; he lifted his hand to tuck a loose tendril of hair back into the knot at the back of my head.

A flash of a memory from Jak doing a similar thing earlier made my heart plummet to my stomach. *How could I be so stupid?*

Anyone could have walked in. What if it had been Jak? Or worse, my father? Pulling the skirt right, I fixed my dress and stepped around Dracho, putting space between us, facing the door where Roux had just been.

"I'm—I'm sorry." Dracho ran his hands through his hair, brushing it out of his face. His eyes had returned to normal. "I shouldn't have spoken to you like that."

I nodded, unsure how else to reply. *I didn't mind it,* whispered a dark voice in the recess of my mind.

"This... this won't happen again. This *never* happened," I told him. The words were like ash in my mouth, that wild part of me screaming at me for denying us.

I heard him move slightly behind me. A rough exhale. "Yes. You're right."

My heart twinged. *Am I?* I didn't know anymore. He'd always been able to leave my head in a spin.

I turned to look at his beautiful face.

"What do you *want,* Dracho?" I asked softly. I wasn't sure if I really wanted to know.

His gaze was piercing, his brow furrowed. He glanced down. "I thought that would have been obvious by now."

Revenge? But there was a sorrowful longing in his tone—in his very face.

"What—" I started.

Dracho interrupted. "Have you heard the fable of the boy who flew too close to the sun?"

I was taken aback by the bizarre question. I had read the tale as a young girl, but the memory was fuzzy. I tried to make sense of what he was saying. "Are you comparing me to the boy or the sun in this story?"

"Neither. The flying."

"You can already fly, Dracho," I said impatiently, not understanding.

He shook his head in exasperation, running a hand through his raven hair again. His blue eyes pleaded with me.

"The boy craved the ability to fly. I'm saying—you're my flying, Eliana."

He strode past me—to leave. My heart started to beat like a drum at the thought, my throat thickening with emotion. I tried to stop myself from asking, but—

"And... he couldn't have what he craved?"

One hand on the door handle, he turned to look at me, a sad smile on his lips. He spoke softly.

"No. Because he didn't deserve it."

He walked out, closing the door behind him and leaving me there alone.

I didn't see Dracho again that evening, or his companions, and I assumed they'd retreated to their rooms. The rest of the night was a blur of dancing with noblemen I neither knew nor liked, and being polite whilst trying to pretend I didn't have a raging headache and a heavy heart.

Once the ball had ended and the many guests had left the palace, Vyn, Bas and I took platters of leftover food—and a few too many bottles of champagne—back to Bas's room. There we toasted to my birthday, the two singing a very drunk and indecent rendition of a birthday melody.

When they fell asleep atop Bas's blankets, I slipped back into my room using the hidden pathway, where I found a parcel wrapped in fine green paper on my bed. I opened a new set of throwing knives made from the most beautiful metal I had ever seen, with green-stained steel handles. Reading the accompanying note, I simply sat there, more confused than ever.

My hazy eyes read the words over and over. The note was so simple, but deciphering it was like reading ancient tomes in an unknown language.

To flying.

Chapter 17

Roux was escorted to my room bright and early the next morning, hours before the meeting of rulers was to take place. Cubra entered behind her, purring to himself as he jumped onto a chaise-longue and curled into a ball.

I had almost forgotten the scene Roux had walked in on, willing it to the back of my mind, but as soon as she met my gaze, my cheeks heated. I almost stumbled taking a step towards her. "Roux, I am so sorry—"

She laughed. "Why are you apologising? It was bound to happen sooner or later."

"What?" I blew out a shaky breath.

"C'mon, Eli, there's so much tension between you two—it was only going to result in one of two scenarios."

"And what scenarios are those?" I dared to ask.

"Either you kill each other, or you fu—"

"I get it," I interrupted, holding a hand up, and she laughed again, a sound like pleasant birdsong. Rubbing my hands over my face, I walked over to the armchair by the window, lowering myself into it with a slump. "It was a mistake. One which won't happen again."

"Mm-hmm. And what would be so wrong if it did happen again?" Roux asked, pulling her braids over her shoulder.

I couldn't hold back a flash of annoyance. "Dracho betrayed me—"

"I don't think that's exactly—"

"No, Roux. Please don't stand up for him. No matter our differing opinions on the matter, that is how *I* feel, and my feelings matter too."

She was silent for a moment, her eyes softening with understanding. "I'm sorry, Eli, you're right. Your feelings—of course they matter. I only hope that you can both come to some understanding, or maybe in the future, some semblance of the friendship you once had."

I didn't respond at first; I wasn't sure what to say. I couldn't see a way forward where I could let go of my pain and let him close again.

I looked away from her. "As soon as this Hollow business is under control, we can go our separate ways... and I won't have to see him again."

From the corner of my eye, I glimpsed her nodding. She inhaled deeply. "I'm going to visit Aunt Sizwe in the library. I'll see you at the meeting?" she asked tentatively, and I nodded back. She left, the door closing with a faint click behind her.

As I sat in the blissful silence for a few more moments, I glanced over to the new throwing knives. How many other things would ensure the memory of him remained?

Roux was not the only visitor I had that morning. Less than an hour later, Demetria knocked and poked her head round the door.

I jumped to my feet so that I could pull her in for a hug. We'd had only a brief chance to talk once I'd returned to the ball after my moment with Dracho; I was thrilled she had stayed, even if it was mostly to discuss business with my father.

"How's Adrie?" I asked as I pulled out of her warm arms and took a seat again. I had been disappointed that Demer's partner hadn't come with her to the ball.

She settled into the chair opposite, her perfect white teeth flashing in a grin. "She's good. Holding the fort whilst I'm away."

I laughed. "I'm sure she's loving that."

Demer smirked. "I'm sure she can't wait for my return. So, how was your birthday?"

"You know, it wasn't that bad. Thank you so much for coming."

"I wouldn't have missed it for the world. First ball back in Meridium for years! It was, despite the circumstances, nice to see Dracho again too."

I swallowed. "You spoke with him?"

"Only briefly. He asked how the shipment had fared, offered help and resources if we needed it."

"He did?"

Demer nodded. "We were lucky to get that shipment from Madain—enough grain and stores to last the northern villages and farms for a while. But I told him we'd always appreciate any extra help."

"That's good." I smiled.

Her eyes narrowed playfully. "So… I hear that quite a bit went on between you two?"

"Oh for Goddess's sake, who's been gossiping now?"

Demer looked at me pointedly.

"I swear, one of these days I'm going to kill Bastion Ekker."

Demer laughed, waving a hand. "You know how much of an unintentional gossip he is. He accidentally told me whilst gushing about some woman he described as '*the most beautiful deity you could ever meet, with skin that glowed in the moonlight.*' Safe to say he had inhaled his fair share of ale by that point. I think it was just before I saw the three of you sneaking off to your room."

I laughed. "That would be Roux. She's a mage from Aion."

"Ahhh. I did see her. She looks very much like Sizwe, and her mother."

I nodded, smiling fondly as I thought about the three.

"You didn't answer, by the way."

"Answer what?"

"You and Dracho."

"Demetria!" I scolded, throwing a cushion at her face. She caught it easily, giggling. My exhale was rough. "There isn't much to tell. We were friends. Now we're not."

"Uh-huh," Demer murmured, her tone disbelieving. She was always able to read my facial expressions better than most.

"What?" I asked in frustration.

"Sometimes, Eliana, you're as easy to read as a book."

"Oh, please," I said dismissively. "He's here for answers. And I plan to help him find them as soon as possible, so he can leave my city."

Demer hummed, a perfect blonde brow arching. "Now let your face say the same thing, and people may believe you."

I growled in frustration, launching another cushion at her face as her silvery laugh sounded out once more.

I was enjoying some tea and toast in one of the small breakfast rooms after Demer's departure when a staff member escorted a new guest in. I made an effort to pull myself together, feeling ambushed as I thanked Kael and sent him on his way.

Illyra stared at me, her tongue running across the front of her teeth behind her upper lip, until I greeted her. "Good morning, Illyra. Would you like some tea?"

Her eyes flashed darkly, her hand fidgeting with the gem at the base of her throat. She planted a false smile on her face. "No thank you, Your Highness. Did you have a good time at your ball?"

"I did, thank you. It was lovely to see so many faces after such a long time."

She hummed. "Yes, it was nice of you to be home for one after so long. I know your father missed you terribly whilst you were away."

I blinked at her, resisting the urge to narrow my eyes at the vicious meaning behind her words. "What about you? How was your engagement tour?" I asked sweetly.

Her eyes crinkled a bit at the edges, and I stifled the smirk that started to rise on my lips.

"It was pleasant," she stated coldly.

"Good, good. Well—"

"I just wanted to let you know that I know what happened last night," she rushed out, and I froze.

Jak seriously wouldn't have told her... would he?

"I don't know what—"

"Don't insult my intelligence, Eliana. I know it's not something you would be brave enough to reciprocate, for fear of causing bad blood between King Proditor and your father." *Ouch.* "But it was written all over Jak's face once he got back from wherever he disappeared to. I could sense it as soon as he returned."

"How—"

"I just could." She was agitated, tapping her fingers against her necklace.

"Well..." I stood, brushing down the skirt of the blue gown I wore. "I can assure you it wasn't as bad as you think. But it was wrong."

The words were like ash in my mouth. How could Jak put me in a position where *I* had to apologise to Illyra? But it was the right thing to do.

"I am sorry for the part I played in it," I managed to get out.

Illyra said nothing; she stared at me with no obvious emotion. I looked away awkwardly, accepting that she wouldn't acknowledge my apology.

"I hope you don't mind," I said, walking past her to the door, "but I have duties to attend to. Give Jak my best, and safe travels to you both."

"Thank you, Eliana." Her calm response surprised me. "Safe travels to you too."

I frowned as I left the room. Had I mentioned any travels to her or Jak in passing? I couldn't remember.

Our exchange slipped my mind as I made my way upstairs to the room where Ruvalon's rulers were to meet. A large round table had been placed in the centre of the room before the great stained-glass window that adorned the front of the palace. A smaller window in the centre of it was open, showing the courtyard and city beyond, the statue of my mother visible from where we sat.

Jareth, Bisa, Roux and Sizwe already sat at the table; Jak and Illyra had been sent back home. Jareth was stricter when it came to political matters and had always been hard on his son, claiming he had a soft nature. It was a contrast to how my father treated me, having allowed me from a young age to attend meetings and study the way of ruling.

I'd kept my dress simple, feeling less out of place in it than in the ball gown I had worn last night. Dracho's eyes found me as I entered, assessing me briefly before turning back to Althea and Antares. They stood by one of the glass windows at the side of the room, talking animatedly.

Jareth spoke to no one, sneering around the room as two of his personal guards stood nearby. It was an attitude I was used to—I'd never heard a pleasant word come from his mouth. The man consistently had a metaphorical stick up his arse and acted as if he were better than everyone in the room. It was a wonder how he'd become king in the first place.

Bisa and Roux were smiling as they spoke to each other, Roux stroking the top of Cubra's head; the feline's eyes slowly scanned his surroundings. Taking my own seat next to my fathers at the head of the table, I took a steady breath to ground myself for what was sure to be an eventful meeting.

The double doors opened, my father strolling in with Connaught just beside him. Everyone bowed as he approached the table. Connaught caught my eye whilst Father sat, and I offered him a smile.

"Good morning, everyone. I hope you all enjoyed and feasted at the ball. Eliana, I hope you had a wonderful birthday."

"I did, Father—thank you so much for your generosity."

He smiled lovingly back at me, before turning to the rest of the table. "You all know why we are here. After the Tain, a treaty was formed between the ruling leaders of Ruvalon. There, we all agreed to banish Jandar Morven from the continent, and Jareth was elected as king to rule over Stillmere instead. As a gesture of good faith, the draconi agreed to remain in their city behind the mountains, and that was signed by Eltanin Celesta, the previous emperor of Tenebris. Now that there is a new emperor, a new treaty needs to be signed on behalf of Tenebris." Father held his hand out to Dracho, who nodded. "As rulers of Ruvalon, it is vital that we come together, especially during these trying times, and come up with something that will work for us all."

"What is the point in creating a new treaty, Teyrnon?" Jareth asked, clasping his hands in front of him. "The very person demanding it is the one who broke the last one! How can we trust him to keep his word?"

Jareth wasn't wrong. Dracho's visit south had threatened the alliance between the kingdoms, but we knew realistically there was no way Jareth would try to punish Dracho—and no way Dracho would welcome any such attempt.

"I acknowledge my transgressions, Your Majesty," Dracho said. "I did, knowingly, break the treaty and step foot into the mortal realm. But I did so only with the intention of finding answers about the attacks, which were happening close to my borders. It was never my intention to reveal myself or interfere." He pinned Jareth with a cold gaze.

My father stepped in to mitigate. "Dracho travelled to Ruvalon to assist in finding the cause of the attacks on our villages—"

"*Your* villages," Jareth interrupted. "There have been no attacks on my kingdom in the south."

Dracho's eyes narrowed.

Father smiled tightly. "But in the interests of *all* Ruvalon, Dracho's help was vital in discovering the being we now know as the Hollow. I think to punish him for that would be a disservice, and not something I would look to do. I believe that moving forward with a new treaty, one which suits us all in these difficult times, would be what's best. Can we agree on that?"

Dracho looked slightly surprised.

"I agree," called out Bisa, who had been watching the exchange with quiet interest.

"Fine," said Jareth reluctantly, reminding me of a petulant child.

Father exhaled in relief. "Now—"

"My apologies, Your Majesty," said Dracho, "but before we go into the details of the new treaty, I think there is something we need to discuss with King Proditor."

"By all means, please go ahead, Your Excellency," Father replied as Jareth's brow arched.

Dracho looked at Bisa, who nodded. "During our stay in Aion a week ago, the nearby village of Carew was attacked. The smoke was visible from our location, so we went to investigate. Once we arrived, we found the whole village ablaze. There were no survivors."

Bisa had already told my father, but his face still crumpled in concern. There was a brief pause; Dracho studied Jareth's reaction.

He ran his fingers across the table leisurely, no shocked expression visible. Of course, Carew wasn't one of the villages closest to his city, but it was still in his territory—even if it supplied no trade or resources to Stillmere. So I supposed to him it was expendable. He disgusted me, but I wouldn't cause further discord by voicing my opinion.

"The Hollow arrived whilst we were there," Dracho went on. "Our fears are correct; it *is* the Hollow that is directly controlling the wyverns. It has returned, and the attacks have resumed."

Jareth started to ask, "How could you possibly know—"

"Wyverns, of all manner of creatures, appeared beside it. Not attacking, just still. As if waiting for its command."

"Then how did you all make it out alive?" Jareth asked, his eyes narrowing.

"It didn't attack," I said. "It just stood there, waiting for something."

"It wasn't ordered to attack us," Antares offered from beside Dracho.

I turned, confused, to meet his intense stare.

"A being of the Hollow is created by someone *infecting* those who are close to death. It's a dark and corrupt magick, and it's used to create a slave. Whoever is behind this is only ordering the Hollow to attack those villages. We didn't attack, therefore it did not need to retaliate."

Of course. How had I not realised it sooner? "So that day, before Aion…?" I asked tentatively.

Antares nodded. "Dracho stepped too close with a weapon in hand. The being took it as a threat."

Dracho stiffened in his chair, and Antares's gaze finally left mine, looking to his friend. My chest tightened. Before everything had happened in Tenebris, Dracho had told me he believed Aion to be his fault. By keeping his true nature secret and not transforming, he had allowed the creature to survive, and then go on to attack Aion.

It was far from the truth. As far as we knew, the Hollow was a threat to all life in Ruvalon, and it would not stop until we ended it. That day, we'd had no idea of its true intentions. It could simply have come across us on its way to the great tree. It was something we'd never know, but I hated the idea that Dracho carried the burden of guilt for the whole thing.

"But—" I started, before my mouth snapped shut.

Antares and Dracho both looked at me, seeming to know what I was going to say. *I* had stepped towards it... and if anything, it retreated slightly.

Jareth asked the most important question. "So, how do we go about stopping this... *thing*?" Unfortunately, it was the one we couldn't answer.

"We need to learn everything we can about the situation," Bisa said, her hands clasped in front of her. "Eliana has planned a trip to the temple of the Hollow."

"There's a temple?" Jareth asked, his interest piqued.

Bisa hummed. "There are some... fanatics who built a temple there. People brave enough to venture into the Vildspire—though not many. They believe the natural energy of the actual Hollow to be a god. They're scholars, mostly. They aren't dangerous."

"Unless they knew what was happening when whoever it was turned a poor soul into that creature," Roux pointed out.

"How would one even create or control such a creature as the one you've described?" Jareth asked.

Bisa sighed. "It's corrupt magic. Dark magic. Something I believed had been lost to the ages... but it would be a ritual of some kind. I cannot be sure of the exact method, but the person whose soul they corrupted would have to have been very close to death, navigating the realms between the living and the lost in the Notherworld."

It was difficult to suppress the shiver that slid up my spine.

"Can—can that person be saved?" I asked.

Bisa's eyes softened as she looked at me, a sad smile on her lips. "No. The person's soul is being ridden by the dark magick and the energy of the Hollow, kept between the living world and the Notherworld. Even if we managed to separate them from it, they would die. And we have no idea what would happen to their spirit."

I nodded, feeling a deep, tangible sadness for the poor soul. "As Bisa mentioned, I plan to go to the temple and see what I can find," I announced.

Dracho looked at me from beneath his dark lashes, a half-smile on his face. Father's jaw clenched; he was exasperated with my involvement, and had even tried to change my mind, suggesting that Connaught go in my place—which I'd refused. Bisa and Roux smiled in understanding.

"I shall go with her," Roux announced.

"We shall go also," Dracho said, and my stomach clenched.

"Well, now you have *that* sorted, shall we settle this treaty business? I am keen to return to Stillmere," Jareth drawled, brushing his long crimson hair over his shoulder as his eyes travelled over Dracho and his entourage.

Dracho gave him a tight-lipped smile, though he addressed my father. "That's another thing, Your Majesty. I'm not sure I would like to sign a new treaty whilst my father's murderer still goes free."

I tensed, sensing my father do the same. Despite Althea's words back in Aion, I still had my doubts regarding Dracho's motives—especially when it came to my father.

"I give you my word, I had nothing to do with Elta—"

"I know that, King Cervidae. But I don't want to be restricted while I look for the person behind it."

There was a beat of silence; a heavy atmosphere fell over us as the muscle below father's temple twitched.

"Understood."

A collective breath seemed to be taken in the hall.

"As I told you before, I will do everything in my power to help you find his true killer," my father vowed. "I don't know how my pin came to be where it was—I'd lost it days before—but you have my word, as king, that I would have *never* harmed your father."

Dracho stared at him until the silence became uncomfortable. I knew this was partly for Jareth's benefit, but it still felt like I couldn't take a breath until Dracho spoke.

"I believe you," he said at last, and my heart jumped in my chest.

My anger simmered underneath my skin, swirling with a thinning shred of patience. Dracho's head tilted suddenly towards Bisa, the mage's eyes glowing unnaturally as she pinned her concentration on him, clearly communicating privately. The corners of Dracho's lips curled up slightly as my father noticed at the same time I did.

Jareth waved a lazy hand. "What is going on? It would be nice to be kept in the know."

Dracho's nostrils flared; Bisa looked one second from slapping the king upside the head.

"You pointed out that Dracho broke the treaty because you saw him in Stillmere," I told him impatiently, "but he was here before then. He came south to investigate the attacks that had been happening. We came across one another and travelled together." My eyes met Dracho's across the table, and I resented the flip my stomach did. We had become more than acquaintances, done more than just travel together. We had become... more.

A shaky breath left me. "I was there when we found the emperor, just after he had been assassinated. With my father's pin on his body. Dracho had me questioned before his court"—Father stiffened but I continued, my eyes flicking to Jareth, who was listening intently—"and deemed me innocent, so he let me go."

"He just let you go? With no proof of your or your father's innocence?" Jareth asked in disbelief.

Dracho's head slowly turned to the southern king. "I have my own ways of determining if someone is deceiving me, King Proditor. It's why I myself came south." Dracho's voice was like smoke.

Jareth's eyes flicked to consider him, baulking at the violence in his expression. He nodded.

"And is precisely why I have had this prepared." Father handed a rolled scroll to Connaught, who moved around the table to pass it to Dracho. "In that scroll you will find a writ, signed and sealed by me, offering you diplomatic protection in my territories as you seek answers."

Dracho looked at my father in surprise.

"I promised I would help find your father's killer," Father continued. "I hope this can go some way towards proving I keep my promises. And prove that there is still a relationship to be had between our two kingdoms."

Dracho stared at the scroll for a moment, his thumb brushing over the seal before he turned back to the table. "Thank you," was all he said, but I could see the gratitude in his eyes. He lifted his chin. "The new treaty. What did you have in mind?" he asked calmly.

"The same as before," Jareth declared. "You stay—"

"That won't work," Dracho interrupted. I could tell he was fast losing his patience with the ruler. "The old treaty was signed by my father in good faith, and now someone from the mortal realm has broken that faith. Making a new treaty is an opportunity for us to become allies once more, to rebuild that relationship. Not only that, but I am here to find my father's killer *and* help where I can with the threat of the Hollow. I cannot do so stuck behind the borders of Tenebris."

"I'm sure we are capable of uncovering this conspiracy ourselves," Jareth said dismissively.

"Then why haven't you?"

"Excuse me?"

"Why. Haven't. You?" Dracho enunciated each word slowly, the tension becoming so brittle I was expecting it to shatter at any moment.

"This isn't what we're here for," Jareth argued, though his face was only a shade lighter than his hair under Dracho's stare. "Changing the treaty would give Morven an excuse to try and reclaim his land here in Ruvalon. *My* kingdom."

I swallowed hard. The elf king, Jandar Morven, had started the Tain, spouting vile propaganda about mortals and fairie-folk as he waged war throughout the land in an attempt to restore it to its 'rightful' rulers, the elves. He was the cause of the huge expulsion of magick—both pure and corrupt—that had destroyed Volente and forever marked a part of the land: the Vildspire.

Many had died that day, including my mother and Morgwn. It was a bloody stain on our history, one we all hoped would never be repeated. And it had led to the creation of the treaty, an agreement that was supposed to keep the draconi behind their mountains and Jandar from ever returning to Ruvalon.

Dracho's lips pulled up into a sly grin. "What Morven doesn't know won't hurt him."

"If he doesn't know now, he soon will. Word of your father's death will reach him," my father pointed out.

"True, but he doesn't know that we have left Tenebris."

"He'll likely know that too, after your little show the other week," I remarked, and my father rubbed a palm over his tired face.

Dracho's eyes burned into me for a moment as some emotion flashed across his face, but he turned away. "Fine. I'll agree to the old terms *after*, if it will prevent Morven sailing here, providing I be given unobstructed access to travel in my search for justice. After uncovering the truth, it's not like there's anything I want here anyway."

I almost flinched. The words cut deeper than they should have. I held his icy blue gaze, determined not to react, but I saw Roux wince and the widening of Althea's eyes. Dracho's head inclined just slightly in Antares's direction.

"I can agree to that," Father said.

"We cannot allow—" Jareth blustered.

Dracho's head snapped to Jareth, his eyes changing and flashing in anger, his voice a deep growl. "Do not believe you have any real power here, Proditor. I am trying to do this diplomatically, but know that I am extending you a courtesy by signing your treaty. I will remain. I *will* find those responsible for my parents' deaths and punish them how I see fit—no matter their position or lineage."

After a brief moment, while Jareth's face turned a furious shade of red, he nodded.

Father sat with steel resolve in his expression. There was no ounce of guilt to be found there. Which meant...

Someone was trying to set my father up. But why?

My eyes widened as a thought occurred to me. "When we were in Aion, we determined that the Hollow had been created to create chaos throughout Ruvalon." I looked to Bisa, who nodded in agreement. "The attacks were happening so close to the mountains that of course people would be suspicious of Tenebris. Don't you see?"

Dracho's eyes narrowed as he surveyed me; Antares muttered a realisation.

"The assassination of your father was a way to turn Tenebris against Ruvalon, or more specifically, Meridium. This is the turning point they wanted." I spoke with conviction. "To start war specifically between *our* two cities."

Bisa hummed her agreement as Dracho rubbed his cheek. "But why?" he asked.

My face fell and I shook my head. "I have no idea, but fortunately, you had already ventured south investigating for yourself. They weren't expecting..." I trailed off, cheeks flushing as I looked down, aware of what I'd been about to say.

"Us."

My eyes flicked up to him, his gaze holding mine until I hated the emotion I saw there. I looked away, feeling my father's eyes upon me.

"They weren't expecting us to meet," Dracho went on.

I shook my head. Then I cleared my throat, aware of the awkward atmosphere that had settled over the table.

"Are there any other stipulations you'd like to add to the new treaty?" Father asked Dracho and Jareth. Jareth waved his hand in dismissal, and Dracho seemed to think for a moment before shaking his head. "That will be all, then."

The notary who had been sitting in the corner of the room this whole time approached my father, bearing the large scroll that contained the new treaty. Father indicated that he should place it on the table, taking up the notary's quill and signing along the bottom. The notary poured wax next to his signature; using his royal ring, Father pressed his seal into it. He offered the quill to Jareth, who followed suit, signing quickly and sealing it before hurrying back to his seat, further away from Dracho.

Dracho was the last to sign. The room held a collective breath as he hesitated over the scroll, quill in hand; then his hand floated across the page as he signed it and sealed it with his ring.

The treaty was signed, with a stipulation that it would not need to be remade in the events of a rulers death. Everyone could relax. Now we just had to help find who had planned his father's death, and discover more about the Hollow as soon as possible. The sooner we finished this, the sooner he'd leave.

The sooner I could move on.

Father clapped once loudly. Several members of staff came in, carrying flutes of champagne on silver platters, placing one before each of us. A staff member placed one in front of my father, leaning over my shoulder next to give me mine. He must have been new; I didn't recognise him. I caught his eye, and he winked before leaving.

My brow furrowed. I looked over at Dracho, who was watching the exchange. The lines of his face seemed to sharpen as he raised his own glass, watching the retreating back of the waiter. He turned to Antares, the two of them staring intently in one of their conversations.

Father stood, picking up his glass and tipping his head to our guests. "To Ruvalon!"

Antares's golden eyes blew wide. "Wait!" he called out—just as everyone joined Father in his toast, taking a sip of their champagne.

My glass halted against my bottom lip as my eyes snapped to Antares, who was no longer there. I jumped as he appeared beside me, ripping the glass from my hand and smashing it against the tiled floor.

A rough cough brought me out of my thoughts. Father's hand was pressed flatly against his chest. His mouth moved, but no words came out.

"Your Majesty?" Connaught stepped forward, his face pinched in concern. Antares was scanning everyone in the room.

"Father?" I faltered.

The table fell silent. I was vaguely aware of Antares as he came forward, standing close to me.

Father continued to cough harshly, gaze flickering to each of us before flashing to his glass and then to my face, his eyes widening in bloodshot horror. He pushed away from the table; the chair fell to the floor as Connaught rushed to support him. I wrenched myself to my feet. Shocked gasps and the scraping of chairs vibrated the air around me, but I only had eyes for Father.

His hand clawed at his throat. Black lines were spreading under his skin. His eyes watered as he coughed, a trickle of blood lining his lips. Connaught held him against his chest.

"*Fetch a healer!*" he yelled to the guards behind him at the doors.

"He's been poisoned."

Antares's voice sounded hollow to my ears. I held my father, my hands gripping his arms tightly. "Father? Look at me." Even I could hear the panic in my voice. "Dad? You're going to be fine. Everything's going to be fine! Bisa?"

She rushed forward as I smoothed his greying hair away from his face with shaky hands. His eyes bulged, staring up at me in fear. His skin appeared to pale and waste away before my very eyes.

"No, no, no..." A sob broke from my throat.

A wave of blue light spread from Bisa's hand as it hovered over my father's chest. It did nothing to stem the spread of those vein-like marks.

"Bisa, please!" I cried.

Her fist closed gently, the light going out. My gaze swung to hers, not accepting the sorrow there.

"It's spread too far in his bloodstream. Even if I knew what to do..."

It can't be too late.

I felt the soft brush of fingertips against my cheek. Father lifted a hand weakly, pointing out of the open window towards the statue of my mother. My brow creased and I shook my head, not understanding. His lips pursed, before opening on an unspoken word; my head shook faster, unable to bear the sight.

Shaking, his hand moved to cup my cheek, the panicked look now gone from his eyes.

"No. No, *no!* Don't you dare! You're going to be fine! Everything—everything's going to be fine. Daddy, just—just hold on!"

My father's eyes turned glassy. A solitary tear ran down his cheek. He gazed over my shoulder, eyes full of determination, for a moment before looking back at me. A small smile played on his lips as one final, laboured breath left his mouth...

And he was gone.

Chapter 18

There was a moment.

A moment where the world fell silent. When I couldn't hear the chaos erupting around me as I closed my father's eyes for the last time.

But the silence disappeared when reality set in.

Sizwe burst through the double doors. Jareth shouted behind me, his tone accusatory, and I didn't need to turn to know it was aimed at Dracho, whose presence I could feel close to my back.

Sizwe knelt beside me and her sister, their hands clasping together as Bisa shook her head. She was speaking, but my ears heard nothing. I let go of my father's body to stand, turning. Dracho nodded to Antares, who disappeared through the heavy doors.

"This is treason! I demand he be taken into custody at once!" Jareth continued to shout, his voice grating my returned hearing. His guards moved closer.

"Do you really think the emperor would use poison if he wanted to kill him? And hang around to hear these accusations?" Althea snapped from her position by the window.

"I think you beasts will use whatever manner you can to take over!"

Althea snarled, stomping forward until Roux took a hold of her arm. Cubra stood beside her, hackles raised, his tails lifted in the air as if to strike at any moment.

The room started to close in, and all the noise was making my skin itch.

Jareth and Connaught were shouting at each other; Dracho stood, watching me warily. Waiting to see if I'd crumble before them all.

You do not break.

I held a hand up. Everyone fell silent. I had to swallow the lump in my throat, to force the words past my lips. It felt as though my mouth was full of ash.

"Whilst you are in *my* home, King Jareth, you would be wise not to make demands of me. Especially... especially in *this* moment." My voice was a dark promise as I caught the king's eye, which widened in alarm.

Sizwe and Bisa had placed my father on the ground, laying his hands gently on his chest. Connaught came to stand beside me, his face a promise of vengeance. His fingers brushed against the back of my arm in comfort, but I turned to look at Dracho, finding him silent and pale. His eyes did not leave me as I scrutinised him. *It wasn't you.*

"Where did Antares go?" I asked.

"To find the staff member who served the drinks. We thought your exchange was odd, but... we were too late."

For a brief second, or even less, the irrational part of me was sure he was capable of this. That he had returned to Meridium on a quest for revenge, and he had found it. That somehow, instead of outright killing my father, he had formed this plan to try and remove himself from speculation, waiting for the treaty to be signed before enacting it.

I could do as he had. I could order my guards to seize him—or try to—and I could start a war.

Yet I looked into his cool blue eyes, and I knew him to be speaking the truth.

I almost burst out laughing at the irony in the situation. I had told many what I would do in the same circumstance, never truly believing I would be in it. But now I had a choice... just like Dracho had had.

Despite the pressure of another ruler in the room, I would not make the same mistake.

"The emperor will not be taken into custody, King Proditor."

Jareth's face turned an ugly shade of red as his fury reached its limit. "Princess Eliana, I must insist. It is obvious that this—"

"Nothing is obvious," I said. "Nothing is proved. I will not risk *war* between the realms by seizing one of its rulers—one who may very well be innocent. You are more than welcome to try, though." I held an arm out.

Jareth paled at the prospect.

I turned away from him, facing Dracho. "I have questions for you."

He nodded, shaking off the stunned expression on his face as he took a step closer. I heard a grumble sound in Connaught's chest.

Dracho eyed him, then me. "I will answer anything you want. I will help in any way I can."

I found warmth in his blue eyes, and something else. Empathy. It made me feel nauseous, and I turned away as the heavy doors pushed open.

Antares stormed into the room, carrying a brown-haired man in front of him as easily as if he weighed nothing. Dracho moved to my other side as Antares threw the man forward onto his knees before me and Connaught. He looked up at me, no emotion in his face.

"Who are you?" I asked him, my voice surprisingly steady.

A small smirk played at the corner of his lips as he glanced between Connaught and me. With a tilt of his head, his eyes travelled over me hungrily. My lips curled in disgust.

"No one important." His voice was a whiny thing. "Hired to do a job, tha's all."

My mind worked over that. How had he managed to get into the palace and get close enough to my father? "By who?"

The man stared at me. "That I 'onestly can't tell you. All details were delivered in secret. No names."

"He's telling the truth," said Antares, clearly listening to the man's heart.

"Then why?" I spat at him, my voice breaking slightly.

Leaning forward, the man broke into a wide grin. "Because the pay was enough."

As soon as the final syllable left his mouth, my knees hit the floor and my unsheathed dagger found purchase under his chin. Bubbling blood filling his throat as his eyes widened in shock.

I leaned so close our noses were almost touching. "It's a shame you'll never see a single dram of it."

The man's choking sounds continued until they didn't. I watched, undisturbed, as the light left his eyes. Removing my dagger, I stood; the man's body fell to the floor, his blood pooling around his head.

"You should have kept that vagabond for public execution. The people will hear of this soon," Jareth said. His voice made me want to kill one more.

"And make a spectacle of the king's death? No. We don't do public executions in Meridium," Connaught told him.

Jareth scoffed. "Whyever not?"

My voice was calm. "As rulers, we see enough bloodshed. Become used to it. Why would we encourage bloodlust, and not *peace*, in our own subjects?" I might have taken the man's life into my own hands, but at least this had avoided a messy, public spectacle.

Jareth rolled his eyes, turning to looking out over the city out the window. The wild part inside me wanted to launch my dagger into his face; a long breath left me. I pointed to the man on the floor with my dagger. "Someone clean that up."

I knew I should stay, deal with the fall-out now that one of the kings of Ruvalon was dead. But I couldn't face remaining in the room with his body.

My father's *body*. Not my father—because who he was, his spirit, had gone, leaving behind nothing but some vessel made of flesh and bone.

He was *gone*.

I swayed a little, the sound of Bisa's sniffle reaching my ears. Fingers brushed against my arm above the elbow, righting me. I turned to face him, already knowing who it was from the way goosebumps trailed over my skin. My heart beat a furious storm as I clenched my teeth, trying to control the suffocating panic that started to lace through me.

Dracho's eyes were soft, and did not leave mine as he spoke to the room. "I'm escorting Eliana to her chambers."

Jareth spun. Connaught stepped forward, his mouth opening in protest. Dracho whirled, snarling at them with fangs bared. "Do not think I would ever harm a hair on her head!"

Connaught took another step forward, outraged. "I don't care if you were to worship at her feet! As captain of the guard, *I* will escort Eliana!"

I turned, only partly aware of the altercation. I pressed a hand to my heaving chest, feeling a splintering within.

"*Eliana,* is it, Captain?" Dracho asked, his tone unamused.

Connaught blinked a few times, swallowing.

Dracho continued, "The king has just been assassinated. Until you sweep this castle, I will ensure the rightful heir to this seat—my *ally*—is protected."

Ally. Are we allies? My mind spiralled as it started to process what had just happened. Could I trust the company around me? *More betrayal.*

"Captain," Sizwe said softly, standing beside my father's still form. I couldn't bear to look at it. "Let her go."

Realisation seemed to dawn on Connaught's paling face. He nodded. "O-of course, Your Excellency." He tipped his head forward slightly before turning to my father's body.

I walked away quickly, not willing to crumble in front of everyone.

Dracho nodded towards the door but did not touch me as he walked us out. My legs trembled all the way to my chambers; the walk felt as though it went on forever as my nerves threatened to bring me to my knees at any moment. Members of staff bowed and stared as we walked past, whispers already spreading through the castle. I felt Dracho's eyes upon me the entire time. Two royal guards followed us to my door, their weapons drawn as if expecting another threat.

"Wait," Dracho said, his fingertips gently touching my arm to stop me. He eyed my guards for a moment, before opening my door and slipping into my room. I didn't have the composure to speak out, to ask him what he was doing, but he returned quickly.

"The room is clear."

A rough breath left me as I stepped over the threshold. I spoke without turning. "Thank you for escorting me, Dracho. That will be all."

"Eliana, are you sure—"

"Yes, I'm sure. Thank you. You may take your leave now." I turned, closing the door without a second glance at him, then pressed my forehead to the wood.

Muffled, I heard him sternly order my men to stand guard outside the door and search Bas's room. In any other situation, I would have smiled at his remembering that Bas's room had a secret passage to mine—something I had told him when we were in Crystalwood together. And had it been any other situation, I would have loved to see their faces at being given orders by the dragon emperor.

I faced my room, my eyes scanning every shadow until I was sure I was alone. I sighed in relief, and my eyes fell to the brush my father had given me for my birthday.

Like a wave, the realisation of my father's death washed over me.

I didn't know how to navigate it safely—wasn't sure how to stop my heart from being battered against my ribcage like a ship upon the rocks. The breaths came sharply and quickly, blurring my vision as tears flooded my eyes. The grief was absolute, flowing through every nerve ending in my body. I couldn't even hear the animalistic wails that tore my throat.

Fear. Grief. Loneliness.
I knew in that moment that nothing would ever be the same again.

Chapter 19

Dracho

I watched Eliana closely over the week that followed, hating the lack of life in her forest green eyes. If I thought I had taken it badly when my father died, it was nothing compared to the grief that surrounded Eliana. She undertook her duties with all the grace and propriety of any noble ruler, but there was no love or confidence for the role in her yet. Not whilst forced into it too early and riding the waves of her grief.

I knew how that felt.

I had been stunned when she hadn't ordered my arrest, knowing I would be the first suspect at the table. It doubled my own grief and guilt at how I had treated her back in Tenebris. Despite my dragon taking over in that instant, I had realised almost immediately how foolish I was being. I only hoped that my actions here, helping them with the Hollow and now her father's death, would show her how sorry I was.

I'd always believed she was a better leader than me.

It was obvious to me and Ant that guilt was an emotion Eliana was struggling with. She had run away from home for two years; it had caused a rift between her and her father, which I assumed they had been trying to mend during her time back in Meridium.

I couldn't comprehend what she felt deep down. My father was my idol—had been. We had been close at the time of his death... I couldn't imagine how painful it would be to lose a parent just as you were beginning to know them again.

After the attack, the *captain* had ordered a sweep of the castle and the staff to be questioned. A young wood nymph called Kael had been found in a hardly used pantry, his throat slit by the assassin who had taken his place. Said assassin, killed by Eliana, had carried a note upon his person. No location or names—just an amount and a promise to pay a second half upon confirmation of the king's death. The amount given was enough for someone to live two wealthy lives, and we hadn't found the first payment he had received. Whoever wanted the king dead had plenty of resources.

Connaught had taken it particularly hard, and his guilty conscience was evident. He had moved around a lot of his men since our arrival, and because of that, someone had slipped through the cracks. He had been naive to overlook the staff as a way of entering the castle. He was older than me, but still young to undertake a role with such responsibility. I could tell he had been questioning his capabilities since, and he hadn't left Eliana's side.

The whole castle and city seemed to mourn alongside the princess, despair setting in amongst the people. Teyrnon had been a beloved ruler, and his death left a dark cloud. Whispers of discontent came from the shadows of the streets, rumours that perhaps this was a threat of war to come.

Eliana didn't address the gossip. She kept busy, heavily guarded—usually by the captain and a large troll named Marcus—as she planned her father's funeral and stepped into the city streets to speak to and comfort the people. Bisa and Sizwe remained in the palace, assisting her where they could, hiding the depth of their own sorrow.

But Eliana... she drank her own grief like it was the richest wine. Wore it like armour. From the dark circles under her eyes, and the nightmares that caused her to scream out in the night, I knew she was dying inside. Even in a separate wing of the palace, I lay awake at night, listening for the smallest noise, waiting for her to wake from those stars-forsaken dreams.

Bastion was shocked when I approached him for advice after we had finished sparring in the training arena. I had invited him the evening before, knowing that besides Vyn, he would be the best person to discuss Eliana's current state. Vyn was still a little frosty towards me.

"You're coming to *me* for advice?"

"I didn't say I'd take it." I chuckled weakly. "I just wanted to ask."

He shrugged. "That's fair." But he had no idea how to deal with the current situation. He had been close to the king himself, and was dealing with his own grief. Feeling it so strongly himself, he could only worry about the intensity of what Eliana was feeling.

"What do *you* think we should do?" Bas asked.

I wiped my brow of the slight sheen that had grown there; the arena air was humid. "I'm hoping the funeral and her coronation will give her some closure. But if personal experiences have taught me anything... she won't rest until the person responsible is found."

"That's what I'm afraid of," Bas muttered. "We've already got so much on our plate, with the Hollow and everything else."

We did. The Hollow, my father's assassination and now King Cervidaes', along with the need for resources in the north. I nodded. "I want to help, but after everything..."

Bas winced. He slapped me on the shoulder. "We all make mistakes, but have you tried to make amends for yours? Have you thanked her for not throwing you in the dungeons?"

My heart twisted. I felt like slapping myself. "I haven't. I am trying."

Bas hummed, seeing my expression. "I know. I suppose you're only human, after all. Well..."

I huffed a laugh. "Thanks, Bas."

"How has she been?" Ant's deep tone called, his eyes fixed on Bas. He sat on the ground not too far away, his back resting against a wooden post.

I knew what he meant. We had all seen her, but how had she been in the private company of her friends? I hadn't been alone with her since escorting her back to her room immediately after her father's death. I believed the captain, Connaught, was to blame for that.

Bas rubbed the back of his neck. "I'm not entirely sure. Even when we're alone, she's determined not to talk about it. She rattles off about getting the funeral done and leaving Sizwe in charge of the city so we can go to this temple."

"She's keeping busy," Ant said. *You saw how Althea was after her father's death. How* you *were after yours,* he added to me.

"You know her nightmares?" Bas said.

I nodded.

"Well, they've been keeping me up more often than not."

"We've heard," Ant stated.

"You can hear them?"

I nodded. "It's hard to miss, if we're in tune with our senses."

His face crumpled. "They've been worse for a while, but nothing like this."

"A while?" I asked, with morbid curiosity. Bas gave me an awkward, pointed gaze.

'Cause of your betrayal, dickhead, Ant whispered into my mind.

Fuck you. A surge of guilt made me feel queasy for a moment.

Right here, or shall we go somewhere private? Antares mockingly replied, echoing my words to Eliana the night of her ball.

Thanks for the reminder you were listening that *closely.*

Who d'you think pointed Roux to the correct room? Your dragon side was riding you because of your jealousy. It was a complication we didn't need.

Despite being furious at the interruption at the time, I couldn't disagree with him. My possessive nature had come out to play, and had Roux not entered that room, stars knew how far I would have taken it. From the way Eliana's body had responded to my touch, I knew she wouldn't have stopped me—but likely would have regretted it, even if I hadn't.

I hesitated for only a moment before asking my next question. "If you don't mind me asking, Bas, how… how did you and Eli happen?"

How *did I not know about this?* Ant asked, genuinely surprised.

Eliana mentioned it back in Morcroft.

I thought that was a joke.

You really need to work on your sense of humour.

Eliana quite enjoyed mine on her birthday, he teased, the corner of his lips turning up subtly as he sent me a brief image of her laughing.

Again, fuck you. My chest ached as I thought back to my favourite memory of her: dancing in Stillmere, her head thrown back in a laugh that was freedom, her cheeks flushed and eyes clenched shut. Making her laugh was something I desperately wanted to do again. Even if it was the last thing I ever did.

Bas's cheeks had darkened, and he was clearly unaware of our private exchange. He exhaled slowly through his nose. "It was before she met Jak."

I nodded, although slightly surprised. My brow furrowed as I thought it over. "So were you her—"

"First, yes," he said quickly, his lips thinning.

I did not expect that. "Oh," was all I could verbalise.

He coughed, clearing his throat. "After what happened with…" He trailed off, giving me a pointed look, and I understood. He meant the night she'd been attacked.

Ant eyed us both carefully, but didn't intrude. I had shared a tiny part of her story with Ant—he knew that she had experienced some trauma at the hands of men. He had been sickened by what little I'd told him; his knuckles had turned white in his clenched grip as he listened, and the molten fury in his eyes had matched my own. I hadn't told him of the scar she now bore, or the full details. I wouldn't betray her trust, even if I wanted Ant's opinion on what had happened. I still didn't believe the men responsible had been civilians.

Bas continued, "There was no one around that she trusted or clicked with. Not in Meridium, anyway. And she didn't think it was some special *thing* she had to give to someone. After everything that happened, I think she wanted to take control of the situation. Lose it on her terms—not in some symbolic consummation of marriage, if that ever happened. She wanted to feel in control."

I nodded, respecting how mature that decision was. Ant pursed his lips, and I knew he agreed too.

"When she first asked me, I laughed. Thought she was joking. I was kind of mortified once I realised she was being serious. But then she told me she hadn't thought of asking anyone else. I was one of her best friends, and she said she knew she could trust me, and that we'd be all right after. Honestly, I felt kind of honoured. I told her so, and she punched me in the gut. Told me to stop being a soppy prick."

I laughed.

"We continued for a little while after. The physical side of it was just a bit of fun. There was no deep, emotional connection—besides us being best friends, obviously. We ended it when she got serious with Jak, when I could see that she started genuinely smiling again."

"And you didn't resent the ending of it?"

"No! Never. I never saw her in a romantic way. That sounds silly, considering what we did, but no. I still have my best friend. She's like my *friend* soulmate. I'll always have her."

I smiled widely, understanding what he meant completely. I felt the same about Althea, and when we were younger something similar had almost happened between us. We'd decided against it, understanding that it was more from the expectation of our families that we would end up together than an actual desire to be with each other in that way.

"So, what about you two?"

I pointed to myself. "Eliana and me?"

He nodded. "Obviously I know you became close before... you know, everything. But do you think you'll get there again? Is that even something you want?"

Is that even something I deserve?

Ant's eyes narrowed, as if sensing the direction my mind had taken.

I shoved those thoughts from my head and sighed. "Honestly, I have no idea. All I was concerned about was finding out who murdered my father." I ran a hand through my hair. "But there always seems to be more and more complications. Despite everything that's happened... I can't keep away."

Bas smiled knowingly, and Ant rolled his eyes.

Shut up. You know your feelings have changed too, I directed at him.

Her stubbornness is... admirable.

I almost laughed loudly at that. Of course it would be a trait others found frustrating that drew Ant in.

Bas clapped his hands, his muscles tensing beneath his inked biceps. "Well, if there's one sure-fire way to melt her cold heart again, it'll be helping to find out who killed her dad." A solemn expression passed over his face; he looked down for a moment, then shook his head. "I have every faith in you, brother."

I huffed again, this time in disbelief. "Thanks, Bas."

The funeral was a sweet sorrow, allowing all those burdened by their raw pain to say goodbye and remember the fond memories they had of their beloved king. The people had gathered in one of the courtyards, turning their faces up to the palace balcony.

Eliana stepped to the edge of the balcony in a breath-taking flowing gown of black. Her face was clear, her hair pulled back into a chignon, braids tucked into the back. Her eyes scanned the crowd gathered below, her form backdropped by a great pyre and the glorious stained-glass window that was built into the front of the palace. Her father had been wrapped and blessed by Bisa, Sizwe and Roux. Eliana had gone to say her final goodbyes and assist them.

Only those paying very close attention—and with my superior vision—would have noticed the way her breath shook as she exhaled before addressing all before her, her voice ringing out clearly. Measured. Strong.

"My father was more than deserving of the title he bore each day. He was not a man who sought riches or glory." She took a breath. "Though his name was known almost everywhere. He thrived mostly in doing good—caring for all, whether it was his family or his people. I don't think anyone would disagree that he went above and beyond to help."

I saw many in the large crowd nodding their agreement.

"He was honest, hard-working and kind. A loving husband..." She paused. "And an outstanding father. I am ashamed to say I spent the last two years away from him."

Connaught stood a few feet behind; his eyes never strayed from her.

Eliana cleared her throat. "I may not be able to make that up to him in life, but I vow to do so in death by looking after his people, *my* people. My father ruled with honesty, so I shall do the same. The rumours are true. My father was murdered."

Whispered chatter broke out.

"This news may bring about unrest to the usual peacefulness we find in Meridium. But I promise to do all that I can to ease your troubles. I shall find out who is behind these village attacks, and who is behind my father's death. It is not something I take lightly. And I will ensure peace returns to Meridium once more, with the help of my allies."

I sensed many eyes landing on myself, Bisa and Jareth as we stood to the side of the balcony, feeling rather than seeing their gazes.

"I promise to do all that I can to ensure the peace of Meridium, from now until my end."

A silence fell over the crowd as she finished, lasting a few brief moments. My jaw clenched. I wished I could take a step forward and comfort her, but I knew that in front of so many people, including Jareth and Bisa, it would not be appreciated.

"Long live the heir!" a lone voice called out from the crowd. A young man's fist rose high into the air.

"Long live the heir!" a woman joined in, raising her own hand. Suddenly cries of the same words came from all over, until the whole crowd was unified in their support of Eliana.

Eliana turned in graceful silence, the calls still coming. Her knuckles were white, but only a couple of tears escaped, trailing their way down her cheeks. She was inspirational with her courage in the face of grief. She faced it down like a raging bull, never wavering or giving in.

I knew there would come a time when she would need to unburden herself, and I vowed to myself to be there in that moment.

My heart constricted with the memory of preparing my father's body, and I clenched my jaw. That realisation of being alone, of being the last remaining member of your bloodline and heritage… It came with a burden all its own. A crushing weight.

If I could help her share the load, no matter her feelings towards me, then I'd try.

Her head lowered as she took a few steps forward, a rough exhalation leaving her lips, and took a flaming torch from Connaught. The smell from the oil on the pyre was strong to my senses as she lowered the torch, lighting the wood that rested below her father. The flames licked the white wrap that enshrouded his body, and Eliana stepped back to Connaught's side. Sizwe, Bisa and Roux stood by me, holding hands, their heads lowered in prayer.

Eliana's face remained emotionless as she watched the pyre, the flames causing flickers of light to cross her features. I couldn't tear my eyes away from her.

She was an inspiration to all. She didn't need power to be strong, didn't need to be dominant to show leadership. I knew she would make an amazing queen, and I hoped that fact was obvious to all in attendance. It showed the importance of having the right person as ruler. Not someone there by solely blood or birth, but by what her spirit proved her to be.

A queen of the people. Mortal or fairie folk alike.

And as she bowed her head, mumbling a prayer, I tipped my head to the sky, whispering one of my own.

"May the light of the stars shine upon you."

Chapter 20

Eliana

The messenger came from Solva Bay, brought in from a traders boat.

The air was so brittle from the tension, it felt like it could crack at any moment. No one spoke as my visitor climbed the steps towards the dais, but the guards around the hall stiffened as their eyes wandered over the traveller.

It had only been a week since I had laid my father to rest, collecting his ashes and placing them in an ornate urn in the crypt below my mother's statue. Seeing their urns together had sliced viciously at my heart, but I found comfort in knowing that they would find each other again.

My nightmares had not given me a reprieve, plaguing me almost every night with images of my father clawing at his throat. Comparing stories, we had agreed that whatever substance had been used by the assassin was related to the deformed creatures used by the Hollow and the poison used on the blade that killed Dracho's father. So far, no amount of reading or searching had provided results as to what it could be. The healers of Meridium had never seen anything like it. It made me worry that more death would result from such a lethal poison.

My anger urged me to flee Meridium, to head straight to the temple of the Hollow and find answers. My thirst for retribution and knowledge had been stemmed by Roux, who'd reminded me that my people needed me right now—and that rushing out to unknown territories in a rage was reckless.

It was just after breakfast one morning when Tomas found me, barging into the small tea room I had taken my meal in. Someone had arrived at the city gates, immediately stopped by some of the guards enquiring his business. He had informed them he wished for an audience with the king and seemed genuinely shocked when he learned of his demise. After learning of my position as Queen Regent, until my coronation, he had requested to meet with me.

Considering who—or rather *what*—the man was, I'd accepted, telling Tomas to bring him to the throne room in an hour.

It hadn't taken long to gather everyone. Dracho and Antares had seemed rather shocked when I asked them to join. Antares had left to fetch Althea, who'd made a habit of visiting Engel in the bay; the latter was surprisingly taken with the draconi. The Aioni women were here too, including Bisa, who should have left a week ago. I knew it had more to do with her worry for me than her desire to stay.

The messenger's long-sleeved, black furred jacket covered him to just below his waist, and was buttoned up completely, slightly off-centre. A single decorative, light blue thread hemmed his jacket and trousers. With his brown boots, made from an unusual fur, it was obvious he came from a colder climate. It wasn't his attire that made him stand out.

It was the sharp point of his ears.

Long, smooth blonde hair rested around a chiselled, tense face. Wide hazel eyes took in the hall as he walked gracefully forward. The man was unmistakably elven. There was something otherworldly about him and his calm aura as he walked.

Connaught took a subconscious step towards the throne, and I fought the urge to roll my eyes. I could dispatch one elf if necessary. Vyn and Bas were studying the male; his eyes snapped to them for a moment, widening, before returning to me. Dracho, Antares and Althea stood to the side of the hall, also watching the visitor with obvious interest, if not a little curiosity. Numerous citizens stood near them, though at a little distance.

The elf stopped just in front of the dais, tipping his head forward as he bowed. The silence in the room starting to make my skin tingle.

"Speak, sir. I was informed that you requested an audience. You have it. What would you ask of me?"

The elf stood straight, a small smile rising on his lips. "Your Highness. Firstly, I thank you for accepting my request, and my presence within your city. I am deeply sorry for your loss."

"Thank you for your condolences. Not *all* elven are banished from these lands. You are of course welcome to go as you please."

"That is... a surprise, Your Highness," he said. My eyes narrowed. "But I fear that not all share your generous view. Many would rather cut my ears from my head than see me walking amongst them."

I winced, unable to suppress it. "You will find no such person here. Whilst you are my guest in Meridium, you shall be protected. I swear it."

The elf bowed again, his eyes twinkling as he came back up. "Thank you, Your Highness. My name is Adven. I come from Akraya, a small island to the south-east. It is where my master lives."

"Your master?"

"Yes, Your Highness. I am here on his behalf."

"And who is your master?"

"His Royal Highness, Prince Cirdan Morven."

The sudden burst of noise from the outraged subjects around me was almost deafening. Adven said nothing more, but his eyes darted around the hall as if expecting an attack at any moment.

The Tain was still fresh in many people's minds, having only ended thirteen years before. The cruelty of Jandar Morven had not yet been forgotten, so it was easy for many to tarnish the son with the actions of the father.

Cirdan was the legitimate son of King Morven, the evil elven king who had started the Tain all those years ago. It was rumoured that he'd held no love for Cirdan's mother, an elven woman as vicious and cruel as Jandar—she had died during the Tain. Jandar did not mourn for her; supposedly their union had been an alliance, a way for him to bear a true heir.

Cirdan had been but seventeen years old when the Tain had begun, and he had been left on the continent of Eshmnor whilst his father waged his war. When he had been defeated, Jandar chose to return to him there. Nothing much was known about Cirdan besides his name.

I raised a hand, silence falling immediately. "And what would the son of Jandar Morven want with me?"

Adven laughed awkwardly. "Begging your pardon, Your Highness, but Cirdan has had nothing to do with his father for many a year now. He has estranged himself from his wicked sire. His only wish was that your father—now you—receive this scroll, and that I convey this message: that he accepts whatever you choose to do afterwards."

He pulled a sealed scroll from the canvas bag at his side, lowering his head once more as he held it out. I waved my hand at Connaught, who took the steps down the dais to fetch it, checking over its seal before handing it to me.

Jandar's royal blue seal shone up at me. The sigil of the wolf, intact. I took a moment to open it, reading the letter in silence.

Your Majesty,

If you are reading this, I thank you for graciously accepting my messenger and my letter. I would have visited myself, but I didn't want word of our conversation reaching my father. I have sent my most trusted advisor, Lord Adven, to deliver this. Please confirm that his place has not been taken by one of my father's men–Adven has a leaf-shaped birthmark on the back of his left hand.

I know due to my lineage that my letter will come with some level of distrust, but I must speak with you. I have been away from my father for many years, but his exploits have started to reach my ears. I have also heard of the attacks that your land has suffered... and I may have the answer to the questions you have been asking. Along with a solution.

I await your answer with the return of Adven. As much as I wish for us to work together, I understand that your trust is a lot to ask for, especially after everything my father did. If you find yourself unable to meet with me, I will at least thank you for reading my letter. I hope you find what you are looking for, for the sake of all Ruvalon.

Yours humbly,

Cirdan Morven

I read over Cirdan's words three times, fully absorbing what he had written.

At first, my impression of his letter was that he was somewhat paranoid, asking to check his advisor's skin. But then from everything I had been taught about the war, it wasn't surprising that Jandar might seek to replace a messenger with a man of his own.

Had Cirdan also implied that his father was somehow connected to the Hollow?

Lifting my eyes, I caught the gaze of Adven, who stood silently waiting. "Adven, please approach."

Connaught took a step forward as Adven obeyed, but I raised a hand.

"Show me your left hand," I demanded.

Adven gave a small smile, but removed the glove he had been wearing, raising his hand. He showed me the back of his hand, as if knowing what his master had written. There, on his pale skin, was a light brown birthmark in the shape of an oak leaf.

"Thank you, Adven."

As if he sensed Connaught's tension at having him so close to me, he took a step backwards off the dais.

"I assume your master has shared with you what he wanted my father to do?" I asked.

"He has, Your Highness."

"This isn't something I can decide lightly. I will require a day to consider it."

Adven's eyes widened in surprise. "I understand completely, Your Highness. Thank you, on behalf of my master, for considering it at all. I shall retire to the city until you have made your decision."

"No, that won't be necessary, Adven. I extend an invitation to remain here, in the palace." Murmurs broke out in the hall. I ignored them. "You shall be my guest until my decision is made."

Adven got down on one knee, placing his hand on his chest. "Thank you very much for your generosity, Your Highness. I would be honoured."

"Milly," I called out. My handmaiden scurried towards me, bowing. "Please escort Lord Adven to one of our guest suites. Ensure he has everything he needs until I call for him."

Her eyes flashed to mine, and she understood my meaning. He was not to leave his room until I deemed it so. She turned to Adven and indicated he should follow her. Adven gave me a last smile, eyeing the draconi curiously before following.

I stood, the guards throughout the room coming to attention as silence fell. "Connaught, my guests from Tenebris and Aion, I require your attendance in the strategy room immediately."

I made my way down the dais, turning to take the doorway towards the staircase, Connaught and Marcus closely behind.

"Is there something we should be worried about, Eliana?" Connaught asked quietly as he ghosted my steps.

My breath left me roughly. "Send some of the men to sweep the city. Tell them to look hard. Any new faces. Any more elves."

"Eliana?" he asked, alarmed.

"Cirdan's letter mentioned spies of Jandar. We need to ensure he wasn't followed."

Connaught nodded at Marcus, who split off, heading towards the barracks to gather some men for a search.

The strategy room was in the centre of the palace on one of the upper floors. In old times it had been called the war room, but my father had deemed that a bit morbid, considering that he used it to discuss every idea to *avoid* war. The walls of the octagonal room were covered in portraits of old kings and queens. In the centre of the room lay a large square table, where a model of Meridium had been built on top of the largest map of Ruvalon I had ever seen. Numerous figures made from various materials sat around the detailed map, indicating where nobility of Ruvalon lived.

Connaught stopped at the nearest edge, but I strolled around the table until I found a small island off to the south-east: the smallest island between Eshmnor and Ruvalon. Picking up one of the pins from a box on the side of the table, I pushed it into the small island.

Akraya. I was not familiar with it, but there were a few other islands off the coast. Judging by the size of this one, there wouldn't be room for more than a small village or a singular castle.

Dracho, Antares and Althea entered the room, followed closely by Bisa, Sizwe and Roux. Vyn and Bas followed, never needing an invitation from me, and closed the door behind them.

Coming to stand along one of the sides of the table, Antares took in the room, which he'd never seen before. I looked on in amusement as he noted every inch of the map and model of Meridium.

Dracho was studying the map too. I was still staring when he froze, his shoulders tensing, before his gaze latched to mine. Our gazes were locked together, a ribbon pulled tightly with us holding either end, neither one relenting. I knew I needed to look away, but I couldn't.

A clearing of a throat redirected his attention. His eyes lowered and stopped on the pin near my hand. I found Bisa watching me from the far wall with a crooked grin.

Taking the scroll, I walked to Dracho, holding it out. Over his shoulder, I spotted Connaught's tight expression and quickly looked elsewhere. Dracho accepted the scroll in silence, reading it over then handing it to Antares and

Althea. It made its way round the rest of the group.

"What do you know of Akraya, Bisa?" Aion was the closest major location to the island.

Bisa's brow furrowed. "It's a rather small island off the coast, about four or five days by boat from here. Not too close to any mainland. I wasn't under the impression anyone lived there. The castle on that island belonged to an old lord of Ruvalon, centuries ago, before his line died out. I believed it had fallen into disrepair."

"I'm guessing Cirdan claimed it after fleeing from his father," Dracho mused. "Either way, the elven prince wants to meet with you."

"Could it be a trap?" Althea asked, her brows pinched.

"That was my initial thought. But his letter seems genuine, and he was willing to put his messenger at risk coming all this way." My teeth found the inside of my cheek.

"I don't think it's worth the risk," Connaught offered.

I wasn't sure I agreed. And the thought of leaving the city for a bit and postponing my coronation... it was a beam of light through a darkened room. I had been tempted on more than one occasion to put off the coronation and head to the temple of the Hollow sooner rather than later. Surely I could justify its importance enough to everyone that they wouldn't realise how terrified I was of finally having that crown upon my head.

I wasn't quite ready to pick up my father's sword just yet. I could leave the city in the capable hands of Sizwe. The city would be vulnerable whilst I delayed my coronation, but I knew Sizwe could handle things... probably better than I could.

Dracho seemed to read my expression. "We will go with you."

"Are you sure?" I would never tell him of the relief I felt in that moment.

He nodded. "If it gets us answers about the Hollow, I don't see why we wouldn't go. You'll have us for extra protection—or a deterrent. Either way."

Antares snorted. "You describe us like weapons."

Roux's tinkling laugh sounded. "Are you not?"

Antares tilted his head in subtle agreement as a small smile pulled at the corner of his mouth. Connaught stood close by, silent. I wasn't the only one who noticed.

"What is it?" Vyn asked him calmly.

Connaught let out a deep sigh. "The timing seems too convenient for me. The Hollow's attacks have been going on for a few years... if he truly believed his father was involved, why only just contact us now?"

"Hmm," said Dracho.

Antares leaned over the map. "The captain is right," he said in his deep voice, pointing to the area surrounding Akraya. "Strategically, Cirdan has chosen a great spot to set up home. It's miles off the mainland of Ruvalon, closer to Eshmnor, and there's no other land close by. It would be the perfect trap to lay for Meridium's ruler, ensuring that no one found out for a long while. Can he not meet us on neutral ground?" He stood, crossing his arms. Vyn was watching him closely.

"I can certainly ask Adven. But time is of the essence," I pointed out.

"True." Antares paused for a second. "I think we should go, just to validate his information. Plus, I don't think he would have anticipated three draconi going with you. You'll have us, and if we find out Jandar is behind the Hollow after all, at least we have a better lead."

It was possibly the most I had ever heard Antares say in one go, and he was completely right.

"But why would Jandar set this thing upon Ruvalon? Why would he attack?" Althea asked.

I caught Bisa and Sizwe's matching stoic expressions.

Bisa coughed. "Jandar always swore he would return one day, after his banishment. Perhaps this is how he intends to take part of Ruvalon back."

Sizwe's lips pursed. "Perhaps he believes if he runs the mortals and fairie folk out of the continent, he can claim it without all-out war?"

"But not everyone would leave," Roux said.

"Meaning he would have less to massacre," Antares replied.

A moment of silence fell. It was a possibility. If the attacks carried on and people continued to die, the inhabitants of Ruvalon would seek safety elsewhere. Whether that meant heading off the mainland to a neighbouring continent, I didn't know. But if the people couldn't rely on its rulers to protect them, why would they stay?

The thought made me doubt my decision to delay my coronation, just for a moment. But the need to resolve the issue pressed down upon me like a heavy weight. Finding answers and ending the chaos would make people feel safe. It was all about the long run. When I glanced to my left, Dracho's expression seemed to say the same thing.

"We'll go," I declared.

Connaught turned towards me. His hand moved, but he clenched it shut just before he touched my arm. “Are you sure?”

I nodded. “Sizwe, would you do me the honour of watching over Meridium with Connaught whilst I am gone?”

Connaught opened his mouth, but the look I gave him silenced him instantly. He was my close friend, but I was also his future queen. Jaw clenched, he nodded.

Sizwe also accepted. She was trusted by the people of Meridium and had spent most of my life helping my father with his rule.

“Bisa, I assume you will be returning to Aion?” I asked.

“Yes. But please update me on what you have found upon your return.”

“Of course.”

Roux held up a hand. She looked so like a small child asking permission to speak that I smothered a laugh, before freezing in shock. All I had felt lately was grief.

“Eliana, I think I’ll go back with my mother.” She gave a small smile at our surprise. “I would like to visit home for a bit, before our journey continues.”

I could understand that. We had no idea where this next stage would take us, or how close we were to finding and defeating the Hollow—if we could. We believed Roux’s magick would play an important part of beating it, but there were no assurances she would survive. I would not begrudge her spending time with her people.

“Of course, Roux. We’ll see you back in Aion on our return?” She nodded. I faced the three from Tenebris. “I know you have made your decision, but you don’t have to come with me. I know this goes beyond what you had planned for your stay here.”

Althea gave me a close-lipped smile; Dracho chuckled lightly, Antares watching him from the corner of his eye.

“I’ve come to expect the unexpected when I’m around you, Princess,” Dracho said.

I sensed Connaught’s stiff posture behind me as I suppressed a smile, shocked once again by a positive emotion. “All right. I’ll inform Cirdan’s messenger. I will insist he leaves with us. We leave in three days’ time from the harbour. Connaught and Sizwe can prepare for my coronation for when we return.”

“Excuse me, Your Highness,” Antares said, startling me with his politeness. “I was wondering if I might accompany you when you speak to Adven?”

If my sceptical expression was a surprise, he didn’t acknowledge it, nor the shocked looks from everyone except his comrades.

"I'd like to get a read on him before we travel," he explained.

That made sense.

"Also, there may be a quicker way, if all deem it appropriate." Antares crossed his arms.

Roux snorted. I felt like I had missed a joke. "Appropriate?" I repeated.

Dracho smiled widely, his white teeth flashing in the candle light. It took me a moment.

"Oh!" My stomach dipped at the reminder of the enormous beasts that lived in the magick beneath their skin. Could I ride one? The sudden nausea in my stomach told me no, along with all the other complex thoughts that ran through my head. "I don't think that's best. They may not have heard of your visit to Ruvalon, and I think arriving on the back of a flying dragon may be a bit of a shock—don't you?" I arched a brow, looking between Dracho and Antares. The latter nodded in agreement, but Dracho pouted.

I sighed, looking around at my companions, a warmth settling in my stomach that I couldn't decipher. It washed over my despair like a soft wave. I wasn't ready to feel it.

"All right. Get to it," I told the room in a strained voice. Turning, I left, with Connaught close behind.

Chapter 21

"You will?" Adven's tone was calm, belying the surprise he obviously felt at my confirmation we would visit Akraya. He glanced over my shoulder, eyes travelling up and down Antares's intimidating figure as he leaned leisurely against the wall behind me. His presence was in addition to my usual guards; Marcus stood guard against the far window.

"I will. We will meet with Cirdan, at the very least to hear his theories."

We were in a small room, drinking tea. We'd passed my mother's portrait on the way, and Adven had paused to take in every detail before giving me a warm smile.

"We?" Adven asked.

Nodding, I took a sip of my tea. "Two of my crew shall be with me, as well as my guests... from Tenebris."

Adven choked on a mouthful of his drink. I heard a small, dark chuckle from behind me whilst he spluttered, apologising before wiping his mouth with the cotton napkin from the table.

"Tenebris?" he asked tentatively, a light blush rising upon his cheeks as he glanced at me, apparently trying to determine whether his lapse in composure bothered me. I would never get used to the royal treatment from outsiders. Most in Meridium treated me as an equal, something I loved. I hated all the airs and graces and formality.

It was part of the reason I was putting off my coronation. Everything would change.

"Yes. They were present in the throne room during your initial visit. My friend Antares here is one of them."

Adven's gaze skipped over my shoulder once more, his throat bobbing as he swallowed.

"They can switch from their dragon form into that of a mortal one." Adven nodded, wide-eyed, but didn't outwardly express surprise at this information, so I continued. "They have been helping with our investigation into the Hollow's attacks—many of them happened close to their border. We thought it prudent to work together."

I rushed the words out, leaving out the parts I didn't feel like sharing. For some reason I felt like I would be stepping over the line by divulging the truth about Eltanin's death, and the fact that one of my guests was the new emperor himself. As much as I wanted to find out if Cirdan knew of Eltanin's death and subsequent crowning of his son, I thought it best to ask the man himself.

Adven cleared his throat. "Well, I'm sure His Highness will be most pleased to meet them. It is a surprise indeed."

"What can we expect of Akraya?"

Adven took another sip of his tea, as if he needed a moment to think of the correct words. "It's a very small island. There aren't many of us there. The castle was rather run-down when we first arrived. His Highness had renovations done immediately. Hired discreet staff from Eshmnor—anyone happy for paid work. It is still a work in progress, but it's comfortable enough."

"And Prince Cirdan?"

His brow rose slightly. "Prince Cirdan?"

"What is he like?"

Adven's teeth flashed into a wide smile. "His Highness is generous indeed. He cares deeply for his people, despite separating from his father, and would do anything to keep them safe. A small number left with him and now reside on the island. He is a good man... unlike his father."

I hummed. "Do you know what solution he wishes to discuss with me?"

"I do not." Adven shook his head almost immediately. "But it must be serious if His Highness has reached out, despite his banishment."

I shook my head. "Cirdan was never banished from Ruvalon. Only Jandar."

Adven's eyes narrowed.

"You didn't know?" I asked, my voice almost a whisper.

"Forgive me, Your Highness. But when Jandar returned from Ruvalon at the end of the Tain, we were informed that all his court had been banished. Including Cirdan."

I shook my head. "That was a lie. We were surprised when most elven left with him for Eshmnor; I suppose that if he was dishonest with you, it makes sense. But Cirdan has never been banished. If he had chosen to live in Ruvalon, he could have."

Adven winced.

"What is it?"

His gaze turned away from mine, as if ashamed. "It's just... Jandar wasn't the most tolerant father. Cirdan had lost his mother, who died during the Tain—and wasn't a very warm woman anyway. After the war, Jandar was worse. It fills me with sorrow that there could have been another way for Cirdan. That he could have escaped his father's shadow."

"You must really care for him."

Adven hummed in agreement. "I practically helped raise the boy. Helped him grow strong in the face of his father's abuse. Discreetly, I tried so hard to navigate him away from his father's poison."

"You must have been so glad when he left him. Escaped his influence."

His smile was almost a grimace. I coughed, aware the conversation had navigated into awkward waters. "We plan to sail in three days. Does that suit you?"

Adven nodded. "That would be excellent, Your Highness. Time is of the utmost importance with these matters, so I'm sure my prince will be thrilled to receive you that soon."

"Then we shall see you before we board. My ship will be moored within Solva Bay. Should you need any supplies or wish to explore the city, now would be the time. I will have a guard escort you." He probably believed that was for his safety, but I also wanted my guards to monitor his comings and goings, confirm we could trust him.

"Thank you from the bottom of my heart for your hospitality, Your Highness. You have been the most gracious host. You remind me of your mother."

An icy awareness swept over me and crawled along my spine.

"You knew her?" I asked quietly, aware of Antares's still form behind me.

"I met her. I am much older than I look." Adven gave me a small smile.

"She was a beautiful woman. Fierce, but kind."

"Thank you," I whispered.

"It is lovely to see you take after her, in character as well as beauty." His intense eyes looked at me pointedly, and a brief silence followed.

I stood. "Thank you for your time, Adven, but we must start preparing. If there is anything you need, please do not hesitate to tell one of my guards." I clasped my hands tightly in front of me as he stood.

He bowed from the waist. "I cannot ever thank you enough for your kindness, or your help. I am eager to see how you and my master will work together and resolve this issue. For now, I bid you farewell until we leave."

"Until we leave," I echoed, tipping my head slightly. I remained standing as he walked to the door, his eyes darting quickly to the side as he passed Antares. Marcus walked him out of the room, following him back to his suite.

A deeper silence fell after the door was closed. If I hadn't been so aware of Antares, feeling his cool presence behind me like a summer breeze, I would have said there was no one else in the room.

"Well?" I asked, keeping my back to him. I heard a small shifting of feet before he walked around the table, gracefully seating himself in Adven's chair. He rested an ankle atop a knee, intertwining his fingers over his stomach.

"Everything he said was honest."

"But?" I asked, hearing his hesitation.

"There was more in what he wouldn't say. His words were very measured. Careful," Antares noted.

"Perhaps he was just worried about divulging his master's secrets?"

"Perhaps. But then you are keeping some of your own, aren't you?"

My nostrils flared; I sucked in a breath. "What is that supposed to mean?"

His bright eyes narrowed. "The man knew your mother."

"He *met* my mother. There's a difference."

"Do you happen to know why?"

I waved a hand, taking a steady breath to slow my heart. "Before the Tain, all the rulers were familiar. Jandar was King of Stillmere, so they likely came across each other before I was born."

Antares's eye twitched, and he made a small noise of scepticism.

"Are we done here?" I asked, my skin itching.

He rubbed a hand along his sharp jawline. "I think it's prudent that we remain vigilant on this journey. But it is still the best way to find out new information."

"I agree." I turned. "Now, if that is all, we have a boat ride to prepare for." I felt sick at the thought.

"Yes we do," he muttered, sounding amused. "Oh, and Princess?"

I halted with my hand upon the doorknob, goosebumps rising upon the back of my neck. His smooth tone was so sensual it felt as if he had whispered against my very skin.

"I will find out what it is you are hiding. It's in my nature," he promised.

My mouth dried, preventing any response. I practically fled the room, his dark promise ensuring I would do my best to avoid him for the days to come.

Chapter 22

I hated the sea.

I wrapped myself tightly in blankets in my cabin, waves of nausea making me miserable over the days we travelled. Not once had I emptied my stomach, but it lurched and gurgled with every ebb and flow of the water.

My party had met Adven at the docks in Solva Bay, where the ship's crew loaded our belongings and supplies from the city. I had been given the boat on my sixteenth birthday; her name—*Little Doe*—was engraved on the hull. An extravagant gift from my father, considering that I had never been on a boat in my life. He'd given her to me in the hopes that one day, he and I would venture to my mother's childhood home to learn more about her upbringing.

We'd never got around to it.

She wasn't one of the largest in the fleet, fitted out more for leisure than any of the work or war ships, which was why I felt it best to take her.

Connaught had cornered me in my father's study—now mine—yesterday, bringing Bisa and Roux along with him. He had been adamant, and somewhat justified, in his argument that I should be crowned before we left. He'd pointed out that the title gave me more protection wherever I went, and it left Meridium in a more stable place.

He wasn't wrong, but I was sure Bisa had sensed my deep-rooted and private reasoning for taking this trip *before* my coronation. Her bright eyes had watched me carefully as I discussed it with Connaught, and she'd given me a small smile of understanding once he gave up. He'd obviously believed they would help him, not accept my decision.

Visiting Sizwe in the library later that evening, after I had said my goodbyes to Roux and Bisa, I'd gone over the duties that needed tending to whilst I was away. She'd nodded and rolled her eyes.

"Silly girl. As if I haven't helped your father rule for the past thirteen years!"

I had laughed. Meridium was probably better off in her hands than my own.

Part of my reasoning that I kept to myself was a small hope that along this journey, I could heal. Even if just a small part of me. It hadn't been long since my father's death, and I wanted to keep busy, but not by being burdened with my mantle of queen. I wanted to get out of the city and explore this new territory of being orphaned, of having neither my parents nor brother to guide me. Before I took up the shackles of queen… I needed more freedom as Eliana.

The door to my cabin creaked open.

"You look awful," Vyn chuckled.

I groaned, bringing the blanket over my head.

He laughed again. "Captain Moustache said we should be there by the morning."

My only response was a grunt. Had I felt better, I would have admonished him for the nickname Vyn had given Captain Bennett. The captain had been a good friend of my father's, taking care of many of the ships in the fleet for almost twenty years. He was in incredibly good shape for his age, his dark blue eyes wrinkled at the edges, and he sported a large, red moustache—which curled at the ends.

"You should really try to eat something," Vyn remarked. The clink of a glass reached my ears.

"Do not talk to me about food, stomachs, or anything right now," I mumbled through the blanket.

Vyn removed it from my face, ruffling my hair. Blearily, I took in his grin.

"I'm glad you find this amusing," I rasped, holding my hand out for the water he had brought in with him.

"Rather you than me." He handed me the glass, taking a seat on the end of my bed. The main cabin was wide, with plenty of space to relax in out of the weather. It was made from a dark wood with accents of sage green running throughout the decor.

Vyn and Bas shared the smallest room, big enough to accommodate three, whilst Dracho, Antares and Althea had the one beside mine. The ship offered all the comforts that one could find in the palace, including a private chef... it was a shame I couldn't bring myself to enjoy his meals.

"I hate boats."

Vyn laughed. "You're the one who denied us the other mode of transport. The *fun* mode of transport."

I rolled my eyes. "You're just disappointed you didn't get to ride Antares—and not in the first way you imagined."

His laugh was short and rough, and he watched me carefully as I reached over him, placing the glass on the bedside table. I knew that look. It was one I'd been on the receiving end of several times over the years. It was one he knew I despised.

"What?" I snapped.

"Are you all right?"

"What a stupid question."

His eyes narrowed, and shame flooded me. "You know better than to snap at me," he pointed out.

"I do. I'm sorry. This seasickness isn't helping my mood."

"And here I thought a foul mood was your everyday disposition."

I glared at him; he smirked and clasped my hand gently, resting it on his lap as he raised his free one.

I supressed a shiver as a cool breeze brushed over my face, like the mist that coats your skin at the bottom of a waterfall. I closed my eyes, sighing deeply, grateful for the freshness.

"Everything will work out," Vyn continued. "I know you're someone who needs answers right this second, but this will take time. Before long you'll have your coronation—" He halted at my sneer and suppressed a grin. "But even before your father died, you were our queen. Always have been, always will be."

"I'm your friend," I whispered.

I had never wanted that position over them. Never wanted to be treated differently. It was partly why I spent so much time with the people of Meridium. I didn't want their reverence, their fear... I wanted their respect. The blood I'd been born into didn't mean I was better than anyone. Didn't mean I had the absolute *right* to rule over them.

It was pure chance.

But with the privilege I had been granted, I could work every day to make their lives better. I felt more suited to do that as a princess, not as queen. There was more freedom. Now it was far more difficult. Protocols and alliances got in the way—as well as other things.

My head throbbed at the thought of it all.

"You are my *best* friend." Vyn squeezed my hand. "That won't change after you're queen."

His words still couldn't rid me of the fear that our closeness would change after taking my role.

"Why don't you come up to the deck? Get some fresh air," Vyn proposed.

"You know I can't do that."

His mouth pulled up in a brief, sad smile.

It had taken everything in me to walk aboard the ship back in Solva Bay, and the journey—over what felt like a lifetime—had stripped back my nerves as much as possible.

Vyn knew of my fear of water, but not why. I couldn't even put my face directly into a flow of it. Ever since the night Engel had found me, I'd had a deep fear of any body of liquid. I hadn't told Dracho or our other guests, but suspected they knew from the way I had run up the gangplank, before my fingernails practically gouged holes into the wooden railing of the ship.

I'd secluded myself in my cabin ever since, refusing to step foot on the deck. The worry of appearing unsociable to the crew was smothered by overwhelming nausea. Vyn and Bas were able to blame it all on my seasickness—which meant some peace from our draconi guests too.

I *had* loved it when Vyn told me how Antares couldn't steady his footing on deck—the draconi, so used to flying, had never been on a ship before. The image of a usually sure-footed Antares stumbling about, his face set in a permanent scowl, had me clutching my stomach as I fought the urge to laugh loudly. A sliver of hope lanced through me at the sensation. Maybe I could navigate my way through my grief.

The healer on board had come in at some point—a lithe young man called Petr. He had made a tonic to calm my gut after too many days of feeling sick, and I couldn't thank him enough for the regular doses. I was due one soon.

As Vyn left, I spotted a familiar figure standing vigil outside my door.

"You can come in," I mumbled, shoving my head into my pillow.

A light chuckle sounded out; I heard the door click shut.

"You look terrible," Dracho said.

"Are you and Vyn conspiring to bully me together or something?" I grumbled.

He laughed. "Not at all—I wanted to check on you. It's just unusual to see you so... un-put-together."

I raised a middle finger in response. "I may have to take you up on your offer to fly when we return to Meridium. I don't think I'll survive another boat trip."

His brows rose in surprise. "Feel free to ride me any time."

I shook my head as he chuckled again.

I felt unnerved by the rather pleasant conversation, and I realised something had changed. We had fallen into a comfortable manner around each other... and that felt dangerous.

I cleared my throat. "If that's all, I think I'll try and get some sleep before we arrive." Maybe he would leave.

He smiled, a rueful expression, as though he had sensed where my thoughts had gone.

"No worries, Eliana. Rest. We'll be there soon."

He left, and my stomach rolled for entirely different reasons.

Chapter 23

Adven hadn't lied when he had said the island was small. It contained nothing but the large manor that was built upon it. Two large towers rose at either end of a long building, all made of dark red stone. Simple windows were scattered here and there around the walls in fairly symmetrical patterns. A great gate with large wooden doors and a couple of guards manned the only passage into the manor. Trees grew close to the gates, providing the manor with valuable wood for all sorts of purposes. Judging by its rough exterior, the building had stood the test of time.

The guards on the gate watched us with suspicious eyes as we entered the main yard, and I marvelled at the size of them. They matched Connaught in height, but were both as bulky as Bas. Adven introduced them as Joff and Erix; they didn't greet us. Oddly, though, one of them gave a long sniff as I wandered past him. A shudder ran through me as I suppressed the urge to cringe away, noticing their very human ears. Unusual to see them guarding the home of an elf.

"It's just through here, to the great hall." I detected a hint of nervousness in Adven's tone. The doors of the manor groaned as they were opened for us by two more human guards.

"What is that smell?" Antares whispered to Dracho, who shook his head.

I leaned forward to catch his eye. "Don't be rude," I hissed. "Adven said they've been renovating. It was left decrepit for years."

"Doesn't explain the wet dog smell," Antares muttered.

"Couldn't you have discussed that using your mind-talk?" I whispered, knowing he could hear me.

"And deny you the pleasure of hearing my voice?" I could hear Antares's smirk. Dracho laughed.

Unfortunately, I couldn't disagree. There *was* a lingering scent of wet hounds, but it improved as we entered a large hall. In the centre was a large oak table, prepared for a meal. In contrast to the rest of the manor, the table was laid with the finest silverware, goblets already full of wine and baskets of bread. I'd eaten very little aboard the ship; I salivated at the sight.

"Please, sit," Adven said. "His Highness will be along shortly." He strolled to a door at the back of the room, besides the wooden dais.

I glanced at Vyn and Bas and they shrugged, taking a seat. When we had all followed suit, some staff entered—still human—to offer water instead of the wine already on the table. Everyone but I accepted, although I noticed Antares take a hidden sniff of each goblet before drinking. His eyes skipped to Dracho, nodding once and taking a small sip. I couldn't deny the sight made me nervous, but nothing happened.

We chatted casually for several minutes, Bas speaking through his mouthfuls of bread as Vyn shook his head, his lip curling in disgust. Adven returned from the door he had gone through, moving to stand by the dais and dipping in a bow.

"May I present His Royal Highness, Prince Cirdan."

We all stood, our gazes trained on the doorway.

The prince swept in with a swish of his black robes, and my breath hitched as everyone bowed. He came to stand at the head of the table, his eyes sweeping around the group before zeroing in on me. The corner of his lips pulled up a fraction before he tipped his head forward.

"My guests." The prince bowed from the waist, sweeping out a long arm, before rising, his eyes meeting mine. "Princess Eliana," he purred. "You honour me with your presence. I cannot thank you all enough for accepting my invitation."

Damn, came Dracho's voice inside my head. I looked at him, exasperated, and he shrugged. *What? I can appreciate an attractive man... elf.*

I shook my head, returning my gaze back to the prince, whose hazel eyes had not left me. Dracho wasn't wrong; he *was* rather good-looking.

He was ethereal and unapologetically elven. A sheet of jet-black hair reached his waist, framing a sharp, thin jaw and high cheekbones. His eyes were fringed with thick lashes… but there was light missing from them. I glanced at Dracho, noting how, even though his eyes were currently the colour of cool water, they still held warmth. It wasn't just the colour of Prince Cirdan's eyes that made me wary, but his aura. Somehow it was shielded or suppressed. I couldn't get a good read on him; I assumed it had something to do with him being an elf. By Antares's furrowed brow, he was having the same issue.

I shook my head and cleared my throat. "Prince Cirdan, these are my companions, Vyn and Bas, and my guests, Antares, Althea, and Dracho." Cirdan's eyes travelled over the others. "It's a pleasure to meet you, though I cannot lie—it was a surprise to receive your messenger."

A smile tugged at the corner of Cirdan's lips as he held a hand out, indicating that we should sit. Adven walked over to take the seat opposite me, on Cirdan's right.

"Yes, I imagine it was," Cirdan said, amused, as he seated himself. "I must admit that *I* was surprised to learn that I would be meeting Eliana Cervidae, and not Teyrnon. Not many would entertain the idea of meeting with me. But I'm glad you did."

A shiver crawled up my spine, knotting between my shoulders as his eyes travelled over my face and hair. Dracho's awkward chuckle sounded out in the silence, Cirdan's eyes skipping to him.

"Ah yes. Your guests from Tenebris." Cirdan bowed his head so minutely it almost appeared that he was mocking Dracho, who stiffened. I was surprised at the casual way he addressed Dracho, considering that Adven must have only just told him about the draconi accompanying me on the journey—and that they could assume mortal form. But also Dracho's hesitation to introduce himself *and* his proper title. I took in his thin-lipped smile and the severe glint in his eyes.

I coughed. "I give my thanks for your gracious welcome."

"It is my pleasure. Please, eat, drink. Tomorrow we shall discuss this awful business that has been going on."

Before I had time to argue that time was of the utmost importance, several members of staff made their way in through various doors, carrying trays of food. The smell of baked fish, vegetables and roasted potatoes was a pleasure to the senses; I shovelled them onto my plate once I saw Antares give Dracho another subtle nod.

Looking up, I noticed Vyn's satisfied smile as he surveyed the amount of food on my plate. The glass of white wine was a welcome taste upon my tongue, a hint of honey in the smoothness of it.

When I'd cleared half my plate and was feeling much more like myself, I watched Cirdan study Dracho and Antares intently as he took small bites of his food. When he caught my gaze, he almost looked bashful.

"So," I started, wiping the corner of my mouth with my napkin, "Your Highness—"

"Please, call me Cirdan."

I smiled. "Cirdan"—his teeth flashed in a wide grin—"how long have you been here?"

Cirdan clasped his hands in front of him as he leaned forward. "Since last summer. Before that we were situated on a different island. I've been slowly renovating this manor, trying to bring it back to its former glory."

"It's a beautiful building," I offered.

"It is, though it needs some work. Have you heard of the story behind it?"

"I can't say I had time to look into its history prior to arriving. But I was told it used to belong to a Lord of Ruvalon."

Cirdan made a noise of confirmation. "It was before my father's time, but the lord who presided over this island acted as a middleman between the elven king of Stillmere, and the lupera alpha in Eshmnor."

"Lupera alpha?" Althea asked suddenly. Her cheeks turned a pretty shade of pink when Cirdan's thoughtful gaze rounded on her.

"Yes. An old species of wolf who were able to change into mortal form. They used to be feral, unchecked. The lord tried to establish peace between them. Unfortunately the wolves ended up killing him and taking this very manor for themselves."

How have I never heard of this? "What happened to the lupera?" I asked.

I had heard of the creatures, of course—described in books as mortal-seeming men who could transform into terrible, violent beasts. They hadn't been seen for hundreds of years, and it was widely believed they had died out.

"The elven king at the time, my grandfather Haldir, had been rather fond of the mortal lord, so he took revenge. He laid waste to the lupera on the island, killing the alpha, and taking those who remained into his service until they died."

An uncomfortable silence fell, the only sound the use of cutlery around the table and pouring of drinks.

Bas laughed awkwardly. "You can tell you don't have company often, Your

Highness. S'not really a dinner story."

Dracho's lips tugged at the corners, hiding a smirk, but I gave Bas a look of disbelief. His eyes widened in realisation; I tensed, dreading Cirdan's reaction. But to my surprise and relief, Cirdan burst into deep laughter.

"No, perhaps not. Thank you—I have not laughed like that in some time."

Clearly doesn't get out much.

I stifled a gasp and coughed as Dracho breezed into my mind. Cirdan looked at me enquiringly, and I gave him a warm grin.

"So." Cirdan took a mouthful of wine before continuing. "Dracho."

Dracho's head turned slowly to face the elven prince, as if he didn't want to entertain the conversation.

"What brought you to Ruvalon?"

Dracho took a deep breath. "Women with a penchant for violence."

The air turned icy around us, as if I'd been caught between a freezing wind and an immoveable glacier. I prevented myself from saying something that wouldn't have been appropriate for the dinner table. Instead, I continued to watch Cirdan, refusing to look at the draconi.

Cirdan's hazel eyes roamed over Dracho inquisitively, and his parted lips lifted dangerously at the corner, showing a hint of a lengthened fang. Adven glanced between the two.

"I'll admit," Dracho drawled, breaking the tension, "I thought your reaction to my current form to be rather... subdued."

"Adven explained when he retrieved me from my study. It was a rather unexpected surprise to hear that the 'beasts from Tenebris' can change their form. Rather useful, I would say, hmm?"

Dracho nodded stiffly.

"I did not want to make you feel uncomfortable with my questioning. After all, for centuries your kind have been considered almost like gods to some in Ruvalon." Dracho shrugged; Cirdan continued. "However, I am most interested in how you became involved with Eliana?" Leaning forward to rest his chin upon his clasped hands, Cirdan kept his gaze trained on Dracho. His voice purred again on my name.

Dracho huffed darkly. "Involved?"

I swallowed. "Dracho was sent to investigate the Hollow's attacks. They are happening so close to hi—their border. Naturally they wanted to find out information."

Cirdan's eyes flicked lazily to mine. "Even if it broke the treaty in the process?"

A low growl sounded from Antares, and I froze.

Cirdan laughed, waving a hand. "Do not fret. I am not my father. Rumour had reached me from our supply captain that the new emperor had made quite the scene in Meridium weeks ago. I was confused at first as to such a minimal reaction to a *dragon* arriving, but now... well, it all makes sense."

"I understand that your journey into Ruvalon was beneficial to the continent, Your Excellency. You will receive no trouble from me for that." Cirdan raised a goblet, tipping it towards Dracho before taking a sip. Dracho nodded in response, eyes narrowed.

I started, "Speaking of the Hollow—"

"Ah, yes. This business with the awful attacks."

"I was surprised you had heard of them," I told him.

"Why, of course. Even though I am no longer familiar with Ruvalon myself, I have made many friends who tell me stories of my ancestors' land."

"How *did* you come to learn about the Hollow?" Dracho demanded.

Cirdan inhaled, but before he could speak, Adven broke in. "Perhaps we should save this official business until tomorrow? Your guests have had a long journey, Your Highness, and I have yet to show them to their rooms."

Cirdan smiled. "You are right, as usual, Adven. Please, enjoy yourselves this evening. Princess Eliana, Your Excellency... would you be so kind as to join me for a private lunch tomorrow, in my study?"

Dracho looked suspicious, and Cirdan seemed to sense his hesitation. "Anything I share you are most welcome to divulge to the rest of your group. I just wish to discuss a more private matter with the two of you alone, as rulers of Ruvalon."

Antares was looking at Dracho, brows furrowed in a way that showed he did not like the idea. There was a moment of silence before Dracho's teeth flashed in a grin.

"That would be no trouble at all with me, Your Highness. Eliana?" His silver eyes warmed as his gaze pinned me.

"Yes, that would be fine."

"Excellent!" Cirdan wiped his mouth with a white napkin before standing swiftly. "Then I shall bid you goodnight and retire. Please, enjoy yourselves. Should you need anything, ask one of my men or Adven, whom I am entrusting with your care." He bowed his head, his robe swishing behind him as he floated gracefully out of the room.

I blew out a long breath. Adven smiled, leaning forward in his seat. "Different to what you expected?"

I nodded with a blush. "After hearing tales of Jandar's cruelty, I must admit I expected someone different."

"Cirdan is far superior to his father in many ways. His generosity is one of them."

"He was rather pleasant." Though there was a seed of something more under the surface. The fact that his aura was guarded made me wary, but that could be because of his discomfort at having the draconi here.

"I'm sure he will be glad to hear that." Adven laughed, which made me blush. I could feel Dracho's stillness beside me as he listened to every word.

I decided there'd been enough tension for the day. "Adven, would you please show me to my room? I was rather seasick on the journey, and I'd like to get an early night."

Adven stood promptly. "Of course. It would be my pleasure."

I stood, surprised when Althea did the same.

"I'm rather tired too," she declared, smiling brightly at us.

Adven returned her smile and walked towards the double doors. Following him out of the room, I didn't look back at Dracho, but I felt his gaze on me the entire time.

Signs of age were visible throughout the manor. Considering that Cirdan had been here six months, I was surprised by how little renovation had been done. Perhaps it was hard to get supplies from overseas, considering who it was for.

We started ascending a curling stone staircase, and Adven told us, "You two are sharing a room."

I halted, and he glanced at me in concern. "If that's all right, Your Highness? We are still renovating, and there are only so many rooms available."

I was accustomed to having my own space, but if there was no alternative, then we would have to make do. *I* would have to make do. "That is more than all right, Adven. Thank you again for all this."

Something flashed across his eyes, so quickly I wasn't sure I had seen anything at all. He smiled at me, tipping his head forward, and paused before a wooden doorway, gesturing inside.

In a cosy, well-decorated room sat a large four poster bed against the far wall. Curtains were tied to each post, accents of blue and grey running through the fabric. A lit fireplace graced the wall opposite; I was glad for the warmth.

A closed door to my right caught my eye. Adven noticed where my gaze fell. "The bathing chamber lies through there. I apologise, but there is no electricity in this manor, with it being so old; during dinner I had some of the servants bring up some hot water. It should still be warm, but if not, please do not hesitate to ask."

"Thank you, Adven, it's lovely."

Althea strolled past me, kicking off her boots and opening the door to peek into the bathing chamber.

"What time does Cirdan usually meet for lunch?" I asked.

"Just after midday, Your Highness. Breakfast is an hour after dawn, though the prince will not be in attendance, as he is meeting with the captain who brings in offshore supplies. You are more than welcome to explore the manor grounds before your audience with him—though please avoid the basements below. The flooring needs to be repaired, and it is rather unsafe to walk."

"No problem at all. Thank you. I shall see you tomorrow."

He bowed once more before leaving and closing the door.

"Althea, do you wish to bathe—?"

"Isn't it weird that a guest room has been renovated the most, instead of the public areas or the rest of the manor?" she interrupted, returning to the room and removing her weapon.

I had seen the blade before; she had sharpened it whilst camping before Aion. A short, crescent-shaped blade, the cross-guard simple except for the violet-jewelled horn on either side. The silver of the blade was bright and unmarred, its edge viciously sharp. It was obvious she took care of it. A beautiful blade, for a beautiful woman.

"Perhaps he had been planning to invite my father for a while," I suggested.

"Or maybe he knew you would be a possible visitor?" Her brows waggled at me.

Choosing to ignore her, I strode to the bathroom, humming in satisfaction when I saw small steam rising from the bathwater.

"Do you mind if I jump in? Or do you want the first tubful?" I asked, looking over my shoulder.

"No, go ahead," she said, flopping backwards onto the bed.

"Don't you want to clean up?"

She leaned up onto her elbows, feigning shock. "Didn't you know?

Draconi lick themselves clean... like a cat."

I heard her tinkling laugh as I closed the door, giving her a rude gesture.

Chapter 24

"Why do you all have to go?" I whined, trying to be strong and withhold the tears I could feel building.

"You know why, my little doe." Mother's eyes had never looked so sad as she stroked the top of my head. "I love you, my darling." She glanced over at my father, an indecipherable look passing between them.

"You'll be all right, little sister!" Morgwn smiled widely, walking over to stand beside me. "Vyn is with you. You'll look out for each other." He bent down to whisper in my ear. "I'm sure Bastion will sneak in to spend time with the two of you as well."

I smiled, wrapping my arms around his neck. "Be safe."

His arms squeezed me; I adored the feeling of safety within his arms. "You know me, little doe. No one can beat me."

I laughed as he stood, nudging my arm gently. I scanned my brother and parents, in awe at how imposing they looked in their armour. Mother's white-plated armour fit her like a glove, the stag sigil embossed beautifully on the breastplate. Her dual short swords were sheathed at either side. She looked like a goddess incarnate, her helmet proudly atop her head, short antlers protruding from either side.

Father's armour was just as beautiful; in a dark grey, the sigil over his own chest stained green. The sword of Meridium was strapped to his side, and he moved it slightly as he came to kneel before me.

"Be good for Farley," he told me, suppressing a smile when I childishly rolled my eyes. Farley would try to make me carry out my duties whilst they were away, but he would likely fail. My father knew that. "Look after Vyn, and Bastion. I'm relying on you."

"Yes, Father." I nodded eagerly. He smiled brightly, leaning forward to kiss me on top of my head, just like Mother.

"Tell Bastion he can stay in my room when he inevitably moves in for the summer!" Morgwn beamed as my mother shook her head. The plates of his light-grey armour made a noise as he crossed his arms. The sigil on his showed a doe, instead of a stag. My dagger was at his side.

"Take care of that," I warned him. Mother looked at it disapprovingly for a second.

"Do not *lose that dagger," she said sternly as she mounted her Madainian horse, Morgana. Morgana was a chestnut mare that had been with her for years; the two had met in the south-west of Ruvalon when my mother was around my age. Father's own horse, Nara, stood proudly beside her, awaiting its rider.*

A tear finally broke free as I watched my parents, ready to ride off to a battle I was too young to understand. As if sensing my crumpling resilience, Morgwn wrapped a strong arm around me.

"It's all right, little doe. It will all work out." His eyes filled with some emotion I couldn't understand, seeing beyond me and all that was happening. "I love you, little sister. Be strong and remember—"

"I do not break."

"That's right." He smiled.

"Come on, Morgwn, we must make haste," Father said, knowing that if he wasn't told, he would stay by my side forever.

Morgwn eyed them over his shoulder as they spoke to the royal guards, turning to me and whispering hurriedly. "Whilst we are gone, remember, Eliana—you alone were given this life, because you are strong enough to bear it. You will be happy, but first you will be strong. Do not break."

He pressed a long kiss to my head, and my face crumpled. I was too young to understand the fear behind his words, but old enough to hear his desperation.

Morgwn turned to join my parents, taking the reins from a steward and mounting his horse, Caspar—a brilliant white horse that could only be tamed by my brother.

The edges of my vision blurred. My mother's voice whispered words of strength as they turned, leaving Meridium, leaving me.

If I let them go, they will die.

I tried to run after them in a panic, scrambling at the ground as my feet sank into wet mud. I cried, trying to fight the bog that pulled me under, prevented me from going to them. Their shapes grew farther and farther away, and I screamed. Cried for help, for them to stay.

They are going to die.

They disappeared from view as I sank, the mud coming over my chin. I gasped for a final breath, screaming into the black abyss before I was choked by it.

"I didn't know what to do. I didn't want anyone to hear." A soft voice like the tinkling of bells spoke in the darkness.

You're dying, a voice in my head said. *This is what death feels like.*

The choking dizziness had me clenching my eyes shut, my lungs wheezing with every breath I tried to take. My hands clawed at my neck. Strong arms pulled them away, making me gasp.

Don't. I need to stop it! I wanted to cry out.

"Go," a voice like smooth liquor, not smoke, called out roughly. I heard the quick click of the door closing as those strong hands pulled me up, sitting me against something hard.

Something breathing, *living*.

"You're all right. Feel my breath. Breathe, Eliana," the voice urged, the tone calm and soothing.

My arms tensed as I tried to pull them back to my neck. One of the hands holding my wrists tightly lifted and flattened itself over the clammy skin of my chest, against my breastbone. I was pushed back against the living wall behind me.

"*Breathe*, Eliana. Feel my own breath beneath you."

Somewhere in the panic-laced fog of my brain, my consciousness started to listen to that voice.

"Feel my heart. Feel my breath. Replicate it with your own," the voice whispered against my lower ear. Somewhere my panic was tinged with fear for a moment, wanting to swat them away.

That hand moved slightly, bringing me back to what was real as I felt warmth radiate from it. I concentrated on that warmth, realised I felt it against my back, and managed my first inhale. It was a harsh gasp; my lungs thirsted for air.

"That's it. In, and out."

I followed the command, forcing my breathing to sync with theirs. *In, and out.*

My heart began to slow, my body relaxing from the stiff posture it had kept during my panic attack. My muscles ached, a bead of sweat dripped down my spine, and I was aware of it all. But I focused on that breathing.

In, and out.

The hand holding my wrists released them, coming to gently hold my shoulder. Not restricting my movement, but calming. Reassuring.

In, and out.

I groaned in relief as I opened my eyes. I could hardly see; the only light in the room was a small candle lit by the door. I squinted, spotting long legs outstretched to either side of me. We were on the large bed I had fallen asleep in, his back against the headboard and mine resting against his chest.

"Antares." My voice came out in a heavy whisper.

"Eliana," he exhaled in what sounded like relief.

"H-how?" I rasped, mindful of taking my breaths slowly, mirroring his behind me.

"Althea couldn't wake you once you started having your nightmare." His chest vibrated against me, the soothing timbre of his voice relaxing me more. "She called me as soon as you started screaming."

That explained why my throat was so sore. "Did anyone else hear?"

"No. If they did, they certainly haven't made an effort to come check on you." He sounded bitter.

"Where is Dracho?" I asked, wondering how Antares had ended up in my bed and not him.

"Out flying. Needed to unwind. I can call him if you—"

"No." I was unsure if I wanted to know what Dracho needed to unwind about, but I knew I didn't need him here at this moment. I didn't need another person to see me weak and vulnerable. I knew the other two would likely tell him, but I couldn't deal with rehashing it. Not somewhere new and unfamiliar. I sniffed. "You didn't have to—"

"I wanted to."

"Oh." That surprised me, and every nerve in my body was dying to ask why. Antares, as usual, seemed to know.

"I have helped Althea many times, as has Dracho, with attacks like yours.

Although Althea has not had one for a few years, they are not pleasant to witness. I hate seeing people in such pain. A pain caused by their own mind."

My throat tightened, and I swallowed the thick lump that seemed to have formed there, taken back by his selflessness and consideration for other people. He usually seemed so distant from those not in his inner circle. I glanced down, realising that his hand was still against my chest...

And my legs were bare.

My scar was visible in the low light, under the hem of my long bed-shirt, which had ridden up. My blood ran cold, but it was too late to hide the thudding of my heart under his palm. I cleared my throat, sitting forward a bit and moving his hand from my chest.

I felt the brush of fingertips against my cheek and turned. My breath froze in my chest as I found myself inches from Antares's concentrating expression. I was about to ask what he was doing when his gentle fingers brushed softly along my skin once more, just under my jaw.

I almost winced, realising the skin was sore there. I remembered suddenly the feeling of clawing at my neck and realised I must have scratched myself. Antares's eyes travelled up the expanse of it; I remained still under his gaze. His luminous eyes glanced quickly at my leg, before returning to my face.

"Don't be ashamed of your scars. They define your story as a survivor."

I clenched my teeth, feeling my eyes turn glassy.

"I *know*, Eliana."

What it is to be a survivor? I blinked in the low light, still able to see the bright glow of his golden eyes as they flicked to mine. "You know what?" How I'd got the scars? Or...

His chin tipped down ever so slightly, his eyes speaking more words than his mouth ever had to. I sucked in a sharp breath.

"You know *nothing*," I hissed, enraged at his audacity. Pulling out of his hold, I scooted back towards the centre of the bed, anxious to remove myself from his proximity.

"I may know something."

"Then you will keep your sharp tongue behind your teeth!" I bared my own at him, and his eyes widened.

My chest felt tight again. I couldn't look at him, afraid to see judgment and hate there now that he knew the secret I avoided even thinking about, let alone speaking of to anyone.

My hands fidgeted in my lap. "Will you tell—"

"No."

My head jerked to him.

"It is not my place. Though I think *you* should. It won't be long before he finds out for himself. I am surprised he hasn't already... but clearly his feelings for you have blinded his instincts."

I nodded, but refused to have this argument with him. "I... I will tell him soon."

"Hm." His face was emotionless as he stood slowly to walk across the room. I realised that his careful movements were for my benefit, and for a second I was almost overcome by gratitude. He paused before the door, but didn't turn to look in my direction.

"Will you be all right?" he asked, his deep voice unnaturally soft for once.

I thought it over. "Yes."

As he walked out and turned to close the door, I raised my voice ever so slightly. "Thank you, Antares."

His amber eyes glanced at me through the gap for a second, then he nodded and disappeared, leaving me alone with a new panic building inside my chest.

Chapter 25

"Are you all right, E? You've hardly eaten anything." Bas used his fork to point at the plate of fruit and sweet breads that sat before me.

I blushed, feeling Dracho's gaze brushing over me again. I wondered if Althea or Antares had told him about the night before.

"Yes." I coughed, shoving a piece of crisp apple into my mouth. "New place, different bed. I didn't sleep the best."

Vyn gave me a quick, concerned look. His eyes kept jumping to the skin on my neck, and I cursed myself, hoping that the scratch marks would soon fade. I was glad their room had been far enough away that I hadn't woken them, but they would want to know about the grazes.

After Antares's departure, I had slept with my back to Althea for the rest of the night. Neither of us had spoken when she re-entered the room, though I was sure she knew I was awake. She'd fallen asleep long before me and I was grateful for it, though I knew I needed to thank her for her help. When I'd woken, feeling overwhelmed with exhaustion, she'd already left the room. Dressing in one of the simple gowns I had brought, I had loosely pinned my braids at the back of my head, too tired to bother with anything more intricate. It did nothing to ease my discomfort—if anything, I felt worse.

"What time are we meeting Cirdan?" Dracho suddenly asked, not looking up as he served himself from the various foods before us.

Once more the table had been laid with the finest silverware, with water and juice poured by the staff as we filled our plates with freshly cooked sausages and lightly salted eggs. Our host was nowhere to be seen, which made me feel uneasy, but Adven had greeted us briefly before we sat, reminding us of our engagement with Cirdan later.

I blinked a few times, watching Dracho's calm expression. "Um, just after midday. Adven said we could explore the manor grounds if we wished, but to avoid the basement due to renovations."

Dracho continued to spread butter over a piece of bread, though his brows rose and fell in quick succession. "How generous."

The noise around the table stuttered for a second as I glared at the side of his head.

"*Anyway,*" Vyn said, drawing the word out, "I think I'd like a nosey around... Eliana, would you like to join me?"

I looked at him, catching his pointed expression. "Y-yes. I would. Dracho, I'll meet you for lunch?"

He said nothing but hummed in agreement, still not meeting my gaze.

"Who pissed in *his* porridge?" I muttered quietly under my breath, catching Antares's eye. He covered his mouth, hiding an uncharacteristic grin.

Dracho did look at me then. No one spoke.

The silence held until the scraping of chair legs broke it, tearing my gaze from Dracho's.

"All right, I'm done. Eliana?" Vyn asked, the tips of his fingers pressing against the table top. His sharp eyes were narrowed.

"Yes, me too." I stood and followed Vyn out into the main courtyard, where I closed my eyes and took a deep breath of the fresher air.

"A nightmare?" Vyn asked, straight to the point. When I opened my eyes, he nodded to my neck. He already knew the answer, but wanted confirmation that I was all right.

Uncertainty swirled in my gut as I debated whether to tell him of my conversation with Antares the night before. I decided against it. He didn't need to share that burden of worry. It was enough for me to carry it.

"Antares helped me."

"Antares?" His tone went up an octave.

"Dracho was out flying. Althea didn't know what to do."

"And was he? Helpful?"

We wandered to a broken wall, staring out at the calm sea waters.

Was he? He had certainly succeeded in bringing me out of my nightmare, his technique effective at calming my panicked breathing. I had avoided thinking about our position and my state of dress once I had come around, but Goddess, I'd be lying if I said I hadn't found comfort against his hard chest, his hand on me. Or that I'd had to resist the strange urge to lean further back into him.

Vyn clicked his tongue. "I'll take that as a yes?" he purred slyly.

Heat filled my face. "Not funny." Vyn cackled like it was the funniest thing in the world. "He was… gentle."

"Gentle?" Surprise was on his face again, and I focused on keeping my breathing steady.

In, and out.

It had been real. Antares had helped me get over my panic; he had spoken to me softly. I knew it was for Dracho's benefit that he was trying to be amicable with me, but it felt like something else.

It felt unnerving that my gut told me to trust Antares. It was all I could hope to do after our conversation the night before.

"Maybe I'm just growing on him," I suggested.

Vyn snorted. "I know someone you've already grown on."

My brows lowered. "Who?"

"Why, Prince Cirdan, of course."

Shoving at his arm, I shook my head. "Don't be so ridiculous. He merely looks at me—"

"Like you're one of Marie's chocolate muffins."

"Oh, shush! That's the last thing I need. Another man to add to my problems."

"True, you have had a few." He winced and laughed when I punched his arm. "But perhaps this one is a bit more… *suited* for you?"

I cringed. "I just want to find answers for now. All of that can wait for when this is over."

A slight nod. Vyn stared off into the distance. "Sometimes, Eli, things happen you could never anticipate. I hope you're ready for them."

I gnawed at my lower lip before releasing a sigh. "I hope so too."

At midday I returned to the dining hall, my steps practically punching holes in the floor. My face warmed as I avoided Antares's gaze; flashes of my conversation with him kept attacking my mind. Dracho was already there, taking to his feet when he saw me and Adven and following us through the door beside the dais.

Cirdan's study was quite large, with a limestone-tiled floor. A small desk and winged-back chair sat near the back wall. The air in the room was clear but cold.

Not three feet inside, my head jerked back as I collided with a hard chest which had appeared before me with blinding speed. My gasp was audible as I looked up.

Cirdan's brow was low as his eyes travelled over my neck. His eyes rose to meet mine and a shiver ran up my spine; his elf features had sharpened as he released a hold on his glamour—an elf magick that allowed him to look more human. His ears lengthened and came to a point at the top. I swallowed hard.

"Did someone here harm you?" His tone promised violence, his eyes skipping over my head for a second.

I shook my head quickly, trying to take a small step back. Dracho stood only a couple of paces behind me, looking around the room. I didn't need to see them to know that his silver eyes shone.

"I... I did this to myself."

Cirdan's features softened. "To yourself?"

I nodded, lifting my chin. "I suffer with dry skin. Sometimes it irritates me something terrible."

"Dry... skin?"

What kind of excuse is that? Dracho whispered in my mind. I ignored him. He hadn't mentioned the marks, so I assumed Althea had told him of my nightmare.

"Mm-hm." I forced a smile, before looking around Cirdan's large frame. "Is this for us, Your Highness?" My heart pounded in a relentless rhythm against my ribs as I manoeuvred around him, heading for the smaller, much more intimate table set up for lunch.

"Please, sit," Cirdan called behind me, thankfully putting aside my ridiculous excuse for now.

We sat in a somewhat awkward silence until the staff came in. The table was spacious, but still small enough that I could feel the tense auras of both men sitting to either side of me. Cooked pastries, sandwiches and a large pot of tea were placed in the centre of the circular table. Cirdan picked the latter up and offered it to me; I graciously accepted.

Dracho's rising irritation was obvious, but Cirdan continued to pour us all a cup, a small smile on his lips. I kept my breath even and took a sip, determined that this lunch would go well and we would hear the solution Cirdan had to offer.

"Your Highness—"

"Please, call me Cirdan."

I laughed lightly. I'd forgotten. "Cirdan," I repeated, and he smiled. "Your letter said you may have information and a solution. Please, would you share it with us now?"

Cirdan swallowed a mouthful of tea, lowering his cup to the table. "Of course. Before my father and I became estranged, I was privy to certain information. Most of the mages that fled Ruvalon after the war did not stay with my father, but one of importance did. One who had belonged to the Xolani family."

"Kanu," Dracho said with certainty, an echo of guilt crossing his eyes. We had encountered Kanu in Stillmere. Dracho had not sensed any trace of the Hollow surrounding him, but had been so spooked by whatever Kanu had said to him that we had fled the room before I could ask any questions of my own.

Cirdan nodded, only showing slight surprise. "Both he and my father were enraged at being exiled from their homeland, and vowed to get their revenge."

"And what makes you believe your father and Kanu are behind this?"

"During the Tain, I had heard Kanu talk about an ancient power he had come across."

Dracho and I shared a look.

"He was obsessed with it, and my father grew to be too. During the war, they believed that if they uncovered its secrets, they could turn the tide of war... it ended before that happened."

"You say you've been estranged from your father for years. Why only inform us of this now?"

"I only heard about the attacks recently. Would you have believed me if I had shown up in Ruvalon to provide my concerns and not facts? Would I have been welcomed with open arms?"

No, he wouldn't. He looked so much like the images of his father I had seen in books that he likely would have been mistaken for him and lynched before he even reached Meridium.

"When I was younger, I never believed they would go through with whatever they were planning—I never thought they would truly risk breaking the treaty and causing an even greater war, after we'd lost so many. But these recent attacks were too suspicious to ignore. Though it's been many years since the war, my father's anger has not diminished. I knew he would not want to wage war against King Cervidae again… but I'm more convinced he could be behind this now that I've learned—"

"That my father is dead."

"Mm. And I fear this destruction will only get worse."

"Why tell us all this? Do you truly believe your father is behind the Hollow's attacks? That he and Kanu are controlling it?" Dracho asked, scepticism leaking into his tone. For a split second I thought I saw a shadow fall over Cirdan's eyes, but it was gone before I could be sure.

"I'm afraid I don't have the facts. But what I know from before points to them. So does my gut."

"And you're willing to help?" I asked hopefully.

"As much as I can, of course, Eliana." His hand gently pressed mine, his eyes shining. "I am at your disposal. Unfortunately, I do not have many soldiers." I nodded in understanding as I carefully slipped my hand from under his, picking up my cup. "But… I believe I could arrange a… negotiation."

"A *negotiation*. With your father?" Dracho asked in disbelief.

Cirdan nodded, gaze fixed upon my face. "I believe the two of us could barter for peace throughout the land. Undo the mistake that was made by your parents. If you were to… pick up the sword."

My cup clinked loudly as I placed it down. My heart jumped in my chest. I'd known that this would happen at some point—known I would have to explain it to Dracho. But I'd wanted to do it on my terms, and I'd never expected it to be so soon.

"Mistake? What's he talking about?" Dracho asked. I could feel his eyes on me.

Cirdan lifted a brow at me. Dracho swung his gaze to the prince, who smiled slightly, never looking away from me. "You did not know?"

Dracho shook his head.

Cirdan opened his mouth but I held a hand up, silencing him. I took a deep breath before looking into those icy blue eyes. Familiar panic bloomed in my chest, knowing I was about to voice part of a secret I had kept my whole life. But Antares already knew… and I would not allow a stranger to tell Dracho. If anyone was going to tell him, it would be me.

"The war started because of my mother."

Whatever Dracho had expected to hear, it evidently hadn't been that. "Your mother?" he repeated.

I nodded. "My mother... was betrothed to King Jandar, Cirdan's father. But before the wedding could take place, she visited Meridium and met my father. They fell in love and married in secret."

Dracho's lips parted as he listened intently.

"Whilst my grandparents were alive, King Morven dared not seek revenge... but when they passed—well, you know."

The Tain.

Dracho frowned as his mind worked over my words. I caught Cirdan's tight-lipped grin and gave him a warning look before he decided to open his mouth and spill any further information.

"But... who was your mother? To be betrothed to a prince?" Dracho asked.

Cirdan laughed, his bright eyes still on me. "*That's* the question right there."

My jaw clenched. "*Enough.* This conversation is postponed. We'll see you this evening at dinner."

"Yes, I apologise for revealing such sensitive information prematurely. It seems that you have much to discuss." Cirdan tipped his head.

I stood, ordering Dracho to follow as I stormed back through the dining hall, ignoring the surprised expressions of the others. I led Dracho to the gardens Vyn and I had found that morning. My heart was thumping.

"Eliana. Wait."

I didn't stop or slow as I continued my mission through the gardens, avoiding overgrown bushes and tree roots in search of somewhere no one could hear us. I grunted as his hand gently caught my arm, pulling me to a stop.

"What's going on?"

My heart clenched at the genuine concern and curiosity on his face. "I'll tell you shortly. Come on."

He let out a dark, humourless laugh. "More secrets, huh? They've always put us in good situations."

I glared at him. "It's nothing I won't tell you when I'm ready, and where we won't have ears listening."

"Yet Cirdan can know?" he pointed out, furious and impatient. "You know, now that I think about it, I do find it incredibly strange that he'd invite us here… and why is the prince taking such an *interest* in you? Judging by the way he can't take his eyes off you! Not that it's unusual for any male to be interested in you. But *he's*—"

"Anyone would think you were jealous. It's clearly my charm." I smiled smugly at him, trying to navigate the conversation into safer territory. "I mean, what man could resist?"

Shrugging his hand off, I turned to leave. He tried to touch my shoulder a second too late. Instead, I felt a relief of weight against the back of my head as thick braids fell loose, the hair tumbling down the sides of my face.

My hairpin.

Putting my hands to the loose hair, I rounded on him. "Give it back!"

He held up the pin. "You mean this little thing?" Holding it between his finger and thumb, he waved it back and forth, teasing. "Knowing you, you'll likely try and stab me with it. I think I'll keep—"

A vicious rage burned its way through me. I lunged for it, and him. Wrapping my fingers as tightly as I could around his wrist, I pushed him backwards.

His outburst of laughter irritated me further. I inhaled, trying to temper my anger. "Give. It. Back. Before I take your hand," I told him, my voice a quiet threat.

His lips were suddenly inches from mine. "I think you'd rather enjoy *taking* my hand, no?" His voice was like dark smoke. He held the pin higher above our heads, forcing my arm to stretch painfully.

"Tell me." His tone turned from playful to sad. "Why is it that *Cirdan* can know more about you than I do?"

My eyes met his own, and I didn't miss the hurt that flashed across his gaze. I could feel my cheeks starting to burn. *Damn him for affecting me like this.*

I rushed to speak as I released him and took a step back. "I wanted to. I just didn't want you to look at me—"

The words and my breath were sucked out of me as my heel caught on a root. Dracho's eyes widened and he reached for me, but I grabbed a fistful of his shirt and pulled, trying to save myself.

His eyes widened. Faster than I could see, he twisted as we fell to the ground, a curse leaving his lips as his back hit the grass. He started laughing as I pushed myself off his hard chest, but not before I could feel every inch of our lower bodies touching, causing heat to pool in my stomach. I rolled onto the grass next to him with a thud, releasing the breath I had been holding when we fell. Dracho moved onto his side to face me, still chuckling.

An eerie silence fell.

I turned to find him staring at me. His eyes were blown wide, the whites visible and that icy blue full of awareness, as if all the answers to the world's biggest questions had just come to him.

Realisation dawned, and blind panic settled in. I froze.

Dracho's breaths came heavy as he reached out, his eyes dancing with emotion, scanning my features as if seeing me for the first time. His fingers travelled softly along the side of my throat, the action causing me to swallow nervously. His fingertips tickled as they moved tenderly up over my cheek.

My lips parted; I inhaled shakily.

He traced the outside of my lower ear. Goosebumps rose all over my body as he moved upwards agonisingly slowly.

Until he came to the sharp point at the top.

Chapter 26

"So *that's* what you are," he whispered, almost as if in awe, his blue eyes a reflection of the iciest waters.

A shudder worked its way through my body. I had always hidden my elf heritage with my hair, sometimes unable to keep control of the glamour I held over my image; the ears were the hardest part to hide. Right now my emotions were so frayed it was almost impossible to keep them hidden.

I knew I wasn't supposed to feel relief, but I couldn't help it. It washed through me, mingled with surprise at my own feelings. My deepest, darkest secret had just been unveiled.

But I felt *relief*.

I pushed his hand away, wrenching myself to my feet as my heart rammed against my chest.

In a flash he was bending before me to stare into my eyes, his own bright and curious as raven strands fell over them. "You're immortal."

Wrong. I could be killed. But I was blessed with long life, like my mother. And being less than thirty summers old, I still had many years left to live.

I tried to decipher the hopeful look in his eyes, but he spoke again. "Why would you hide?"

His words pulled me up short. "W-what?"

His hands grasped my arms, a firm but gentle grip. "*Why* would you hide yourself? This explains so much."

Pulling from his hold, I burned with incredulity. "Are you dense?"

"You're an *elf*—"

"*Exactly*! Even if they had stayed in Ruvalon, many despise them, and most at least distrust them. Even before the war. No one knew about my mother. They believed her to be a lady from a distant continent, and Jandar was too full of pride to reveal the truth. The public reason for the war wasn't a lie; he hates mortals and other fairie-folk, but it wasn't his only motivation. He was too ashamed to admit that an elven woman had left him for a *mortal*, fearing he'd be the laughingstock of the elves. So why would I, a future *ruler* of Ruvalon, announce that I am a half-breed? Descendant of a race the people hate? Part of a species they believe wanted to wipe them out? How can you not understand this?"

My voice rose as I continued my tirade. "When I release my glamour and look in the mirror, I see only what I heard for most of my life. That the elves were monstrous—evil. That they all had a darkness in them. That I can *feel* that wickedness deep within, told by my family to suppress it for years for fear of being exposed. That it was the only way to be accepted and to survive."

His surprise turned into something else—something softer. "No one could hate you, Princess. And you could never be wicked."

My chest tightened. "It wouldn't matter what I said. The distrust would already be there," I told him.

"I think you have too little faith in people."

"After everything I've been through, are you surprised?"

His lips pursed. "That's why I can converse with you."

"What?"

"With my mind-talk. It's because you're magick. Not celestral, but still... you have elven magick."

My mouth opened and closed a few times, perplexed. I'd never considered my elven heritage to be connected to the draconi magick. Their magick was gifted and blessed by the celestral energy of the planet itself. Elven magick was tied to our bloodlines, gifted a long time ago by those who had been forgotten. But it did explain a lot of things—like how I'd been able to pray to the ancestors on the Aioni people's behalf. They'd syphoned the elven energy from my body in order to perform the rites.

"So, who was your mother?"

I let out a long breath before tipping my chin up. "My mother's real name was Lorelai Orinan. She changed her name to Laurellen once she married my father."

"Oh shit."

Why hadn't I told him sooner? My shoulders sagged with the weight removed, the relief instant. I could tell by the look on his face that he knew how significant that name was. Not only was my mother fully elven, but she had been descended from the oldest elven family that had ever lived on Adref, the continent to the northeast.

"So you're not only Ruvalon royalty... but like, *world* royalty?"

I nodded.

"And you are now the sole living direct descendant of the oldest elven family ever known." It wasn't a question. "Well, no wonder Cirdan's interested in you." His eyes left mine as he spoke more to himself. "These are your kind. The two of you could bring together all elves under one family."

Now he knew almost everything.

My mother, Lorelai Orinan, had been only in her second decade of life when she had been betrothed to Jandar Morven. The couple had courted for several years, but no official engagement had been made; Lorelai's parents were unsure about the elven king from Ruvalon. Then, during a private tour of the continent with her parents, Lorelai happened to meet the young king of Meridium, Teyrnon Cervidae. My father. During her stay there, they had fallen in love.

Once Lorelai had returned to Adref, she'd known she wouldn't be able to go through with a marriage to Jandar. She wanted my father, but she knew war would break out between Adref and the elves of Ruvalon and Eshmnor should her parents break the promise to Jandar. Adref would win. But they would lose many in the process.

She did what she thought best. She fled.

Without saying goodbye; without her belongings. An elven princess showed up on the doorstep of King Cervidae, and he took her in with no hesitation. He'd fallen in love with her long before.

They kept her identity hidden, though her parents were notified once they'd been married in secret. The rulers of Adref did not visit, nor did they write, but it wasn't easy to hide her real identity from Jandar. He usually avoided visiting human territories—but he'd found out the truth when he'd come to Meridium for a political meeting.

His wrath was great, but his pride was greater. Instead of revealing my mother's identity, he bided his time. He didn't dare seek revenge on her whilst my grandparents were alive, knowing the elves would unite under their banner to eradicate him should he do so.

But my grandparents' life-force and power dwindled, heartbroken over the absence of their daughter. Someone—and it didn't take much to work out who—took advantage of this and murdered them whilst they slept. Immediately, Jandar took charge of the situation and waged war on Meridium—on my parents.

He had started the Tain because my mother had dared to fall in love with a human. Now, decades after she had shunned their betrothal, he still carried that hate and resentment, entangling thousands into a war that would change Ruvalon forever.

But it hadn't only been revenge he'd sought.

"When Cirdan advised I picked up the sword, he was being literal. My mother stole the symbol of the elves. And only that sword could unite all elves under one call."

The sword of Orian.

It was an ancient family heirloom, named after the first king of the elves. My mother had taken it when she'd fled the continent. Only she and my father had known where it was buried, and I knew she'd taken it to prevent Jandar's twisted ideologies from spreading further than Ruvalon. She'd wanted those residing in Adref to live in peace, not be ruled by a tyrant.

"Do you know where it is?" he asked.

"No. And even if I did, I wouldn't wield it."

"Why not? Think of all those you could—"

"That sword, and my mother's refusal to marry Jandar, is precisely why the Tain happened."

"Eliana, your mother fell in love." His eyes softened.

"I know that, and I don't blame her. But I will not try to rule those I have no right to rule."

"You wouldn't just be ruling them. Think about it. You could unite *all* elves, humans and fairie folk alike."

A swirling sickness floated in my stomach at the thought. Of having that much responsibility. That much pressure.

"Think of what we could achieve together if we united the people," he continued.

"We?"

His expression turned confused. "Our... our shared dream? To bring the people of Ruvalon together."

The laugh bubbled up out of me unexpectedly. "Dracho, that dream died when you decided to throw me into a cell."

"I didn't—"

"We're working towards a similar goal right now, to find the Hollow. But as soon as all this is done, you go home and I do the same. There is no *shared* dream. No *us* to bring the people together."

He swallowed. His eyes fell for a moment, but then returned to mine.

"I think you're being selfish," he said.

My mouth fell open.

"And you're scared. Scared of the responsibility. I get it. I had to step up before I was ready too. But if anyone can do it, and unite everyone, it—"

"Enough. One thing you can't accuse me of is being selfish."

"But you are. You could unite the elves with the rest of your people, and yet you're choosing not to. Why?"

My teeth gritted. "It's not as simple as that."

He took a step closer. "It could be. All you need—"

My patience wore out. "What does it matter to you, anyway? You have your kingdom, your rule. Why does what I do with mine matter so much to you? Is *your* wish to unite your people with the rest of Ruvalon so you can lord over us all?"

He recoiled as if I had spat on him.

I knew it was low, and untrue. Also uncalled for. But his attitude was irritating the hell out of me.

"Eliana, that's not true—"

"Your truth, my truth, everyone else's truth... they're all a version of what's real."

His eyes hardened. "Don't deflect. You're saying these things to avoid talking about the *actual* truth. You're scared. Scared of ruling—that's why you didn't go through with the coronation before we left. Scared of restrictions. Of being in a cage"—I winced—"of revealing yourself."

I scowled at him.

"Scared of letting me in again, in case—"

"In case what? You betray me? Hmm, I wonder why."

His shame was written across his face. "That was a mistake... and I am so sorry, Eliana."

My breath hitched.

"You've had plenty of opportunities to apologise, Dracho." I swallowed. "You even said sorry to Bas when you first arrived in Meridium. But people throw around apologies and '*sorry*' as if the words can just fix everything that has happened. When the fact of the matter is, your actions are yours. You chose to throw me into a cell, no matter how short the period of time. You knew my pain. I know you may not have meant to, but you made your choice at the expense of my emotions and that—that is not all right. Nor do I have to be all right with it. Some people may live by their rules of forgiveness, but not me. I remember and recover, not forgive and forget. And… and I do not forgive you for what you did. You don't deserve the closure."

"You're right," Dracho whispered. "I don't, and I'm not saying this to ease my own conscience. I'm saying this because I am genuinely sorry, Eliana. It was the biggest mistake I have ever made in my life, and I have regretted it every day since. I hadn't said sorry yet because I knew I was undeserving of your forgiveness, and because I've been dealing with all these mixed feelings since my merging. I know I'm a different person, and I'm trying to come to terms with that. Frankly, I've been blessed to have remained in your company for so long since my return. All I can do is show you every day how sorry I am. Even if it's just as your ally."

I stayed silent. My heart felt like it had broken, finally hearing those words from his mouth. And yet it felt like a good breaking… one that potentially led to healing.

I cleared my throat. "Thank you."

But letting my guard down again was not something I could risk.

His face crumpled. "It's too late, isn't it?"

I didn't know. My mind was as tumultuous as the sea. "I just… I'm not sure I can fully trust you not to betray me again. As you said, you're a new person."

He shook his head. "I think I have proved, perhaps just a little, that even if you cannot trust me with your heart, Eliana, you can trust me to help. Do you honestly believe that I would betray your kingdom? *My* kingdom, by risking conflict?"

"I don't know what to believe, Dracho. I believe you want to find out answers about the Hollow. But let's not forget that you returned to Meridium under the guise of accusing my father. You have your own answers to find.

Perhaps you should go and look for them."

"What?" he asked, incredulous.

"I think perhaps you should leave," I repeated, almost shrinking away from his outraged expression.

"I didn't come here for just you. Or did you forget my father was killed too?! The Hollow is connected to *both* our fathers' deaths, and now allegedly to Jandar."

"I know that Dracho!" I bit back, my voice like acid. "I just think that maybe our history is a bit too complicated to work so closely together on this."

"Because you can't accept my apology?"

I nodded.

"Too bad you don't always get your way, Princess. I'm staying."

"This isn't about me getting my own way. This is about what's best for everyone."

"What's best for you, you mean," he scoffed.

"That's not fair, Dracho. I didn't ask for any of this to happen."

"Your lack of trust is only going to hurt you in the long run," he muttered. "You need to let people get close."

"I do." I stared him down. "But I will ensure it's the right people."

He huffed humourlessly. "Well, then... perhaps, if you can't trust in the company you keep, it *is* futile for us to work together to face the Hollow."

"Perhaps you're right."

His jaw clenched.

"I'm not your responsibility, Dracho. You don't need to delay your own quest for information or your vengeance. Cirdan and Adven have welcomed us warmly, and I have Bas and Vyn here with me. You can go. Find answers in whatever manner you see fit."

He considered it for a moment. "Maybe... maybe you're right. I could save you a trip and visit the temple of the Hollow. We could always reunite here to discuss everything later?"

"That sounds good," I rasped, unable to deny his hopeful eyes.

"Okay," he said. An uncomfortable silence fell between us for a moment. "We'll leave, then."

"Good."

The silence was brittle, the only sound the combined heaving of our breathing.

He turned, and I closed my eyes. It wasn't until I heard the rustle of leaves that I realised he had gone. My chest constricted as I opened my eyes. I had never questioned my own decisions as much as I did when around him.

Only this time, it felt like I had made the wrong one.

Chapter 27

Antares

Dracho burst through the double doors. "We leave. Now," he barked, and left.

I looked to Bastion and Vyn, who wore matching perplexed expressions, then threw my cards onto the table, taking to my feet to follow my emperor.

Dracho!

I found him in the main courtyard, holding his rucksack and sheathed glaive. A couple of the manor members of staff wandered past, giving him concerned looks. I wasn't surprised—Dracho's unnatural pacing across the cobbled stones and his clear distress had my senses on edge.

What is it, brother? I asked him.

His pacing stopped, his cold eyes finding mine. My back straightened in realisation.

You know, I said.

You knew she was elven? The hurt in his eyes made me feel paper-thin.

I suspected. I confirmed it last night. I sent him an image of her face as she snarled at me, fangs visible as her sharpened features showed.

Why didn't you say anything?

It wasn't my story to tell.

He nodded—albeit reluctantly—knowing I would never betray someone's trust like that.

Does it... bother you? I asked. I had been sure it wouldn't, yet whatever had just happened between them had obviously left him reeling.

Of course not. He ran a hand through his hair, huffing in frustration. My eyes travelled over him, noting the slight tremble in his fingers and the restless legs. He would need to fly soon.

Then why—

She doesn't trust me.

I remained silent. This, I knew. What had happened had affected Eliana deeply. It was something she hid well, but I could read it easily from the conflicted emotions that flashed across her eyes whenever she looked at Dracho.

I left it too late, he said.

I winced.

We both agreed I should leave and visit the temple of the Hollow.

Why?

It'll give us space. Get us answers quickly. I apologised to her, Ant... but I hurt her too much. His sadness was like a bruise, bleeding and spreading through his hope like a poison.

We can't leave her with these strangers, Dracho.

They're her people. She said she has Vyn and Bas. Perhaps if I can find answers at the temple, I can return to her and it'll make amends.

That was a stretch, but I could see the desperation in his eyes. *Brother...* I whispered into his mind. *I don't think she truly wants you to leave. We all say things we don't mean in the heat of the moment.*

You never do. How do I know she doesn't speak the truth?

I had no answer for that, no insight into Eliana's mind. I could guess, judging by the way she looked at Dracho, but I feared her heart was too wounded by the betrayal in Tenebris. A grudge was a powerful thing to hang on to. It could keep you living in pain, unable to find happiness. It seemed that deep down, Eliana preferred that to the alternative—opening herself up and being vulnerable to hurt again.

What do you want to do? I asked, willing to do anything to ease his suffering.

He was getting worked up, his breathing heavy and his silver eyes shining. *Fuck it. If she thinks she can trust Cirdan more than me, then so be it. I won't stay where I'm obviously not wanted. I won't stay and watch as she is courted by someone else.*

I followed his logic. Cirdan and Eliana were both elves; the prince had shown an obvious interest in her. The thought of remaining and being witness to such behaviour was causing his dragon to ride his emotions.

Dracho, it's not true she doesn't want you here. What about your goals? Your father?

Exactly! Cirdan isn't offering anything worthwhile, so I can pursue my own information at the temple.

A blinding glow caused me to shield my eyes momentarily as he transformed. I took a few steps back; his obsidian form took up space in the large courtyard. His silver eyes caught me once more as he picked up his discarded clothes with his claws.

Dracho, don't—

I clenched my eyes as the movement of his wings buffeted me with wind. When the dust cleared, I watched him rise higher and higher in the direction of Ruvalon.

Shit, shit, shit. I turned and fled up the circular stone steps to where I knew Eliana's room was.

Althea's squeal as I burst through the door would have made me laugh, had the situation not been so dire.

"Antares! What is it?" she asked, eyes blown wide in astonishment.

I leaned against the door, panting. "Dracho has gone."

"What do you mean, gone?"

"All I know is, Eliana told him to leave, and he was angry enough that he has. He's flown back to Ruvalon. We must go."

She nodded in agreement, heading towards me, then pulled up short. "What about the others?"

My jaw clenched. It was unnerving to realise that for the first time in a long time, I had no idea what to do. A tug in my chest warned me to stay, but...

Duty.

"He's our emperor," I told her, mind made up.

With sad eyes, she nodded, turning to gather her belongings. It didn't take me long to get mine, and we headed out.

Vyn came towards us we approached the courtyard doors, and I stopped, though Althea continued.

"What's going on?" he asked, sharp eyes narrowed on my belongings.

"Vyn," I breathed out, "I'm not sure on the full details, but we're leaving."

“What?” He jerked back.

Reaching out, I pulled him closer, his windswept floral scent enveloping my senses. “Dracho has already left. We follow. Listen, I’ll try to change his mind, but be careful. Look after each other.”

“Antares, what is going—”

“Vyn.” My voice rose. “Please. Take care of each other.”

His eyes scanned mine with concern, jaw hard, but he nodded.

I exhaled roughly before taking a step back. “Find Eliana. Ensure she’s all right. I *will* see you again soon.” Without another look back, I rushed to the courtyard, finding Althea in her lavender dragon form.

As we flew away, I looked back to the manor, watching as it disappeared through the clouds and wondering if we had made a grave mistake.

Chapter 28

Eliana

"He found out who I am. *What* I am."

Bas rubbed his brow with ragged tiredness as Vyn listened intently to my tale. They had come to find me in the gardens immediately after Dracho had left, and remained with me there for a few hours. My mind kept tormenting me with all the things I should have said instead of the words that had come out of my mouth. I'd really believed that a couple of hours to cool down would do us good. It wasn't until Vyn and Bas had come rushing towards me that I'd realised the gravity of what I had done.

"And he was angered by that?" Vyn asked.

"No. I told him I couldn't trust him... and that he should leave."

Despite the anger I felt towards myself for pushing him, I couldn't believe he had actually left. A creeping loneliness ran up my spine, reminding me of how I'd felt when my mother, father and brother had gone off to war and left me at home.

"Why, E?" Bas asked.

I wasn't sure myself. "There's so much hurt still there. It was a stupid fight, and I pushed too far."

"Perhaps he'll return soon."

I wanted to believe that. I really did.

A small cough behind us caused us to turn.

"Your Highness." Adven bowed, his eyes travelling over Vyn and Bas for a second. "Prince Cirdan asks if you would join him for a dinner this evening, to continue your conversation?"

I smiled politely. "Of course."

"And Emperor Celesta—do you know where I could find him?"

I swallowed. "He has left."

"Left?" Adven's eyes shone as they widened. He seemed genuinely surprised, or else doing a good job of pretending to be.

"Yes, I'm afraid he had some business to attend to back in Ruvalon."

"And his companions?"

I nodded.

"What a shame. I'm sure His Highness will be saddened to hear of it. Dinner is at sundown. Masters Ekker and Kaze, yours will be served in the dining hall."

"Thank you, Adven." Vyn smiled; Adven hurried away.

"What do you wanna do?" Bas asked, reaching forward to take my hand.

"I want to find out more about this solution Cirdan has. So we'll stay for that." They both nodded in agreement. "From there… we shall see."

Before my dinner with Cirdan, I took some time to reflect in my room. The air still smelled of Althea's perfume, the scent of freesia lingering in the air and causing my chest to hurt. Feeling confined by the blue gown I had been wearing, I decided to slip into something more comfortable. The dark brown breeches clung to my legs as I pulled a white shirt on, the hem brushing my leg mid-thigh. My eyes hesitated on my dagger and its sheath, but I decided to leave it—it wouldn't be proper etiquette to wear weapons at a private dinner between two rulers. Not that it had ever stopped me before. But if I was to be a queen soon, perhaps I should try to act like it.

I had left Bas and Vyn in the main dining hall, the two wishing me luck. Adven was nowhere to be seen; it was the two guards from the front gate who directed me to the study, and they remained at either side of the dais as I entered.

The same table I had sat at for lunch had been laid for dinner, a crisp white sheet beneath the polished silverware, and a lit candelabra—that was new. The oil lamps around the room had been dimly lit, and the atmosphere of the room felt rather… intimate. A shiver swam between my shoulder blades, and I steeled myself for whatever was about to be discussed.

There was an air of excitement to Cirdan as he entered the room, closing the door behind him. Turning, he sighed deeply as he took in my frozen form at the dining table.

"Eliana, I must apologise for this morning. Adven has told me of Dracho's departure. I hope our conversation wasn't the cause?"

"Thank you for your apology, Cirdan. No, Dracho has returned to Ruvalon to pursue another line of enquiry regarding the Hollow."

"Did he say if he will return?"

"He may, if he finds answers. But I'm not sure," I replied.

"Well." He clasped his hands before him. "I suppose all will end well. No secrets between friends and all that."

I smiled tightly, unsure how to take that.

"Thank you for coming to dinner." He walked over, taking the seat beside me at the table and pouring me a glass of red wine from the goblet before him. "I know you've probably wondered why I invited your father here. Why I was determined to help a mortal and a half-breed."

The words were jarring, shocking me from my silence and causing the blood beneath my skin to warm. "Call me that again and you'll find my blade somewhere uncomfortable."

His eyes widened as he stared at me and my cheeks flamed, cursing that violent part of me that had jumped to threaten him. He bowed his head. "My apologies, Eliana, I truly meant no offence."

I took a calming breath. "I apologise. I should not have threatened you."

He laughed, his eyes narrowing playfully. "I must admit, I was taken slightly by surprise. I had heard that the warrior princess of Meridium had a feisty side, but never hoped to experience it for myself."

My cheeks heated for an entirely different reason now. "You had heard of me?"

"Well, of course. Knowing that there was a half-elven princess ruling in Ruvalon certainly piqued my interest." He looked at me flirtatiously through his dark lashes.

I nodded in response. "If you don't mind me asking… is my heritage known to many of your people?"

"No." He shook his head. "Adven knows, of course; he met your mother when she was courting my father. My father told me when I was younger, but as you can imagine, his pride was rather damaged by your mother's actions. He kept it hidden well enough, but I certainly wanted to know more. Especially once I learned about how beautiful you were."

I coughed, ignoring the compliment and feeling a little lighter knowing that my identity was not known to many. But the conversation was going in a direction I hadn't anticipated. I eyed the goblet of rich, reddish wine before me and the bowl of apples in the centre of the table, but ignored it, choosing instead to pour myself a cup of water.

"I fear I must apologise again. I have made you uncomfortable." Cirdan's brows met in the middle.

Shaking my head, I swallowed the mouthful of water. "No. It's quite all right. I'm just... not used to compliments."

"Truly?" he asked in mild astonishment.

"Well, except from my friends and family, yes."

"You are uncomfortable when it comes from men?"

"Or women. Just... anyone who is not known to me."

His lips pursed in amusement. "Well then, hopefully you will learn to accept them... once you come to know me more."

"Perhaps."

"I hope so, Eliana. For that is what I wanted to talk to you about. The solution to all that is going on in Ruvalon, and to the negotiation with my father."

"What?" I asked, leaning forward in confusion.

Cirdan stood, his large frame towering over me... then he dropped to one knee, clasping my hand within his.

"Princess Eliana, heir to both the thrones of Meridium and Adref, I offer you my hand in marriage."

Chapter 29

A laugh burst from my throat, slowly dying when I saw Cirdan's curt expression.

"Oh, you're serious," I said blankly.

"Quite," he said, sounding as if he now wished he wasn't. He moved to stand, and I clasped his hand tighter.

"Cirdan, I am truly sorry. I did not mean to offend, but I really don't think that's a good idea."

"Why not?" he asked slowly.

"Well, we don't even know each other, for one," I pointed out, thinking it was rather obvious.

"Arranged marriages have always been made amongst the elves, proving quite successful. Just think what we could achieve. We could bring the continent together. My father's revenge would be rendered pointless if we united all the fae and returned to Ruvalon. We'd be the most powerful rulers in the world."

I understood what he was saying, but his voice was cutting and sharp. Something lay beyond his words I couldn't decipher. Some powerful emotion he wasn't fully revealing.

"Your father is the current ruler of the fae on Eshmnor... why would our marriage satisfy his need for revenge?" Did Cirdan have any real power over his people while Jandar was their king?

"He wouldn't really have a choice if we united the elves of Eshmnor with those on Adref."

"Uh-huh," I drawled, not fully believing him. "Let's just say I'm a bit too *lively* to be a good, dutiful wife to an elven prince."

He chuckled deeply, his features sharpening, and leaned closer.

"Eliana..." He drew out my name seductively, but it only caused a nervous shiver to run up my spine. "Deep down I think we both know that every confident woman like yourself wants a man that can make her feel a little—unsure. Perhaps... intimidated?"

I removed my hand from his, pressing myself away from him as much as possible as I stood. A muffled shouting came from outside the door, but Cirdan ignored the commotion, and I had bigger issues to worry about.

"You don't intimidate me," I told him confidently, ignoring the creeping sensation building in my gut telling me to run.

He rose, walking behind me in a slow circle and daring to trace a finger along the back of my neck. Alarm bells were chiming in my brain. I turned in a fluid motion, for once not bothering to hide my speed—faster than a mortal's, thanks to my elven side—as I captured his wrist and stared into his autumnal eyes.

He smirked before pulling his wrist gently from my grasp, turning and putting his back to me. "Is it the draconi?"

I jerked back.

"If so... you should be with your own kind."

A flash of hot rage burst through me, and I started to realise his slip of the tongue had been no accident. "My kind? I am a *half-breed*, as you put it. I'm not accepted by the elves, nor will I ever truly be accepted by the humans. My kind *are* the half-breed creatures. The many that continue to be mistreated across the realms. Mistreated by the likes of your father."

My mind thought of Vyn—his half-Djinn nature. Cirdan turned, amusement in his cold gaze. "You say that as if you stand with them. From what I hear, you remain hidden in the shadows. No one knows who you truly are."

My jaw clenched as his words sank in, like shards of broken glass. His smile was almost feline.

"It would be... *prudent* for you to seriously consider my proposal."

My head turned as the sound of the heavy door opening then closing reached my ears. The two large guards named Joff and Erix stood in the way of the only exit. An anxious fluttering started to tighten my chest.

"After all," Cirdan continued, "better to be united by blood and marriage… than divided by blood and chaos."

I swallowed thickly as my heart beat wildly in my chest, scanning the room for any way out as my hand drifting to my thigh where my dagger would usually sit. and cursing that I had left it in my room.

Had I not learned my lesson from the last time I had forgotten my dagger?

Anger built, my blood roiling as I realised the predicament I had put my friends in.

Coming here was a trap, like we feared, and I've just sent away the only protection I had.

I finally turned to catch Cirdan's eye. My vision was starting to blur slightly at the edges. I glanced down at my glass of water.

"He'll find me," I promised, finding it hard to enunciate.

Cirdan's eyes flashed in challenge. "I would like to see him try."

"You know, just because you cage something, it doesn't make it yours," I whispered, knowing he would hear me despite the slurring of my words.

His eyes flashed wickedly. "No…" The corners of his mouth curled up cruelly as he leaned close to me, his breath cold against the shell of my ear. "But you always enjoy the experience of taming the beast."

I pushed forward, sprinting for the guards by the door before my body gave in to whatever I had been poisoned with. Satisfied smiles greeted me as the bigger one swung his arms out to catch me. I dropped, kicking his knee, hearing the grunt leave him as his leg buckled. I shot up again, facing the remaining guard whose yellowing teeth flashed at me.

The cracking of bones that drew my eyes back to the larger man. Not his leg where I'd kicked him—but what sounded like the cracking of *every* bone in his body.

My eyes widened as I seemed to watch in slow motion. As his body contorted, his moans of pain should have been music to my ears, but I was transfixed by the spectacle. The blood drained from my face as his skin appeared to bubble, stretching painfully with him as his body grew, lengthened and started to sprout tufts of dark fur along his exposed flesh. As his back arched, his neck cracking with the effort, his clothes ripped apart at the seams, dropping to the floor in scraps of fabric.

My brain stuttered as I comprehended what now stood before me—on four legs, not two. The remaining guard, Joff, chuckled darkly as he took a step towards me. There was no way I could fight my way out of this room unarmed. A blunt force to the back of my head knocked me to my knees as I realised for the second time in my life, I had just witnessed the transformation of man into beast.

Chapter 30

My stomach tumbled when I came to. I was dizzy, and the urge to throw up tightened my throat. *Why is the room bobbing up and down?*

I scanned my surroundings—difficult in the non-existent lighting, but I made out the wooden planks beneath me, musty and covered in a greasy layer of filth. The walls on either side of me curved slightly, creaking as they seemed to move. The chopping of water slapped against the outside of the room I was in, making it groan, and I almost retched.

I'm on a ship.

Barrels stood off to the side, and I realised I must be in a storeroom. I tried to glance around in search of Vyn and Bas, but as I pulled forward my wrists burned. They were bound tightly behind me, my back resting against a wooden pillar. I cursed loudly.

Where are they taking me?

Panic raced through me, the back of my head pounding. How long had I been out for? I opened my mouth to shout just as a door swung open. I squinted as the tall figure walked leisurely towards me, a glass lantern held in its hand.

As he knelt before me, his features became clear.

"You," I said through clenched teeth. "Where are you taking me?"

Adven smiled as he placed the lantern on the floor beside him. He balanced on his feet, resting his elbows on his knees as he clasped his hands together.

"What are we going to do with you, hmm?" he mused.

He spoke like I was a misbehaving child, not his captive. Had he forgotten that his master had struck me over the head and kidnapped me? If I hadn't been so dumbstruck by his casual attitude, I would have been terrified.

"Well." My tongue ran over my cracked bottom lip. "You could always release me, considering you all *abducted* me!"

He laughed. "I don't think raising your voice is warranted."

Is he out of his fucking mind? "No? Unbind me and I'll show you exactly how I feel without using any words."

He found that positively hilarious. "Whilst the idea amuses me," he said as my lip curled at him, "I would never willingly put myself in a position where you could harm me. Even if you are only *half* elf."

I tutted. "Shame."

"The elven blood that runs through your veins is more potent than that of most who live in Adref. More valuable."

"Lucky me," I drawled.

"Yes... lucky you, Eliana. You have no idea what power you could hold, if only you were to take your birthright and join Cirdan."

"I don't want it. I want nothing to do with him."

"But you will. He cannot claim rule over your entire people, not without the sword... and even if he did have it, he does not carry any blood of Orinan."

"So all the flattery and pomp were because I'm a means to an end?"

"Well..." He unclasped his hands, bringing a calloused finger up to brush a strand of hair over my shoulder, his finger touching my skin for a second longer than necessary. "I wouldn't say he's displeased by his future wife."

I jerked my shoulder back. "You're a vile prick! If you think for a second I would *ever* let him touch me—"

A loud, cruel laugh burst from his chest. "My dear Eliana, don't you understand? By the time he is finished with you, you'll be begging for a pleasant touch as a reprieve from that which will undoubtedly *break* you."

My eyes widened, my mind emptying of all thought. His lips pulled up at the corner, and I swallowed hard.

"Where are you taking me?" My voice was a whisper.

"No concern of yours. Just a little castle of Cirdan's on one of the islands. Don't worry, your friends from Tenebris won't find you. We had to accelerate our plans as soon as we learned they had left. How things worked out! You did our job for us by getting rid of the dragons." He laughed again. "We'll be long gone by the time they even realise you are missing."

"Where are Vyn and Bas?" I demanded.

His lips turned down. "Now, Eliana. Had you just behaved... well, your friends would have been fine."

I hissed at him, my wrists screaming as I wrenched forward. "I'll kill you, I swear! You piece of—"

Adven's hand whipped forward, gripping my cheeks so hard my words were cut off and my jaw ached. "Don't test us before we've even arrived home." He pushed my face away, wiping his hand on his trousers. The temptation to spit in his face was high, but my chest started heaving as something clicked.

"Wait," I wheezed, "you said *your* people. Not ours."

His grin was sadistic as he stood. "Because they are not my people."

"Wh-what? I don't under—"

Before my very eyes, his form began to change. His hair and ears shortened, his features morphing into something more mortal-looking as his eyes sharpened. As his irises turned yellow, a faint rouge appeared in the skin around them.

Blood pounded in my ears; my hands shook against my restraints. "You're a djinn."

His white teeth flashed in the low light as he bent before me. "And not just any djinn."

I squinted at him in the light, watching as it flickered over his silver-blonde hair. He waited for me to figure it out.

"You're Vyn's father," I whispered in horror.

He stood straighter. "I must admit I was surprised to see my spawn in your throne room that day we met. I was intrigued to find out if he had grown worthy of the blood of my species running through his veins. From what I have seen, I am disappointed."

"Fuck you! He's more than you'll ever be!"

"He *was*. Not is."

"You fucking prick. I'll kill you if you have touched him!" I screamed, blinking as I tried to focus on Adven's face, but his features had started to blur. If they had harmed Vyn and Bas, I was truly alone. They had been taken from me. There was no one left.

The loneliness was a squeezing pressure upon my heart that became a constant pain. Breathing was hard. Really hard.

For a moment, his brows furrowed, as if trying to work out what was wrong with me. Then realisation dawned, and he rolled his eyes. "There's no need to be so dramatic."

"F-fuck... you," I wheezed out between laboured breaths as I continued the fight against my own mind and body.

I was stranded. I was lost. There was no one coming for me.

He wasn't coming for me, and my final words to him had all been a lie.

My head swayed as Adven's blurred form retreated. "Sleep tight, Eliana. We'll all be home soon."

The edges of my vision darkened, my panic attack overcoming me. I was pulled back into unconsciousness.

Chapter 31

We reached our destination a day later. I laughed maniacally when Joff tried to pull me out of the ship, only to fall to his knees, his hands gripping his nose tightly from where my head had connected with it. Unfortunately, three other guards surged forward. Still, it was only when Joff transformed into a wolf that I faltered, and they managed to grab me. My futile attempts to rip myself from their hands were almost laughable, even with my elven strength.

I did my best to take in all the detail I could as they dragged me towards a castle, the dark wolf trailing behind, his teeth snapping at my back. Anything to work out an escape or a position. Large boulders littered the ground, the path to and from the castle snaking around them. The castle was obviously old, sporting patches of different stonework from where repairs had been carried out. There was nothing else around; this was another small island, the walk from the ship to the castle only taking twenty minutes, even with me slowing them down. *They must get supplies from offshore.*

Five narrow, round towers formed a protective barrier all around the castle, connected by low, chunky walls made of dark brown stone. Crude windows dotted the walls in perfect symmetry, along with holes for archers. I was dragged through the large wooden gates and past several shocked women carrying laundry. One caught my eye; her lips turned down in a frown, and her hand flattened against her chest. I wondered if they truly knew the character of their master.

Once we had reached a very dark corner of the castle, I was dragged down a set of stairs into a cold, dank area where one of the guards unlocked a wooden door. I cursed at the sharp burst of pain that shot through my knees as they threw me to the floor. I looked around the room. Besides a bucket in the corner, there was nothing. Nothing except two metal rings, embedded into the wall—for chains. Panic made my blood run cold.

The heavy wooden door shook as it slammed shut. I rushed to it, hearing the metal bolt locking on the other side.

I screamed for a while, my throat growing hoarse as I demanded to be released. Pure, unadulterated fear coursed through me when I received no answer. I even tried using my mind, screaming internally and thinking of Dracho, testing whether his ability to speak to me in my head worked both ways. But nothing happened.

Eventually my shouting stopped, and I opted to pace instead as my mind drifted to my friends. Something in my gut told me they weren't dead, but I wasn't sure if that was me holding onto vain hope. I had severely underestimated Cirdan and Adven.

If anything has *happened to them, I'll never forgive myself.*

I had no idea how many hours I had been pacing the small room when steps sounded from outside. They stopped outside my door, a guard unlocking it. Prince Cirdan himself entered. His smile was victorious.

"Welcome to Fallstone. I hope you've calmed down."

"Fuck you," I spat at him, knowing that if I struck him I'd likely never leave this room.

He exhaled through his nose, his brows lowering in clear disappointment. "Your behaviour is very unbecoming of my future bride."

"I am not, nor will I *ever* be, your future bride, you sanctimonious prick." I lifted my chin defiantly as rage simmered under my skin.

He laughed. "I wonder what will get you killed first, your mouth or your stubbornness?"

My voice was flat and cold. "Probably both."

I saw the flash of his smirk before a grunt left me, my back slamming against the cold cell wall. His hand gripped my throat, his fingers squeezing. I clawed at his hand, kicking out to find purchase, but as he held me off the floor, I found none.

Panic once again flooded me.

"I think you *will* be my wife. We simply need to convince you first."

"Where are Bas and Vyn?" I croaked weakly, as the back of my head throbbed painfully.

My knees buckled when he dropped me, my back sliding roughly down the stones. My hand brushed over the skin of my neck as I coughed.

"That doesn't concern you," Cirdan replied. "I left their fate to Adven. After all, it is his son."

"Vyn was *never* his son."

He tutted. "Now, now, Eliana. They suffered for *your* behaviour—"

"Suffered how?!"

He ignored me. "I'll leave you to get acquainted with your new home... I have to go and write to my father and let him know that you're here."

"Jandar?" The word left my mouth in a gasp. I berated myself for not having spotted the clues before. The pieces had been there, but I'd failed to put them together.

"Hmm, yes. Would you ever have met with me had I been in my father's affections? No, I don't think so." His laugh mocked me as he looked me up and down. "I'll need to make sure you're presentable by then."

I spat at his feet. "I'm going to kill you."

He bent down to scrutinise my face. "Yes. I believe you think you will. But we'll soon get that out of you."

He stood, sweeping out of the room in a single motion, but pausing in the doorway. "Make sure everyone knows she is to remain *unspoiled*," he instructed the guard.

Though I tried not to show it, a jolt of fear made its way into my thoughts. A tangle of memories—unwanted hands, clawing their way up my legs. I gritted my teeth, staring at Cirdan with all the hate I could muster.

I will not break.

His smirk returned. "But if she gives you any trouble, feel free to punish her. Leave her face unmarked. And do not allow your hands to *wander*. She is still mine."

He turned and left. The guard turned to shut the door, but not before giving me a wide smile full of yellow teeth. As he slammed the heavy door, I slumped back against the wall, staring dully into the darkness.

Sleep had found me for only a few hours when my cell door opened quietly. A human ear might not have heard the slight creak of the hinges, but to my elven ears, the sound was as loud as tower bells at noon.

It was the guard—Joff. The one I had struck back in Akraya and on the boat.

He chuckled quietly in the silence, pulling the door behind him until only a sliver of torchlight came from the crack. "I was hoping you'd sleep a little longer."

"What do you want?" I grumbled, blinking my dry eyes.

His gaze across the exposed skin of my neck was enough to cause a wave of nausea. I shot to my feet. Cirdan may have commanded I be left unspoiled, but there were other violations of the body that sick men could enact. Even if commanded not to.

"You wouldn't," I hissed at him. "Cirdan will kill you."

"Like anyone would believe you anyway." He grinned, stalking towards me.

Just as I raised my fists and prepared to scream myself hoarse, the door hit the cell wall with thunderous force, the wood cracking.

Joff flattened himself against the wall instantly. Cirdan leaned casually against the open door frame, one hand behind his back. He wore a simple black shirt and pair of trousers, a bare foot crossed over the other. A young guard, smaller than the others, stood outside, his fidgeting revealing his nerves.

"Your High—"

Cirdan clicked his tongue a few times, wagging his finger in the air. His steps made no sound as he entered the cell, his frame seeming to grow larger when illuminated by the torch's firelight outside.

"I made my wishes very clear. Were you about to touch *my* intended, Joff?" His voice had taken on an eerie quality. The low tone was just as unnerving as the hiss of his words.

"N-n-no, Cird—"

"Please don't embarrass yourself by lying." Cirdan's eyes flashed, his teeth bared.

"I'm s-sorry, Your Highness, it won't hap—"

He didn't get an opportunity to finish his sentence. Faster than thought,

Cirdan stepped before him, using a silver dagger to open Joff from navel to neck. An agonised and surprised cry left Joff's mouth, his hands trying to prevent his innards from falling out.

My back hit the wall as Cirdan grinned ferociously in the guard's face, paying no mind to the blood and tissue that spilled over his bare toes. The sight made me want to vomit. Once Joff's hands fell from his stomach, his head slumping in death, Cirdan released his blade and allowed him to fall.

He gave a bored sniff, turning in my direction. The hand holding his dagger, covered in blood up to his forearm, waved at Joff's body. "Sorry about that, Eliana. I'll have someone come and clean that up."

I shook my head, unable to look away from that bloody arm of his. "You're insane."

His laugh sent a shiver along my spine. "I am merely protecting what is mine. I put rules in place, and I expect them to be followed. Maybe you should keep that in mind."

My eyes dropped to the guard's prostrate form. I didn't respond.

"Now," Cirdan continued, "off to bed. Busy week ahead."

"W-what's happening this week?" I dared to ask.

Had he not been a sadistic fucker who wanted to use me for my lineage or subjugate my body, the excited smile he sent me would have been both handsome and charming.

As it was, it terrified me more than anything I'd ever experienced.

Chapter 32

Fortune had been in my favour for a few days. Cirdan—and the guards—had left me in my cell, only dropping in to bring me meals and water and to change the waste bucket. The dead guard had been removed by his peers—their eyes showing the fear that Cirdan had no doubt wanted to instil in them as they cleaned his entrails—but the acrid smell of blood and death remained.

It was on the fourth day that his guards came to collect me, dragging me kicking and screaming to a private chamber in one of the towers. There were several elven maids there; their eyes widened when they saw me fighting the guards, who dumped me roughly onto the stone floor.

"Don't even think about running. There's no other way out and we'll be outside the door."

"Fuck you," I hissed. The maids gasped.

The guard, Erix—he seemed to lead the others—laughed. "I suggest you get ready, or I'll come and bathe you myself."

I cringed as he slammed the door shut, then turned to face the women. Their eyes were cast down, a young one on the end blushing as she chewed her lip nervously. I did my best to get them to speak to me, to beg for their help, but their frightened glances proved they were just as terrified of Cirdan as I was. They would not incur his wrath.

I didn't give them trouble, allowing them to bathe me. They scrubbed my hair with lavender shampoo and brushed it until it was as smooth as silk. One maid offered me a simple blush gown to wear, but I refused and another handed me a clean pair of breeches and white shirt instead. I muttered a small 'thank you', dressing myself and relishing the clean feeling of them on my skin.

I ignored Erix's appraisal when he entered the room, though it made my skin crawl, and I didn't give them the satisfaction of dragging me again. "I'll walk. I won't run."

I would face Jandar with my head held high.

They walked me, one in front, one behind, to a large throne hall. Eight sandstone columns lined the walls, a slender brazier between each one coating everything in an orange glimmer. Intricately carved woodwork hung from the slanted ceiling, while sculptures and gargoyles looked down upon the tiled floor. We reached the centre of the room, and the guard in front of me moved.

Jandar Morven, the cruel former king of Stillmere who now ruled from Farcross on Eshmnor, was sitting in the large throne upon the raised dais.

It was made up of thick tree branches, all twisting and coiling into a towering chair that looked as if it belonged in some mythical fairie tale. Not in the cold throne room of a monster.

Adven leaned casually against the throne, a satisfied grin on his face. Cirdan stood off to the side, as silent as death as he waited for his father's reaction. It was remarkable how similar the two looked. Jandar's black hair was tied at the back of his head, not a strand out of place. The only true difference between them was Jandar's dark blue eyes. If I'd thought Cirdan's eyes held no warmth or love in them, it was nothing compared to the blatant animosity and cruelty in Jandar's.

My ability to sense a person's aura was a rare ability gifted to me by my elven magick, and not one many knew I possessed. For years, it had allowed me to judge the characters of those around me—assessing whether someone was kind, or merely getting closer to me for selfish reasons. It had come in handy more than a few times. Now I almost wished I couldn't see Jandar's. Unlike Cirdan's shielded aura, his father's was a beacon of darkness, a slick oily thing that had consumed any goodness around it.

"Well done, Cirdan. Finally you have done something useful," Jandar said, head resting lazily on his fist. I saw a muscle twitch in Cirdan's jaw. "You look just like your mother."

"That must bring back good memories for you," I drawled.

His head rose, eyes flashing dangerously, as Adven chuckled darkly. Cirdan looked to the floor, his lips turning up at the corners.

Taking a slow breath through his nostrils, Jandar clasped the arms of his chair, pushing himself to his feet. "I hope you've found your stay here comfortable." His eyes shone with amusement as he looked down at me.

I clasped my hands together in front of me. "Perfect, thank you. My room could do with a few home furnishings, though. Some flowers, a bed, maybe a *window*... but otherwise, lovely."

Cirdan was trying very hard to contain his laughter—whether at my expense or his father's, I didn't know—but Jandar wasn't taking my sarcasm well. He was a blur as he came down the few steps to appear in front of me, bending at the waist slightly to lean over.

"Your mother would never have dared to speak with such insolence." He spat the words in my face.

"I think, *Your Majesty*, that you clearly didn't know my mother very well."

My head snapped to the side. I tasted blood as I threw my hands out to prevent my fall; the impact of my knees on the hard stone made me wince. I looked up, winded, my cheek stinging from the punishing backhand.

"Perhaps not... I must admit I never expected her to run off with your *mortal* father." His lips stretched into a vile grin. "But he's gone too, isn't he? And you're all alone."

"Fuck you!" I bared my teeth at him, feeling the sharp tips of fangs against my lower lip.

Jandar scoffed. "There's the better half of you showing her face. I know they want your death—"

"Who?"

"—but it would be a waste, Eliana. It would be so easy for you to join us."

They. There was something bigger going on. Others who were involved.

Jandar smiled. "Take your place by my son's side. I know you have grown up with the delusion that all life in Ruvalon was created equal. This is a falsehood. If you just open your eyes, you'll realise the world wasn't created that way—"

I spat at his feet. "Yes, it was. But some decided they were better than everyone else."

He sneered. "Maybe you'll understand if you come to rule over your real people."

"Human, elves or fairie folk, it doesn't matter. They are not all mine to rule, but they are *all* my people."

"Admirable," he said dryly. "But I wonder, who will you really choose when it comes down to it?"

"What?"

"You are free to go. If, and *only* if, you pledge your hand to my son Cirdan and return to Meridium with him as your king."

My eyes widened. I looked between the pair, then laughed. "Do you truly believe I would allow your poison into my kingdom?"

"Well, it's either that, or you can spend the rest of your days in the dungeon—however long that will be—whilst I deal with Meridium myself."

"Why don't you just kill me?" I asked.

He grinned, a perfect black brow lifting as if the answer was obvious.

And it was. I was the last heir to the house of Orinan. The only elf who could raise the sword of Orian and unite the elves under one banner. He wanted that house under his control.

"How are you so cruel that you would forsake *all* other races just to ensure the welfare of the elves?!"

He didn't answer my question directly. "I will do very questionable things to ensure the prosperity of my people, yes. Of *your* people. Humans aside."

"Is that a threat?"

"I don't need threats, dear girl."

He indicated for the guards to open the door. I looked over my shoulder as the double doors opened; the two guards wore identical masks of fear. My back stiffened, fear crawling its way through my entire body. A shocked whisper left me.

"*No.*"

The atmosphere in the room guttered, as if someone had sucked out every bit of air left. An unnatural darkness fell over the room, shrouding the being that entered. Its steps were almost silent as it stalked in.

If an onlooker didn't know better, they would assume it was a human beneath the light grey armour, so light it almost appeared white. But my previous experiences had taught me that there was nothing but evil there. Evil and corrupt magick, shoved inside the dying body of a poor mortal. Its aura was non-existent, revealing there was no soul.

The Hollow.

"It *has* been you all along," I whispered.

I had thought Cirdan's words a lie to get my attention. But it was true. It was *Jandar* who had summoned the creature; the jealous, jilted, violent instigator of the Tain had ordered the recent attacks throughout Ruvalon. The monster whose actions had taken my grandparents, my mother, brother, and now my father from me. Anger boiled within me, overriding my terror.

The steps of the creature we had named after the Hollow energy that resided within it stuttered. Surprise washed through me. Was it looking at me? I felt a pulse of *something,* like raw energy, as its helmet turned from me to Jandar, its steel-covered hands shaking. A hissing sound escaped it, impatient and furious.

I felt cold. How had Jandar achieved this?

Jandar rolled his eyes at the creature, and I bared my teeth at him. "So, what? Your plan was to destroy *everything* in Ruvalon? Decimate the towns and people and then return for the scraps?!"

"Well, it wasn't my initial plan. Your draconi lover made sure of that."

I flinched, looking at him in confusion.

"Don't be so naïve, girl. Why do you think we had this creature attack villages in the north first?"

I put the pieces together. My voice was barely a whisper. "You were trying to frame Tenebris."

He grinned.

"You were trying to instigate a war between Meridium and Tenebris. Dracho's presence ruined that plan, so you murdered his father. Then *mine*!"

He hummed. "Well, whilst *your* father wasn't *my* idea"—my eyes flicked to Cirdan, who stood watching, but not confirming—"I can't say it hasn't been without its benefits."

"You fucking prick!"

I gasped and had to catch myself again, this time the other cheek stinging from the impact of Jandar's hand. I heard a creak of the Hollow's armour from behind me but when I snapped my gaze to it in fear, it hadn't moved.

Jandar admired the blue-gemmed ring that adorned his finger. "You are starting to bore me, and that is very dangerous. As I was saying, I now have the future Queen of Meridium in my hands. Be wise, Eliana, unlike your mother. Join our family, and we can unite all elven kind, returning them to their rightful home in Ruvalon."

He was insane. They all were.

"If you don't... well, are you still a queen if your kingdom is in ruins? If there is no one to rule over but corpses? It doesn't matter. It will happen either way." He exhaled lazily. "So, what will it be, girl?"

I hissed at him, baring my teeth. "*Fuck* you! You might as well kill me. I'll never cower or kneel to a king whose rule only continues because of every life he has ever spent!"

Jandar grinned, as if I had given him the answer he was waiting for.

"So be it. You." He nodded at the Hollow, who showed no reaction. "There's a small village called Coed. It lies between Meridium and Asaph."

My whole body started to tremble. Aunt Lys lived in Asaph; she knew Coed well, as it was within her territory. There was an orphanage there for children who had lost parents during the war. Meridium funded it, making sure those children grew up wanting for nothing. For the sacrifice their parents had given for the city.

Jandar somehow knew this.

"*That* is your next target."

The creature didn't speak, but turned to walk out the door.

"No!" I shouted at it.

How was it that this being, created from an ancient and corrupt magick, took orders from a weak king so easily? I wanted to scream at it, tell it to turn its attention on those who were trying to master it. Even to turn its attention to me. Anything to prevent it from harming Coed.

To my surprise, it halted. It turned, its head tilting in my direction.

Even though I couldn't see its face underneath the helmet, I still pleaded with whatever it was. "Please. Please, you can't."

"What do you think you're doing? Go," Jandar commanded it irritably.

The creature only hesitated for a moment, its head still facing in my direction, before it turned, leaving the room.

"You're a fucking monster!" I screamed at Jandar.

His fingernails dug into my cheeks as he suddenly knelt before me, squeezing my face in his grip. "You have no idea." His white teeth flashed in a wide, eerie smile.

For a moment, I understood why my mother had escaped him. Praised the Goddess that she had.

His voice lowered, full of disturbing promise. "But you will. I was hoping to be done with this business sooner rather than later. Oh well; it won't take long to deal with you. Guards, return *Her Highness* to her room."

The guards came swaggering in, confidence returned after the Hollow had left. They dragged me up off the floor.

"We will break that spirit of yours. Once we do, you will marry Cirdan, and finally Ruvalon will be ours." Jandar turned his back on me as he walked back up to his throne.

The last thing I saw as the guards dragged me backwards out of the room was Cirdan's triumphant smile.

Chapter 33

Dracho

Two weeks had passed since we'd left that dreary manor. Two weeks since I had left her, and I regretted every single moment not in her presence. I had been restless ever since, my wings dying to burst out and return me to her. Even just to scold her stubborn arse.

In the end I asked Althea to return, while Ant and I went on to the temple. I just wanted her to check on her. For a moment. Ever since I'd left, a sickening feeling had overcome me, one I couldn't shake. But I wasn't sure if I was just being paranoid, and—not wanting to show up empty-handed—I vowed to explore the temple before returning to her.

Antares and I had continued alone, but the dry, suffocating sands of the Vildspire weren't harsh enough to rid my thoughts of her. The harrowing magick left on the cursed land bore down upon me, making my own emotions worse.

We found the temple of the Hollow towards the coastline: a place of worship carved out of a huge formation of rocks, the very energy surrounding it causing my skin to tingle. Ant and I transformed several feet from the entrance, and I used my newer magickal ability to dress us instantly with a click of my fingers. Ant pulled a sack over his shoulder, keeping his dagger tightly in his grip.

The atmosphere was heavy, reminding me of the time I'd spent in Volente when Roux had gained her extra magick. I'd warned Ant about the way the angry spirits trapped in the Vildspire could have an adverse effect on your mood. And that was putting it lightly.

A figure appeared from the temple: a slimly built male, his white robe hanging loosely on his frame and tied around his waist with a simple rope. His skin was tanned from spending so much time in the desert, the contours of his face sharp. His green-blue eyes shone as we approached him cautiously, his smile unnerving in an environment that didn't really feel positive.

"Greetings," he called softly. "My name is Hale. It has been many years since we received a visitor. Are you believers?"

"Uh—" I looked at Antares, who nodded. "Yes! My name is Dracho; my friend is Antares."

The man clapped his hands together. "Fantastic news!" He seemed genuinely excited. "Come, come. I shall show you to it."

I exchanged a quick glance with Ant before we followed Hale out of the sandy, biting wind and through the sandstone building. The space expanded massively as we entered the mountain, but there was no decor, no personality, save for the lit braziers that lined the centre of the large hall. The floor was covered in a layer of coarse sand; Hale walked over it barefoot.

The further we walked, the more worshippers we saw. People emerged from carved holes in the walls, muttering and chattering excitedly at our presence. We walked until the hall started to narrow, where we came to a long staircase that led down to a pit in a darkened cavern.

My feet carried me down the stairs almost before I knew it, for the pit at the bottom was not dark. It was full of light.

A brilliant orb of equally swirling light and darkness hovered before us in mid-air over the centre of the pit, dwarfing us. It was so beautiful it was difficult not to reach out and touch it. I stopped quite a way from it, unsure whether it was good or evil.

"This is it?" Antares asked, awe in his voice as he came to stand beside me.

"The Hollow," Hale replied with a nod. "It has been here since the beginning. It is neither life nor death. It just is."

"Does it *do* anything?" I asked in concern, feeling like the aura surrounding it was alive. As if it were considering us as much as we were considering it.

Hale shook his head. "It's not sentient. It's just energy."

In my experience, energy could be sentient. Like the magick that ran through my veins.

"Has anyone ever used its energy? Created something bad from it?" Antares asked.

Hale's face fell, realising what we were here for. "How do you know about that?"

"Did you allow them to create that monster?" I growled, taking a step closer and feeling my magick slither underneath my skin.

Hale held his hands up. "We do not speak of it. They came and killed many who lived here. Many tried to stop them from turning that poor, dying soul into... into something else. I warned them not to use such corrupt magick here. But *they did not listen!*"

"Why didn't you warn anyone? King Cervidae?" I asked.

"We have taken a vow of seclusion here. We do not leave—have no method of sending letters. And why would he believe me? The mage who performed the ritual told us it was simply an experiment. That he was going to destroy the creature."

"Well, he lied."

Hale's face crumpled. "I am so sorry. The Hollow here is not evil. That mage abused his magick to manipulate it. W-we had no power to stop them, or to follow them. Not after what they had done."

"What did the mage look like?" I asked him, fearing I already knew the answer.

"He had cold eyes. His skin was dark, and he had scars littering his head."

Ant's voice brushed against my mind. *Kanu.*

Heavy guilt settled in my stomach. I hadn't sensed any corrupt magick or trace of the Hollow when I had come across Kanu in Stillmere. He was creepy, and had been following Eliana around Ruvalon, but he hadn't shown any evidence of evildoing. In my unease and hurry to get Eliana away from him, I had failed us all.

"Do you know how we can stop it?" I asked in desperation.

Hale's eyes turned glassy. "If they have used this creature for evil, I cannot think of anything to stop it. I have never seen anything like it in all my years—have never seen magick used in such a way. Perhaps pure magick is the answer."

Roux. In her altercation with the ancestors in Volente, she had promised to help restore the balance. It was why they had given her more power. Whatever her role was in this, it was an important one... but she wasn't strong enough right now. I wouldn't risk her life so soon.

Perhaps we have a chance, Ant whispered against my mind.

My exhalation was shaky. Where did we go from here?

"Hale," Ant said suddenly. "You said *they*. Who was with the mage?"

I held my breath as Hale's brows met. "The two who slaughtered my brothers and sisters... they looked so alike, their long black hair like shadows as they rolled though the people who stood against them. As if they hated nothing more than the mortals who live here."

"Why do you think they hated mortals?" Ant asked, a sliver of urgency in his tone.

Hale sighed, the sound full of remembered pain. "Because they were elven."

I met Ant's gaze, and some thread pulled taut.

Eliana.

I didn't care what game Eliana and I were playing, skirting around each other and speaking only through our anger. I would always want her safe—even if that meant being as far away from me as possible. And I would always go out of my way to protect her, even if that meant destroying an elven prince.

With the knowledge that it was likely Cirdan and his father, King Morven, who had—with Kanu's help—created the being of the Hollow, we left in a hurry, intent on getting some backup before we returned to Akraya. So first—Tenebris.

My uncle and Boone were astonished to see me land on the palace balcony.

"What do you know?" Uncle Thuban demanded as soon as I transformed, his dark eyes wary as I dressed us.

"I need five of the best from the guards, now," I announced, strolling past him. Boone bowed as I swept through the throne room.

"What? Why?" Thuban asked. "Dracho, wait!"

I exhaled impatiently and came to a stop, nodding to Ant, who left to gather my guards.

"Eliana is in trouble," I told Thuban and Boone.

"The *princess*? I don't understand. I thought you left to accuse her father of your father's assassination?"

"Her father was innocent—"

Thuban scoffed. "Her father's pin was found on Eltanin's body."

I bared my teeth in anger. "I remember! But King Cervidae is dead. This goes much deeper than we all thought."

A silence rang out. Boone's eyes travelled over my face, and he frowned. Thuban remained still, no discernible emotion on his face.

I hadn't expected any sorrow from the man, even though a good man had been murdered, but saying it aloud hurt. A man who had welcomed me into his city, and palace, without truly knowing who I was, had died. A man who had offered his help once he had found out about my father, as if it had affected him personally. Seeing Eliana deal with his loss had reminded me of my own father's death, and Uncle Thuban's stoicism stung. Perhaps King Cervidae's death had upset me more than I'd realised.

"I don't have time to waste, Uncle. I promise to tell you everything upon my return." I turned to leave again.

"Where are you going?" he called after me.

Once again, my steps faltered. "We met with Prince Cirdan."

"Morven?" Thuban asked, eyes wide.

I ignored him. "Before I could discover what he really wanted, I left... and I left Eliana with him. Ant and I went to the temple of the Hollow. It's Jandar Morven. It's been him all along."

"How do you know?" Boone asked, taking a step towards me.

"We met with someone at the temple—a worshipper. He was there when the creature was made. There were two elves, and they sound like Jandar and Cirdan."

Thuban started, "But we don't know that for sure—"

"I will not risk leaving her in the hands of those behind our fathers' deaths!"

Thuban's jaw clenched. "So you will put *yourself* at risk for that woman?" he asked, his tone low.

My magick thrummed under my skin, roiling and warming. My eyes flashed silver, a pull in my chest tugging me towards an unknown path.

"I will risk *everything* for that woman," I hissed, that deep, possessive nature roaring in my ears as my fangs lengthened.

Thuban's eyes widened, his head jerking back. "You are blinded, nephew. You will doom us all."

I turned my back to them, my footsteps quiet as I headed towards the exit. "Perhaps. But not before I've torn Morven's kingdom to shreds."

Chapter 34

Dracho

After obtaining five of my best soldiers—two draconi, three mortal—we returned to Meridium, which went into meltdown as four dragons approached the palace. A full military unit had rushed to protect the steps that ascended the front of the palace doors by the time we landed in the courtyard. My respect for Connaught grew; his soldiers were well-trained and brave enough to face down dragons for their city.

Connaught stood before them, his sword drawn, demanding to know where Eliana was, but I remained in my dragon form. Sizwe rushed down the steps, full of concern, and I explained everything to her with a heavy heart.

She translated for Connaught, who was beside himself with worry for Eliana's safety, and insisted that we take him with us. At first I was going to refuse, but I could see that there was no swaying the captain from his decision—and if a fight with Cirdan's men was inevitable, his presence would be invaluable.

Our final stop was Aion. If Roux's magick could give us an edge, I wanted her by my side. The Aioni were taken aback but not scared as the four of us landed on their beach, Connaught on my back.

Bisa rushed across the sands to greet us; as with Sizwe, I used my magick to communicate, not wanting to waste time transforming. *Jandar Morven is behind the Hollow.*

"What?! Are you sure?" Bisa asked in alarm.

I gruffed in confirmation. *I... I left Eliana with Cirdan.*

A sharp inhalation was her only response.

Roux joined us. From her determined expression, she could tell there was trouble.

"Where are we going?" she asked, and my heart twinged in gratitude for my friend. My friend, who was always there, no questions asked.

They have Eliana.

"We'll get her back," she said fiercely, kissing her mother's cheek before rushing to my side. I lowered a wing, allowing her to climb up and situate herself behind Connaught.

"Bring her home, Dracho," Bisa commanded, her hand shading her eyes as she looked up.

I nodded and took to the skies.

With the wind on our side and how quick we flew, it only took a few hours for that small island to come into view, but before we reached it, a form became visible in the afternoon sky. A flying vision in lavender.

I could see the confusion on Althea's draconi face as she neared, before turning and flying in the same direction. *Why are the others here? Jeshwa, Skaze, Tosen... what have you found?*

Everything points to Jandar creating the Hollow, I told her. *Where is Eliana?*

Althea's silence was deafening, causing a rising, conflicting tide of fury and fear. I snarled, *What, Althea?*

She's gone.

I heard Roux's gasp as I dropped slightly in mid-air, my head snapping in Althea's direction.

We'll find her, brother, Ant said, his tone concerned.

One of my worst fears had come true. And it was all my fault. Fury raged through my veins, fuelling a fire I had not realised existed there.

Althea flew straight, her gaze avoiding mine. *Dracho, there was no one there. But...*

But what?

Althea's nostrils flared. *There were signs of a struggle... and blood.*

My heart raced; a feral snarl escaped my throat. Roux squealed in frightened surprise, and Althea winced mid-flight. I met her terrified eyes.

"What is it?" Connaught demanded loudly. Roux started to update him.

Tell me everything you found, Althea. Now.

Perhaps we could wait until we arrive—

Please.

It belonged to Bas, Althea blurted out. *And...*

And?

In Cirdan's study... there were some drops of Eliana's.

My claws curled in on themselves, that sick feeling in my gut increasing and threatening to climb out through my throat. *What about Vyn?*

She shook her head. *No sign of him either. Looks like they put up a fight, whatever happened. The place was a mess.*

We never should have left, I whispered.

It's not your fault, Dracho.

We'll find them, Ant chimed in. Turning, I noted a muscle twitching in Ant's jaw, and I guessed he needed to find them as much as I did.

Althea's blue eyes were scanning my face. *Wherever you go, I will follow,* she said.

I tipped my head to her in thanks.

I *would* find her, one way or another. My nostrils flared as I inhaled deeply, allowing that deep thrum of power to spread, like darkness slithering through my veins. I could almost hear the beast I'd once shared my consciousness with, before my merging. That awareness of power and magick filled my entire body until a hazy shadow seemed to form over my vision, and I vowed to rip out the throat of anyone who had caused her harm.

Chapter 35

Eliana

My mind was always the loudest when my surroundings were silent.

Beside the blinding torches that announced the morsels of leftover meals dumped before me, no glimmer of light offered me the comfort of using my sight; all that surrounded me and my mind was darkness. All I had left was the endless journey of my thoughts.

I had no grasp on the passage of time since my imprisonment. Days or weeks, it didn't matter. In the darkness they blurred into one another. In the first couple of days after seeing Jandar, I'd scraped my fingers raw, scouring every inch of the small cell for anything I could use as a weapon. Any loose stone I could find along the rough walls.

But there was nothing, and I was never able to get more than a few punches in against the lupera guards. The punishments were severe—my ribs were still tender and bruised from the most recent beating. After attacking the last guard who'd brought my food, he had poured the small bowl of hot soup over me on purpose, laughing as I screamed and ripped the breeches from my body. After I'd tried to attack him in retaliation, he and two other guards shackled me to the two steel rings that protruded from the wall, the length of chain attached only granting me a little movement to use the bucket beside me. To add to my humiliation, my breeches remained in the corner of the cell, out of my reach. It was demeaning and left me feeling too vulnerable, sitting on the filthy floor practically naked, even if my shirt covered most of my modesty.

The voices of my mother and Morgwn sounded in my head. *You will not break.*

I was fighting as well as I could. But it wasn't enough.

I knew something was different when boots stomped down the hallway outside. Not enough time had passed since my last meal for it to be another one. A light flickered from the tiny gap underneath the cell door as two guards whispered to each other.

A blinding light forced my eyes shut as the guard pushed open the door, holding his flaming torch high and carrying the usual tray of food.

"Well, well." His voice was grating. He moved closer, placing the torch in the wall bracket with a scraping sound. "These must be different accommodations to what you're used to, hmm?"

Squinting through the light, I recognised Erix—the wolf. My shoulders rose in a half shrug. "I don't know. I've had worse."

He chuckled darkly. "Still some balls left. Impressive."

"Well, one of us has to have them. Actually, no. Balls are weak—you can keep yours." I laughed.

A snort sounded from outside my cell. Erix gave me a tight smile, kneeling in front of me. His muddy brown eyes travelled over my bare legs, causing my back to stiffen.

His smile was a vicious, twisted thing, all manners of perversions and violence present in his ugly gaze. He glanced back at the second guard, standing out of view in the hallway.

"You know…" he started, leaning forward to whisper into my ear.

My heart pounded at the opportunity. It wasn't wise, but I would show them that the fight wasn't out of me yet.

"…I don't see why Cirdan gets to keep you all to himself."

His voice sent a shiver across the skin of my neck, and not a pleasant one. But I turned my head slightly in his direction, as if listening intently. *Just a little closer.*

His head tipped forward an inch, the stubble of his cheek rubbing against mine. "I think I could have a taste, and he would never—"

Now!

Wrenching forward in my shackles—a burning tightness erupting between my shoulder blades—I clamped my teeth down on his ear.

Oh, how I basked in his howl of pain! The taste of iron slipped over my tongue as I ripped into his flesh, tearing it as he yanked away. I spat out skin and sinew as he backed up against the opposite wall, his hand covering the bloody remains of his ear.

"You fucking bitch!" he spat through gritted teeth. I smiled, feeling his blood run down my chin. "That's gonna be a prick to heal!"

My smile faded.

His tone was angry, but he laughed. "Didn't realise we wolves healed, did you? Stupid little girl."

I spat out more blood. "Worth it."

"Was it?" His eyes promised death, but I knew he wouldn't kill me. He'd face the wrath of both Cirdan and Jandar if he did.

He got to his feet, moving deliberately back over to me and kneeling again. A rough hand reached out, running a calloused finger over the thick scar of my right leg. I tried to kick out, to remove his touch.

"Interesting. What a pretty scar."

"Fuck you!" I screeched at him.

"Been around lupera before, have you?"

"What?" In spite of myself, I stopped moving. "No."

He laughed. "It's rare for your kind to scar. Your elven gifts usually heal you quickly. If you weren't scratched by a lupera, then whoever did this must have done so with a lupera blade."

I couldn't comprehend what he was saying. Frozen, I watched a long, black claw burst from the tip of his finger, sharp enough to shred skin and slice bone. My mind drifted back, back to a time when a young girl could never have hoped to fight off a grown man.

A grown man with a black clawed blade.

"I think you deserve a matching set," Erix growled.

Flesh tore. Pain surged through every nerve-ending until all I could feel was the searing misery in my leg. The scent of iron and salt reached my nose as my head rocked back, hitting the wall with a thud. Through the unbearable pain, I couldn't hear my own scream, but my throat burned with it.

The pain was still agonising, down to my very bones, but it lifted enough for me to move and glance down. My heart stopped. The once-smooth skin of my unmarked thigh was covered in crimson blood. Amongst the red was a gash, so ugly and vicious looking that I had to tear my gaze away.

My teeth clenched as the guard smirked, never taking his eyes away from my face. From my pain.

Steps hurried in from the doorway.

"What are you doing, Erix?!" the young guard shouted, his eyes darting between my leg and the claw that still protruded from Erix's finger.

He scoffed. "Keep out of it, Mal."

"Cirdan will kill you!"

"Cirdan told us not to mark up her pretty face. It will practically be healed by the time he sees it. He'll be fine."

"You cut too deep! What if she dies?" The young male was panicking.

"She won't die, you fucking idiot. She may only be a half-breed, but she has their gift of healing. She'll just have a pretty scar to match the other. Now shut your mouth before I give you one."

My head started to swim, my eyes unfocused.

Erix huffed. "Or maybe she dies. Like I give a shit."

Black edged the corners of my vision as he got to his feet to leave.

The sound of my cell door opening shocked me awake. I winced as I tried to move back—I'd forgotten my new wound. I tried to assess the damage in the dark before the flame of a new torch made me squeeze them shut. *Goddess, what if Erix is back?*

Someone tutted. "Trust you, Erix." The voice got closer as he knelt before me. "I warned you about things like this. Always quick to temper."

I rested my head back against the wall. "What do you want, Cirdan?"

"I thought I'd pop in. See how you were doing." I heard him suck a breath through his lips as he examined my thigh.

"Not so good, by the look of it," Erix muttered.

I opened my eyes. He was by the door, his face perfectly clean.

"What's that? I can't hear you!" I laughed hysterically as rage filled Erix's face, his hand drifting towards the healing stump where his ear had been. Why hadn't Cirdan punished him like he had the other guard?

Cirdan studied my face. My vision was still swimming. Dizzy from the blood loss.

"You're delirious," Cirdan muttered. Fury in his eyes, he glanced back at Erix, who slunk out of the room with the first hint of fear in his expression I'd seen.

My head fell onto my shoulder. "Do me a favour. Will you hit him with your knife?" With tremendous effort, I nodded towards the dagger at Cirdan's side.

Cirdan smiled. "I believe the correct term is *stab.*"

"That's it." I laughed again, the dizziness worsening. Memories floated to the surface. "Did *you* send them?"

Cirdan's brow furrowed in confusion.

"No. Too young. Mus've been your father," I slurred.

He watched as my eyes drifted to the healed skin of my thigh, and his lips thinned. "A rash decision, I'm afraid. Knowing your parents and brother had run off to fight in the war, my father paid some mercenaries to assassinate you. No one knew the lupera still lived, so he was convinced they would be successful. We always wondered why they weren't."

I grinned sleepily. "Lucky, I guess."

"It was my idea, you know. To join us in marriage. Father had no qualms about killing you until I offered an alternative."

"Well, you have my gratitude." I mustered every ounce of sarcasm for my reply, thinking it would have made Vyn proud. It hurt to think of him, and I realised I was starting to believe that he was dead. Had been tortured and beaten and murdered, along with Bas.

"Eliana, be smart. All this can be over right now, if you just accept. I can have you moved immediately into your suite. You can bathe and have your leg treated—"

It was getting harder to talk. "I would rather throw myself... from the highest rise in Meridium... than subject my people to you or your vile father."

It was a lie. I was extremely tempted by the thought of being seen by a healer, by the idea of a warm bath.

"Could you stop being so stubborn for one moment?" Cirdan growled.

"Hmmm. Sorry. Not possible."

He growled under his breath as he stood in one swift motion. "Fine. It seems more time alone is needed."

He turned, his cloak sweeping across the floor, but paused in the doorway by Erix. "Reduce her meals." He glanced at me once more before walking out.

I swallowed hard, determined not to grimace until the door had closed on Erix's satisfied smile. Panic lanced through me. If Erix hadn't been punished for this, what else could he or others do to me without incurring Cirdan's wrath?

Once more, I allowed myself to succumb to the blackness.

Chapter 36

Soft fingertips brushed against my leg. I shot awake in a panic.

"It's all right."

I opened my eyes. I knew that voice. My vision adjusted as his fingers continued to move my leg gently, burgundy eyes studying the gash there. It was the young guard from before—the one who had scolded Erix.

My eyes narrowed as exhausted curiosity eroded the fear. *Is this some kind of trick?*

His bright eyes reached mine. "It's all right," he repeated with a small smile. He reached behind him to a small bowl I hadn't noticed until now. "My name is Malzan. I'll do my best, but I'm afraid I'm no healer."

I didn't speak or react, watching through wary eyes. He exhaled deeply, brushing his short maroon hair out of his eyes as if steeling himself. Dipping a bit of clean cloth into the bowl, he brought it towards my leg, pushing my shirt further up my thigh.

I didn't have it in me to feel conscious about my appearance—didn't care that his eyes skipped to the healed scar upon my good leg. His cheeks flushed as his eyes avoided mine; had I been more lucid, I probably would have felt grateful for his care, or taken his embarrassment as an indication I was safe with him.

I *did* feel safe, oddly. Perhaps it was because he had tried to stop Erix... or perhaps that I was that far gone. Any small amount of kindness could now trick me into a false sense of security.

"Are you a wolf?" I asked, fear causing me to become more alert at the thought—no matter how gentle he was being.

He nodded with a tight smile.

My leg throbbed, and a hiss pushed its way between my teeth as he placed the cloth to the skin around the new wound.

"Sorry," he said, and it sounded genuine.

The pain subsided a little, my breath coming out in a sigh as the coolness of the water eased some of the soreness of my flesh.

"I'm so sorry," he repeated in a whisper, his brow pinched. "If I could, I would stitch it for you. Help you heal faster. But I'd likely do more harm than good."

"They'd... they'd question who helped me," I wheezed.

"That too."

"Why?" My voice was hoarse. My tongue dipped out to try and moisten my cracked lips.

Confusion lined his face as he looked up at me.

"Why didn't Cirdan punish him?"

Malzan exhaled roughly. "Erix is an alpha of one of the packs. The biggest pack. Cirdan would lose a lot of support from the wolves if he killed him. Erix leads with fear, but it's a strategy that has kept everyone in line. Meaning more soldiers for Cirdan's army."

"Army?"

Malzan nodded. "Cirdan and Jandar have been building a force to take over Ruvalon. Several packs of the lupera are part of it."

"Then why are you helping me?"

His eyes widened slightly. "Because... you don't deserve any of this. No one would deserve *this*."

My head sagged back against the wall, relief relaxing my shoulders. I thanked the Goddess that not everyone here despised me. Maybe I was already broken, if I was feeling grateful that one of my captors had a shred of compassion. But his gentle hands continued to clean my leg, and I allowed my eyes to close.

A pair of blue eyes flashed behind my eyelids; my chest tightened. My thoughts drifted to Vyn and Bas. Had they suffered a similar torture before Adven killed them? My wound hadn't killed me because of my elven heritage... Bas and Vyn had no such luck. A small sob broke out before I could prevent it, and I bit down on my lip to stop any more.

Malzen's hand paused. "Don't worry, Your Majesty—"

"Don't call me that," I hissed. My title and name had got me into this trouble in the first place. My suffering was due to the mistakes of those before me. All I wanted was to slip back to a time spent in the middle of a crystal forest... when I was just Eli.

"Sorry... Eliana. You won't be here forever."

I didn't know whether to feel grateful for that.

When my eyes opened again, I was alone, save for a shimmer in the corner that pulled my gaze: a small splattering of light that looked like shining stars. Pulling forward, I cried out at the pain that lanced through my leg. My neck ached from the position I'd slept in, burning as I stretched it out before squinting in the darkness to look closer. The shimmer grew before my very eyes, the edges of the growing form blurry. I leaned back, pressing into the wall as much as possible.

I struggled to make sense of what I was seeing, shock and horror parting my lips as the form stepped forward. A soft smile full of sadness rested on her beautiful face. She waited for me to speak.

"Mammy?" I whispered.

Her eyes crinkled as she smiled wider. She nodded.

"H-how are you here?"

Her hand came up to rest over her heart, as if to say, *Love*. I nodded, suppressing my sobs, looking to the ground.

You must fight, little doe.

My gasp sounded harsh in the silence of my cell, my eyes capturing hers immediately as her words sounded in my mind. I didn't understand how I could recall her voice so perfectly. Her intonation, her softness... it was too perfect.

I studied her features and, though the colour was dimmed, her beautiful blue eyes stared back at me. I took her in hungrily, ashamed that I had forgotten the finer details of her face.

She seemed to read the emotions that filled me. *I have missed you... so much.*

My fingers stretched out, as if I could reach out towards her despite my irons. "I've missed you, Mammy. You and Morgwn."

Her smile fell, utter devastation written within her face.

"I don't have much fight left in me, Mammy," I whispered, looking away from her. A shameful confession.

She took a step towards me, kneeling before me as the men had. Her long-sleeved white shirt moved unnaturally, as if carried on some breeze that didn't exist in the dark cell. It was tucked into a pair of brown breeches and her feet were bare, which brought a smile to my face. This creation in front of me, clearly formed from the blood loss I had sustained, was so accurate. I had so many memories of my mother walking barefoot through the palace gardens.

My body felt boneless. Exhaustion weighed on my eyelids. It took such effort to keep them open—to keep looking at my mother's form.

You must fight, Eliana.

"I-I will try." My lids drifted, burning with the effort of avoiding sleep. I caught my mother's smile as her hand reached forward, as if to tuck my hair behind my ear. Madness must have taken hold of me, because I could have sworn I felt the ghost of her fingers brush against my skin.

I must go. Remember, take it with you; it's more important than you know.

"T-take what, Mammy? I don't understand."

Take it with you. My little doe, you do not break. Her voice grew quieter; she started to dim in the darkness.

"Mammy don't go! Please." The words were weak but desperate, urging my brain to keep its hallucination intact so I could gaze upon her face for longer. But my exhaustion was too strong, and she continued to dim, her words only an indiscernible whisper.

Alone, I sobbed into the darkness.

Chapter 37

Dracho

I vowed to never stop hunting for her.

The only sound I could hear was the thundering of my own feet as I paced back and forth in the great hall where we had first met Cirdan. Even thoughts of his name caused a well of rage to boil within me, threatening to bubble over and scald anyone who dared provoke my wrath.

A week had passed since I had learned of her disappearance. No trace had been found.

I would tear it *all* apart until I found her. I would destroy all Cirdan cared about. Even if she was alive, my gut told me over and over that she was in trouble.

I only had myself to blame. Had I never left, Cirdan wouldn't have dared to touch a hair on her glorious head. Not whilst the threat of dragons remained in his home.

Roux strolled over, placing a warm hand upon my arm, halting my pacing. "We'll find her, Dracho."

I swallowed hard, not wanting to voice my fears but unable to stop them. "What if we don't?" My voice broke.

Roux's slender arms came to wrap around my waist; she laid her head on my chest. "Don't think like that. We *will* find her."

I embraced her in return and brushed a kiss on the top of her head, my chest tight with anxiousness, as if it was trying to extinguish any hope I felt within.

Loud, hurried steps came from outside the double doors. Jeshwa burst through them. "Your Excellency!"

We turned to him eagerly; he jogged towards us, face flushed, holding a piece of parchment out.

"We received this!"

Taking the crumpled paper, I opened it, reading the words quicker than any mortal could.

To friends of the princess: she doesn't have much time. You'll find her on the smallest island east of Akraya. I will leave the way open for you. Hurry.

"Who delivered this?" I asked, my voice desperate.

"He wouldn't give a name, sire. Only said that Eliana had friends on the island she has been taken to, and he was acting on their behalf. He says the information comes from someone within Cirdan's circle. And, when the time comes, he'll let us into the castle."

"Did you detain him?" I asked, my magick swirling at the thought of having someone to interrogate over her disappearance.

"Antares let him go," Jeshwa replied.

What?! "Why?" I asked, my tone dangerous.

"The messenger came from Cirdan's location, Your Excellency. He was putting himself at risk. Antares believed if we kept him here, Cirdan would become suspicious."

That makes sense. I cursed myself internally for doubting Ant's strategic prowess, even for a second.

"Very well. Round up the men immediately," I told him.

"Dracho, what if it's a trap?" Roux asked.

"Then we'll burn them all."

Chapter 38

Eliana

It had been several hours since my last beating. The guards had grown braver and braver since Erix had taken his claw to my leg, and had got away with it. I was pretty sure I had a broken rib from their kicks, and it seemed Cirdan's order to keep my face clean had been rescinded—the tender apple of my cheek attested to that. Apparently spitting in a guard's face was frowned upon.

Still, I was constantly relieved that it was neither Cirdan nor Erix who visited my cell. I could no longer feel the chafing of the shackles, though my wrists were raw, the skin blistered.

I am so tired.

The gloom and stench that surrounded me, in these walls created by pure hatred, threatened to drown me. I knew Jandar was here, had heard the guards whispering in the hallway. But days and nights bled together so that all I knew now was the darkness that surrounded me and the plague of nightmares that visited me with each sleep.

I was just so tired.

That was what Cirdan wanted. To wear me down until I finally gave him what he wanted.

I thought I was stronger than this.

My physical maladies weren't so troubling—it was the prison of my mind I'd been left in. The torture that came from my own thoughts. I drifted off sometimes, into sweeter memories. Quiet afternoons in the library with Vyn. Breakfasts in the palace kitchen with Bas, laughing as he ate too quickly and was reprimanded by Marie. Training with Connaught.

Are Vyn and Bas alive?

I wondered if Roux was still with her mother in Aion. I pondered how quickly I had grown close to Althea, feeling as if I had met a soul sister. I thought of Antares, and his eyes that could look right through you. I wondered if we could have been friends...

I thought of Dracho.

I thought of how his every smile and touch felt like it lit up something inside me. I thought of how he was *trying*... despite my stubbornness.

I still believed I couldn't trust him with my heart, but I should have trusted him with everything else. With keeping our kingdoms safe. I shouldn't have pushed him away. Then my friends wouldn't have been harmed, and I wouldn't have been captured. Did they even know that I was gone? People must be aware that I was missing by now.

Stop fighting, a voice that sounded like my own seemed to whisper in the dark.

My body would not perish, thanks to its elven gift of healing. But my mind was dying. My soul was breaking. I no longer had the energy to cry for what I was losing. To grieve for what I had already lost.

I don't want to be here anymore.

The loneliness became a vice on my heart, the pressure just enough to cause constant pain. With every new day spent in darkness, I lost some of my light, and I wasn't sure when I would run out. I just knew it would be soon.

Eliana. A low whisper floated across my mind, like the brush of gentle fingers.

I know that voice...

I had hallucinated it so many times while in this unending darkness that at first I didn't believe it was real—but the rumbling and terrible roar somewhere deep in the heart of the castle woke me fully from my restless slumber, and real hope flickered in my heart.

Then the screaming started.

The clash of steel was drowned out by a howling that came from no human. Another terrifying roar sounded from outside the castle, mixed with the yelp of hounds. It didn't sound like the fight was lasting long. My heart pounded against my rib cage, as if trying to burst out of my chest. I had no idea what was happening down the hallway, but the terrifying cries were getting closer.

Thundering boots sounded outside my cell. There was a final shout as a body crashed into the door, and then—silence.

Eliana, the same low voice whispered again.

No... *pleaded*.

My heart squeezed, pain and disbelief lancing through me. I prayed that the voice and shadow that appeared under the small gap of my door was death herself, instead of another hallucination. Coming to take away the pain and escort me to the Notherworld, where I could journey until I found my peace.

No peace came. Blinding light burst into the room from the doorway, where the door had been kicked off its hinges.

"Fuck." The voice broke on the word.

I pressed myself into the corner, the chains dragging against my skin. Footsteps hurried towards me, and panicked breaths rose into my throat, choking any sound that threatened to escape. Firm hands grasped my arms as my body finally gave in; a shaky cry left me. *There's no fight left in me.*

That was when I felt the shackles snap away from my wrists. The relief was so instant that I cried out. And I smelt it—citrus and smoke.

A charge ran through my veins, stimulating my mind and body as if waking me from the deepest nightmare. Calloused fingers tilted my chin up.

"Open your eyes, Princess."

Princess.

I shook my head, eyes squeezing tighter, not trusting the heartbreakingly tender but broken voice that I was hearing. *It isn't real. You're slipping away.* He was the last ghost to visit me before I left this plane, and a welcome one. The only one I wanted to see before the end. Before I was reunited with my family.

The grip tightened, holding my face firmly. "Open them, *now*."

It was a command, not a request, and the authority in his voice sent a jolt through me. *If this were my dream, he wouldn't be raising his voice at me.*

My crusty eyelids snapped open, my gaze meeting cool silver that shone despite the darkness of my cell. Nothing in that moment could have torn my gaze away as sobs started to wrack my aching body.

He looked at me like I was the answer to everything. But at that moment, he was mine.

"*Dracho.*" It slipped out on a soft breath.

It didn't feel real. Speaking his name again.

His hold was firm, but so careful, and I savoured it. If this turned out to be a dream or my death, I would be happy in the knowledge that I'd greedily accepted whatever this version of him would give me in the end. My eyes hungered for him—the black shirt tight across his muscled chest, his bare feet filthy, covered in mud and what I assumed was blood. He must have dressed quickly after transforming.

Brows lowered, he studied my face in the dark, nostrils flaring as he took in a deep breath. "What have they done?" he whispered, more to himself, as if something greater than his worst nightmare had torn at his heart, leaving him damaged.

I didn't answer. Because *he had come*. He was here to save me. *I'm alive.*

"You came." I winced at the hoarseness of my own voice, my cracked lips hurting as they moved around the words.

His face crumpled. "Of course I came."

"Why?" The question came out breathy. I was still trying to convince myself that this was a dream I needed to wake from. Because I had hurt him. I had said awful lies.

He huffed, taking a gentle hold of my face with his large hands and pressing his forehead to mine. His thumb brushed gently over my tender cheek. "I thought you would have realised by now. You can banish me from your side, hate me, strike me as much as you want—" His eyes flashed in the low light. "But there is *nothing* I wouldn't do, and no one in this world that would keep me from you, *mia estra*."

Someone spoke outside. I panicked, trying to hide, using Dracho as a shield. His expression revealed that he knew who approached, but he moved anyway, wanting to block me from the light of the doorway.

"We found them. How is she?" I heard a voice like smooth liquor ask.

Dracho looked at our new visitor. I leaned over, looking at the shape in the light. "Antares?"

Holding a flaming torch, he stood by the door in a loose shirt and breeches, his feet bare too. A rough exhalation parted his lips as he made his way forward. "Eliana. We've been—"

He froze as the light reached me, staring down as a threatening growl made its way out of his throat. Dracho followed his gaze, his eyes suddenly full of blazing silver fury, black pupils thin.

I had forgotten what state I was in. Left in only my long white shirt and underwear, the old scar on my thigh was quite visible… as was the new wound Erix had given me.

It was still healing, visible amongst the remaining blisters from the boiling soup that had burned me. Congealed blood covered the floor and me, despite Malzan's efforts to clean me.

Flinching at the rage in Dracho's eyes, I tried weakly to pull my shirt down. He caught my arm gently, his fangs elongating with his anger, but his gaze had softened.

"Names. Fuck that—it doesn't matter. Everyone in this stars-forsaken place will die for this." His voice wasn't his own, but that of some ancient, violent entity that promised death.

My shoulders bunched, I looked down, tears trickling down my cheeks.

"Dracho," Antares warned, his voice uncharacteristically soft.

"Did they…?" Dracho trailed off, his voice snagging on the words.

I shook my head. "I was to remain… *unspoiled*." Nausea rolled through me, the words like ash in my mouth. "For Cirdan." A relief, but not a consolation for what *had* been done to me.

His hands cupped my cheeks once more. "I *will* kill them all," he vowed, and I almost shrank back from the violence in his eyes.

"That's what I came to tell you, Dracho," said Antares.

"What?" he asked, not taking his hands from me, his eyes a raging storm as they held mine.

"We have him."

Overwhelming relief hit me. We both turned to focus on Antares.

"Jandar is upstairs."

My disappointment was bitter, but Dracho broke into a cruel smile, his fangs showing. "Well, well. Looks like the fun will begin shortly."

Chapter 39

Light stabbed through my eyelids as Dracho carried me through the castle, his heavy cloak wrapped around me. So used to being in the dark, I couldn't bear to open my eyes, the brightness still too painful.

And I couldn't bear to see all their expressions at what had become of me.

Numerous voices muttered around me as he walked, and the smell of blood and death reached my nose. Whatever Dracho had done to take the castle, it hadn't gone well for Cirdan's men.

"Not now, Jeshwa," he said to someone. I pressed myself into him further, not wanting anyone else near me.

A door opened, and the light faded. Opening one eye, I found velvet red curtains and soft candlelight. Dracho placed me down upon a lavish bed as I took in every corner of the room.

I baulked when he turned and headed straight for the door, a terror of being alone overwhelming me all at once.

"Where—" I started to ask.

"Someone will be along shortly." His voice was cold, unfeeling.

"But—"

I jumped when Roux burst into the room. Her bright, brown eyes found Dracho, then me. A sob wracked my body. As she rushed to climb on the bed, wrapping her slender arms around me, my eyes caught Dracho's for a split second before he left. He looked as broken as I felt.

"It's all right," Roux kept repeating. "We've got you. It's all right."

Seeing Roux again felt like a dream, but the feeling of her arms wrapped around me anchored me to the fact that it was all real. When my tears had subsided, I lay down in her embrace, her soft hand smoothing my hair as I stared up at the ceiling.

"How did you find me?" I asked eventually.

"Someone sent Dracho a letter. We were prepared for it to be a trap, but when we arrived, the gates were open. We just... walked right in. Then the fighting started. Although it wasn't much of a fight, despite the wolves. Many of them started to flee once they realised there were dragons."

I nodded. "The wolves... that's how they captured me."

Roux was silent.

"Who's left?"

"We aren't sure. Not many alive."

I swallowed, catching her eye. "How long?"

Devastation marred her beautiful features. "Almost a month."

I breathed out harshly. What had I missed in all that time?

She squeezed me tighter. "Don't think of any of that now. You need to focus on healing."

Her hand brushed over the top of my ear as she continued to smooth my hair.

"Did you know?" I asked.

She smiled, realising what I meant immediately. "I had an inkling after the Uhane ceremony. The ancestors wouldn't accept just anyone's prayer. But after Volente, I could sense something different about you."

I nodded. Once I'd awakened from my recovery back in Aion after the Uhane ceremony, I had panicked, wondering if my glamour had faded away during my unconsciousness and if anyone had noticed my ears. Bisa had clearly been careful in ensuring my secret stayed that way. I'd guessed that Bisa had known of my lineage, having been close friends with my mother—but if Roux had known for all that time...

But she didn't care?

"I'm sorry I kept it from you," I whispered.

"Don't be. It was your secret to tell, when you were ready." Roux smiled.

With a kiss to the top of my head, she removed herself from my bed, walking over to a doorway in the corner. My heart constricted until I heard running water. It must be a bathroom.

I looked over myself, noting that underneath Dracho's cloak, I still wore my filthy shirt and simple underwear. Feeling the soft, thick material of the cloak, I couldn't help but bring the material to my nose, breathing in his scent.

This is real. They're here.

It was my new mantra. I repeated it many times whilst Roux ran the bath. After a few minutes, a small knock at the door made me drop the cloak.

Roux's head poked around the doorway. "Do you want me to get that?"

I shook my head, calling in my croaked voice for the visitor to come in. The door opened slowly.

Dazed, I scrambled to my knees on the bed. A whimper sounded from my throat; my hands covered my face, muffling my sobs.

Strong, muscled arms wrapped around me, encasing my arms and picking me up with ease as someone smoothed my back. My hands cupped his cheeks, feeling the scruff of his dark, untrimmed beard brush my fingers. Roux watched from the bathroom doorway, a soft smile on her face.

"How?" It was all I could get out.

Bas chuckled, the sound breaking. "We put up one hell of a fight..."

Vyn chimed in. "But the wolves overwhelmed us. They nearly killed us, but then they started arguing about whether we would be useful leverage. In the end they stuck us on the ship and took us to the castle. Antares found us in the cells. Just think—this entire time we were probably no more than fifty feet away from you, and we never knew!" He tried to make his tone cheerful, but his face was pale, his yellow eyes tight.

Emotion knotted in my throat at the idea of them being kept alive just to be dangled in front of me to extract my obedience, but for now all I could focus on was the fact that they had survived. They were here.

Bas set me on my feet and I turned to hug Vyn, squeezing him tightly before I took a careful seat on the edge of the bed. From their cuts and bruises, I could see their beatings had been bad. I could see the exhaustion in the dark circles under their eyes, but only concern for me radiated from them.

Bas's eyes flitted to the corner of the room, lightening when he saw Roux. "Hello, little mage."

"Hey, big man," she said quietly.

Bas noted the looks Vyn and I were giving him and cleared his throat. "Dracho caught us up as soon as he found us. He, um... he's notifying Connaught now."

"Connaught is here?" I asked, bewildered.

"As soon as Dracho found out about your disappearance, he picked Connaught up from Meridium. Then me from Aion," Roux said.

"What about Meridiu—"

"Aunt Sizwe has taken care of everything. The city is fine."

The city. "What about Coed?"

Roux frowned, and my stomach dipped. "What about Coed?" she asked.

"It's... it wasn't attacked?"

She shook her head. "Coed is fine... but Ruthun was destroyed."

My heart dropped to my stomach. The large town to the south of Meridum was a major supplier to the city.

"How do you know there was another attack?" Roux asked.

"But..." I skimmed through my memories, sure I'd heard Jandar give the order to the Hollow to go for *Coed*, not Ruthun. Perhaps he'd changed his mind? I blinked, looking into Roux's concerned eyes. "It's Jandar. It's all been Jandar. I have so much to tell you!" I rushed out, taking a step but stumbling.

"Not now, you don't," Vyn said sternly. "As we speak, Dracho and Antares are no doubt venting some stress and extracting information from the wolves left." He took a gentle hold of my arms, his eyes darting down to my exposed thigh. I winced. "First, we need to get you cleaned up and tended to by a healer. We need you strong and healthy so you can tell us everything you remember, all right?"

"Yeah. Sorry, E, but you stink." Bas waved a hand across his nose, and I sent him a glare. "If it makes you feel better, you can hit me. *Lightly.*" Bas stuck his neck out, offering me his cheek, which I kissed instead.

"Sort yourself out, *then* we'll talk," Vyn added.

"But—"

"No buts," Bas ordered, bringing his hands up to cup my cheeks. "You've got this. You're the strongest person I know, and you'll get through all this shit. We'll see you in a bit."

Vyn kissed the top of my head with a whispered *I love you*, and I watched silently as they left the room. Even with my elven strength, my legs were shaky and weak from lack of use, and it was a struggle to take a few steps forward.

A laugh bubbled up from my chest, bursting out of my mouth before I could stop it. I could feel Roux's stare from the doorway, but the laughter continued until I held my stomach, hardly able to breathe. I realised tears were falling down my cheeks just before the laughter turned into loud sobs. My strength failed, my legs giving out beneath me as I fell to my knees. I wrapped my arms around myself, relishing the sensation of my fingernails digging into the skin underneath my shirt. Something real.

Slim, warm arms wrapped around me from behind, holding me tightly. I cried harder.

I continued to cry as Roux carried me into the bathing chamber, her magick tingling my arms as she used it to boost her strength. I cried as she washed away the grime from my hair and skin, as she cleansed my wound and wrapped it before putting me to bed.

I cried for what had happened, for the relief I felt that Bas and Vyn were alive.

But also in disappointment... that *I* was alive along with them.

Hushed voices outside the room woke me. My hearing was still extremely sensitive after my time in that cell, picking up on the tiniest noise. My eyes darted around the room in disbelief. I was sleeping in an actual bed?

"She's... in all honesty, I'm not sure." It was Roux, talking to someone.

"I know."

That low voice caused a shiver to run through my body, and I focused on keeping my breathing steady so he wouldn't pick up on my heart racing.

"I heard," he continued.

"You were listening earlier." It wasn't a question.

Dracho didn't respond.

"You shouldn't punish yourself, Dracho."

I narrowed my eyes, wondering what he was punishing himself for.

"Why shouldn't I? Isn't this all my fault? Isn't everything, since—"

"You can't think like that. We saved her. We saved them. You can't think of leaving them now."

My heart skipped a beat; my stomach twisted, nausea setting in. Silence fell outside the door for a moment.

Dracho sighed. "I'll stay with her. As long as she wishes, until we find answers and I can ensure her safety. I'll see you in the morning. Goodnight, Roux."

"Goodnight, Dracho."

I closed my eyes, taking a calming breath as Roux re-entered the room. The bed dipped behind me as she climbed in, but I was still awake hours after the sound of her softer sleep-breathing started.

Chapter 40

I felt ridiculous in the dress that Roux had procured from one of the many rooms in the castle, but it was far better than my filthy shirt I had been wearing. The light blue fabric fell to my ankles; in the mirror, I could see it was big on my frame, showing how much weight I had lost. I was still thick in the leg and arse area, but my collarbones and jawline were more pronounced, standing out even more when you took in the dark circles under my sunken eyes.

My once rich brown hair fell flat, and I didn't bother to put in my usual braids. No one to hide it from now.

Roux had asked me countless times if I truly wanted to head down to the great hall. Not for breakfast, but to watch as Dracho doled out punishment to those who had wronged me. To Jandar.

It wasn't that I thirsted for blood; I craved the information he might give. Craved it like a dying man longed for relief. Where had Cirdan fled to? How were they controlling the Hollow? How could we end it?

The spiral staircase was empty as we descended, seeing no one until we reached the big double doors to the great hall. Two men stood on either side, both encased in silver armour bearing the crest of Tenebris. Their eyes remained fixed forward as they opened the doors for us.

My heart raced as I walked in beside Roux, the hall suddenly feeling a lot smaller once I saw how many people it held. A few sets of eyes turned to me as

I entered, and I caught Althea's as she stood near the raised dais at the front. She gave me a small, empathetic smile, and my jaw clenched.

A small clearing of a throat made me jump, and I realised that Antares now stood by my side. He cringed slightly, then held out his arm in offering. I looked down at it and back up to his face; he smiled, nodding to his crooked elbow.

He's safe, some instinct seemed to whisper in my mind. I linked my arm with him, glancing at Roux, who smiled encouragingly before heading towards the dais.

Antares walked me silently to the side of the room, not far from the dais. I appreciated the silence; my fingers were clasping his bare forearm rather tightly. His skin was warm under my touch, and I allowed it to ground me amid all these strangers whose eyes I could feel on me. Maids from within the castle; soldiers who had obviously arrived with Dracho. I couldn't see Bas, Vyn, or Connaught anywhere, and a momentary panic shot through me.

The steel bolt of a door sounded, and from a corner of the room, a couple of Dracho's guards dragged someone in.

Jandar.

My breath hitched as I looked over at the elven king. Far from his previous splendour, his hair was messy, falling over his sharp features, his jacket ripped and breeches stained from where he had been kept in a cell—I presumed. His cold, calculating eyes captured mine, and a sneer turned his upper lip before they threw him before the dais and the ornate wooden throne atop it.

The double doors opened once more, but I felt Dracho's presence before I saw him, a pull in my chest warming me from the inside. I looked up anyway, and I sucked in a breath, because there he was.

I had no idea what had happened over the weeks we had been apart, but at this moment, the man before me was mostly beast. His power and aura pulsed with rage; scaled, obsidian wings spread from his back, flaring slightly. He walked into the hall flanked by a smiling blonde man and a female with a sheet of long black hair.

He certainly did like to make an entrance. Glancing at the dais, I saw Althea roll her eyes.

But I could see beyond the swagger. Dracho's knuckles were white, red marks visible on his clenched fists from where his blows had landed on whatever poor soul he had dealt with earlier. The light fighting leathers he wore were covered in blood.

I had never seen such emotion cross his face. Pure white fangs were just visible beneath his top lip, a vicious smile growing on his lips as he sauntered towards Jandar. I was surprised to find that his fury didn't frighten me. I realised that the temperamental, possessive beast that lay beneath his skin made me feel safe.

His eyes skipped to me ever so briefly before he launched himself forward. Jandar found himself hanging in mid-air by his neck.

My breath caught in my throat; Antares scoffed from beside me. I could have sworn he muttered the word 'show-off' under his breath.

"Where's Cirdan?" Dracho drawled casually, staring at the claws on his free hand as if already bored of the conversation.

"F-fuck you," Jandar choked out. The curse sounded strange coming from his mouth.

Dracho rolled his eyes. "I'll find him one way or another, and end your rotten line. You may as well be of some use in your final breaths." That vicious grin was back.

Jandar's eyes widened as he clawed at Dracho's hand. "I'll never tell you."

"I thought you would perhaps see it my way... but alas." Dracho dropped him to the ground.

Jandar fell into a heap, before pushing himself onto all fours. The bastard actually started to laugh hoarsely through his heavy breathing. "You're all going to die," he wheezed.

Dracho didn't look worried in the slightest. He merely arched a brow, looking down at the former king.

"You have no idea what you're up against. No matter what you do to me, they will kill you all." Jandar rose to his knees, looking Dracho in the eye as he panted.

I stepped forward, aware of several pairs of eyes turning to me. "Who are *they*—?"

"You'll die," Jandar interrupted. He turned to me. "And Cirdan will break the half-breed whore right before he slits her—"

"Dracho!" Antares shouted.

I tried to lunge towards them, my legs failing me; I fell forward, Antares's arms wrapping around my waist to catch me. "No!" I cried.

I didn't see Dracho move, but the inhuman sound that escaped his throat made me jump. He lifted Jandar in a flash, his mouth descending on his neck, a fleshy, tearing noise echoing through the hall. He pulled his head back, tearing Jandar's throat out before releasing a bone-shaking roar at the man's petrified face, his fangs bloody.

Jandar's hands fluttered to try and cover the wound, blood pouring over his fingers. It didn't take long for the light to leave his eyes, his hands falling limply to his sides. Dracho dropped him unceremoniously to the floor.

"Well," Antares muttered, "that didn't go as planned."

Jandar was gone. No information, no answers to Cirdan's whereabouts... It was all gone. My mind spiralled. Would the plague of the Hollow stop, now that its master was dead? Or had Cirdan taken over the beast?

My stomach churned, sick of the sight of blood and violence. I didn't realise I was shaking until Antares pulled me closer. His brows were heavy over his golden eyes, his lips pursed thoughtfully. I pulled myself free, turning to flee the room, back to the safety of my chambers.

"Eliana... I have a gift for you," Dracho called, halting my steps. Everyone's eyes turned to me again, making my skin itch.

The sound of metal chains reached my ears and I flinched, instantly on alert. I knew Dracho wouldn't dare put me in chains, but I couldn't shake the instinct to hide. I caught Antares's glance, and I despised the softening of his eyes. The understanding.

From a door at the corner of the hall, two men were dragged before the throne. The larger man raised his head, his dull eyes finding me straight away, and my breath hitched.

It was Erix—gagged. And beside him was Malzan.

The hatred in Erix's eyes as he stared at me could not be measured. Nor the pain. For where his hands had been, there were now two tightly wrapped stumps, the bandages drenched in oozing blood. My eyes skipped to Dracho; his face was the epitome of satisfaction.

I realised the only reason Erix was still alive was for me.

A darkness seemed to creep through my blood, that ancient, feral part of my elven lineage bolstering me. The human mask slipped off me like a warm cloak, my fangs lengthening. I had never felt such hatred or anger.

It made me strong. I supported myself on my own legs, my feet carrying me forward, the skirt of my long dress swishing about my ankles. Just before I reached Erix, a breeze ruffled my hair; Dracho appeared in front of me, blocking my view of the guard.

I caught the rage mixed with concern in his gaze as he held an object towards me. I gasped, my hands darting up, hovering a few inches over the hilt of the dagger.

My dagger.

Tears sprang to my eyes. "How did you—"

"It was with the guard," Dracho said. "He acquired it when you were captured."

I tried to get a glimpse of Erix over his shoulder. Dracho leaned forward, and I jerked back instinctively from his bloody mouth before I relaxed enough for him to whisper something close to my ear.

"You can finish this in private, if you wish? I know you take no satisfaction from this, so there is no need for all to see. It's up to you."

He released my dagger, and I relished the weight of it in my hands, holding it up for a moment and spinning it in my palm. Closing my eyes, I took a deep breath, clasping the hilt tightly.

"What about his wolf?" I asked, looking up at Dracho.

He smiled. "Roux is preventing that from happening."

Turning to the dais, I could see that Roux was holding her hand out, a wicked grin on her face as she stared at the guard.

"Now is fine," I told Dracho, who nodded and stepped aside.

I steeled myself for what I was about to do. A thousand things ran through my head as Erix's eyes burned into me, his expression hateful and cruel. He was lightly shrouded in a black and gold mist from Roux's magick.

I walked slowly towards the man who had given me another scar to add to my collection.

"And you're wrong," I called, without looking away from him.

"About?" Dracho asked from behind me, never straying too far.

I stopped a foot away from Erix, staring down at his ugly face, rage boiling in my blood. "I *will* take satisfaction in this."

Dropping to my knees, I punched Erix straight in his uneven teeth with all my elven strength, knocking some out and giving me the chance to get a firm grip on his tongue. He tried to yell as I yanked it out, bringing my dagger up to slice clean through it.

Erix tried to scream, the sound strange as it escaped his throat. Still clasping the end of his tongue, I shoved it back into his mouth, as far as I could, before dropping my dagger and clasping my hands over his mouth and nose.

I watched the rising panic in his eyes closely, enjoyed the jerking of his body as he choked and tried to push himself away from me. I wanted him to know how it felt to be helpless, fighting to take a breath that wouldn't come. Roux held him still and I was using my entire strength, digging my sharp, broken nails into the skin of his face.

Leaning in, I bared my lengthened teeth. "You tried to take something from me. You failed," I whispered.

His eyes widened for the last time; tears sprang into them. My mind flashed back to everything I had gone through. The lupera blade used to mark my skin when I was a young girl. The loss of my mother and Morgwn. The distance between my father; his death. Everything that had happened with Dracho. And now Cirdan.

My exhalation was shaky. "By the time you walked into my cell, there was nothing left to take."

It felt like an hour for him to succumb to the lack of oxygen. His eyes dulled, glassing over as he stopped moving, but I held his face for a moment longer than I needed to as his shoulders slumped and his head bowed. Before his body could touch me, I shoved him back and sucked in a breath.

In, and out.

Getting up, my steps a bit unsteady, I looked to the ceiling and took another deep breath. I felt rather than saw Dracho walk past me, but my attention snapped to him at his next words.

"Your turn," he stated confidently, stalking to the final guard remaining.

Malzan.

"No!" I yelled, stumbling forward and nearly falling. A set of firm hands gripped my arms from behind. For a moment panic was all I knew, until the smell of oak and vanilla told me it was Antares, who righted my footing before releasing me immediately.

Dracho's clawed hand had stopped a mere inch from Malzan's throat, his breathing heavy.

"Why?" His furious whisper was like smoke on the wind.

"He helped me. Cleaned my wound after Erix had—"

A snarl ripped from Dracho's throat before I could tell him exactly what Erix had done, and Malzan's eyes closed as he flinched.

Perhaps not the best thing to start with.

I raised my voice. "He made sure it didn't get infected. That's all. He never hurt me. He never touched me inappropriately."

"He stood by and watched whilst others did," Dracho snapped, his claw brushing against the skin of Malzan's neck.

That I couldn't deny. But he had never joined in on my torment, and only treated me with kindness.

"He was kind," I said, my chin tipping up. "More so than any other guard. This is your chance to stop the violence here." I took a step forward, ignoring the muttering of our audience around the room. "You once said you'd do anything to prevent a life being taken… Malzan's actions demand a different fate."

Dracho turned to meet my gaze for a second, his brow creasing in concentration. The night before we entered Stillmere, he had said those words to Vyn after we'd seen the sujin—after he'd stopped us from taking its life. I hoped and prayed there was some of that Dracho left now.

"Other than his cowardly absence from your torture, why is this filth deserving of such mercy?" Dracho asked, his eyes a molten silver.

"He… he—" I turned my gaze to Malzan, and with my eyes I pleaded for him to say something that would save his life.

"It was me," he croaked.

My heart lurched, unsure of his meaning.

"It was me who let you in and sent the message." Malzan's voice was steady as he continued. No lie in his words.

"Why?" Dracho asked, his voice a low rumble as he turned back to the wolf.

"I know something of the situation Eliana found herself in. Being tortured to breaking point."

I froze, hearing the truth and pain in his words.

Malzan's head dropped. "Erix was our alpha, but not our alpha by choice. He was cruel to our pack. I wasn't strong enough to fight him. So when he commanded us to, we started working for Cirdan. I wasn't as strong as Eliana. She didn't deserve what happened to her. No one would deserve that."

I felt exposed, as though every person in the room had just discovered a secret laid bare for all. As someone rather private, I felt like an imposter in my own skin, wanting to claw my way out.

Dracho looked to Antares before he took a deep breath, lowering his hand. Turning, he nodded to the Tenebris guards who rushed forward, unlocking the chains that kept Malzan's hands bound. Malzan stood, rubbing his wrists. My own itched at the sight.

"You may go. I grant you freedom *only* because the future queen has vouched for you. But I suggest you leave this place, and leave this land," Dracho said, his tone deadly. Remembering that day we'd been attacked by bandits, I could see it was killing him to set Malzan free, even if he'd led them to me.

My body sagged in relief, a shaky breath leaving me. Malzan looked at me as if he wanted to say something, and I sent him a small smile, mouthing the words *thank you*. He smiled tentatively back, stopping when a low growl vibrated through Dracho's throat. Without another word, Malzan turned and fled the room.

My body seemed to crash. I almost crumpled, but Antares held me up again as Dracho bent to retrieve my dagger. I was shaking—with adrenaline or shock, I wasn't sure—and my vision swirled before a strong arm wrapped beneath my legs, picking me up and pulling me against a hard chest. I wanted to push them away, to show I was strong enough to walk out of that hall by myself. But the truth was, I still wasn't.

"Return her to her room, please," Dracho said coldly as he handed me my bloody dagger. I clutched it to my chest with both hands, not caring if Erix's blood dripped onto my dress.

Antares turned, leaving the room, which burst into loud chatter. I turned my head into his chest, closing my eyes. It was a relief to leave them behind.

"I know what it feels like." Antares's voice curled around my tired form.

"What?" I mumbled.

"To feel like there is nothing left."

I lifted my head, my breath catching in my throat as all my muscles locked. I hadn't meant for anyone to hear that. I'd forgotten what a shadow Antares could be, seeing and hearing all—never missing a trick.

"Years ago," his voice was gruff, "I found out that my friend was being abused... by her own father."

"Althea?" I asked softly.

He nodded. "Once Dracho and I figured it out, we ran to her house. She lay on the floor, covered in blood. Understand, it's hard to truly harm a draconi, so to inflict the kind of damage he had that night..."

I could see this was a difficult subject for him and toyed with the idea of moving my hand to comfort him, and try to rid his face of that haunted expression. Antares wasn't fond of too much touchy behaviour.

But he's touching me... And he had quite a bit since he'd returned with Dracho to Meridium. I wondered if he had started to see me as more than just the woman who'd distracted his friend on their original mission to Ruvalon.

I didn't ask, and I gave him the space to continue if he wanted, without the shock of my touch or voice to add to his discomfort. I was moved that he was sharing so much with me.

"In that moment, my dragon took over. That rage was like nothing I had ever felt before. It triggered my merge, and—I killed her father."

From my conversation with Althea in Meridium, I had deduced this was the ending of her father's story. Nor was I surprised in the least that Antares was capable of it. But to hear him say it out loud was something different. There was shame in his tone.

"He deserved it," I murmured.

Antares nodded, his eyes dropping to me. "Perhaps we are more alike than I first thought."

I remained silent as he held me tightly, and I wondered if my closeness was as comforting to him as it was to me. His confession had calmed my ragged nerves after witnessing all the horror of the throne room. He'd helped me take my mind off it, whilst offering up a piece of himself. I knew how much of a sacrifice it was to do that.

For a moment he watched me carefully, as if I were a jungle cat preparing to pounce. Then his golden eyes stared ahead of us.

"It wasn't just my rage that triggered the merge," he told me. "It was my shame."

My brows flew up.

"I am known for my ability to sense things," he admitted. "My skills as a soldier, both in and out of my draconi form... but they failed me when it was most important. When it came to my friend." His jaw flexed. "I was ashamed that I hadn't noticed the signs, that I had allowed it to go on for so long."

"You have nothing to feel ashamed about, Antares."

His steps paused for a minute, and he looked down at me.

"Althea said the same." He continued walking. "And I have come to accept that, even if I never believed it myself. But back then, it made me feel like a monster. Guilt for having taken her father from her—her only living parent, even if he was a *prick*"—he bit out the insult—"and shame, for not knowing my friend was in pain. I distanced myself, no matter how hard they tried to help or talk me out of it. My mind... suffered."

"How did you get out of it?"

Antares's eyes flickered to me again. He inhaled deeply. "As if drowning alone out at sea, I had to realise that only *I* could pull myself to shore. I could only do so in finding my own strength."

I frowned. I didn't think I was strong enough for that right now.

"It's not a case of getting over the wave that tried to drown you in the first place. It's the agony of learning to swim and keep swimming."

I was still frowning, but I understood what he was saying. We started to ascend the spiral staircase to my room, and my ears pricked as hurried steps came down them.

"Eliana," a voice breathed out in relief.

The crimson of his hair caught my eye first, then his heartbreaking expression. "Connaught." I smiled.

Connaught hesitated once he saw who carried me but took another step down. Antares nodded in greeting. "I was escorting her to her room, but you probably have things to discuss."

He lowered me to my feet slowly, so I could gather my bearings. Connaught's hand reached out to rest against the middle of my back.

Antares turned to leave. My hand shot out, clasping his firmly. He turned in shock.

"Thank you," I told him.

He simply nodded before turning to retreat down the stairs, staring at his hand intently where I had touched him.

Connaught offered me his hand tentatively and I took it, following him slowly up the remaining steps into my room. Once inside, he closed the door and opened his arms for a hug.

I embraced him gladly. He bent down, wrapping his arms tightly around my waist and burying his head into my neck. He took a long inhale through his nose, and I knew he was trying not to cry.

Releasing me, he held me gently, his brown eyes glassy. "I almost didn't believe them when they told me you were alive. I'm so sorry I wasn't in that hall with you. I was debriefing with Vyn and Bas, and then I came up here to guard you. I didn't think you'd go and watch that."

I shook my head, reaching up to cup his cheek. "You're here now."

"And so are you," he breathed.

"How is everything? Is the city all right?"

His eyes closed as he shook his head, a humourless laugh breaking free. "The city is fine. Don't worry about that. Are *you* all right?"

His eyes shone with concern, and I felt undeserving. I knew what he was asking—had my mind drifted back to where it had been when I was a young girl, the night I'd met Engel? Something I had not shared with anyone but him.

I wouldn't talk about it with him, though, not now. I hoped I'd be able to one day. My hand fell as I glanced towards his feet, chewing the inside of my cheek. "I will be."

He inhaled sharply, pulling me towards his sturdy body, holding me tight, as if letting me go meant he would lose me forever. "I can't say I'm not angry at you for sending the emperor and his friends away. I'm furious. More so at him for leaving you. But I won't burden you with my anger. From now on, I will always be there. Whenever you need me. Just call my name, and I'll be by your side."

I wrapped my hands around his broad back.

"I know," I told him, leaving out that this time around, it was so much worse than he knew.

A presence in the room and a cold breeze from the open window woke me from my slumber. Sitting up quickly, I dropped Dracho's cloak—I'd been holding it tightly—and squinted around in the low light. I didn't see anyone.

I must have fallen asleep early; I caught sight of the moon behind clouds high in the sky. Roux was absent, and I trod slowly over the wooden floor to look out the open window, my legs feeling stronger as the first drops of rain started to fall. As I stood there, I remembered that I hadn't opened the window, and a shiver ran along my spine. Roux must have done so at some point; I didn't like the idea that I'd been sleeping so deeply, I hadn't stirred.

Breathing in the fresh air, I stood for a moment, longing to stand in the rain. Longing to wash everything away.

Mind made up, I slipped out of the room—and faltered. On a chair a few feet away from the door was Bas, lightly snoring, head awkwardly resting on his shoulder. I shook my head, smiling, then wondered where Connaught was, slightly annoyed that Bas was here when he should have been resting. Cringing at the creak of the wooden door as it closed, I tiptoed past Bas and down the staircase, keeping out of sight from anyone else awake as I made my way through the castle.

Pushing open a door, I walked into a huge courtyard. An oak tree grew in the far corner, its leaves swaying with the wind as rain poured down. Unhesitatingly, I walked out from underneath the shelter of the castle walls.

The rain pelted my skin. I closed my eyes, tilting my face towards the grey clouds, taking a deep breath and feeling each cold splash as it hit my face. My hair began to stick to my cheeks as the rain soaked every strand, a strangely exhilarating feeling.

A scuffle of feet before me made my eyes shoot open. He was just inches away.

Close enough to touch. To smell—that sweet, addictive scent of citrus, smoke and cedar wood permeating the electrified air as it mixed with the delicious smell of petrichor.

"How... how long have you been standing there?" I asked him.

Dracho didn't answer immediately. "Longer than you'd like."

My lips parted slightly as I stared up at his icy blue eyes; he gazed down at me, and it occurred to me that for a man now so talented at killing, his eyes were remarkably soft.

He looked away. "How are you?"

"Fine," I answered too quickly.

His eyes returned to mine. "If you don't want to talk about it, that's all right. But don't lie. Not to me."

"I thought that's what we did."

"What?"

"Lie to each other."

He sucked his teeth, anger turning his eyes cold, before they travelled all over me, realisation settling onto his face. He exhaled impatiently. Before I could utter a word, he'd used his inhuman speed to lift me into his arms and carry me out of the rain.

I barely had a moment to wrap my arms around him, burying my face into his neck so as not to feel sick from the speed before he was putting me down—onto my bed. Anger lanced through me that he had removed me from outside, where I had wanted to be.

"What in the name of the Goddess do you think—" My eyes skipped past Dracho's form. Bas was no longer outside the open door, his chair empty.

Dracho closed the door. "Eliana, not that I don't enjoy you having some fire back, but for once in your life, shut the fuck up," he called as he walked into the bathroom, returning with a towel.

My mouth snapped shut, nerves creeping into my stomach. I became aware of how drenched I was from my little trip outside.

"Take off your clothes."

"Excuse me?"

With a sigh, he held out the towel. "Take your clothes off. You'll catch a sickness if you stay in your wet clothes. Especially since you're malnourished and recovering."

"Why do you care? You've avoided me at every opportunity since you rescued me," I snapped at him childishly.

Dracho closed his eyes, inhaling through his nose. When the thick lashes lifted again, that sliver of silver around his eyes was glowing. "I care. And if you think for one moment I won't spend every free second I have ensuring you return to your healthy, *deliciously* curvy self, you are mistaken. Now take. Off. Your. Clothes."

My mouth parted; heat trailed up my spine. I snatched the towel from his hand and headed to the bathroom, where I halted and stared at the steaming tub in the corner. The rounded bath was large enough to fit four people, and it had obviously been filled recently.

I turned. "When did you—"

"I returned to fill it once I knew you were heading outside."

Returned? Roux hadn't left that window open. He had been in my room, watching me sleep. *Curled up with his damn cloak in my grasp.*

I just nodded and shut the door behind me, resting my forehead against the rough wood for a moment, trying to calm my breathing. Having him so near, in my chamber, was unnerving. With how we'd left things, and all that had happened since, I didn't know how to act around him. Nothing had changed. My imprisonment hadn't taken away anything that had happened.

But he'd saved me. That had to mean something.

Breathe, I told myself. *In, and out.*

We were two stars colliding, and I felt like there would be no surviving it—only an endless emptiness left from the destruction.

But he'd saved me.

What did he save, exactly? I was numb. Broken. It would have been better if I *had* died. My city, my friends... *everyone* would be better off if I had died. Not stuck taking care of my broken self.

It was a lonely thought.

My mind spiralled as my brain and heart fought over pushing him away or wanting him near. I had been alone for so long with little interaction that it felt... disingenuous. As if my mind couldn't comprehend that people would actually want to help me. Take care of me.

I shook it all away as I peeled the wet gown away from my skin, realising that it must have left very little to the imagination. It was a relief when it pooled around my feet on the floor.

A slash of red caught my eye. The fresh, jagged cut stood out against the flesh of my thigh. My chest heaved as I looked at it. A twin to match the other.

My vision blurred, my breath coming in pants. Memories—sounds, scents, emotions—overwhelmed me.

There was a knock at the door. "Eliana, I'm coming in."

I glanced at it and realised that I was on the ground, my cheeks wet from tears. I didn't have the energy to stop him, so I just wrapped the towel loosely over myself as the handle turned.

He held a smaller towel tight in his hand. Brows scrunching, he walked to my side, indicating for me to stand.

Confused and dazed, I just frowned at him. He huffed at me. "Stand up."

My eyes widened. "This towel isn't wrapped around me."

He shook his head lightly, walking over and lifting me with ease as I clasped the towel to my front as tightly as possible.

"I've seen it all before, Princess. And trust me, seeing you hurt isn't exactly a turn-on."

I didn't have it in me to reprimand him for the nickname. *Give in. Let him help.* He was staring at me, waiting for me to drop the towel. With a shaky huff I lowered it to the floor, ridiculously grateful that he made a show of not looking as he helped me into the hot tub, where the bubbles hid my form from his eyes.

Once I was in he left the room, and I took the opportunity to lean my head back on the edge of the tub, resting my arms along the rim as a relieved sigh left my mouth. I stretched my legs out, pleased that they didn't even reach the other end. Beside the sting of the wound on my leg and other small cuts across my skin, the hot, sudsy water was perfect. I picked up a soap bar from the side of the tub, relishing the sensation of it gliding over my skin. For weeks I had felt layers of dirt and grime clinging to me like a second skin. Now, even though I had bathed since my rescue, I still felt the need to erase every speck of dust from that cell, remove every trace of it from my thoughts.

The hairs on my neck prickled as I heard Dracho's steps grow louder, and I turned to see him kneeling behind me, another rough bar of soap in his hand. His hand tentatively weighed on my shoulder as I started to sit up.

"I just want to take care of you," he whispered.

I turned to face him, eyes wide. "But I need to be strong on my own." I had always dealt with everything on my own, without leaning on anyone. I prided myself on not being a burden.

"I know you're strong," he said, "and the bravest person I've ever met. But sometimes it's all right to lean on people. It's all right to need people, Eli."

I swallowed the knot of emotion that formed in my throat.

"Just... for now. Let *me* take care of you."

My eyes travelled over his face, pausing at the emotion in his eyes, and I knew the reason he had been cold and distant. I could see how he blamed himself. How he hated himself for leaving me.

But *I* had sent him away. I had suggested it.

My heart sank to my stomach, guilt overriding most of my other warring emotions as I nodded, turning away from him so he could wash my hair. I hugged my knees close, my cheeks heating as his hand ran slowly through its wet strands. I hadn't let anyone else wash it since I was a young girl, always worried about trusting anyone near my ears—worried about revealing my heritage. I didn't even let Beatrice or Milly, who had always known, wash my hair, disturbed by thoughts of their disgust at my elven features. Not that they, Sizwe or Connaught had ever expressed such a thing—but still.

He's only doing it because he feels guilty. It's the only reason he's still here.

He sighed. The sound of the water being disturbed didn't bother me as he scooped handfuls and poured it over my head, warming my scalp.

My head tipped back to give him more access, and I closed my eyes to the silence. Dracho's hands were gentle, washing my hair in a comfortable rhythm as his fingers ran through the tangles. A relaxed breath slipped out, and he paused, but only for a moment.

After several minutes, his hands disappeared—but not for long. My muscles bunched as his hands found my shoulders, rubbing the tension away.

"Relax," Dracho said softly. "We can go back to hating each other tomorrow. For now, rest."

Ice crawled through my veins at his words; I remained tense for a moment but allowed myself to relax wordlessly into his hands.

I shouldn't have been surprised by his kindness. The old Dracho had always been a kind man—thoughtful and caring. I knew that—but this moment between us, as his soft fingers caressed my aching shoulders, had my edges fraying.

And for some reason that made things worse. The relaxation chipped away at the wall I'd built, releasing some of the pressure that had been hiding behind it—making me feel exposed. I hated feeling vulnerable around him.

Why hasn't he asked me anything about being imprisoned? My breathing sped up slightly as his ministrations along my shoulders and upper back continued. *Does he view me as broken now too?*

I wouldn't voice the words, as if to do so would give them power. Acknowledge the reality, despite the proof of it being marked again upon my skin. I'd never be able to hide what had happened to me, forever etched into my body.

Into my very soul.

I didn't even realise I was shaking until Dracho's hands wrapped around my shoulders tightly. Firm but gentle. My teeth felt like they would crack from the way I was clenching them, as I fought hard for the fractured shield around me to remain intact.

My heart constricted when he removed his hands, but I flinched when I heard the sloshing of the water as he stepped into the tub, nudging me forward to settle behind me—clothes and all. His arms came around me, gentle across the top of my chest as he pulled me back against his warm chest, his chin resting atop my head.

"*Mia estra*," he murmured. "Let go."

That was what shattered the shield—what broke the dam holding back my tears. He hadn't dared to tell me it was all right, because it wasn't. None of what had happened was all right. But he'd given me the freedom to grieve in front of him.

To grieve who I had been. Because there was no doubt I was forever changed.

I turned to bury my face in his neck, sobs wracking my body as they tore from my throat. He said nothing as his arms tightened around me, giving me space to breathe but reassuring me he was there.

I didn't have the energy to tell him that many of my tears were precisely because I didn't hate him at all.

Chapter 41

Dracho held me in the tub, allowing me to empty that dam of emotion until it was mostly spent. Only when the water started to cool did he stand, removing me with him. My breath was sharp as the chill air hit my skin, and I found that I no longer cared I was naked. Carrying me to the white fur rug in front of a roaring fire that had not been lit when I first entered this room, he left to fetch a towel, which he draped around my back and shoulders, laying a silk robe at my side.

A soft sigh left me as I watched the flames dance, the wood crackling beneath them.

Once the warmth started to heat my cheeks, I pulled the robe on. The material was so light that it felt like my own skin. Dracho came to sit behind me, brushing my hair in silence before splitting it into three parts and braiding it. The slight tug on my scalp helped me feel something other than the drowning sorrow.

"What do you want to do?" Dracho's voice asked softly.

He didn't mean right now; I knew what he was asking. Did I want to seek out Cirdan?

Do I?

What was the other option? Roux had updated me on what Dracho had done during our separation. They'd discovered what I already knew—that Jandar was behind the Hollow... and they didn't know a way to stop it. Perhaps it already had with Jandar's death, but I didn't hold out hope for that.

"I'm not in the mood to do anything," I told him honestly, unwilling to have that conversation.

"All right. Just say the word, and we'll stay right here doing nothing. I'll braid your hair every night, and the outside world can burn, for all I care." He read the expression on my face.

I didn't want to stay here. But it sounded nice... doing nothing.

"Nothing," I whispered.

"Then we'll do nothing." I twisted my head slightly, looking at him. "And tomorrow we'll do nothing. And every day that follows we'll do nothing."

"Until?"

"Until nothing turns into something."

"I have a gift for you." Morgwn's voice sounded higher, filled with excitement as he held his hands behind his back.

"If this is a trick again, I'm gonna tell Mammy," I threatened.

Morgwn laughed loudly, clearly remembering when he had placed a slimy frog into my hands, terrifying my five-year-old self. Six years later, I was used to my brother's pranks.

"No. I promise. This is a nice surprise." Morgwn grinned, and my eyes narrowed at him, slightly doubtful. "Close your eyes and hold your hands out."

My lips pouted, and his head tilted. "C'mon, little doe. I pinky swear."

Huffing, I held my hands out nervously, peeking through one eye before clenching them shut.

Morgwn blew out a shaky breath. I felt something heavy and made of cold metal rest in my hands. Opening my eyes, I couldn't stop the gasp that escaped.

"I asked for Mother's permission, but um, this was made for you. You're only to practice using it when I'm around, and then it will stay with me at all times, do you understand?"

I nodded silently, unable to take my eyes off the gift; the most beautiful dagger I had ever seen. I moved to unsheathe the blade.

"Careful," warned Morgwn, and when I looked up he seemed nervous. As if I could ever dislike a gift like this, from him!

Pulling it free, I marvelled at the double-edged blade, so bright it glowed. It was fixed onto a stunning silver hilt, the handle made of grey oak wood. At the end of the hilt sat a bright green emerald. My eyes savoured every smooth pane of its blade, turning it over in my hands until an inscription caught my gaze.

Looking up at my big brother—my sun and my constant for all my days—I felt so very loved. I threw my arms around his neck, dagger still in hand.

"Woah, careful!" he laughed, leaning back but wrapping his arms around my middle. "So, you like it?" he asked eagerly.

I hugged him tightly, feeling his chest rumble as he chuckled. "I love it. Thank you, Morgwn. You're the best brother ever!"

I released him, pulling back—and saw the face of a stranger smiling wickedly at me.

I let go, but the stranger's hands dug into the skin of my waist. I struggled to pull myself free as his face morphed, the brown hair growing into a sheet of smooth, black strands. I was staring at the handsome, but cold features of an elven prince.

Cirdan.

My eleven-year-old self didn't have the strength to rip herself away. Cirdan's hand released my waist to brush a finger along the apple of my cheek.

"You'll be mine," he promised, before clasping my throat tightly.

My eyes tried to adapt to the dark space around me as I panted. It took a few moments to work out that I was sitting upright in my bed, cold sweat running down my spine as I held my dagger out in front of me.

Dracho stood in the moonlight streaming through the window, his sculpted chest illuminated by the light. His eyes were sad as he stared out at the world, standing so still he looked like a heartbroken statue of old.

I lowered my dagger, holding it in my lap as I looked down at it, releasing my white-knuckled grip.

"I never realised it had an inscription," he said quietly.

I nodded, my fingers brushing over the letters on the blade. Still as clear as they'd been when I received it.

Little doe.

"It was my nickname," I murmured.

"From your mother?"

I shook my head. "From Morgwn. But it stuck."

"Your brother."

I nodded. "I used to train with him when I was younger. He knew how much I wanted my own dagger. He said he had this one made for me, provided I only used it during training with him. He took it with him when he rode off to war."

Dracho frowned, and I knew what he was thinking. How had I retrieved it?

"It was the only thing my father found when he went looking for Morgwn, after the blast at Volente. He was surprised it hadn't been destroyed... brought it home for me. Knew how much it meant to me," I told him.

"It's an elven blade."

My eyes widened in shock. How had I never known? How could Dracho tell?

"There's only one kind of metal that could pierce a draconi's mortal flesh that *easily*," he said. "I was immediately suspicious after you stabbed me in Meridium. I should have put everything together then." He laughed and I blushed, remembering when my blade had cut through his fine suit.

"After I... *left* you..." Dracho's jaw clenched. "And we returned to Akraya—Antares found information about it in Cirdan's study. It's called argentium. It's a metal crafted long ago by the elves. Made by magick, the weapons never dull, never lose their sharpness. They're the only weapons ever made that could kill a draconi in both mortal and draconi form."

I swallowed hard, still wondering why Morgwn or my mother had never told me. "Did you know?"

"That there were weapons out there that could kill me? Yes. But I wasn't sure of their true existence until after you had stabbed me." He laughed again, pointing to his shoulder and revealing a small silver scar. I gasped.

"I'm sorry." Could I have killed him if I had struck his heart? I suddenly felt sick to my stomach. "So that day I almost *did* commit treason and murder an emperor?"

It was intended as a joke, but it came out unsure. Dracho's smile was playful, though.

"How... I don't understand how Morgwn could have had it made. This was after my mother had left Adref. And there were no elves living in Meridium at the time."

"Perhaps it was a skill your brother picked up? Maybe he made it himself?"

I hummed, sceptical. Smithing was never a talent or interest that Morgwn had ever expressed. "Perhaps it was just a family heirloom of my mother's."

Dracho smiled. "You must have loved him very much."

"Morgwn was my best friend."

"Tell me about him."

A shaky breath left my mouth. "Sometimes... sometimes the memory of him makes me sad... and then I feel guilty. I don't want to forget him. It's so hard when my best dreams and worst nightmares have the same people in them... the people I care about. But it hurts more when it's Morgwn. He was the best brother anyone could ask for." I swallowed, looking to the ceiling.

Dracho walked silently over to the bed, sitting on the edge as he faced me.

"He was protective, fierce and so loyal," I told him. "But more than that, he was fun. When we were both supposed to be undertaking our royal studies, he would break me out of the palace to steal horses from the stables and go riding."

Dracho's hand slid across the blanket to cover mine.

I laughed humourlessly. "Sometimes I half expect him to come running around the corner laughing... but then I'm filled with such rage and bitterness, wishing he was still here. And I wonder... how is it fair that someone as good as Morgwn was taken from me, but Jandar was allowed to live that day?"

A few tears fell from the corners of my eyes, leaving my cheeks feeling cold. Dracho crawled to sit beside me, leaning against the headboard and stretching his long legs out in front of him.

"But then I try to remember how lucky I was to know someone like him. How blessed I was. How blessed I was to have them all. Now, I'm alone."

A brief silence fell between us. I wiped the tears from my face.

"You're never alone, Eliana."

My breath was stolen when I caught his eye. Some gazes were the promise of home, protection and company. His was all of that—and more.

It made me feel exposed.

Placing the dagger down upon the side table, I wriggled down, moving over to wrap my arm over Dracho, resting my head on his hip. He stilled briefly before bringing his arm over me, his fingers brushing lightly up and down my shoulder. The embrace was comforting. His arm, firm but gentle, allowed me space to breathe, whilst still making me feel secure.

"Are you all right?" he asked softly.

I stared without seeing. I didn't know what I was. I felt broken and lost, and I couldn't deny it. Underneath it all, I could feel familiar tears in my soul and a bone-deep weariness clouding my soul. The thought of getting up every morning from now on and simply living my life was exhausting. That flame that usually burned within me was all but a smouldering ember. I wasn't sure how to reignite it.

If I ever could.

Dracho and Antares could somehow sense that. “No,” I whispered, being honest with him and myself.

“You will be,” he promised, his voice falling.

And maybe, just for a moment... I believed him.

“And Eliana?”

“Mmm-hmm.” My eyelids felt heavy.

“I prefer *Princess* to little doe.”

For the first time in a while, a genuine laugh left my mouth.

Chapter 42

“Are you ready?” Bas asked.

Nodding, I squeezed his hand. “I’m definitely ready to leave this place.”

I was done with hiding. It had been a week since Dracho and the others had rescued me. A week being dragged down to the great hall for breakfast, where the blond guard of Dracho’s—I had since found out his name was Jeshwa—had endeavoured to spend as much time with me and Roux as possible, his eyes straying to the latter quite often. If I had been in the right headspace, I would have laughed at the glares Bas kept sending his way.

“On to our next adventure, eh?” Bas asked, nudging me with his elbow.

“I think I’ve had enough adventure for a little bit.” I chuckled, letting go of him to slip my arms into the heavy cloak Dracho had given me.

Vyn walked towards us. “Um, about that....”

My back stiffened. “What?”

“Well, your ride is here.”

He indicated the double doors at the end of the hall that led to the outside courtyard. Giving him a curious look, I pushed them open.

Standing in the courtyard was an azure dragon with dark navy scales lining its spine. Its barbed tail ended in a gentle point and was covered in the same narrow scales as its body.

I took a step back, shaking my head. “No fucking way. You are not getting me on that thing.”

"Hey!" a low voice called out from behind us. Dracho headed past us, a playful smile on his full lips. "That *thing* is Jeshwa."

The blue dragon was looking straight at me. It bared its teeth in what I assumed was a smile, but just left me feeling more unnerved; I suppressed a shiver.

A rough noise came from Jeshwa's mouth. He shook his large, horned head as if laughing. It was hard to imagine the playful man I'd met had become this colossal beast. Smaller than Dracho's, but still large enough to intimidate.

"The woman over there is Skaze," Dracho said, indicating the woman I had seen with him in the hall. She gave a small wave. "And that's Tosen." He pointed to a severe, older-looking man beside Skaze. "Those are my fellow draconi. Finn, Jules and Caleb are mortal. They're fetching the last of our supplies." He walked backwards until he stood alone in a wide space of the courtyard. "And if you think I'm letting you ride one of the guys, you have another thing coming."

I breathed in relief, glancing around for Althea even as colour bloomed on my face at his words.

"You'll be riding me," Dracho added with a wicked grin, and before I could object, his loose shirt and trousers shredded from his body as he transformed.

His skin lit up, as if luminous stars had erupted beneath it, and I shielded my eyes as his form grew, stretching and morphing into a beast with four legs and wings. A large, black dragon now stood before me, spreading those gorgeous wings out as if stretching. Dracho shook his head, his silver horns shining in the morning sun.

"Fucking Goddess above," Bas muttered beside me as Connaught stepped into the courtyard. Vyn crossed his arms, looking impressed.

Dracho's silver eyes opened, staring at me. *Well, Princess, I don't think I've ever seen you so speechless. You've seen me before.*

He was right; I had. But I'd forgotten the sheer magick of the moment. Looking upon a real-life dragon—it wasn't something I'd ever thought I'd do in my lifetime. And that was a long time.

I realised my mouth was hanging open. I cleared my throat. "Yes, but that was before you said I should ride you."

Even his grin in his dragon form was wicked, and I rolled my eyes.

"Um, am I missing something?" Bas asked.

"Dracho's using his mind talk."

"And you can hear it? Whilst he's in dragon form?" Connaught asked.

I shrugged, realising I had never told them.

Now we know it's because you're elven.

I nodded. "It's because of my heritage," I explained aloud for the others' benefit.

So, Dracho continued, *I kind of need to do damage control back in Tenebris. I left rather abruptly after fetching my guards. And... I would like you to come with me. We can return to Meridium as soon as you're ready.*

I frowned, thinking it over.

"What is it?" Vyn asked.

"Dracho needs to return to Tenebris. He's invited... us?" I glanced back to Dracho, unsure if he meant for us all to go. His large head nodded in confirmation.

"Well, I wouldn't mind visiting again." Bas clapped his hands together. "Provided we have better accommodation this time around." He gave me a conspiratorial wink, and I heard a low groan from Dracho.

Did I want to go back to Tenebris? I had some bad memories from my time in the palace, but from my brief glances at the city, I most definitely wanted to see a place that differed so much to Meridium. It also meant I didn't have to rush into a coronation I wasn't ready for.

My eyes found Connaught's; there was a wrinkle between his brows. "What do you think?" I asked.

Connaught exhaled deeply. He looked from me to Dracho before taking a step forward, gripping my arms gently. "I *want* you to return home... but what do *you* want? Whatever it is, we'll make it happen."

I caught Bas's eye, and he gave me a small smile, nodding. I swallowed hard, surprised at the emotion that swelled in my throat. "I think... I want to go to Tenebris?"

I didn't explain that I couldn't handle the pressure of a coronation and being queen right now—that it weighed enough on me now to know I *could* go home. I still felt like I was letting my court and city down. At least I could spend some time in Tenebris just to heal, so I didn't look too sickly once I returned to my people.

"Eliana," Connaught said, reading my expression, "you have given more to your people already than most rulers could give in a lifetime. It's okay to let people look after you." I smiled slightly at the echo of what Dracho had said to me. "Meridium will still be there. I'll return to update Sizwe and prepare for your coronation."

I gave him a wider smile, glad that not only was he an amazing captain, but an amazing friend. Turning, I looked into Dracho's silver eyes.

"Okay," I told him.

If dragons could smile, I was sure that was what Dracho did. *Well then, climb aboard, Your Majesty. Your carriage awaits.*

A great obsidian wing lowered until it was resting on the ground like a makeshift ramp, one of the talons that lined the top of his wing stopping a few feet in front of me.

"Really? Can't we just get a boat?"

And risk your weak stomach? Dracho teased. *This is the fastest way we're getting to our location. So stop wasting time arguing and get on.*

Crossing my arms, I huffed like a petulant child.

Vyn turned, smirking. "Eli, it'll be the easiest way out of here." He sniffed, and I noticed that the end of his nose was slightly red.

"Are you all right?" I asked, frowning.

He waved me off. "I'm fine, just feeling a little under the weather. Go on, get up. Also"—his eyes skipped sideways to Antares, who passed us at that moment, loosening the ties at the top of his shirt—"*I'm* not going to complain about riding anyone."

"Won't I hurt you climbing your wing?" I asked Dracho.

He scoffed in both my mind and in dragon form, the sound rough. *My wings are made of tougher stuff than that.*

Sighing internally, I took a step closer, a flush rising on my cheeks at the other draconi getting naked in front of us. A rumble sounded from Dracho's chest, but his body remained perfectly still, head resting on the ground.

Standing at the edge of his black-scaled wing, I hesitated. "Um, how exactly do I do this?"

His wing flattened a bit more, a breath leaving his nostrils. *Slowly. Avoid the bones and stick to the thick membrane.*

"Uh-huh," I said, as if I did this every day.

Taking my time, I took a first gentle step onto the membrane, releasing a breath when he didn't react in pain. I probably took extra time I didn't need to as I climbed up, eventually using my hands towards the top of his shoulder. As relieved as I was to be off his wings, I now discovered a new problem: where to sit.

Just settle in the divot between my shoulders, in front of the wings. And hold on tight.

"Have you done this before?" I asked, my voice unsteady as I obeyed, avoiding the sharp points by his shoulders and settling onto smooth scales. "Perhaps you should have a saddle made."

Antares snorted from the courtyard as Dracho's dark chuckle brushed against the edges of my mind.

With Connaught. And Roux.

Well… they were still alive. Glancing down at the ground made me feel a little dizzy, my equilibrium off-centre as he rose to his feet. Goddess above, I was sitting on a dragon.

Bas and Vyn will be travelling with Althea.

I laughed, watching as the woman in question entered the courtyard from the double doors, knowing how disappointed that would make Vyn. Bas would just be ecstatic to ride a dragon.

Dracho seemed to sense where my thoughts went. *Antares would never allow anyone to ride him.*

"Why?" The word came out before I could stop it.

Dracho's wings rose and fell in imitation of a shrug.

"Do you think he'd be able to talk to me? The way you do?" I asked quietly, suddenly curious, and I felt the burning focus of golden eyes settle on me from where Antares stood, waiting for room to transform.

Hmph. I'm not sure. But I wouldn't count on him trying. He likes a quiet flight.

I'd expected that. Antares was a deeply private person. We'd only just started to speak amicably, so I couldn't imagine this more intimate way of speaking was on the agenda for us any time soon. Looking over to Jeshwa, I could see that Roux and Connaught had settled upon his back. I sent Roux a wave when she beamed at me.

"I'll see you in Tenebris!" she called.

Tighten your thighs, Princess.

Before I could scold him and his amused tone, Dracho's wings rose in a swift motion, his strong legs kicking off from the ground. I fell forward, clasping some of the smaller spikes on his shoulders, and squeezed my legs as tightly as I could. I no longer felt like the idea of a saddle was a joke. My eyes closed at the strange feeling.

Dracho's wings beat against the air in long swipes until he found a rhythm. Once he steadied, my eyes opened and I marvelled at the open skies around us, the cloudless sky that reached as far as the eye could see, the small breaks in the sea waves far below.

Straightening, feeling Dracho's strong muscles between my thighs and the jolt of each flap of his wings, I tipped my head back, feeling the cool wind brush my hair over my shoulders. Tentatively, I lifted my hands from his back, reaching my arms out wide to either side of me. As if he knew what I was doing, he flew as calmly as possible, maintaining his straight course.

The feeling could never be explained. It wasn't a sensation of falling; it was freedom. Jealousy shot through me at the thought that Dracho had the ability to do this whenever he wanted. Answering the pull I felt in my chest, I reached out to the bit of his wing that rested by my calf, running my fingers over the smooth membrane there.

A tremble seemed to roll between Dracho's shoulders, and he dropped a few feet in the air, causing me to quickly remove my hand.

"Sorry!" I yelled.

That... you didn't hurt me.

"Oh?"

It's... distracting. His inner voice sounded breathless.

"*Oh!*" I laughed. Maybe it was best to keep my hands to myself.

The emotion that overcame me as Ruvalon came into view surprised me, and I wiped away the tears that sprang to my eyes. Turning my head slightly, I took in the convoy that followed—Jeshwa in his blue form and Althea a beautiful shade of lavender that highlighted the blue of her reptilian eyes. My breath hitched as I watched her, stunned by the soft fur that adorned the top of her head and spine.

"Althea has fur!" I exclaimed.

Dracho laughed. *Did you expect all draconi to look the same?*

"Well, not the same, but... similar, yes."

There are many different types of draconi. From the fire dragons of the mountains to the windweavers of Venrus forest, beyond the palace... we are not all the same.

"That sounds amazing. What's Althea?"

She is a water dragon.

My mind was officially scrambled. "So she... shoots water at you?"

I could sense Dracho's smirk. *Scalding water, yes. Trust me, you wouldn't want to get a faceful of that.*

I wouldn't want to get a face full of water at all, no matter the temperature. I pondered in amazement what I had learned, tempted to ask what kind

Dracho was, but as I looked back over to Althea, Antares caught my eye. The only part of his dragon I had ever seen were the dark green claws that had escaped his control all those months ago, when he'd found out I knew about Dracho.

The quiet dragon caught up to us, the vertical pupil of his eye spying us for a moment. His scales were a beautiful forest green, with numerous spikes along his chest and the tops of his wings that hooked over. He had a thinner build than Dracho, and as he flew off ahead of us I noted the spiked, whip-like tail that trailed behind him.

Dracho laughed in my mind. *He's enjoying this.*

"What?" I called out over the wind.

Despite the size difference, I'm the fastest draconi alive. He's enjoying being able to pull ahead for once.

"Why don't you catch up?" I asked, pulling the cloak around me tighter and suppressing a shudder.

I wouldn't put you at any more risk than is necessary, Princess. It's also rather cold up here, even for an elf.

I nodded in agreement, though he couldn't see it. I was extremely grateful for the thick, fur-lined cloak he had given me; whatever it was made of was perfect for keeping heat in.

We flew steadily over the Vildspire dunes, the broken tree of Volente a speck below us. The air became dry and hot, and even this high up I could feel my lungs burning with every breath. Further to the south-west, Aion's bright green canopy shone above the rest of the forest.

As we flew further inland, I gazed in amazement at the small villages, rivers and farms below and wondered how the people would react to a dragon flying above them. I laughed as Meridium came into view a few hours later, feeling emotional as we flew over it. Jeshwa descended towards the palace, and I waved at Roux and Connaught on his back.

"So," I called, "why did you want me to come to Tenebris?"

Do you trust me, Princess? was all he said.

I only had a second of hesitation. There was one thing I didn't trust him with—my heart. But with my safety... Unquestionably.

"Yes."

If I'd thought Tenebris was beautiful when I first saw it, it was nothing compared to the beauty of it from above. I looked down at the river dividing into waterfalls that flowed through the centre, and an awed breath left me as the palace was backdropped by clear skies. The setting sun glinted off the tall spires, blinding me for a moment. I rubbed my chest for warmth after flying through the biting winds of the Ballaraan mountains.

Dracho eased into a glide. He was approaching one of the balconies that protruded from the spires towards the top of the palace, Antares for one a floor lower. I held on tightly to the spikes on his shoulder as he hovered several feet above it.

A blinding light, and then I was in freefall.

A terrified scream left my throat as I plummeted towards the balcony floor— before two strong arms captured me, holding me as easily as a feather pillow. My heart pounded, Dracho's dark chuckle infuriating me as I clambered out of his arms, turning to face his... very naked body. I shrieked again, covering my eyes and spinning, still feeling slightly dizzy.

"You scared me, you arse! And put some bloody clothes on!" I cried.

I felt a slight breeze kiss my neck; his lips, close to my ear, startled me.

"If I remember correctly, you were practically begging to remove my clothes in that tent. What's wrong? Nervous now you have me naked?"

My hands dropped, and I bared my sharpened teeth at him. He'd retreated several feet—still naked. Keeping my eyes from his corded muscles, I swiftly removed the cloak from my shoulders, walking over to shove it at him. I turned and stormed into the room, and my steps faltered.

It was gorgeous.

The floors were white marble, the large table-top matching. A golden goblet sat atop the table, with two crystal wine glasses beside it. A breathtaking and ornate golden four-poster bed stood on a slightly raised platform in the corner of the room, a doorway not too far from it which I assumed led to a bathroom. Scattered around were several small pots of greenery, adding a pleasing splash of colour to the room.

I felt the hairs rise on my skin as Dracho strolled past me, tossing the cloak onto a chaise-longue before clicking his fingers. A gasp escaped me as a pair of breeches and a white shirt suddenly appeared on his body.

"How did you do that?"

He grinned, happy to have impressed me. "It came with the upgrade in power. I must admit, it's been useful. Though I miss the draught through my nether regions." He laughed when I scrunched my nose.

"Can Ant do it too?" He had already merged with his dragon.

Dracho shook his head, his expression gleefully smug. "He's jealous."

I smiled. "So... why did you want me to return here?"

"I figured..." He exhaled, watching me closely as I looked around the room. "You needed time to recuperate... and you'd be too stubborn to step back from royal duties if we were in Meridium."

"Wow—rude."

He walked into my field of view, his lips tugging at the corner as I fought hard not to let my gaze drop to his undone shirt, where his muscled chest showed. "Just think of it as some much-needed relaxation away. I need to explain to the council why I took off with five of my best soldiers," he admitted, rubbing the back of his neck. "And let them know Jandar is dead."

"And what about when they hear I'm here?" I raised an eyebrow at him.

"Hmm. Think of it as a diplomatic visit."

"Uh-huh. And after my last visit here, how are you going to explain our *relationship* to your council?"

His eyes turned gentle. "I'll tell them you're a friend."

I laughed softly. "Are we friends?"

"I'd like to think so." His blue eyes twinkled, and my stomach dipped. "If not, what are we?"

My chest felt tight, and I swallowed thickly. "I think... we are two people who happened to meet, with similar interests," I told him, only somewhat joking.

I didn't think I could risk letting him become more. I still didn't think I could trust him with my feelings.

Yet the biggest reason I fought it was that not only was I about to become queen of Meridium, but he was already emperor of Tenebris—and had just signed a treaty agreeing that he would remain there after finding his father's killer.

"That's all?" he asked, trying not to smile.

"That's all." I nodded.

"I'd agree with you, but then we'd both be incorrect," he quipped, and I genuinely laughed—it felt strange.

"But I mean it, Eliana. I want you to use this time to recuperate—enjoy yourself a bit. I know you weren't exactly looking forward to your coronation." He held his hands out, the fabric of his shirt pulling tight over his defined arms as he motioned to the space around him. "Here's a relaxing interlude before you have to commit to your duties."

I rolled my eyes playfully at him and turned, looking around the room. "Is this my room for the time I spend here?"

His full lips twitched. "This is *my* room, Princess. But please, feel free to spend as much time as you want here." He looked at me from under his lashes, pouring a glass of some red liquid I assumed was wine.

I scoffed, turning to hide the heat flaming upon my cheeks. "Perhaps you could show me to *my* chambers, then? I am rather tired from our flight."

"From *our* flight?" he laughed. I looked over my shoulder, breath hitching at the sensual smile he was giving me. "If I remember rightly, *I* was doing all the work."

"That makes a change," I grumbled under my breath, earning a chuckle as I strolled out of the main door and into a white stone hallway. I glanced left and right before Dracho whispered against my neck, giving me goosebumps again.

"To your left."

I pointedly ignored the flush caused by his proximity and headed in that direction, though I had hardly gone twenty feet before I came to the very next door, where he halted me.

"What?" I asked.

Dracho nodded towards the cream door, ornately carved with vines and wings.

"This one?" I asked, my voice rising an octave as his grin widened. The room next door to his own? Having him so close would be too much of a temptation—even if I would never admit that. But how could I explain that it was a terrible idea? Resigned, I placed my hand on the cool handle, entering the room.

It was stunning.

Walls of light cream and furniture accented with champagne fabrics adorned the room. Thin, gauzy curtains drifted in the cool breeze from the open balcony doors, the late afternoon sun pouring in. A fur comforter was laid over the bottom of the white oak four-poster bed, ending just before it touched the tiled floor. A bathing chamber sat off in the corner, though I couldn't see inside from the door.

The room felt light—so in contrast to how I had felt inside recently—and a thick swell of emotion grew in my throat at the comfort it seemed to immediately bring me. Whoever had owned this room before my visit had clearly loved it, and it was obviously still taken care of.

"It was my mother's," Dracho said quietly behind me.

I turned to face him, my shock pulling back the wave of emotion. He took a few steps forwards until he stood beside me, the warmth of his body seeping into my own.

"It was her room whilst she was courting my father. She used it as a workspace and relaxation room after they were officially together. I continued its upkeep after she had gone."

"It's beautiful," I breathed. *And I can't possibly stay here.*

As if reading my thoughts, Dracho smiled at me so warmly that my blood heated, and I couldn't help but give him a small smile of my own.

My mother would have loved for you to stay here.

This time it shocked me less when he spoke. I was getting used to hearing his mental voice, and somewhat comforted by the softness of it. I just nodded, deciding not to fight such a personal offer, turning to peruse the room some more. A window seat had been crafted in the deep-set sill opposite the bed, either side of it furnished with two large bookshelves, filled with books I had never heard of and some in languages I did not know.

"Vyn and Bas should be settled by now. Do you want to see them, or would you like a moment alone?"

Despair threatened at the thought of being alone, but I pressed down upon the emotion, hiding it from the lines of my face. "I want to see them."

His light eyes studied my face for a long second before offering his arm. "Then this way, *Princess.*"

I scoffed but took it.

As we wandered through the halls, heading down a spiral staircase until we arrived on a lower floor, I was surprised by the lack of treasures around. The palace wasn't showy, like that of Stillmere, nor as decorated as my own in Meridium. The walls, steps and floor were made of natural marble, the whites and cream of the stone blending magnificently and creating a beautiful effect. There was no art hanging along the walls, no gold or silver decor. Each door was finely carved with florals, vines or wings as the one to my own room. It was light. It was beautiful.

Voices from up ahead reached me as we approached a large open area between two rooms. Chaise-lounges were scattered about, and several large cushions were placed on the floor, laid on top of an eye-catching ivory rug.

Bas had already made himself comfortable; he lounged on one of the cushions, his legs stretched before him and crossed at the ankle. Althea had joined him on the floor, sitting cross-legged as she laughed at something he said. A twinge of jealousy ran through me, seeing her laugh so freely. I wished I could be like that after everything.

Feeling eyes on me, I glanced at Antares, who was leaning against the stone wall. I froze, feeling a tug in my chest as I became very aware that he was studying every emotion passing over my face, every minute movement. I looked away quickly, finding Vyn as he lay back on one of the lounges.

"It won't be long before Roux is back, but I need to go and do damage control with Thuban," Dracho told them before turning to me, his hand brushing over my arm. "You are free to explore the city; you aren't confined to the palace. If you'd like someone to show you around, I'm sure I can find a guide."

"I'll take her!" Althea raised her hand. "Would you like a tour?"

"That would be lovely, thank you." I grinned, looking at Bas, who nodded eagerly.

"We'll go now." Althea jumped up eagerly—which startled me; I wasn't entirely sure I had worked myself up to it yet. "C'mon, then. See you later, boys!"

"Am I not invited?" Antares teased.

"No," Althea said bluntly, "Eliana wants to see all the fun things. Not to be bored by you divulging the history of every street in the city." I laughed as Ant scowled at her. "Bas, Vyn, you coming?"

Bas looked at Vyn hopefully, but the latter shook his head, fingers rubbing at his temple.

"You know, I think I actually need to lie down for a while," he said weakly.

Releasing Dracho's arm, I went to his side, noting the paleness of his skin. When I put a hand to his forehead, all I could feel was heat.

"Goddess, you're burning up, Vyn!"

He batted my hand away with his own. "I'm fine," he sniffled.

Dracho and Antares wore matching expressions of concern.

"Ant, escort Vyn to his room," Dracho ordered. "I'll send up a healer."

Antares nodded, walking forward to wrap Vyn's arm around his shoulders.

"If you wanted to grope me, you need only have asked." Vyn laughed weakly as Bas grabbed his other arm. Antares rolled his eyes.

Dracho nodded at him, some unspoken conversation between them, and I stepped aside, allowing the two to carry Vyn from the room. Dracho must have seen my rising panic.

"Vyn will be fine, Eliana. He's sick, malnourished, and he needs rest. The healers will look after him."

I nodded a bit too much, pretending that fear hadn't taken a sharp grasp of my heart. "I'm going to follow them."

His warm arm wrapped around my shoulders. "Althea, your tour will have to wait. Gather the council. Inform I'll be in the throne room within the hour." He swept me through the palace to where Vyn was staying.

It was similar in layout to my own room, but with accents of blue and silver throughout. Antares and Bas had placed Vyn in the large bed.

His teeth chattered as he tried to pull up the thick blanket. "I-I'm cold."

"Brother, you have a fever. I can't let you wrap up warm or you'll get hotter," Bas told him, his brow lowering in worry. He draped a sheet carefully over our friend.

"I'll fetch the healers," Dracho said, hurrying off.

I had never seen Vyn ill in all our years together. I knew he was malnourished and had been through far too much; it was likely just a small fever, but having been away from them and believed they were dead, I couldn't help but feel anxious. I walked forward to climb on the bed and offer Vyn some comfort, but Antares's hand caught my arm.

"No, Eli," Vyn wheezed, and my chest constricted. Bas rubbed the back of his neck as he watched.

I glared at Antares, whose gaze hardened. "Eliana, you are wounded and starved. You cannot risk getting sick," he said with authority.

I didn't even attempt to stop my teeth from lengthening, snarling at him. "If anyone can risk getting sick, surely it's me. *I* will heal."

"Ant is right, E." My head swung to Bas as he rushed to finish his point. "You need to take care of yourself. Vyn will be fine; it's just something he picked up. I'll keep you updated."

"But—"

"No buts." Bas's eyes narrowed as he scolded me. "It's time for rest. That includes you too. You're not doing Vyn or anyone any favours if you get ill. So take this time to get better."

I sighed, looking down in surrender, and Antares's hand left my arm. Bas was right. I hated that he was, but I could feel the exhaustion running through my bones and the ever-present ache of the wound on my thigh, though it was healing quicker than mortals would. Bas's boots stepped into my vision, and I felt the softest brush of lips against my head.

"Do you want to go back to your room?" Antares asked, and I nodded.

"Vyn," I called as I headed out the door, "get better or I'll kill you."

A weak laugh sounded from the bed. "There she is... I love you," he whispered.

Antares silently followed me all the way up the stairs, only speaking once to remind me which direction to head in. He leaned around me to open my door, watching me like I was a pending explosion as I hovered in the middle of the room, feeling lost. Loneliness crept around my heart like a vice, returning me to that windowless cell and trying to smother that flicker of light left within until there was nothing but shadow.

"Are... are you all right?" Antares asked, his voice rough.

"I..." I trailed off. How could I explain it?

But as usual, he knew what I needed without me voicing it. He strolled over to the desk, poured a glass of water, and pushed it to the edge of the desk.

"Drink," was all he said before taking a book from one of the shelves and settling himself into the window seat.

That was where he stayed. He was silent company as I drank the water and devoured the food that was brought up at some point—strawberries, cheese, and a few slices of bread. His eyes lifted every now and then from the pages to his book to flick between me and my plate.

I contemplated picking up a book to read myself, but my brain turned foggy as exhaustion slipped in. I collapsed bonelessly on top of the bed in my dress, far more comfortable with Antares in the room than if he hadn't been. As I drifted off, I saw his shoulders relax, a sigh leaving him as he continued to read.

Chapter 43

When I awoke, I was momentarily confused by the rows of tight brown braids in front of my face. The sound of a relaxed woman's breathing made me sit upright, placing my hand on her shoulder to turn her over. I grinned as Roux's sleepy eyes opened.

"What time is it?" she mumbled, before letting out a rough grunt as I threw myself on her.

"I missed you too," she laughed.

"I am so glad to see you," I breathed. "Have you heard anything about Vyn?"

"He's fine." Roux sat up straighter. "He's got a fever and a tight chest, but the healers say he should be fine in a few days with the tonics they're giving him."

I fell back against the pillows, my hair fanning out about my face as I sighed in relief.

"How are you feeling?" Roux asked, and I blinked up at the ceiling.

"Like an exposed nerve," I told her, wondering if she knew what I meant.

She hummed. "I think Tenebris will be good for you. Althea and I plan to take you out today." I shot up at that. "But first, bath. Breakfast is on its way, and then we get to explore."

I chewed the inside of my cheek, my mind spinning and my stomach twisting in knots. Again, I had the feeling of not being able to explain. How to start the conversation and explain that being alone made me anxious, but also that the thought of being around so many people seemed equally terrifying? It didn't make sense to me, so I had no idea how to articulate it.

So I remained silent, walking into the large bathroom. I turned the golden faucets, running a hot bath with jasmine-scented soap before taking care of my morning needs, pondering the difference in my surroundings in less than a week. Cold grey stone and iron rings flashed before my eyes, but I shook my head before the panic could grip me. When the bath was full, I practically threw myself into the hot water. My eyes found the healing wound on my leg under the water and my skin felt cold, despite the steam that rose from my skin. The rest of my body had healed pretty quickly, the blisters almost gone and my cheek no longer bruised. My ribs still felt tight from the beatings I had taken, but each day it was a little easier to breathe.

Could I do it? Could I leave the palace and explore the city like any normal person—like someone who hadn't just spent almost a month in captivity, abused and starved to the point of breaking? My throat tightened, like a shackle constricting my airway, as I thought about it. But then my mind drifted to that hallucination which had kept me awake, had reinstated in me a sliver of hope. My mother, reminding me that I would never break.

How easy it felt to break a person. How long they took to repair. Had I not been broken enough by the traumas of my past? Tears burned my eyes as my hands found purchase on the edges of the tub, gripping tightly as if I could be thrown out at any moment. Why did *I* deserve such breaking? Why had this happened to me again? A family name tied to my blood and a title bestowed by my father's death—that was hardly a justified reason to have treated me no better than the beasts the Hollow used.

I looked down at myself, seeing but feeling nothing, as if I had been truly turned into the ghost I felt like. I wondered what would happen if I were to fall away and become nothing.

You do not break. My mother's voice whispered in my mind. I remembered the devastation in her eyes when she'd appeared in that cell. I was broken, but perhaps I could heal. For them. I had healed before, not fully, but enough to live.

I wanted to. I wanted to live—but for myself, not for others.

My hand sloshed through the water, my thoughts drifting to Antares's amber eyes as he comforted me back in Fallstone. *It's not a case of getting over the wave that tried to drown you in the first place, it's the agony of learning to swim and keep swimming.*

Perhaps that was how I should start. By taking the slow strokes.

As I exited the bathroom dressed in a thin white robe, Roux's glowing smile fuelled my determination. I dressed quickly, letting every fear and worry flow out of my mind as soon as they appeared. I hadn't realised how refreshing it would be to be out of a gown until I stepped into the pair of brown breeches and flowing white shirt that Roux must have placed on my bed. My hands travelled to my hair out of habit, as if to hide my ears. Instead, I tucked it behind them, allowing my glamour to melt away.

I can do this.

It would be the first time I stepped out in public as *me*. For a moment I almost changed my mind. But at least while in Tenebris, I would be me. I would refuse to hide myself. Perhaps I could use this time to test how people truly felt about the real me.

I felt as though I had stepped into my own skin again, and when I turned to find Roux holding my dagger out to me, I had to hold back more tears. As I finished tightening the strap around my thigh, relief rushed through me. With a shaky exhalation, I steeled myself for whatever came next.

"Let's go." I nodded to Roux, whose proud smile and bright eyes could have made the Goddess kneel.

"Let's go," she repeated, holding her hand out and grasping my own in its warmth.

Althea was waiting at the entrance to the palace, practically bouncing on the balls of her feet. She and Roux walked me through the trade district, which was ten minutes away from the palace. The sandstone buildings to either side of me were full of various businesses—galleries, clothing and craft stores which displayed their wares outside on stalls with birchwood rooftops. I ran my hand over smooth, luxurious fabrics in colours I had never seen in my life. Business was healthy, judging by the bustling street, and if anyone noticed my ears, no one reacted to them. My unease faded away as warm smiles greeted me and people conversed with Althea whilst we walked.

Roux skipped from stall to stall, telling me about the craftsmanship of the jewellery and instruments on display. Her enthusiasm kept a smile on my face; I realised how much she had fallen in love with this place. I could see it too—

the warmness. It reminded me of Aion.

We walked further into the city, the day passing quickly, until we reached the Ryu district. It was glorious. The sight and aromas of the food being cooked was like a warm embrace to my soul. A large open space was in the centre of the buildings, full of wooden benches and tables where people ate and conversed. Each building around it had a large open window where people would order and collect food. Althea took me around each one, where they offered me samples of delicacies I had never seen or smelled before. Roux dragged me to one, greeting the old woman serving with a blown kiss. I politely refused the full portion of food she offered, not wanting to take something for free.

"Nonsense," the middle-aged woman told me from behind a multitude of sauté pans, the sizzling food a delicious assault on my senses. "Any friend of Althea is a friend of ours."

Althea chuckled. "Thanks, Miriam."

Miriam offered me a taste of the food on a skewer, checking I liked it. The woman didn't even blink when I tucked my hair, which had fallen around my face, behind my ears before taking it gladly, offering a smile in return. Rich flavours burst across my tastebuds as I chewed the piece of fried meat she offered. It was the perfect mixture of sweet and spicy. Roux moaned loudly around her own mouthful, nodding in satisfaction.

"Can we get some?" I whispered to Althea, who laughed along with Miriam as she handed over the full plate. She gave me a conspiratorial wink when I thanked her.

We wandered through more of the brightly lit streets, eating our plates of food as we went in silence—and it was nice. No dark thoughts plagued me; there was no taunting over my heritage as people noticed me. I felt... normal.

Taverns and unusual places with flashing lights and loud music lined the sides of one street, the people going in and out wearing some scandalous clothing.

Althea laughed at my wide-eyed expression. "This is the heart of the Ryu district. This is where we come to dance, drink... let off some steam."

"It's incredible!" Roux exclaimed, her eyes twinkling.

"That's not like any music I've ever heard," I admitted.

"You don't have music like that down south?" Althea asked, her head tilting when I shook mine. "Huh, well, that's given me an idea."

"Why don't I like the sound of that?"

She laughed, the sound like a beautiful songbird. "Come on, both of you. There's more to see." She stepped between us, linking our arms and pulling us forward.

As the noise and thrum of the Ryu district faded behind us, we approached a cliff-edge protected with a wooden fence; the sound of roaring water reached my ears. My breath was stolen from me as we gazed over the viewpoint. Several small waterfalls poured out from *inside* the cliff, ending in a large expanse of water. Boats floated atop the calmer surface further out, the brilliant warm lights looking like stars upon the dark water. We could still hear the pleasant chatter of people from the Ryu district behind us, adding to the happy atmosphere.

"I'm always struck by how beautiful it is," Roux whispered, eyes bright as she looked over the water.

"This is one of my favourite views in all of Tenebris." Althea smiled.

"I can see why." I nudged her with my shoulder. Squinting into the darkness, I eyed something in the distance. "What's that?"

"That's where the falls end, and where the blossom trees grow."

Blossom trees? That sounded amazing. "Can we go?"

Althea shook her head. "There's not enough time left in the day. Climbing back out would be impossible in the dark."

I nodded, biting down my disappointment.

Dracho had apparently meant it when he said I was free to roam where I wanted. The guards didn't look at me twice as I left my room the next morning, heading out of the front doors and retracing my steps through the city.

I felt slightly guilty for not asking Althea to accompany me, but something from the cliff edge the night before had called to me, and I felt like I had to see it alone. Finding the rocky edge of the falls was easy; I followed the flow of water through the city, smiling at the warm greetings I received along the way.

Looking out over the cliff edge, I could see a rough trail down the cliffside. My gaze was drawn to the beautiful lake for a moment. Cherry willow trees lined the banks, and there was an enticing grassy knoll in the middle of the ravine—a perfect place to sit under the trees.

Before starting the descent, I inhaled deeply to calm myself. It was a lot higher than it had looked the previous night. Adrenaline coursed through my body as I took careful steps down. The sound of the waterfall roared in my ears, and cold droplets of spray kissed my skin in the most delicious way.

A few rocks fell away beneath my next step, and I sucked in a gasp. Closing my eyes, I focused my senses, adapting to the elven gifts I knew were available to me but had been unused for a long time. Glancing down again, I spotted a smoother part of the trail, and I used the jagged edges beside me as a natural handhold to get there. My nimble feet carried me down steadily until I hit the solid stones at the side of the lake. Gravel crunched underneath my boots as I wandered past the lake, towards the grassy knoll in the middle of the ravine, and tiny raindrops started to fall from the sky.

A small, breathless laugh left me as I jogged gently to reach the cover of the trees, the pastel blossom-covered branches swaying in the misty breeze carried over from the waterfalls. Occasional drops of rain fell through the small gaps of the trees, each one sending a shiver through me.

I settled myself down between two thick tree roots, arms resting on top of my knees, feeling the earth rumble with the water's force as I watched the relentless movement of the falls. My soul and spirit seemed to breathe for themselves in this place. In such a bustling, busy city, it was nice to find an area of peace—something that seemed untouched.

Magick and power seemed to radiate around me, its aura a comforting embrace. It was in everything: the breeze brushing against my skin, the light mist that floated atop the lake, and the soft petals of the cherry trees that seemed to whisper. As I rested my head on my arms, for the first time I felt that ember within flare a little and grow stronger. Felt my aura reach out into the nature around me, and how the energy that flowed back rejuvenated me.

My peace didn't last long. The sound of wings on the wind reached my ears, and I looked to the sky just as a great shadow flew over the lake. He must have sensed my presence; his wings beat against the air for a few times, hovering, as if hesitating to intrude on my peace. Then those spectacular dark green wings of his slowed, easing him down until his clawed feet landed on the rocky water edge.

His scaled green head considered me for a few moments in silence. I frowned as the silence held, until his head dropped with an impatient huff through his large nostrils.

Oh, right. Noticing the bag tied to his leg, I gave him some privacy by looking away as he transformed, hearing the rustle of clothes. I said nothing as his steps neared me, only taking a quick glance as he settled on the other side of the tree root next to me, his feet bare and rubbing into the soil underneath them.

What surprised me most was that his company felt like sinking into warm water, like that of my bath that morning. It was peaceful—a feeling I'd never thought to have around Antares.

"It's strange." His voice was a breath of smoke that floated away in the wind.

"What is?" I turned my head slightly, seeing the hint of a smile on his face as his golden eyes stared at the water.

"You are both drawn to the same place."

Looking at him fully, I stared, dumbfounded, until his eyes met mine fully—a world of unspoken words twinkling in his sly expression.

It hit me like a brick. That rainy night before Stillmere—the night Dracho had stopped us killing the Sujin—he had come to my tent, and talked to me about why I loved the rain so much. He'd shared that there was a special place for him in Tenebris, where the cherry willows were: the stillness so peaceful, even in the roar of the water. It was a place he'd come to after his mother had died, finding peace in the clear skies when the stars shone above.

"I, um..." I cleared my throat. "I can see why he likes it here."

Antares hummed.

"Did he send you?"

Small beads of water dropped from the strands of hair that fell over his eyes as he shook his head.

"Then how?"

His head tilted, looking at me like it was obvious. "You worried Roux when she couldn't find you in your room. So I tracked you."

"Ah. I almost forgot about your impressive skills—as if being a dragon wasn't enough," I teased.

Antares laughed deeply, but the peace that had settled over me lifted for a moment. Why *was* he here?

"I thought I was free to go where I wanted within the city?" My chin tipped up slightly.

He gave me a sharp little cocksure smile that pissed me off.

"You are." His hand ran through his hair, clearing it from his view. "That doesn't mean you won't be protected, Eliana. By more than just Dracho."

My anger dissipated almost immediately, but the unease remained. "I thought I was safe here?"

"You are," he repeated, "but the Hollow got in once before..."

My heart tripped. I had almost forgotten that the Hollow had entered Tenebris—that it had assassinated the emperor and caused the rift between me and Dracho. What if Cirdan had sent it after me? Panic leeched through me, sucking away my peace and strength as I realised I was putting people in danger. Putting my *friends* in danger.

"Hey, hey," Antares said, his large warm hand suddenly enveloping my own. "Breathe, Eliana."

In, and out. The shortness of breath wasn't awful this time. The skin of my hand tingled as Antares soothed small circles just above my thumb; my eyes closed, and I focused on my beating heart.

"I'm sorry, I shouldn't have said anything."

I stared at him. He was capable of apologising?

"You are safe here, Eliana." He squeezed my hand once before letting it go. All I could do was nod in response. "Vyn is feeling somewhat better," he offered.

"He is?" I croaked.

He nodded. "I think you should be able to see him when we return to the palace."

"I'd like that," I told him brightly, feeling happy that Vyn was better, and as I realised that Antares and I had perhaps become friends.

Chapter 44

Once Antares had walked me back to the palace—no one in the streets of Tenebris seemed bothered by his bare feet—I ran as hard and fast as I could, dodging palace staff, who exclaimed in shock, and guards, who didn't baulk. Reaching Vyn's door, I knocked twice.

"Come in," his voice called out, lazily but sounding stronger than when I had last seen him.

Tears sprang to my eyes at seeing him sitting up at a small, rounded table, drinking from a cup. A grin spread across his face as I rushed over, wrapping my arms around his lithe frame and squeezing him.

"How are you feeling?" I asked, taking a seat beside him. The healers must have done an amazing job; his skin looked a much better colour than the pallor of before.

"I'm better." He smiled, taking my hand within his own. "How about you?"

I waved him off. "Forget about me—"

"No. We never forget about you... Are you all right?"

I chewed the inside of my cheek for a second. "I'm fighting."

"And we would expect nothing less," he said, leaning forward to peck my cheek.

I sighed, my eyes roaming over the table and the empty bowl before him. "Are you eating well? Do you need anything?"

His head shook. "I'm fine. I ate not too long ago—Dracho brought me up a bowl of soup."

I hadn't seen Dracho since he had left Vyn's room a couple days before, and I had knocked his room once or twice. Althea had told me he had meetings to attend to, and I knew he was busy. I felt moved that he had taken some time to visit Vyn, but... why hadn't he come to see me?

"Dracho? The *emperor* of Tenebris brought you food?" I was equally awed and amused.

A small, fond smile tugged at Vyn's lips, a dimple appearing in his cheek. "He hasn't long gone back to his chambers, if you wish to see him."

"He stayed?"

"He kept me company whilst I ate."

I swallowed the lump of unfamiliar emotion that had appeared in my throat.

"Seemed a bit distant though. Stressed."

"Did he say why?" I remembered what Dracho had said about *damage control*. It must have been serious if he was still dealing with it.

Vyn shook his head. "He mentioned a meeting with the council yesterday, but nothing specific."

I hummed, just as the door to Vyn's room was thrown wide open and Bas thundered in. "Hey, E! Come to see the drama queen in all his glory, after he had us so worried?"

Vyn rolled his eyes as I laughed.

"Bastion," I drawled. "Where *have* you been disappearing to the past couple days?" His cheeks darkened as if I had asked him something scandalous. "Does it have something to do with... Roux, perhaps?"

He stood straighter, squaring his shoulders. "That is none of your business."

I failed to hold back the laugh that bubbled up. "All right, all right."

My grin dropped as I caught Vyn inclining his chin in my direction.

"What?" I asked, not liking his expression.

"You should speak with him, Eli."

My mouth went dry. "What do you mean?"

"I mean..." His gaze dropped to his lap. "You've been angry for so long, you've been hurt so much. It's time to let it all go."

I jerked back. "W-what are you saying?"

"I'm saying," Vyn said softly, as if talking to a skittish animal, "I want to see you happy… I think Dracho could make you happy. At the very least, he would take care of you."

"I don't *need* anyone to take care of me," I argued, wondering what in all Ruvalon Vyn and Dracho had spoken about.

Bas waved his hands. "We're not saying that, E. But sometimes, you know, it's nice to have someone look after you for a change."

Let me take care of you.

In the chaos of my mind, I pondered a life where my heart was not damaged but healed. Where I could easily accept what I wanted—what I craved. My heart pounded an irregular rhythm against my ribcage as I thought about that life. Whether it even was a realistic possibility.

It wasn't.

I was going to be queen soon; he was an emperor. Even if our two separate kingdoms hadn't been an issue, the treaty would be. Dracho had agreed to remain in Tenebris after we had finished dealing with the Hollow. In his old fear of the draconi, I couldn't see King Jareth agreeing to change the terms just so we could be together—if that was even something Dracho wanted. If it was, living in two separate kingdoms would be too difficult. And it wasn't like one of us would abdicate our thrones. Not after we had both been through so much to get them.

Everything was too complicated. I clenched my hands in my lap to bring myself back to reality. To stop myself from running to his room and to what could hurt me again.

I didn't know what to do or say—and all that scared me far more than any elven prince or lupera blade ever could. Because if I truly chose for myself, allowed the hurt to heal and started to hope for a future, there was no guarantee. No guarantee we wouldn't *both* mess it up. This was bigger than us. This was kingdoms and people spread across an entire continent.

Was it worth the risk?

I was stubborn. I was a mess. I was broken. I could barely deal with my own trauma and healing; would I be able to carry the burden of someone else's too?

Vyn's fingers brushed through the loose strands of my hair.

"E," Bas said softly, leaning down to clasp my free hand. "We know you're dealing with a lot."

I almost scoffed. They had stuff to deal with too. I hated that they treated my trauma as more important than their own.

Bas continued. "So much has happened to you in such a short amount of time."

But it's not as if I'm the only person things have happened to, I wanted to say. My head turned, my glassy eyes finding those yellow irises of my best friend and mirror. He could see exactly what I was feeling.

"How... how did you cope?" I asked him. "When we were younger and you found out about your mother and father?"

As a young girl who had recently lost her mother and sibling, I'd had no idea how to help Vyn when the orphanage he'd been left at had told him the truth of his heritage. But he'd stayed with me anyway, and somehow, his haunted expression eventually disappeared. Our situations were completely different, but I'd always wondered how he had the strength.

"How did you get over the loneliness?" I whispered.

Vyn laughed softly. "Eli, I was never alone. I had you, I had Bas. We may not have been related by blood, but you were all my family by choice."

Hot tears sprang to my eyes. Bas's large, warm hand came to rest gently on my shoulder. "That's right, E. No matter what you're facing, or what you're going through, you're never alone."

My head found Vyn's shoulder as great sobs wracked my body. That unyielding tightness that had overwhelmed me ever since that night when my innocent and naïve view of the world had been shattered was finally released. I grieved for what I had lost, for what I had pushed away and for what had been taken from me. But instead of focusing on the bitter energy that had swirled in my gut and the recesses of my mind for so long, I concentrated on my friends' faces, and the love there. That love spread through my body as my grief curled in on itself—a tiny thing in the face of the love surrounding me.

I exhaled deeply with a final sniff, raising my head to look at them both. "I love you guys."

Bas teeth flashed into a wide smile. "We love you too, E."

"Don't you have somewhere to go?" Vyn asked, a smirk growing on his lips.

Clearing my throat, I stood, smoothing down the fabric of my shirt. "I... I'll see you later."

"Uh-huh." Bas winked, and my cheeks flamed as I practically ran from the room.

I had no plans to follow through with what they'd insinuated. But... maybe I could start to bridge a working relationship with Dracho. Put aside my stubbornness and grudge to try and build a better future for both of us *and* our kingdoms.

My hands fidgeted restlessly as I wandered back up a floor to his room, hesitating outside his door. I obviously waited for far too long, because before I knew it, the door had been pulled open.

My breath caught as my gaze wandered over his face, a lock of hair falling over his bright eyes.

"Eliana," he said in surprise and smiled, the charming expression warming the beauty of his features.

I followed him almost against my will as he turned, leaving the door open for me to enter the room behind him. From the shadows under his eyes, the scattered papers on the desk, a half-empty liquor bottle and the fact that he was still in his clothes from the day before, I guessed that he'd been up most of the night, perusing whatever royal duties were calling his name.

Running a hand through his hair, he turned, his gaze widening in alarm once he saw my puffy red eyes.

"Is everything all right?" he asked, his voice low.

Now that I was in his room, I had no idea how to begin. How to start mending the gap. My fingers fidgeted in front of me.

Dracho stepped forward in a flash, reaching out to calm my restless hands. "Eliana, is everything all right? You know you can tell me and I'll—"

"It was nice of you," I blurted out.

The corner of his parted lips rose in an awkward smile.

"To take Vyn soup," I clarified. *Why in all Ruvalon did my brain decide to say that?*

He chuckled, and all my senses immediately became aware of how close he stood, the heat of his body, the flex of his jaw as he swallowed.

"It was no problem at all. It's nice to see him feeling better. I thought my mother's recipe would cheer—"

"Your mother's recipe?" I asked, surprised at the throatiness of my voice.

He nodded with a half-shrug, his thumb rubbing a soothing circle into the skin of my hand. I didn't think he even realised he was doing it. "She always used to make it for me when I was sick; I thought I'd extend the favour after all Vyn has been through."

"Y-you made it?"

Head tilting slightly, he raised a brow. "Yes, I—"

I kissed him.

His lips—warm and smooth—were firm as he jerked slightly in shock. He didn't pull himself away, but his entire body was rigid, his eyes were blown wide with surprise. I traced my tongue over his lower lip, and with a deep groan he was suddenly kissing me back. No, he didn't kiss me—he devoured me, as if he craved the taste of me more than anything.

My back arched towards him, and he wrapped his warm arms around my waist, lifting me gently until the tips of my boots brushed against the floor. My hand moved towards his jaw, holding his face to mine. I kissed him like I'd been waiting my whole life for it, and he met it with so much fervour that I wondered who had been craving it the most.

I needed more. I needed his warmth. Needed less between our bodies. My free hand wove through the silky black hair at the nape of his neck and he moaned into my mouth, the sound causing heat to build in my centre.

I pulled away, gasping as his lips trailed hot kisses along the skin of my neck.

"You drive me so wild." His voice was like smoke, causing my stomach to dip as he gave me another kiss. "I thought I would have to beg for this." Another. "And I would have. I would have thrown away my crown and begged before all Tenebris for you."

His raw, whispered words made my whole body shiver. I tipped my head back, a groan leaving my mouth. He kissed along the collar of my shirt as I clung to him.

I jumped as a knock sounded at the door, suddenly realising the position we were in. Dracho's head was buried against the skin of my neck, and when I tried removing myself a low growl sounded from him. I laughed, pushing him slightly until he lowered me.

There were so many things that shone in his blue eyes—emotions that I would never be able to decipher. But that knock sounded again.

"Enter," Dracho called, gritting his teeth but never taking his eyes from mine. I took a step back so there was an appropriate distance between us as the door swung open.

"Your Excellency—uh, Your Highness?" Jeshwa's words came out like a question; I turned, smiling.

"What is it, Jeshwa?" Dracho asked impatiently.

Jeshwa's eyes flicked between us, his lips pursing as if he was worried about his next words. Apprehension rose in my chest.

"It's all right," Dracho reassured him.

"The council has requested another meeting." I felt Dracho stiffen beside me. "And they want to meet the princess."

I frowned, wondering why Jeshwa looked regretful, and why Dracho appeared so spooked.

"That's... good, right?" I asked.

The silence between us was almost comical.

"Jeshwa. Tell them we shall convene after lunch."

"Yes, Your Excellency. Your Highness." Jeshwa bowed before leaving the room.

With just the two of us left in the room, the awkward tension heightened, almost making me cringe. I fiddled with the loose sleeve of my shirt, clearing my throat. "What was that about?" I managed to ask.

A solemn expression passed over Dracho's features, and he looked away. "I never wanted to involve you in any of this," he muttered, his light eyes dulling.

"In what?" I asked, walking forward and taking his hand.

His sigh was resigned, nervous. "The council want to meet you. Officially."

"All right, what's wrong with that?" I was a ruler from another part of the continent. It wasn't unusual for leaders to visit each other.

But the last time I was here...

How could I have forgotten? My hands started trembling, and Dracho's eyes fell in devastation. The last time I had been in Tenebris, I had been questioned about the death of the emperor—of Dracho's father. It was clear from his uncle's reaction that day that setting me free was not something they'd wanted. And from my conversations with Roux and Althea, I had my own suspicions on Dracho's decision to free us that day; we just hadn't had the conversation to clear the air yet... which was mostly my fault. But my returning to Tenebris, after I had been banished—and even if it was in the company of the emperor—was likely a big thing to those who helped him lead.

If they even knew about it...

"They didn't know we were working together," I whispered, my hand lifting to rest against my throat.

Dracho winced.

"You never told them there was a chance I was coming here?"

He shook his head, his face the epitome of regret. "It'll be fine. I've already explained everything that happened whilst I was south. They *know* your father wasn't responsible for my father's death."

"Then why do you look so worried?" I asked quietly.

Dracho huffed. "Some of the council members are... old. They're traditional. They're not happy with the idea of outsiders being here. And..."

"And?" I pressed.

He exhaled deeply. "And the Tain is still fresh in their minds. Some of them… hold on to their dislike of the elves, hating that my father had to involve himself to put a stop to it. They know that if Jandar had had an opportunity to rid the world of draconi, he would have taken it."

"So they blame *all* elves for that?"

"No. But now they know the true reason why the Tain started…" He trailed off.

Ah. My mother's choices. But I could understand that, so why was he so nervous?

"I'm just… concerned," he said.

"About what else?"

He breathed in deeply, pulling me forward into a tight embrace that made the air rush from my lungs. His voice was muffled as he pressed his face against my hair. "I'm worried that they'll scare you off."

I laughed shakily a little, pulling back to see his face. To my own surprise, my laughter continued, the sound deep and throaty as it stretched out until my stomach hurt. Dracho looked at me as if I had gone mad whilst I straightened my spine, wiping a tear that had sprung from my eye.

"Dracho," I breathed, "if nothing has scared me off so far, do you really think politicians will?"

He took in my lopsided grin. "Well… some of them are… dragons."

"I'm not scared, Dracho."

It was a lie. I *was* afraid, but not of what he thought. I was a mess, but I was stubborn. I worried that I wouldn't be able to bite my tongue under an insult or that somehow I would offend one of them. I worried that they would see through my tough facade and see the broken girl beneath—one not worthy of ruling a city of Ruvalon. Someone not worthy of being close to their emperor.

But I shoved it all down, swallowing it like a hard pill until it refused to show on my face.

Dracho seemed to believe the mask. "All right." He nodded. "Then we'll go. Together."

Chapter 45

Nothing had changed in the throne room since I had last been there, save for the coloured banners. They had been a lovely jade colour when Eltanin was emperor, but now were a shimmery black; I kept a smile to myself, realising they reminded me of Dracho's dragon.

He sat upon the marble throne as if he had been born into it. He hadn't bothered to wear the robe of the emperor, remaining in his breeches and a black shirt, which reassured me that this wouldn't be such a formal meeting. At his instruction, I stood off to the side of the dais, facing the stairs that the council would walk up. Not a spectacle, but on show nevertheless.

A man entered first, taller than even Antares and Dracho, wearing a long robe of deep purple, a silver sash tied around his waist. Golden hoops shone from both his nose and ears, and his eyes were soft as he caught my gaze.

"Eliana," Dracho said, "this is Boone. One of my advisors, and my father's oldest friend."

My smile was sad at that, but the man's eyes twinkled as he turned to face his emperor. "Are you calling me old, Your Excellency?" Boone had a relaxed aura, as if the whole world would wait for when he was ready.

"Well, if the shoe fits..." Dracho laughed lightly. "Boone is a mage," he added to me.

"Oh." I wondered if he knew Bisa.

He tipped his head forward. "Pleasure to meet you, Your Highness."

I shooed my nerves to the back of my mind. Flipping my *princess* mask on, I smiled brightly and sent a *thank you* in his direction, but a sudden shiver ran up my spine as the rest of the council entered—more of them than I'd expected. Their faces were a mixture of politeness and disdain as they spread out before the throne, nodding to their emperor, though several gazes kept skipping back to me.

I kept my chin up, straightening my shoulders and refusing to remove my gaze from them. I would show them I was unafraid.

One woman caught my eye. Her hair was gathered into a tight bun, casting her severe features into sharp relief as her savage eyes roamed the hall. She wore a long-sleeved dress of shadow-black, the skirts floating just shy of the floor around her heeled shoes. Awareness crept through me as her eyes found mine, contempt curling her lip. And as the final guest stalked up the stairs, his amber eyes watching all, I realised why.

The resemblance was uncanny. She was Antares's mother. I stood straighter, wondering what I had done to deserve such a look from her.

The sounds of shuffling feet and idle chatter fell as everyone settled and they all bowed towards Dracho. To my surprise, the council included Miriam from the Ryu district. I caught the wide smile she sent me, giving her one in return and feeling some hope.

"Thank you all for meeting me on such short notice," Dracho called out clearly and confidently. None of the nervousness and frustration he had clearly felt at their request showed; he spoke to them with the respect they deserved.

His eyes scanned the crowd, stopping on one man. As I followed his gaze, my stomach dropped. I hadn't noticed his uncle enter the room. He leaned against one of the pillars furthest from me, arms crossed, but not in a way that showed he was bored. His red hair was brushed back off his face, his eyes dark and menacing.

"I appreciate that this meeting has been put off because of me, but as you can see now," Dracho lifted a hand from the throne to gesture at me, "Queen Eliana is here to greet you."

"Princess," a voice called, and my head turned to the short, grey-haired man who had spoken up.

Dracho ushered the man forward with a flick of his fingers. A couple of the people around him exchanged nervous glances as he pushed through, his eyes darting between me and Dracho.

"Please, speak, Lin," Dracho told him.

The man cleared his throat. "Apologies, Your Excellency. But it was my understanding that the lady had not been crowned yet."

"No apology necessary; you are correct. But Eliana will be queen soon, when she returns to Meridium."

"And when will that be?" A harsh, feminine voice joined the fray. My hands clenched shut as Antares's mother stepped forward into view.

"Lara." Dracho tipped his head towards her in greeting, but I spotted the quick flash of silver across his eyes. "It has not yet been decided—"

"I think now is a prudent time to decide, don't you?" she interrupted, and a muscle in Dracho's jaw twitched. "Now the woman is here." She threw her hand in my direction.

My nerves spiked, and I glanced at Antares. He made a tiny movement, as if his hand had inched towards me, but then stood still.

Dracho's nostrils flared; he inhaled deeply. "Eliana is my guest and will be treated as such."

"The last time she was here, she was being questioned for treason. Over the death of *your* father."

"And from my own investigation, I have concluded that she played no part in that. In fact, as I shared with you days ago, we now know that Jandar Morven has been in control of the Hollow this entire time."

"That still doesn't negate the fact that the people are uneasy with her here," she answered loudly.

I clenched my fists. I had left the palace and mingled with the people. Not a single person had paid me any mind or mentioned my presence at all, at least to my face. I noticed Miriam's irate stare as she shook her head in Lara's direction; in fact, only a couple of council members seemed to empathise with what Lara was saying. The majority appeared ambivalent.

You look like you want to say something?

I didn't react to Dracho's low, smoky voice as it brushed against my mind, but he was right. I coughed, taking a step forward as several pairs of eyes landed on me.

"Excuse me—Lara, is it?"

Her eyes narrowed.

"I've been lucky enough to spend a few days exploring and admiring the city, *and* the fine people within it. I cannot praise them more for the warm welcome I have received. To a stranger—and an elf, I may add." I swallowed hard, disbelief striking me that I'd said it out loud. "However, if anyone feels genuine unease at my presence, I would love the opportunity to assuage their concerns by speaking with them. I may be a future ruler, but the people always come first."

The intensity of Lara's dislike didn't leave her eyes, but several of the members of the council now looked at me with something akin to respect.

You are... breathtaking.

I turned, catching Dracho's gaze,

He blinked a few times before frowning, his eyes travelling over Lara's scowling face. "I believe you are using the people as a scapegoat for your *own* feelings, Lara."

Colour rose on Lara's cheeks. The woman's chest heaved with outrage; I was surprised steam wasn't billowing from her nostrils.

Dracho's uncle coughed. Her gaze snapped to him, the two sharing a look for a moment. Thuban uncrossed his arms as he stepped forward into the space, holding them out in a placating manner.

"Perhaps we should bring the tone down a bit, Lara."

"Why?" Lara spat. "Why should I, when the elf is whoring herself out to our—"

I jumped as a snarl sounded from my left, and Lara cut off, turning to her son as he glared at her with a murderous expression. It seemed there wasn't much love lost between the two.

My heart thumped as both Lara and I glanced back to Dracho, who was on his feet. Great scaled wings burst from his back with the sound of fabric tearing; black talons darkened the ends of his fingers.

"I would watch your words from now on, Lara Sterre." The slits of Dracho's pupils seemed to expand, making his eyes look almost black as his head twitched to the side, like a snake watching its meal. I took dark satisfaction in the bobbing of her throat as she swallowed hard, even though the anger in her eyes was palpable.

Sterre? So that's Antares's family name.

"Apologise," Dracho ordered, his voice full of violence and smoke as his aura pierced the room with a thrum of power, as it had when he'd killed Jandar. It reminded me of what lay underneath that smooth skin of his. What beast lay in wait until it was called forth.

Lara scoffed. "You can't be serious—"

Dracho moved an inch forward. She dropped to her knees, her objection dying in her mouth; eyes clenched shut, she bowed her head. My foot moved minutely as I suppressed the urge to step forward and tell Dracho this was not necessary. But this was his court; I would not undermine him in front of them.

"I will not ask again," he whispered as storms gathered in his darkened eyes.

"I apologise," she mumbled.

"To her," he commanded in a dangerously low tone.

She turned to face me, and I could see the disdain in her eyes—the humiliation that she clearly blamed on me. Through gritted teeth, she muttered an apology, her form practically shaking with rage.

"Thank you," I told her, not wanting to provoke the draconi further. This was enough.

"Now." Dracho turned, his hand flexing. "Princess Eliana will be staying here for the foreseeable future whilst we discuss plans to defeat Cirdan, and the plague he and his father have set upon the land. This is of the utmost importance. We cannot allow this evil to spread further than it already has."

Murmurs of assent sounded out around the hall. His fist clenched as he turned to lean against the throne, his wings held high. Lara raised her head from the floor, her eyes wandering over them in envy, and I wondered if it was a skill only the emperor had.

"Does anyone have a problem with this?" Dracho asked.

The air grew cold in the silence, Dracho's silver eyes flicking between everyone in the room.

"Good. Some of you wanted to meet Eliana. You have met her. Then please, go about your business." It was a dismissal, leaving no room for argument.

Scattered chatter broke out as the council left. I stayed rigid as Thuban walked forward, helping Lara to her feet with a pointed look; they descended the steps and left the throne room. Her last defiant act was to throw me a scornful gaze before she rounded the doors.

When they had all gone, I exhaled the long breath that I had been holding and watched Dracho walk towards me, my stomach dipping in awe at the talons he was retracting, his stunning wings still visible behind him as he pulled them in tightly.

"Are you all right?" His tone was apologetic as he brushed his scale-free fingers against my hand.

"To be honest," I started, and he looked nervous. "...I thought that went better than it could have."

Dracho chuckled. "You handled yourself beautifully." He squeezed my hand. Antares hummed in agreement from his new position, leaning against one of the pillars and twirling a small knife between his fingers.

"But Dracho... I don't want to cause conflict between you and your court. If it maintains the peace, then perhaps I should—"

"My court should mind their own business and focus on what's important, not on who I have as my guest." My lips pursed as he lifted a hand to twirl a strand of my hair around his fingers. "There is a stubborn minority. They'll come around once they know you."

"But why would you stand against your council for me?"

"Because you are my equal. Whether they see that this thing between us will benefit all Ruvalon or not, I don't care. Because I know that it will. Don't you feel it too?"

I did. I felt way too much, way too quickly. It terrified me. I glanced to Antares, whose attention was on the knife in his hand.

Dracho's face turned regretful, and unease swirled in my gut. "I've been putting this off, hoping I wouldn't have to do it at all... But I think we need to."

The movement of Antares's blade halted.

"What?" I asked.

"I gathered enough information from the guards to establish what happened back on Jandar's island. Back in Fallstone, Eliana..."

I dropped his hand as I stumbled back a step, that wicked part of me inside hissing in warning for what was coming.

"I need to hear it from your own mouth, Princess. I need to know everything that happened to you."

A deep ache throbbed in my thigh, and for a second I wanted to lash out. To bare my teeth and curl up into a tight ball and forget what had happened.

I focused on a deep breath, because I wouldn't do that. I had decided to fight, to take little steps at a time. That meant opening myself up to the trauma. I had wondered why Dracho hadn't questioned me before, and now I had my answer; once again, he had been protecting me. He hadn't pushed, hadn't demanded. None of them had. They had put my needs before those of the people of Ruvalon.

I felt selfish suddenly. They had allowed me to process what had happened as best as I could up to this point, not even one of them asking for too much. It was time to give back.

The lump in my throat was hard to swallow. "I can tell you."

Dracho nodded, his eyes soft. A small, genuine smile pulled up Antares's mouth, making him look younger.

I sat on the edge of the dais, wrapping my arms around my legs. They followed suit, taking up a seat upon the floor, not too close—giving me the room to breathe and express myself—but not too far.

Tears flowed down my face as I told them of Cirdan's proposal, of my defiance and learning that Cirdan had lupera serving him. I sniffed as I told them of the boat, of learning of Adven and his connection to Vyn. I sucked in a sharp breath, my teeth clenching as I told them of the Hollow. Guards they had beaten for information had already given that up. They knew that Cirdan and Jandar controlled the Hollow, but not how.

"Wait." Antares stopped me, though until now they had both remained quiet. "Jandar commanded the Hollow to destroy Coed?"

I nodded.

"But it *didn't*. It attacked Ruthun instead. That must mean something," he said.

"That the Hollow is bad at geography?" Dracho offered, and I rolled my eyes.

"Did anything else happen, Eliana? Did Jandar call off the attack?" Antares pressed.

"Not in front of me, no. He gave me an offer, I refused. He commanded the Hollow to go for Coed, and I screamed at it to stop. But it left. I didn't see it again after that."

Antares's brow furrowed, his eyes alight with something.

"What is it, Ant?" Dracho asked.

"The Hollow retreated after Eliana took a step towards it, back when it destroyed Carew." He leaned forward eagerly. "And after she told it to stop, it didn't follow *orders*. It destroyed a different village. Eliana... I think there's a link between you and the Hollow."

"What?" I breathed out. "Like... like I can control it?"

"Or maybe that it's frightened of you?" Dracho suggested.

I laughed at that. "Why? I'm no one—"

"Don't say that," he said, irritated.

"You're clearly important, Eliana. We just have to find out what the connection is," Antares said.

"That'll be difficult without proximity to the Hollow," I pointed out.

An uncomfortable silence held until I took a deep breath, filing that information away for later, and continued giving them all the information I could. The lupera who had entered my cell with his own pleasure in mind, until Cirdan had gutted him before my eyes. Erix, and that black claw that had given me my wound. Malzan, who had been kind.

Erix's comment about the night I'd been attacked, and Cirdan's confirmation, made Dracho gasp, his eyes hardening. "I always suspected there was more to the attack on you when you were a girl. Getting into the palace like that... they were clearly too skilled to be anything other than mercenaries."

I nodded, feeling stupid that I had never discussed it with my father. He must have had his own suspicions, but he'd been living in a world of grief at the time.

I didn't tell them about the shade of my mother who had appeared to me in the depths of my delirious despair. I didn't want the looks of pity. I did talk about the starvation, the determination to break me and use my name and blood to control the elves of Adref. To find the sword of Orian, though knowledge of its whereabouts had died with my father. My tale ended with the sound of Cirdan's men being torn apart as Dracho and Antares arrived to save me.

We were all silent for a few minutes once I'd finished, my fingers picking at the hem of my shirt. Before I could break it, calloused fingers brushed against my hand, before turning it over and holding it within its grasp. I looked up into golden irises studying me with an intensity that was difficult to meet. I smiled at him gratefully.

Another hand brushed my free one, a charge running through my fingers and up my arm as Dracho took it within his grip. My gaze turned to meet his; there was torment in his eyes.

"*Thank you,*" he breathed.

They both held my hands tightly, grounding me as hot tears trailed like fire down my face. As I grieved once more for all that had occurred. For all that had changed me for good.

Chapter 46

The days that followed were full of peace and laughter, a stark contrast to the previous weeks. Still, the memories of that cell invaded my nightmares, strange men morphing into Cirdan, or Jandar, or Erix. No matter how I tried to fight it, I would wake up in Dracho's arms as he whispered sweet words against my hair. I felt bad that I obviously kept waking him, but I couldn't deny the safety I felt within his arms.

We shared a few more heated kisses whilst tangled in my sheets, but he would always pull back, expressing how much he wanted me but reminding me that I needed to rest and heal. The next morning we would wake as if nothing had happened, Dracho leaving with a small kiss pressed to my head—which was perfectly fine with me as I avoided considering the implications of a relationship between us.

I continued to try and enjoy myself, frequently visiting the city. Althea showed Bas and Vyn around the districts now that Vyn was better; Bas celebrated with all the different flavours of ales available, often returning rather inebriated with an amused Roux following in his wake.

I often spent the morning before breakfast underneath the blossom trees by the falls, Antares sometimes accompanying me once more in silence; we enjoyed the peace, away from the hustle and bustle. Dracho took me on a tour of the palace, grinning when he showed me the library—a magnificent feast for the eyes of white stone and old books. Like the ones in my room, there were many I couldn't read, but even just absorbing myself in their illustrations was a thrill. It was a balm to my soul, spending that time with him with no pressure to be anything other than myself. Yet the nightmares didn't not leave me.

Roux's concerned gaze found me every now and again, but I avoided it and any deep conversation with her. It felt good not to dwell on all my grief and trauma. Keeping busy was keeping me sane.

We had been in Tenebris just over a week when a craving for more of Miriam's food hit me, and I remembered that Vyn hadn't tried it yet. With a growling stomach, I headed down to his room, ready to drag him out with me.

I didn't knock before I shoved open the door. "Do you want to come—"

A high-pitched gasp left my mouth. I snapped my head away, but found I was unable to erase what I had just witnessed. My hand came up to cover my eyes as I backed out, my shoulder painfully hitting the door frame.

"Never mind! I'll see you later!" I squeaked, hearing a dark chuckle as I yanked the door closed.

I had never walked so fast in my life. I made it to Dracho's room, bursting through the door and closing it behind me, leaning against it for a moment to catch my breath.

"Everything all right?" he asked, a brow arched, from where he sat before his large desk covered in letters and papers.

Letting out a long breath and beginning to laugh, I took the chair opposite him. "I just saw something I think I shouldn't have."

"Oh? Anything I should be worried about?"

"Well... I know where Antares's mark is now." I tried to say it casually, but my voice was too high-pitched for it to sound natural.

It was a mark all draconi carried; Dracho had once told me it had been given to the *chosen*, those blessed by the first mages, long ago. I couldn't see Dracho's properly underneath his hairline on the back of his neck, but the small bit I had seen looked so familiar to me. The memory evaded me, like a mist before my eyes I couldn't touch.

Dracho's eyes widened, but he returned to his work.

"I'm... Did you know—" I stuttered before taking a breath. "I caught Vyn and Antares together," I rushed out, feeling my face grow hot.

Fortunately, I had arrived before anything too graphic had started. In fact, if it hadn't been for Vyn's wicked smirk, I would have been worried about the situation. But the image of a shirtless Antares, the corded muscles of his back and shoulders standing out as he held Vyn by the throat against a wall—the latter's breeches around his ankles—was certainly an image I wouldn't be able to erase anytime soon.

"And?" Dracho drawled, not even looking up from the correspondence in front of him.

"Uh... well—I thought you didn't know?" *I* certainly hadn't realised their relationship had progressed to that extent. If I was completely honest with myself, I'd thought the attraction was rather one-sided—an unrequited crush of Vyn's. I hadn't even realised Antares favoured men.

"It was bound to happen sooner or later," Dracho added.

"And it doesn't bother you?" I asked tentatively, glad that my best friend had found some happiness but nervous of the reaction to it. Below Tenebris' borders, Vyn didn't really hide who he was, but was cautious about expressing it openly. Meridium didn't frown on same-sex relationships, but there were still many throughout the land, especially in places like Stillmere, who weren't afraid to express outdated opinions on things that had nothing to do with them.

Dracho's eyes found me, amusement twinkling in them, before he bent to write. "We don't conform to inane societal concepts such as gender or sexuality in Tenebris. Everyone is whatever they want or whomever they want to be, and it has always been that way. No one would bat an eye."

"Oh. That sounds... liberating."

"I'm used to it, so I wouldn't know..." The hand holding his pen paused; his bright eyes were intense as they rose to mine again. "Why?"

I shrugged nonchalantly. "No reason. Just curious."

His teeth flashed in a wicked grin, and my stomach dipped. "Yes, I bet you are."

I scoffed, standing. "I'm going to visit Althea if you're just going to be crass. She wants me to try on outfits."

Dracho laughed deeply now, the sound like a warm blanket wrapping around me. "A little warning. If you tell Althea you're *curious*, she'll have you out of your clothes faster than I would."

My face was on fire now. Ignoring him, I pulled open the door, but a rush of wind sent a shiver up my spine. Dracho was suddenly leaning over me, his smoky voice murmuring into my ear.

"But maybe you'd like that, *Eliana*?"

His laugh followed as I rushed out the room, pulling the door closed behind me.

"Know what you need? Besides a good night between the sheets?" Althea wagged her eyebrows.

I gave her an impatient look, trying to subdue the flush on my neck and cheeks as I remembered Dracho's comment. I hadn't told her what had occurred, nor did I plan to.

"Oh c'mon, just humour me?"

I huffed. "All right, what?"

She grinned. "Dancing."

"Absolutely not. I'm in no mood for a ball."

"Not that fancy shit you do in your swanky balls. I mean *proper* dancing."

Colour me intrigued. "What do you mean?"

Her smile was positively feline, her eyes twinkling with excitement. "Prepare yourself, Eliana. We're off to the Ryu district tonight. But first, we've got to get you ready."

My brows rose high on my forehead as she yanked open the doors of her huge, cream wardrobe and started flicking through the huge quantity of clothes—too many for one person to wear in one lifetime. Well, unless you were a draconi… or an elf. I wandered over, suddenly feeling like a prude when I realised how revealing the outfits were.

"I-I hope you're not expecting me to put on any of *that*!"

"Eliana, you have curves I would fall to my knees for." Great, now I was blushing again. "So, yes. I am expecting you to wear one of these." She took out a black dress that appeared to be made of night and starlight with little straps instead of sleeves—it looked barely longer than one of my shirts, let alone a dress.

"And do people in Tenebris often wear these?"

Althea rolled her eyes. "I wouldn't put you in something that would make you stand out." She took in my expression and laughed. "All right, maybe I would. But let's be fair—with your features and body you'd stand out in a bathrobe, and I don't mean because of the ears. I promise, you will have the best time. Just trust me?"

I gave a resigned sigh. "All right. But I have a condition."

"Anything you want." She nodded enthusiastically.

"Can I wear something slightly longer?" My eyes drifted down to the still-recovering wound on my thigh, hidden beneath my trousers. Whilst the pain had eased tremendously, the redness still stood out against the rest of my tanned skin. Despite my elven ability to heal, there would be a scar. I didn't think I could stomach the looks I would get if it was on show.

She nodded with a soft smile, turning back to the wardrobe. "You know, it doesn't matter what I dress you in. It will still drive Dracho mad."

I scoffed.

"What?"

"I don't think I need an outfit to drive Dracho mad."

Her laugh was like a bell. "That's true. But I'll enjoy watching either way. Maybe you should just put the poor boy out of his misery! Man's probably got the worst case of blue balls in history. And stars know you need a good time."

I winced. "We're definitely not there yet."

She raised a brow, continuing to rummage through a mountain of dresses.

"I mean it. Physical chemistry we have, sure—I can't deny what everyone can see. But as for anything else... A relationship?" I laughed humourlessly, and her smile fell. "No, we have a lot of baggage to work through. Most of all my trust issues. I can't help but internally doubt anything that leaves his mouth. We're better than we were, but—"

"Eliana, you must realise how obvious it is that you feel for one another."

"It's complicated," I insisted, turning away from her.

Althea's impatient huff sounded behind me. "Sure, all right. All I'm trying to say is, don't underestimate your feelings for him. You may both dance around each other and hide your deeper feelings, put it down as sexual attraction. But put all the games aside—when you're alone, lying awake at night, and you dig deep down... you'll realise the extent of what you would do for him. You'd let the world burn." Out of the corner of my eye, I caught the sad smile playing on her lips. "And what's worse? What could end us all is that that he would do the same. I think..."

She trailed off once she saw me staring at her.

"I'll be right back," she announced suddenly, twirling on her graceful toes and leaving me to ponder what she'd said, wondering if I'd missed something.

Chapter 47

Dracho

"I don't know why I bother playing with you. We both know I'll never win," I grumbled, throwing my remaining cards onto the table between us and giving up on our game of papst.

Ant smirked, picking up his small knife with a cocksure shrug. He'd joined me after I had retired to my chambers. I'd wanted to play a game to relax, but I flexed my shoulders, still feeling that restless urge to unfurl my wings.

The doors burst inwards suddenly. Althea stormed towards me with determination and fury set upon her face. The pupils of her dragon form flashed at me, and I almost fell out of my chair in my rush to get out of her way.

I failed. Sharp pain shot through my arm as her fist made contact, my hand flying up to rub the sore spot.

"Ow! What the fuck, Althea?" I was used to her playful beatings, but this one had hurt a little.

"You're a *stupid* prick, you know that?"

"You're only just figuring this out?" Ant drawled, spinning the small knife between his hands.

"What did I do?" I asked, incredulous.

Althea snorted. "You haven't told Eliana exactly how you feel yet!"

My cheeks heated, and I leaned forward in my chair. "Why? What did she say?"

"Nothing. But it should be obvious!"

Why did I feel like I was being scolded by one of my childhood mentors? The brief pause that fell between us made Ant scoff. "As you can see, my darling Althea, it is not."

I fired him a vulgar gesture, keeping my attention on Althea. "What?"

"That she's completely infatuated with you. Probably just as much as you are with her!" she shouted, flicking my forehead.

Ant's blade stilled in his hand; his head tilted. "To be honest, even I'm shocked you haven't declared your undying love for her yet."

I looked between them. "I thought it was obvious how much I l—like her?"

Ant laughed so hard he clutched his stomach. Althea ran a hand over her face.

"*What?*" I directed the question at Ant as his laughter abated.

His intense eyes pinned me. "Dracho. You can't just *expect* women to know how you feel. I know it's been more difficult since your merging, but communication is kind of important."

"Says you," I muttered, pouting. "No one ever knows how you feel."

Ant shrugged, his lips turning up at the edges.

"You're such a man sometimes, Dracho," growled Althea. "Your actions lately may have *shown* her how you feel, and yes, it's just words, but you should have expressed *to* her exactly how you feel, *and* what you want."

I winked at her playfully, trying to ease the tension, but her patience was obviously running out; she jerked forward as if about to hit me again. I flung myself into the back of the chair, holding my hands up defensively. "Wait, wait, wait! So... should I go and tell her now?"

"No!" they both said in unison.

"If you do it now, it's just obvious that I've said something," Althea huffed, placing her hands on her hips.

"So... when?" I demanded, eager to fix the fractured relationship between us.

"When it feels right, Dracho," Althea told me. "But not tonight. *Tonight,* we're going to Drakes."

Even Ant looked up at that, curious. "What?"

A sly grin crept onto Althea's face. "I managed to convince Eliana to go."

Ant sucked his teeth. "Interesting. Have you informed her of the atmosphere there?"

She rolled her eyes. "Not everyone needs a detailed run-down before they do something, Antares."

I shifted forward in my seat, eager to know more. Drakes was a dance hall in the centre of the Ryu district known for its music and amazing beverages. I'd never witnessed a place like it in the mortal realm, and wondered how Eliana would fare in such a different venue.

"Are you joining us?" Althea asked Ant. Nine times out of ten, we both knew he'd say no.

He looked thoughtful for a moment before giving us a crooked grin. "Yes. I think I shall."

"Good, because we leave at eight. Make sure you dress up. Oh, and Dracho… she's borrowing one of my dresses."

I groaned, covering my face with my hands. "You're just trying to punish me, aren't you?"

Ant laughed.

Althea's teeth flashed victoriously. "Just get ready, boys. And Dracho, don't mess this up. If you leave it too late, you could lose her."

Chapter 48

With a nod and a wicked smile from Althea, the man at the front door waved us in, and we all slipped past him. The walk here had been slow, since Althea had forced me into the most ridiculously high-heeled shoes I had ever seen in my life. How people walked in them I had no idea, and it had taken a hell of a lot of pouting for her to allow me a lower pair than the original ones she'd offered.

The blonde demon had had Roux visit the trading district earlier in the day, bringing me a bag that I'd almost shoved underneath my bed once I saw what was inside. I had always been a fan of lace underwear, opting for aesthetics more than comfort, but the scraps of fabric she had brought me were practically sinful.

But with a black pair I couldn't refuse, a plum-coloured knee-length dress with a neckline that stopped just above my navel, and the shoes, I had to admit I felt like a new woman. I wasn't quite used to outfits that silhouetted my shape and bared my legs so brazenly. I felt naked, yet found that I quite liked it. Althea had looked thoroughly pleased with herself when I'd admired her makeup, which made my eyes look darker against the nude lipstick she'd chosen.

Still, something inside whispered that it was all a mask. A pretty cover for the broken ugliness lurking underneath. I exhaled deeply, trying to shove those thoughts away as I turned to the others.

Roux looked like a vision in a long black dress. The butterfly sleeves ended at her elbows; golden embroidered flowers decorated her waist and shoulders. Althea, as usual, looked like a goddess incarnate, her lilac dress appearing as though it had been painted on her light skin. A slit ran up her thigh, and thin straps crisscrossed over her lower back.

I followed the two gorgeous women as they pulled me further into the building, taking a wide staircase up to another level. A regular beat like a drum pounded beneath my feet. When we walked through a marble archway, my eyes widened and my heart seemed to stop for a second. The circular room was laid out with three bars curving around the outside walls, and a ring of white stone steps leading down into a wide, empty area where too many people to count were dancing to the loud music.

Roux caught my eye and grinned at my astonishment. A feeling like electricity ran up my spine as I scanned the room, spotting Vyn and Bas standing over by the bar, a drink in their hands.

Watching my feet carefully, I took each step one at a time, Althea holding my hand the whole way. When we reached the dance floor, the ground beneath my feet seemed to vibrate with the music. I schooled my shocked expression into one of nonchalance as I followed Roux further into the space.

"I'm assuming this is your first time in such an establishment?"

Dracho spoke so closely to my ear that when I turned, my nose almost brushed against his. Breath hitching, I spun and almost stumbled; his hand darted out to right me. My mouth went dry before I could thank him.

He was a god of night in his black shirt and trousers, both fitting him like a glove and flowing deliciously over the muscles of his arms. He had left a couple of buttons loose at the top of his shirt, the creamy skin of his chest showing and making me want to run my tongue along it.

His own eyes travelled over me like a loving caress, his eyes darkening. A lopsided smirk appeared on his face.

You are possibly the brightest star I've ever seen.

I sucked in a breath at his inner voice.

"Remind me to thank Althea." His actual voice was husky.

I laughed, accepting his hand when he offered it and joining the others at the bar. Althea was smiling at Antares, who wore a plain black collarless shirt, with rolled-up sleeves that ensured his tattoos were on full display. A black metal earring hung from one of his ears, twinkling in the light. Roux, her eyes dancing with excitement, was scanning the room; Jeshwa appeared beside her, placing his hand on her lower back to guide her towards a quieter bar on the opposite side of the room. Bas scowled at the action, moving to follow them through the crowd. I suppressed a laugh.

"Come now, Princess."

I rolled my eyes at Dracho, aware of a drop of sweat travelling down my spine as I eyed the crowd. "I don't know what to do," I muttered.

His expression made me bite my tongue. Leaning forward an inch—still enough to set every nerve in my body on edge—he spoke quietly. "You don't have to. There's no thinking here. Just feel."

I didn't have time to think at all. Althea grabbed my hand tightly and yanked me into the throng of people on the dance floor, passing through until we came to a roped-off raised area, apparently private for our group. We stood by ourselves as she handed me a tall glass filled with a pale blue liquid. I took a careful sip. The flavour tasted of brightness, as if each sip were a collection of brilliant stars, bursting on my tongue.

"Slowly," Althea said, nodding enthusiastically.

"Is this alcoholic?" I asked loudly above the music, thinking of how ale lowered my inhibitions and made it easier to relax. She nodded with a laugh.

Before she could stop me, I emptied the slim glass to the last drop.

Althea huffed, her eyes wide. "It's a bit stronger than ale!"

I shrugged, handing her my glass; she disposed of it on a tall table nearby. I glanced around, hugging my arms as dancers moved around on the floor below us. The others were still at the bar, and I watched as Dracho joined Antares in ordering.

I felt awkwardly out of place, standing still above the moving people, and Althea laughed at my wide-eyed expression. She pulled me close, her hands on my hips as she encouraged me to move. The invasion of space would have been claustrophobic if the music hadn't been so entrancing. The drumming vibrations under my feet and in my chest felt like another heartbeat. It felt as if the music was a living thing of its own, the thrum and melodies a translation of its very soul.

It was like no music I had ever heard.

My mood elevated, and I felt all the muscles in my body relax. I moved awkwardly, following her guidance and laughing in embarrassment.

She leaned in, her eyes twinkling. "Just *feel.*" Her words echoed Dracho's.

I inhaled deeply before letting it out slowly. Wrapping my arms around her neck, I took a step closer and started to move my body.

The more we danced, the more my blood seemed to warm. How had I never experienced this before? My mind felt like it had switched off a part of itself as I threw my head back in a laugh, my hips moving like they were made to sway, as if the music were made for me, as if this was the only way my body knew how to speak. Everything felt electric, and the joy was like a shot of pure adrenaline.

There were no rules to follow, no structure to the dance, just pure enjoyment. I felt no trickle of trepidation when Jeshwa took my hand, joining us. He swayed us to the music, pulling a laugh from me as he twirled me. Bas caught me next, his deep laugh warming my heart as he lifted me off the floor to swing me tightly in a circle. I rested my head against his chest, chuckling, before he placed me down carefully on my heeled shoes. We laughed as we kept dancing, and he spun me—right into Antares's arms.

In the dim light, Ant was all high cheekbones and mischievous eyes, surprising me with a genuine close-lipped smile. He said nothing as I whispered a greeting. Instead, he brought his hands up to gently rest on my waist. I stiffened slightly, then realised I had stopped dancing. I moved my hips once more, guided by his strong hands. It felt strange to have my arms loose by my sides, so I lifted them instinctively, the alcohol making me brave. When I saw the bright flash in his eyes, I paused.

"Is this all right?" I asked—too quietly for the volume of the music, but of course he heard me.

His eyes travelled over my face for a second, then he nodded. I rested my hands around his neck, wrapping my fingers together to stop them from fidgeting. From the serious look in his eyes, it was obvious he wasn't drinking. Ever the protector, staying sober to look after everyone.

"You'd be correct."

I sucked in a gasp, realising I had said the words out loud, then giggled. "I, um… didn't think this would be your sort of thing."

Antares nodded. "It isn't often. I have to be in the right mood, and with the right people."

I snorted unattractively. "And am I classified as that?"

Antares's teeth flashed. He spun me, and I gasped as my back pressed up against his hard chest. His hands lowered to hold my hips as he bent his head, speaking into my ear. "Maybe I haven't decided yet."

My throat felt tight. I swallowed, but continued the sway of my hips, mindful not to push back any further into him. I suddenly realised I felt as comfortable dancing with Antares as I would with Bas—or Vyn. I glanced around, looking for Vyn, but when I found him he was on the dancefloor below, dancing with a stranger. His yellow eyes met mine and sent me a wink. I blew out a breath, relieved. The last thing I needed was to piss off my friend for dancing with someone he was sleeping with. Bas and Roux swayed to their own rhythm nearby, lost to the music as their hands travelled over one another.

Antares's dark chuckle sent a trail of goosebumps along my neck. "*Someone* is jealous," he whispered slyly.

My eyes shot up, finding blazing silver staring at me from the bar. Dracho leaned back, arms crossed. There was jealousy there, yes, but something else was more prominent as Dracho watched me—us.

Hunger.

I couldn't breathe under that beautiful stare. Suddenly that familiar, powerful feeling I had been missing since before Cirdan—the feeling of control—returned to me. At that moment I felt strong, as if *I* held the power within my hands. It was probably just the drink I had consumed, but I flashed him a smirk and turned my head sideways, my nose accidentally brushing the edge of Antares's jaw.

"He doesn't look nearly jealous enough," I murmured as my cheeks flamed.

Antares froze for a second in surprise; then he gave a low laugh. "You're asking for trouble. But yes, I think we could take it up a notch. Don't you?"

I hummed, capturing his hands and raising them to my waist. Closing my eyes, I lost myself to the beat of the music, moving my hips along with Antares behind me. He pulled me closer; my breath caught in my chest when I felt his nose skim along the skin of my neck. A rumble came from somewhere on the dancefloor, but my eyes remained closed, relishing the throb of pleasure that fired through me at the sound. Pleasure I had not felt in a long time.

"It's nice to see you swim, Eliana."

I frowned for a second, before realising what he meant. I felt like I *had* started that long swim.

I leaned back onto his shoulder and raised my hands to wrap them around his neck, my fingers brushing the soft strands of his tied-back hair. Antares's hands started moving, trailing a slow, torturous journey up my waist, his fingers just brushing the skin of my ribs through my dress. My breath caught when I felt the sharp scrape of elongated fangs brushing over the skin of my neck—

—and my stomach lurched as I found myself torn out of his arms. I almost stumbled in Althea's shoes but turned my head, sending Antares a grin as he threw his head back in laughter. Althea was behind him, shaking her head.

Dracho's hand was firm around mine as he dragged me back up the stone steps. I laughed as he pulled me through an exit and along an empty hallway; he kicked open a door, tugging me inside and closing it behind him.

He was on me before I could speak, his forehead against mine, his breathing hard as his eyes shone with yearning.

"Please," he begged. I felt his nose skim softly across my cheek. He inhaled deeply. "Please?"

I focused on nothing but the movement of his lips as he repeated the word, knowing exactly what he was asking. I gave him a small nod.

"Thank fuck," he breathed, pulling me to him.

His lips took what they wanted, leaving nothing as he tried to claim me. My hands found purchase in his hair, pulling to bring him closer. He resisted, his firm hands gripping my waist as he backed me up until I hit a barrier. I realised we were in some empty private area, my back resting against a bar. Dracho's hands were gentle as he cupped my face, his hazy eyes a cool silver as he peppered my mouth with kisses.

"If I hadn't already shared with Antares in the past—"

Wait, what?

He was breathless as he continued. "—didn't trust him implicitly—his blood would be covering that dance floor right now." Kiss. "You drive me crazy." Kiss. "Watching you dance with everyone else *but* me..." Kiss.

"You didn't ask," I breathed, not quite believing what was happening.

He ignored me. "Allowing them to feel the way you move—" Kiss. "I couldn't take it. Do you know how hard it was not to take you from them and show them who you belong to?"

I moved away from his next kiss, tipping my chin up and moving my hands to rest over his. "I belong to no one."

Dracho snarled, and I jumped.

"Shit, sorry. I know you don't. I won't lie—it's in my nature to be possessive. I may have merged with my dragon, but those tendencies to claim all your pleasure for myself are still there. Fuck, I wanted to take you right there on the dancefloor." His thumb blazed a warm path over my lower lip, a groan leaving him as I whimpered. "Wanted to show them all how you call my name, *so* prettily."

My breath hitched as his lips curled up.

"Will you say it for me now?"

My blood heated, an ache gathering between my legs. I needed him—there was no question about it. This tension between us had reached a knife's edge. I could run from it, or I could embrace it.

No thinking. Just feel.

Would it be so wrong? To let him close again.

His eyes softened slightly, as if sensing my dilemma.

"Let me please you," he whispered, the back of his finger brushing down the skin of my cheek. He watched me carefully, as if I were some skittish animal that could run at any moment. His dragon's silver eyes glinted in the low light like uncut diamonds. I knew I should drop my gaze, should say no and protect my heart... but I didn't.

I want this.

I took his hand, running it slowly between the valley of my breasts.

He gritted his teeth, watching the movement with darkened eyes. As his gaze flickered to mine, his eyes widened with sudden realisation. He pulled away like I had burned him, running his hand through his hair instead.

"Shit," he hissed. "We can't. I won't. You've had a drink. I've had a drink." He moved his hands and gripped mine gently. "I'm sorry, that was wrong—"

Something in my chest tugged towards him, and emotion flooded me. Memories of our time together in Ruvalon; of how gentle he'd always been, how tender. Under all his swagger, his posturing, he was only ever kind and considerate when it came to intimacy. Overcome, I wrenched my hands out of his and cupped his cheeks. He froze under my hold, his expression terrified.

"Just feel," I whispered in the dimly lit room.

"Just feel?" he asked, his eyes pleading.

I nodded, suddenly sober.

That was all the permission he needed. He spun me, pressing a hand flat between my shoulder blades until my chest rested against the cold bar. The cool air took me by surprise as it kissed the bare skin of my arse, his hands lifting my dress and exposing me to the room. A pained groan sounded in his throat as he took in my lacy underwear.

"Fucking stars," he hissed.

I laughed as his weight pressed down on me, realising how much I'd needed to feel it again.

He leaned in to whisper against my ear. "Last chance, Princess?"

I pressed back into him. His answering growl caused heat to build in my core. Nudging my knees with his so I'd spread my legs further, he brought a hand around to gently hold my throat, lifting my head slightly.

"As soon as I saw you, I imagined you in this position. Imagined your body clenching me as I took you from behind."

A shocked whimper left my throat.

"But not now. I'm not going to remove these." His free hand brushed along the lacy edge of my barely-there underwear. "I want them soaking wet before I let you come. So when we return to the dance floor, you'll be able to feel it and remember that *I* did that. Do you understand?"

Holy Goddess. I'd never felt so hot in all my life. All I could do was nod through my panted breaths, aware it wouldn't take long. An intense need had built up in my stomach, in my legs... Goddess, everywhere.

His hand moved until it was flat against me, his fingers rubbing against my most sensitive spot. I was burning. I was burning so much I was surprised I wasn't a flame incarnate. I was burning from the inside out, and I never wanted it to end. I bucked, trying to get more friction from his hand, but he removed it.

"Ah, ah, *mia estra*. Stay still."

I stopped moving obediently, sighing when his fingers returned to trace carefully over me.

"Such a good girl." He hummed in satisfaction at the groan that left me. "I think you like being praised, Princess."

I writhed under his touch, crying out at the sensitivity of it. When I tried to push up off the bar, he stopped me, claiming my wrists. A sliver of panic shot through me as he gently held them, his thumb rubbing soothing circles over the almost-healed bruises. I choked back emotion as he kissed each one, before laying them flat against the bar.

"One day," he said breathlessly, "I'm going to erase those memories from your mind. I'm going to remind you that there is pleasure in being restrained. Not only pain."

A tear ran down my cheek at his soft tone. His hand trailed back along the skin of my arse, to where my centre throbbed. He waited, making sure I still wanted this, and I pushed back into him. His hand continued moving against me, and I growled in frustration at the barrier between us.

He laughed. "I told you, Princess, I want you wet for me."

I clenched, craving his fingers inside me as I squirmed against the bar. It felt too good to stop him, though, and I rode against his hand as my chest heaved.

"More," I called out breathlessly, over and over. He applied just a bit more pressure, and I could feel the building of my orgasm. My head hit the bar as I cried out. "Yes. Right there. *Please*."

He groaned, touching me with added fervour. Leaning over me once more, his tongue traced along the outside of my ear, the skin so sensitive it sent a jolt straight to my core.

I moaned loudly as the tell-tale sensations tingled, causing my toes to curl, and he laughed. "That's it, Princess, come so prettily for me."

I called out his name as white-hot pleasure tipped through me, only feeding the flames that blazed through my veins. My vision went black, every thought and memory fleeing my mind.

When my climax eased, Dracho released my hands. I lay on the bar, boneless, feeling his hardened length brush against my backside as he straightened.

He raised me up, my back flush against his chest as he gently pulled the skirt of my dress down. His breath tickled the skin of my neck. "If we didn't have company to return to... if I didn't want you to go out there and have the best time of your life, I would bend you back over that bar until your legs could no longer hold you up."

I was close to that already, if I was completely honest with myself. Dracho helped me to my feet, making sure my dress was in place and my hair was smoothed out. I so badly wanted to accept that offer...

But I also wanted to enjoy myself. Wanted to experience all the freedom and pleasure that I could before I returned home. Before I returned to my duty.

So I did.

Chapter 49

"Oh, sorry." I halted awkwardly, wondering how long Antares had been watching me from where he sat. I'd come to the library to spend some quiet time reading, but it seemed he'd beat me here.

I felt slightly embarrassed to be unexpectedly alone with him after last night, and my cheeks flushed at the memory. Still, it had been the best evening I'd had in years. When Dracho and I had returned to the dancefloor, Althea and Roux had sent me sly smiles, which I'd done my best to ignore. Jeshwa had peeled away from the throng of people, sweat glistening on his head as he approached me. His blonde hair hung over his eyes as he had reached out a hand, which I accepted.

My muscles, which had coiled tight during my time with Dracho, started to loosen as I swayed from left to right with Jeshwa. I laughed loudly when he raised my hand, twirling me in a small circle, catching me and then spinning me once more into Bas's arms. I'd danced with everyone again, riding the exhilarating rush once I ended up in Dracho's arms, loving every second of it.

It had been the most fun I thought I'd ever experienced. I'd even enjoyed returning to the palace with Roux and Vyn—the others had stayed to have a few more drinks—barefoot through the streets, carrying my heels. I had gone to bed with the biggest smile on my face, and I'd intended to stay up, to wait for Dracho. But exhaustion had pulled at my bones, and before I knew it, sunlight was streaming through the gauzy curtains.

Fortunately, I'd awoken to a clear head, in the mood to read in the palace library. Which was where I had found Antares.

He was sitting in one of the alcoves in a cosy-looking wingback chair, a full tea service with two cups and a teapot before him. It was rare to see Antares look relaxed, but here—an ankle resting on top of his other knee, a book laid across his lap and a steaming cup of tea beside him—he'd never looked so normal.

He said nothing but returned to his book. A flash of amusement ran through me as I noticed his face.

"I didn't know you wore focals. I didn't think draconi would need them," I said, taking a few steps towards his table.

He was silent for a moment. When he realised I wasn't leaving, he sighed. "There's no glass in them."

Venturing closer still, I bent slightly to look, noticing the subtle widening of his eyes as I approached. The frames were in fact empty.

"Then why wear them? Style choice?" I teased.

His molten eyes glanced back up at me over the frames. I wondered what he was thinking. "They're a... comfort. Just something that's become part of my routine when reading."

"Ahh." I nodded, understanding that it was one of those unique little things about Antares. He seemed a bit more withdrawn than before, and I guessed it was from a need to recharge after our social outing. Feeling brave, I took a seat opposite him. He had seemed much more comfortable around me in recent times, but that was when we were mostly in a group. I still felt unnerved when we were alone, but it didn't mean I didn't want to know him more.

He arched a brow at me, as if I was being extra audacious.

"Were you expecting anyone?"

His eyes narrowed. "No, why?"

"There are two cups." I pointed to the table.

"Ah." To my astonishment, a faint blush climbed on his cheeks as he shifted in his seat. "Well, then... would you like one?"

I flashed him a smile. "That would be lovely, thank you." Reaching forward to pour myself a cup, I resisted the urge to scold him when he waved my hand away, taking hold of the teapot.

"It's..." Antares cleared his throat and looked away, as if embarrassed. "My own blend. Lavender and chamomile—is that all right?"

"Definitely." I stared at the snake on top of his hand as he poured, the inked animal seeming to move with every flex of his fingers.

"Honey?" His deep tone shook me from my perusal.

I blinked a few times. "Excuse me?"

He rolled his eyes. "Would you like honey? Sugar?"

"Oh! Yes please. One sugar cube and one spoon of honey."

Antares looked offended. "One of each?" he muttered under his breath, but he did what I asked, placing the cup carefully in front of me.

Enjoying the warmth in my fingers as I held the cup with both hands, I blew on the liquid for a moment before taking a sip. I felt like I was in my palace gardens, sharing a cup of chamomile tea with my mother.

"Perfect," I breathed.

"Surely that's too sweet?" he asked with disbelief.

"Nonsense. It's the perfect balance."

He scoffed, opening his book back up. "That cup is a disgrace to tea everywhere. Then again, I have noticed you prefer all things sweet."

"Have you?"

He cleared his throat, pushing a small bowl across the table before lowering his eyes to the text. It was full of strawberries. I popped one into my mouth.

"What are you reading?" I asked, taking another sip of my tea.

His eyes were incredulous as they slid over to me. It seemed like it was unusual for people to bother him while he was reading.

He closed the book, placing it on the table before him and running a large hand over the cover. It was old, the leather aged and its colour dim. "I've been scouring the books of this library for information," he said solemnly.

"On?"

"Poisons," he stated.

"Oh."

Oh. My heart squeezed at the unspoken implications. Ant was looking into the poison that had killed Dracho's mother. And my father.

Something unbelievably like sympathy passed across his face, and I had to look away and clear the sudden lump of emotion that sat in my throat.

"I wondered why this particular poison acted fast in some circumstances..."

I looked back at him.

"But slower in others, such as Dracho's mother."

I bit my cheek in thought and could have sworn the edges of Ant's mouth curled up slightly. "Perhaps it has to do with the dosage used? Or it's form?"

There was no denying the rare, genuine smile that now graced his face, though it was small. "Precisely. I've found no records of such a poison being used in all our history—"

Antares was an extremely beautiful man, but his dangerous aura made people cautious. Now, however, as he continued talking, his entire demeanour changed. His hands moved as he spoke with vigour, leaning forward in his chair. His face lit up as he talked passionately. And I realised: Antares was a seeker of knowledge. Dracho had once made fun of him for it. But I had taken an interest in something he was clearly very passionate about.

It made me smile.

He stopped talking suddenly, blinking a couple of times, his hands still raised. "What?"

I shook my head. "Nothing. What was the last thing you said? Sorry."

His hands dropped. "I think I should take a trip to the Scires. Their library is even more extensive than this one and has older texts. If there's any record of such a poison, it'll be there. I'm hoping that if we find it, we can find the answer to reversing whatever is happening to the wyverns. If it even *can* be reversed."

The Scires was where the scholars trained and earned their titles, located on a small island to the southwest of Tenebris. Not many mortals ventured there unless they were looking to join the League of Scholars. The league sent scholars throughout Ruvalon and beyond, seeking information about the world before housing it in the Scires. It was the most expansive library on the continent. If Tenebris didn't hold the truth about the poison Antares was researching, the Scires was our last hope.

I had never heard of anything that could cause such deformities in wyverns. It was something to be concerned about. The beasts under the Hollow's control weren't natural, and their corruption was leading to the destruction of villages and towns around Ruvalon.

"I think that's an excellent idea," I said.

"You do?" he asked with an eagerness that I would never have associated with him.

I nodded. His teeth flashed as he smiled widely, and my breath was almost taken from me, a sudden tug in my chest making me frown. Why was I experiencing these reactions around Antares? He was attractive—I couldn't deny that. But what was this strange pull?

Was it desire? Was it a longing for his friendship or approval, since he'd once expressed concerns over my closeness to Dracho? I couldn't fully explain my own emotions and decided to file them away. I already had enough on my plate.

I glanced around the packed shelves. "I think if there's any possibility of finding answers, then we should definitely look into it." He nodded, and a thought came to me. "Antares?"

"Yes." He brought his cup to his lips, his eyes not leaving my own.

"What does *'mia estra'* mean?"

Antares nearly choked on his tea. He sat forward, coughing and spluttering into his hand, then laid his cup on the table, his brow creased. "Where did you hear that?"

I waved my hand, as if it wasn't something worth talking about. His eyes narrowed at me suspiciously, but he went on.

"*Mia estra*," his voice purred on the words, "is old draconi. The language isn't spoken much. But it means *my star*."

"My star? Because of your people's love of the stars?" I asked.

He chuckled, the sound pleasant. "It goes beyond that."

I settled back into my chair, eager to hear more, and a crooked smile grew on his face. "I assume Dracho has told you some about the draconi? About the Chosen."

I nodded. "Back... before. He told me there were nine leading families."

A sad look passed over his eyes. "There used to be twelve."

"Dracho said some had died out."

He hummed. "Each family belongs to a cluster of stars in the night sky. The children born are usually named after a star belonging to that constellation. When we die, we return to our ancestors and our place in the sky. There are, of course, exceptions."

My brows rose. "Wait, you're named after a star?"

"My family belongs to the scorpion. Dracho belongs—"

"To the dragon." I nodded.

"But he also belongs to another."

"He told me he was the last born to two of the leading families."

"Yes." His smile turned wistful. "His mother, Irena, belonged to the Heracle family. She was... the kindest woman I had ever met."

"What of your own parents?" I dared to ask, my eyes dropping to the drink in my cup.

"My father is still around, as is my mother—as you know." His eyes darkened. "My father is mortal."

"Oh, wow." I wondered if his father disliked the elves as much as his mother did.

His lips pursed, and I knew there was something else there. I didn't want to push him. The dynamics of the draconi race were extremely interesting to me, and learning about their culture was exciting. The dragons of Tenebris had been feared for centuries; now that I knew they also had a mortal form, I wanted to learn everything I could. Understand them more. "What family does Althea belong to?"

Antares winced. "Althea belongs to the Ox, but is not named for any star."

"Why not?"

He exhaled deeply. "You are familiar with Althea's past." He sucked his teeth when I nodded. I realised this was probably an uncomfortable conversation for him to have, reminding him of what he had done to Althea's father—deservedly so. "Althea's father refused to give Althea a name, and since her mother died during her birth, she had not chosen one. Her father handed her over to a wet nurse, and it was that woman who cared for and named her."

"What happened to the woman?"

"Once Althea was old enough to feed herself, her father removed her from his employment. She now works in the Ryu district."

I blinked. "Miriam?" I guessed.

Antares grinned. "Yes."

A moment of silence passed between us as we each took a sip of our tea. My mind wandered over my conversation with Dracho once I'd found out his real identity, and another thought popped into my head.

"You and Dracho said that you go to your ancestors in the stars when you die..."

A wry smile passed over Antares's face. "You have a lot of questions today, don't you?"

"I'm just curious. Would you rather I didn't ask them?"

Antares waved a hand. "No, no. It's rather refreshing. Go ahead."

"Dracho mentioned something about earning your place?"

"Yes. It's more speculation and belief than known fact, but our people believe that we must live with honour to earn our namesake in the night sky.

So that when we die, we can live within the splendour there, ever eternal. However, if we have disgraced our name, the star dies when we do."

"Do you believe it's true?"

"Mmhm."

"Why?"

He cleared his throat. "Because when I killed Atlas—Althea's father—his star disappeared from the night sky."

I shuddered. "So... why isn't the language spoken much anymore?"

"It was a language used aeons ago before so many mortals lived amongst us. When settlers from the south joined us in our city, we had to adapt. The language has become unused over the centuries, though the old ones still remember it. And we still have our immortal phrases, like the one you found. I assume in a book here?"

"Um," was all I said, nodding guiltily. "So what does it mean?"

"It's sometimes used in old draconi romance fiction, because it's the most significant term of endearment that could be given by one of my kind. It's the biggest declaration of the heart that one of us can give. I suppose it's like saying... 'You are my everything'."

I took another mouthful of tea just to prevent anything from coming out of my mouth. *Oh.* That was... *big.*

I tried to remember the first time Dracho had said it to me but couldn't. If ever there was evidence of his intentions moving forward, I supposed that was it. It was intense, and it scared me that I wanted it as much as I wanted to run away from it.

We sat in silence as I processed the revelation.

"So, what are you two talking about?"

Dracho slowly walked around the end of one of the bookshelves, coming into view of the alcove. His eyes assessed our positions, then lingered on me, my skin shivering at the intensity there.

I looked forward, watching as Antares rolled his eyes before pushing himself to his feet. "We were talking about my next destination."

"Oh?" Dracho asked, glancing lazily at him.

"The Scires."

Dracho nodded, and I realised they must have discussed this before.

"I-I'd like to go," I said, drawing the intense gaze of the draconi.

It was Antares who asked, "You would?"

I nodded, not taking my gaze from Dracho. A spike of fear jolted through my body, as if there was a possibility that he wouldn't let me go, would cage me again. If I couldn't trust him, we could never move forward.

As if he could see my doubt as clear as day, his features softened. "Of course. You can go whenever you're ready. Antares, arrange it."

Antares grinned before exiting the room, leaving the two of us alone.

"It's nice to see you exploring my home. Although I'd prefer that you kept *my* company instead of my best friend's." Dracho said it with humour, but there was an underlying bite to his words.

"Maybe I prefer Antares's company," I teased.

His hand covered his chest. "Ouch." He was quiet for a moment, considering, as if he didn't want to speak his next words. "Be mindful of how you treat Ant, Eliana."

I gave him a sceptical look. *What's that supposed to mean?*

"He's starting to let you in. I've never seen him do that so quickly with anyone, so you've obviously charmed him." My brows reached my hairline. "I just... I don't want to see him hurt."

He raised a hand when I opened my mouth to bite back. "I understand that after everything that's happened, you need to find the answers you seek. And I don't believe for one moment you'd actually use anyone to find them. But Ant is..."

Different. He didn't need to say it aloud.

"If he's letting you near, please... he's my brother."

I couldn't find it in me to yell at him, not with that concern on his face. We had hurt each other, physically and emotionally. I could appreciate that he was worried about Antares. Because I could leave at any moment. Could leave them all. I could see it in the lines of his face that Dracho had been hoping, was still hoping. But he was living in a constant state of fight or flight whilst I was here, expecting me to flee at any moment.

And I couldn't promise that I wouldn't.

Clearing my throat, I promised, "The only thing I am interested in with Antares is friendship. If that's possible. I would never use him, or you... or anyone."

Dracho nodded, walking to take the seat Antares had left. He sighed deeply as he relaxed back into the chair.

"Dracho, you once told me your parents were soulmates?"

"Estellars. Yes."

"What exactly is that?"

"Long ago, when the stars that floated about our cosmos fell to our planet, they eventually turned to dust. We are all made from that dust. Estellars are those who have come from the same star."

"Wow, that's… that's intense. Does it happen often?"

He shook his head, his eyes softening. "My parents have been the only ones in the past two thousand years."

"Oh."

"When it happens, it doesn't mean the people involved are destined to be together romantically. It can mean a friendship that goes beyond blood or loyalty. Like a platonic soulmate."

"How do you know if you're estellars?"

"According to my mother and father, there was always a feeling there. Like knowledge in their very soul. But there is a ceremony that can confirm it."

"That's kind of sweet."

He hummed in agreement. "Why do you want to go to the Scires?" he asked, clasping his hands together in his lap.

"Oh, you know, see the sights." His eyes narrowed as I grinned. "I agree with Antares that's it's our best course of action regarding his investigation into the poison. Also…"

"Also?"

"We all know I'll have to return to Meridium soon. I've been gone way too long already. It's time Meridium had its new ruler. But, before then, I'd like one more opportunity to explore the world."

"You'll have plenty of chances to explore the world when you're queen," he assured me.

"Yes, but there'll be a lot of red tape and people to answer to."

He shrugged. "Accurate."

"So, what can I expect from the Scires?"

"Hmm." Dracho sat back more comfortably. His hand rubbed along his jawline, drawing my eye, and his thumb brushed along his lower lip. My mind drifted back to that room in Drakes, and I crossed my legs in a bid to ignore the heat that built there.

"A lot of attention," he finally said.

"What?" The heat was forgotten. "Why?"

Dracho laughed. "I don't know the last time they had a woman there, let alone an elf—it's typically a vocation that men seem to follow. I imagine they'll have a field day when you walk in. But don't hold it against them. They're constantly surrounded by dusty books, so they'll be grateful to see a gorgeous face."

The warmth in my cheeks spread down my neck as I looked away from him, and Dracho laughed. "And the poor men will definitely lose their senses if you look at them like that."

Chapter 50

"It looks good," Dracho sighed.

Colour rose on his cheeks as he pulled my long black skirt back over my leg. He had requested my presence this evening, so I'd dressed quickly after my bath before heading to his room—where he'd surprised me by asking to check my wound.

"I *am* an elf," I told him with a small smile.

"I know. I just wanted to be sure for myself."

He stood, returning to his large desk and running a hand through his raven hair. Sitting down, he poured himself a small glass of amber liquor.

I could practically taste the stress in the air surrounding him, and a twang of pity ran through me. He had been busy arranging our trip to the Scires—something the scholars were most excited about—but other matters were bothering him. I'd met with a few of the council members at a breakfast Dracho had arranged. The man who had spoken in the throne room—Lin—Miriam, and a couple of others had attended. It had gone very well, and each of them had shaken my hand before leaving. I hoped that Lara hadn't been causing further conflict for him.

All of this did nothing to alleviate my own worries about ruling and the paperwork and policies that would become my life.

"What's wrong?" I asked him, coming to stand beside the desk, resting my hand on the top.

He paused, then offered me some of his drink. "Nothing."

"Doesn't look like it." I shook my head, refusing to shy away from the dry look he gave me.

"It's just the burden of rule and having to answer to people."

"You're Emperor. Who do you truly have to answer to?"

"Everyone," he chuckled without humour.

"Anything I can help with?"

His laugh lifted the hairs on my arms, and my eyes narrowed. He avoided eye contact with me as he downed the drink in his glass.

The realisation was like a quick knife to the gut. "It's still me, isn't it?"

"No. You're perfect," he rushed out. My brow arched at that, and his cheeks flushed. He cleared his throat. "What I mean is... yes. It is you."

"Are some of the council *still* concerned about my presence here?" I tried to shut off the flood of guilt that gathered in my stomach but found it impossible.

"It's just a few people. Nothing I can't handle."

"Maybe I should—"

"No."

"No? I'm going to have to go home soon," I reminded him.

He waved his hands. "I know that. But you also need to recover."

I gave him a disbelieving look, pulling up my skirt once more for emphasis. "Dracho, I'm almost healed—"

In an eye-blink, he was before me to halt the progress of my skirt. I gritted my teeth, realising he probably didn't want to look again at that ugly scar. A muscle ticked in my jaw as I resisted the urge to turn away from him.

"*Almost*. And healing doesn't just take place in the body."

I stilled, releasing my skirt and taking a step back. This wasn't where I'd thought the conversation would go. I was better. I was *trying* to be better.

I didn't need anyone telling me my efforts weren't good enough.

"I don't know what you're talking about—"

"Yes you do, Princess. You need to talk more about—"

"That's the second time you've interrupted me since entering this room. Do so again and you won't be given another opportunity to do so." His mouth snapped shut at that. "Now, I have no idea what conclusion you've come to about the ordeals *I* went through. But I am fine within my mind."

"I have *no* conclusions, since we haven't talked about it since that day in the throne room! I can see how you're ignoring it. You will need to vent eventually, and I want to be there for you when it happens."

He stood, towering over me, whilst I tipped my chin up in defiance. "There is nothing to discuss."

"I'm just trying to help, Eliana—"

"I don't need your help!" I shouted at him. "I don't need to be babied."

"I am not trying to baby you, I'm trying to care! Trying to be your... friend."

My chest seized at the concern laced in his words, and that wicked thing inside me wanted to hurt him. Wanted to push him away so he wouldn't question me further—see that I was still as broken as I was when he'd found me, no matter what I did to forget about it.

I wrapped my arms around myself. "We are barely friends, Dracho," I whispered. What I felt was more than that.

Dracho took a step back, misinterpreting my words. Pain flashed in his eyes but vanished quickly, and my heart twisted.

He huffed through his nose, his eyes hardening. "No? What was the other night then?"

A knot formed in my throat. "A distraction."

"Ouch," he remarked, exhaling deeply.

My lips tightened as I shot him an exasperated look. "After everything, we could never be good friends, Dracho."

Because that would lead to more. And a relationship between us had no future. Not whilst we ruled our own kingdoms and a treaty would soon prevent him from returning south.

His teeth were bared in irritation. "After what? Saving your life? Helping—"

"After imprisoning me!" I shouted.

"And we're back to that!"

"It all comes back to that!" I growled. "I never got over *that*, Dracho."

"I have apologised—"

"And sometimes you just have to accept that people aren't ready to give *you* closure. To talk about things."

Swirling silver dragon eyes locked on mine as he snarled. "You are so stubborn!"

"And you are arrogant!" I shouted back.

We'd stepped closer in our anger; my chest brushed his with every deep breath I took. His eyes lightened as he realised the same thing. My chin rose, eyes shining in challenge.

He accepted it.

With a rumble low in his throat, he bent and caught my lips with his. A tight shudder jolted through me as his hands fisted in my hair, holding me close as his tongue swept over mine—demanding and desperate. He kissed me as if researching, finding out what stroke of his tongue could elicit the deepest groan from me, what sensation could make my eyes roll back. He grunted as I pushed him back into his chair, straddling him and pressing my body to his.

It wasn't long until heated kisses turned into hurried hands, my fingers undoing the buttons of his shirt before finding the strings of his breeches and pulling them loose. A full-body shiver ran through him as I moved back over the thick muscles of his thighs, my hand slipping under the coarse fabric and I finally gripped the length of him. He tipped his head back and whispered a curse into the room.

Despite the aggression we had both begun with, the feel and weight of him in my hand sent a thrill through my blood. I searched for the right combination of pressure and movement until I saw the tension build in his muscles. His hand tightened its grip on the back of my neck, the pleasure of it almost turning to pain.

Sweet noises punched from his lungs as my strokes increased, the strong muscles of his thighs tensing. His eyes shot open, the brilliant silver of them contrasting with black vertical slits as his brow furrowed.

"Eliana, if you don't stop—"

That only encouraged me more. I slid off his lap, coming to rest upon my knees between his legs under the desk.

"W-what are you doing?" he stuttered, wide-eyed.

My smile was wicked as I looked up at him. "Not nervous, are you?"

His response was cut off as I freed him from his breeches, gripping him and taking a swipe with my tongue along his length. His hand clamped down on the edge of the desk, the wood groaning as a hiss left his mouth. He looked down at me, a flush blooming across his cheeks, and I grinned to myself, keeping my eyes on his before I took him fully into my mouth.

"Fuck," he groaned.

I hummed around him in appreciation before I pulled away, eager to elicit more sounds and words from him. Before I could lower my head, the noise of a door opening reached my ears.

"Your Excellency!" Jeshwa's voice called, his steps echoing on the tiled floor.

Dracho jerked forward, leaning on the edge of his desk, pushing me further under its shelter. Fortunately, it had a wooden front blocking me from Jeshwa's view.

"Jeshwa, not now," he stuttered.

"But Your Excellency, Althea went to visit the Princess Eliana, and she's not in her room. Nor is she at the falls. I thought she might be here, but no. No one knows where she is!" Jeshwa stressed, and I almost laughed.

"I'm sure she just went for a walk s-some—" Dracho's words stumbled as I tightened my grip around him.

Eliana, his voice warned breathlessly in my mind.

"She will be fine. I promise," he managed to say aloud.

I leaned forward, sliding my tongue up from base to tip, relishing the choked noise that left his throat.

"Your Excellency?" Jeshwa asked in concern, and I heard his steps come closer.

"I'm fine!" Dracho insisted, his voice rising an octave. He coughed. "Honestly, Jeshwa. Now, please, I have important matters to attend to."

Yes you do. I laughed internally as I pulled him into my mouth, his thighs tightening around me.

"All right, then, Your Excellency." Jeshwa sounded confused, but I heard his retreating steps. I knew when he had left by the way Dracho slumped back in his chair, looking at me under the desk.

"Fucking stars above, you are going to kill me." His voice sounded rough, like thick smoke.

"Then it'll be a good way to die."

He swallowed thickly, strands of raven hair hanging over his eyes as he looked at me wide-eyed.

Holding his stare, I tipped my head forward, swiping my tongue along the broad head of him. His eyes clenched shut, and a delicious noise left him. Encouraged, in one long motion I licked up the smooth skin of his shaft, capturing the bead of moisture that had gathered at the top. My thighs rubbed together as I sought out friction, heat flooding throughout my body at the taste of him. Taking one more lick along his shaft, I placed my mouth over him, filling it as much as I could with his thickness.

"Stars above," he groaned, his hand reaching to fist in my hair. Not pushing, just a gentle hold to encourage my movements.

I realised he was allowing me the space to do what I wanted. Not taking—he was giving as much as I was. That caused a shameless jolt of desire to spread through my entire body. I slid my mouth along his length, almost pulling him out entirely before swallowing him again, taking as much as I could whilst relaxing my throat.

The sound of the door opening again came from behind me and Dracho shot up, knocking his knees against the desk and causing his impressive length to hit the back of my throat. He turned his choke into a cough; it took everything in my power not to make a noise whilst pulling off him.

"Brother, we can't find Eliana. I told Jeshwa she's probably fine, but you know how he gets when he's on guard duty."

I froze at the sound of Antares's voice. If anyone would be suspicious or work out what was going on here, it would be him. My cheeks flamed at the thought of being caught, but it also caused a wave of heat to throb between my legs.

"She's fine, Antares," Dracho said quickly. The hand not grasping the desk—the one that had been wrapped in my hair—tried to remove my hand from him. Grinning to myself, I kissed the soft skin of his thigh before sucking hard, hearing his sharp exhale as his hand fisted shut atop his leg.

"You know where she is?" Antares's smooth voice asked. I rolled my eyes.

"Mmm-hmm," Dracho said, strained.

"And she is safe?"

I took Dracho into my mouth once more, slowly lowering as much as I could.

"Yes," Dracho said tightly through clenched teeth.

"Then where—"

"Antares," Dracho said pointedly, and from my position looking up at him I could see the frustration in his eyes as he glared at his friend. I couldn't see the other, but there was a brief silence. I pictured the scene from Antares's point of view: Dracho's rigid position and the flush upon his cheeks.

"Oh," he said after a minute. A dark chuckle left him. "Want some company?"

My jaw dropped.

"Antares!" Dracho snapped, and Antares laughed once more.

"All right, all right, I'm going." His steps retreated, the door clinking shut behind him, and once more we were alone.

I removed Dracho from my mouth, looking up at him. "Did he mean what I think he meant?"

"Yes," Dracho rushed out as my grip tightened.

"You really need to learn to lock your door," I told him.

"Sorry," he chuckled. "I wasn't expecting to have my dick in your mouth today."

I smiled before swiping my tongue up him. He groaned.

"Eliana, please..."

I returned my mouth to him, wrapping my hand around the length of him that was left. His head fell forward, chest heaving. He looked beautiful.

But I wanted to see him *spent*.

I pulled up him, tongue following my mouth's lead and sliding along his hardness. He muttered curse words and other things I couldn't decipher as his hand tightened in my hair, thrusting his hips forward slightly.

"Eliana, I'm..." he pleaded.

I sucked him again greedily, eager to push him to the edge. My throat constricted as he reached the back of it, and he bucked forward. His eyes shot open, full of lust and other emotions as he looked down at me.

I groaned, still sucking hard, as I dragged my teeth gently along him.

"Fuck," he cursed.

Abruptly, he pushed the desk, the furniture sliding back several feet. I gasped, and Dracho took the opportunity to wrap both hands into my hair, bringing my mouth towards him. I gladly took him, flicking my tongue against the head. I paid attention to the tightening of his legs or twitches as I worked my mouth on him, enjoying his gentle hold on my head. His stomach muscles flexed as I swirled my tongue, his hips thrusting up into my mouth.

I knew he was close when words of praise started falling from his lips breathlessly.

"So good, *mia estra*. Just like that," he panted, every word and sound from him setting each nerve in my body ablaze. My own hips jerked forward in a bid to find some relief from the ache that had built there.

"Fuck, Eliana, I'm—"

I sucked hard, tongue flattening against his length as I pulled him all the way to the back of my throat. With a slight jerk back and a sinful groan, Dracho spilt into my mouth, his hands wrapped tightly within my hair as I swallowed every drop he would give me.

I felt the most incredible satisfaction at his laboured breathing as I laced his breeches as best as I could before leaving the shelter of the desk.

"There," I told him. "Consider us even."

His hazy eyes cleared, though he remained slumped back in his chair, and he looked confused for a moment, his head tilting in thought. I saw when it hit him—that he thought I was returning a favour from the other night.

A debt to be repaid.

Turning, I started to make my way to the door, but a vicious snarl made me jump. I was spun and shoved against the wall, grunting at the impact. *He's pissed.*

There was a sudden spark of excitement in my belly as I noticed that his scaled black wings had burst from him, tearing through the back of his open shirt and flaring wide. He lifted a hand to rip the fabric from his body, and I couldn't stop my eyes from travelling over the sculpted muscles of his chest.

"If you think that we are *even*, you are sorely mistaken. But you gave it a good effort." He smirked, his fangs visible, and I knew all at once that I was in trouble.

Chapter 51

"I made a vow once," Dracho's voice was like warm honey, "that I would spend my time worshipping *every* inch of your skin."

He reached over, locking the bedroom door. I swallowed hard. He grabbed a handful of my hair as my pulse skipped; I could hear my heart pounding in my ears.

His nose skimmed along my neck, raising goosebumps in its wake. "And I intend to fulfil that promise now, *Princess*."

A moment of silence passed between us, my body tightening with the tension. I suppressed the urge to rub my thighs together, still wound up. He pulled back, his silver eyes dropping to my lips, and a small huff left me.

He groaned quietly. It sounded like he was in pain. I stuck my chin out defiantly when his eyes returned to capture my gaze. Snaking my hand into his hair, I pulled harshly.

He hissed before bringing his face close to mine, his lips an inch away. "Tell me to stop," he pleaded, his voice huskier with every ragged breath. "Send me away. I can't bear this torture anymore."

Eyes open and fixed on his, I gripped his hair tightly as his fingers trailed a blazing path up my arm, his thumb brushing the side of my breast.

And I made up my mind.

"This will mean nothing," I told him.

The words made my blood run cold. But it was all I could give. All I could take. Removed from the emotion of it all, I could only use this as a distraction.

Because I couldn't let him in—not fully. I couldn't risk us becoming more, and then having it taken away from me once he returned from his mission against the Hollow. I had been with a prince before, and I had felt the sting of that rejection. Jak's change of mind had wounded me... Dracho's would kill me.

So it was better to give into this desire and put it down to simply physical attraction. Sexual chemistry.

I couldn't admit out loud what my heart screamed at me.

His jaw clenched. "Obviously."

My eyes dropped to those enticing lips, giving myself one last chance to back out, before looking back up to those brilliant eyes of silver, the vertical pupils showing. They considered me so intently, allowing me to make the decision. To make the first move.

"Good," I said.

I pulled him to me, wrapping my hand in a fistful of his silky hair. I could have sworn I heard a small sigh leave him as our chests met and lips collided. It was a clash of teeth and tongues; I pushed my mouth hard against his, biting down on his lower lip.

He growled, pulling away. "Don't." My breath hitched at the ice in his eyes. "It may mean nothing, but don't make this *hateful*."

I swallowed, glancing down. Shame burned through me.

"Let me take care of you." He repeated the words he'd said several times before, and my breaths became uneven as my heart lurched. I came forward, claiming his lips once more.

The kiss stole my breath as he pressed against me, bringing his hand up to untuck my white shirt from the belt of my skirt. His calloused fingers adeptly unfastened the laces of my collar, pulling the shirt off my shoulder. He tore his lips from mine, bringing his head to nip along my collarbone. The scrape of his fangs against my throat made me gasp his name.

He froze for a second, my heart pounding, then dragged his teeth against the skin of my neck again, my hips jerking forward to press against him. A shaky groan left me as he did it a third time.

"What are you doing?" I rasped.

"Experimenting." He chuckled darkly. "Whilst we don't drink from others, like some creatures do with their fangs... I'm starting to think they have more uses than killing."

"Are you really talking about killing right now?" I murmured in a rush of heat as he dragged his tongue over the skin behind my ear.

He laughed, and the sound sent a jolt from my stomach straight to between my legs.

"I'm wondering what other sounds I can bring forth from your delicious body, just by using these." He nipped at the skin on my collarbone again and my hips moved restlessly, pinned between his body and the wall. He kissed behind my ear, and a stroke of his tongue tickled the sharp point at the top. A sound I hadn't known I was capable of making left my mouth.

"This is all I've ever dreamed about," Dracho murmured as his thumb brushed over my lips. "Hearing these sounds from you. Knowing I made them happen." His hand dragged a slow, torturous path down my body, slipping underneath my skirt until his fingers played with the lacy band of my underwear. "I'm going to touch you—give you everything but what you want most—until you're *begging* me for it."

"Then shut the fuck up and do it," I whispered, and he groaned.

My hips jerked violently off the wall as his fingers slid under the thin lace and grazed the dampness between my thighs. The shameless desire that coursed through me was an inferno that couldn't be doused. I gasped as his free hand ripped at my shirt, the fabric tearing right down the middle. His hand closed over my bare breast, kneading the flesh there as my hips jerked against his other hand. He moved his hand further, slipping a finger inside.

Goddess above. The sensation as he moved his finger in and out, curling it as it rubbed gently against that delicious spot, left me dizzy. The way I moved my hips against him was scandalous.

"More," I whispered, opening my eyes.

The hungry look in his own gaze almost brought me to my knees as he eased in another finger, his other hand teasing and playing with my exposed nipple. I rode his hand, my head falling back against the wall.

"That's it," he rasped, his voice smoky and seductive, "fuck my fingers."

A sinful jolt lanced through me; my eyes rolled back in my head as I moaned. My breathing came in short bursts as tension coiled within my stomach and between my thighs.

"*Dracho,*" I gasped as both fingers curled. I reached a hand out, placing it over his shoulder and gently brushing the membrane of one of his wings with my fingertips.

"Fucking stars." He shuddered, and I whimpered. "That's it, *mia estra*," he said thickly, leaning forward to press his face into my neck. "Come for me."

Another graze of his fangs against my neck was all it took for me to fall over that edge. I bit down on the space between his neck and shoulder, the action muffling the sound of my cries as he groaned harshly. I released him a moment later, watching as he eased his fingers from my underwear, bringing them to his mouth… where he closed his full lips over each digit, sucking deeply.

He chuckled at my slack-jawed expression, holding me up on trembling legs with his free hand. My mouth was still open, speechless, as bolts of pleasure rolled through me. Before I could move, he pulled the shirt from my body before gripping my hips, lifting me until I wrapped my legs around his waist.

My arms hung loosely around his shoulders as he walked me to his bed, lowering me gently until I rested in the middle. He placed his palms on the bed on either side of me as he towered over me.

"Do you have any idea how beautiful you are when you're coming undone?" His voice was breathy as he whispered into my ear. He glanced towards the end of the bed, his smile turning wicked. "Here, let me show you."

He bunched his hands in my skirt, wrapping his hands under my knees before dragging me to the edge of the bed. Confusion was my most prevalent emotion, his grin wide as he looked off to the side. Following his view, I realised that we were both now visible in the huge, ornate mirror leaning against the wall. A fiery blush rose on my face as my eyes locked onto his in the reflection.

"You're going to watch in that mirror as I bury myself deep inside you, over and over again."

I whimpered unashamedly.

The air became electrified, filling with his insatiable aura as my skin burned all over once more. His hand skimmed down between my breasts, past my navel, before gripping the sides of my skirt. My hips lifted of their own accord as he removed it and my lacy underwear in one go.

"Fuck, you're perfect," he groaned, head tilted, his finger returning to brush against me.

My trembling hands clawed at the blanket beneath me, my teeth dragging across my lower lip as he continued to brush against me ever so gently—the area sensitive from my last orgasm. My hips jerked upwards, and I almost melted at the dark chuckle that left him. He quickly lowered his breeches, leaning down to place a kiss against the healing flesh of my leg before standing and bringing my legs to rest either side of his hips. I stared boldly.

He was beyond beautiful.

He groaned, dragging the head of his hard length through my wetness. I hissed at the sensitivity of it, a new ache building in my core.

"*Mia estra*?" he breathed, and I almost choked on my breath at those words again.

I swallowed hard, wondering why he waited. Then my eyes fluttered open.

"I-I take a monthly potion," I stuttered out, my face flaming. "Roux made some for me days ago." I had been mortified when Roux had dropped the cup on my desk, having made it herself in the palace kitchens. But suddenly I was grateful.

Dracho looked confused for a moment before laughing.

"I take a tonic." He half-smiled at my surprise, his breath heavy. "But that wasn't what I was asking." His silver eyes shone, but his body was tense as he held himself before me, and realisation finally dawned.

He was asking *permission*.

Because this was different. This was something we had never experienced together, and I swallowed my guilt at his expression. It told me that this meant more to him than I'd ever thought possible.

More than he believed it meant to me.

It made me regret my earlier words. I blew out a rough breath, nodding.

His eyes closed for a second in relief as he pushed forward, his hands tightening on my waist. We both moaned loudly as he entered me slowly, stretching me as his wings stretched wide. His chest heaved with every breath, his eyes clenched shut and a muscle in his jaw twitching as he remained still, allowing me to get used to the size of him. I gyrated my hips, ripping a growl from his throat.

"Move," I commanded him, lifting my hips once more. It was all the encouragement he needed.

So many nights I had spent imagining what this would be like. But this was better. This intimacy set every nerve in my body on fire, a deep pull in my chest causing my breath to hitch as the rest of the world died away. It was as if he had been perfectly made for me, and I for him.

He moved against with an urgency that showed he felt the same. The final vestiges of my control shredded away as my hips tipped up to meet every thrust. His hand was firm against the flesh of my thigh, his other hand raising to wrap itself in my hair as he leaned over me. I turned, giving him access to brush his fangs over the skin of my neck. My gaze caught our reflection in the mirror and I watched, transfixed.

There were many beautiful things I had seen during my short lifetime, but I stared at his stunning form as I would a piece of art. In the throes of passion, as his every move caused a sinful noise to drag up my throat, he was glorious. The tension and tenderness brought tears to my eyes, an agonizing torment to my heart as he entered me slowly, branding my very soul with meaning we'd sworn it wouldn't have.

A wave of dizziness overcame me as he suddenly turned us so that he was sitting on the edge of the bed as I straddled his lap, bringing our faces closer. His lips found mine as he claimed me fiercely, pleasure shooting up my spine at the new angle.

"Eliana," he whispered against my lips, almost pleading as his wings spread high and wide behind him.

My whole body warmed as I reached a precipice, one I was eager to fall over with him. I could feel his muscles tensing in time with mine.

"So perfect," he whispered, kissing along the edge of my jaw. I pulled him closer, running the tips of my fingers over the bone of a wing. He shuddered, and the scrape of fangs against my neck pushed me over.

I cried out, and he followed.

My high came down, returning my senses to me in pieces as we clung to each other, our chests brushing against one another with our heavy breaths. Dracho's fingers threaded through the strands of my hair as he pressed his forehead to mine, silver eyes luminous. He pulled back enough for me to look at him, my cheeks flaming as the heat of the moment cooled, and I noticed how gloriously happy he looked. My body felt content, boneless, but my mind... my mind felt more conflicted than ever.

I wanted him. No. It was more than desire—it felt like an intrinsic *need*. Like something bigger than the both of us was trying to tell me to choose him. That I had *already* chosen him. But I couldn't say it. I couldn't even mumble the words that would change our fates.

Because what realistic relationship could we have together?

He said nothing as he stood suddenly, carrying him with me and turning to place me gently on the bed. I said nothing as he tucked me under the blanket, smiling at me so brightly that my chest tightened.

"I'll be right back," he told me, heading to his desk. There, he poured a cup of water before bringing it to me. "Are you hungry?"

I shook my head. "Tired," was all I could muster. I felt a pang in my chest as he leaned down to place a soft kiss against my forehead.

"Then sleep, Eliana," he said before heading to the bathroom, his wings tucking in tightly.

I didn't resist, too tired to move or to remain awake for conversation. I laid my head upon one of his pillows and succumbed to the darkness.

Chapter 52

My sleep was not restful. I woke in the early hours, the sky still dark and speckled with stars as Dracho slept soundly beside me. His wings had vanished, and I watched the steady rise and fall of his chest as he breathed peacefully and the creamy expanse of his skin, the blanket lying just below his navel.

Dracho awake was ravishing.

Dracho asleep was transcendent.

I could no longer stand the pull in my chest as I looked upon his sleeping form, the urge to bend down and claim his lips once more, so I slipped from the bed and stole one of his shirts from his dresser before leaving. I took one last glance at him before I closed the door, watching as his hand brushed over where I had lain, a crease appearing on his brow as he mumbled in his sleep.

I had only complicated matters. It was a relief that our trip to the Scires would keep us busy, preventing any awkward conversation. A conversation informing him that it wouldn't be wise for us to be together again. A relief—until I remembered our chosen method of transportation.

Antares placed a thick fur on the chair beside me when I arrived at breakfast, where a hot cup of tea was waiting on the table in front of my seat, and a bowl of strawberries. I raised a brow in his direction and he shot me an exasperated look, but his cheeks darkened.

"The Scires is out to sea. The wind can be quite biting, so I had Roux magick this fur to keep you warm."

"She can do that?" I asked, surprised.

Antares nodded. "She can imbue certain objects with some of her flames to warm them. It doesn't last long, but should work until we've returned."

"Thanks, Antares."

He smiled lightly.

Dracho stepped into the room, strolling up to us and swiping a piece of bacon from Antares's plate as he took a seat between us.

"Prick," Antares mumbled as Dracho took great satisfaction in the salty bit of meat.

"Sky's clear. It's a good day to fly." He grinned at me, and I almost looked away from his radiant smile. He'd offered to carry me, since Antares didn't fly with riders.

Antares's eyes kept skipping between us, but I didn't want to worry about what was running through his mind. I pouted. "If I didn't know going by boat would make me sick, I'd demand we go by water."

Dracho leaned over and flicked my nose lightly. "Let's not pretend you don't enjoy riding me." His eyes shone mischievously, and I resisted the urge to punch him... or kiss him.

It was a quiet walk through the palace to the throne room balcony. Before I could say anything, Dracho strolled past me, shedding his clothes and leaving them in a pile on the tiled floor. I barely had time to look away before his skin blazed as brilliantly as the stars and he transformed, shaking his long neck with a rough huff. Antares darted forward to tie a rucksack to Dracho's leg before stepping back, his fingers slipping to the buttons of his own shirt.

With a rosy face, I rushed to Dracho's dragon form. A rough noise that sounded like a laugh left his throat as he lowered a wing, which I climbed to sit between his shoulders. I avoided looking at Antares until his green-scaled dragon stood before us.

The Scires lay a couple of hours to the southeast, over the Ballaraan Mountains and out to sea. It was hard to breathe as I watched the palace and city shrinking away—the place that had become my safe space and home for the last couple of weeks. I made myself take a deep breath, and another, and another, until I felt the tension in my shoulders slip away.

In, and out.

A rumbling sound like a loud purr left Dracho as he soared above the mountains, the cool air filling my lungs and soothing my mind. I pulled the fur around me closer, relishing the heat of it, like the balm of warm water. Beside us, Antares studied me with bright eyes, making a gruff noise before pulling forward.

Dracho didn't use his mind voice to speak to me, and I was grateful to simply enjoy the view. The burnt pink sky of sunrise had vanished, leaving a light blue as shining as a pale ocean.

Eventually, land became visible in the distance as we soared above Lalow Ocean. Even though the Scires sat on an island not much bigger than Fallstone had been, you could spot it from miles out. The great castle walls were bold against the blue beyond—the sight of it was like something from a fairie-tale. The walls were crafted from a mosaic of grey stones, reaching up to form four great towers. I could barely comprehend the amount of knowledge contained within them, and for the first time that day, I was excited.

We circled the castle, Dracho's wings steady through the breeze, and the entrance came into view. A great sculptured bird sat on either side of a set of stone steps, open beaks raised to the sky and wings unfurled, so you would have to pass underneath.

My stomach dipped at the descent; I grasped some of the spikes on Dracho's shoulders tightly until he landed gently on a stretch of rocky ground before the steps. Antares had landed shortly before us but hadn't transformed yet, watching as I climbed down from Dracho's wing. I untied the sack from Dracho's leg, cursing loudly at Antares's almost impossible knots, then dropped the bag to the ground, turning and walking to the steps to give them some privacy. I could hear them chatting quietly as they got dressed.

My eyes scanned the bird sculptures closely, the stone carved in such detail that they almost looked real. Up close, I realised they were phoenixes—a bird of legend thought to be able to bring back the dead, though one hadn't been seen in hundreds of years.

"I'm rather disappointed," Dracho said from behind me as they joined me in front of the steps. "You didn't once try to sneak a look at my nether regions."

I gave him a dry look.

Antares brushed past us to start the ascent. "Come on. I sent word with one of the edjer guards a couple of days ago. Now they've had time to check the tomes, I'm hoping we'll have all the information so we can fly back before sundown."

The staircase curled over the rocky base of the building, each step smooth and steady as we walked towards the brightly lit entrance. Hope swelled within me the nearer we came, warming my insides at the thought of finally finding answers. The sound of my footsteps became louder and louder to my ears as we neared the entrance, anticipation electrifying every nerve and bone in my body.

As we stepped into a large atrium, I covered my eyes from the brightness that threatened to blind me. When my eyes adapted, I lowered my hand and a gasp left me.

A globe almost as big as Dracho's dragon form hung from the ceiling, with multiple golden rings covered in symbols of stars and other celestial objects encircling the replica of our world. A large, circular desk sat below it, the white stone blending beautifully with the light golden flames painted upon the floor around it—a representation of the sun.

A few scholars mulled about, carrying arms full of books or unfamiliar inventions. Some looked at us twice, but it was the gentleman at the desk who jumped when we passed. In his excitement, he stumbled over his robes, wringing his hands and bowing at the waist.

"Your Excellency!" He turned, and surprise bloomed within me when he bowed in my direction too. "Your Highness," he said with a large smile, his cheeks flushing lightly. "It's our pleasure to receive you both. Please, come. Philippe is waiting."

He turned, scurrying towards a stone staircase with a high balustrade that spiralled around the room as we followed. Dracho smirked as he glanced at me from the corner of his eye. "Told you," he whispered, and I elbowed him gently.

"Who is Phillipe?" I whispered back as I walked close to his shoulder.

Antares spoke from behind me. "Phillipe is the lead scholar of the Scires, having taken over when Master Willem died." Of course I should have directed my question at him.

"So if anyone should know...?"

"It would be him."

Well, he sounded like the best person to see. My hope grew stronger.

As we ascended, the scholar from the atrium—his name was Matthieu—spoke eloquently about the history of the Scires, and what a huge honour it was to have us as guests. The conversation drifted away from me; I was distracted by my surroundings.

The broad daylight did not fully reach the main tower. Instead, it was the hanging lights from around the walls that lit the atrium, the light reflecting off the brilliant gold of the sculpture. As we walked further up the steps, we came closer to the globe. Words in languages I did not know were etched upon its surface, the land looking vastly different to modern maps. The rooms that branched off the staircase were filled with murmurs and conversations about, from what I could tell, every branch of philosophical thinking imaginable. Some were indistinguishable, and others easily heard due to their passionate nature.

Matthieu took a turn off the staircase, heading down one of the long corridors until we neared a dark wooden door. He knocked three times before turning to us. "He is waiting for you." With another bow to Dracho and me, he left us.

"Your Excellency! It's a pleasure—come in, come in!" a voice called.

We trudged into the room, and my jaw dropped. The space was much larger than I'd anticipated, shelves of dark mahogany surrounding every wall, stacked with piles and piles of books in varying sizes. In the corner by a window sat a silver telescope, one of the largest I had ever seen, with strange dials attached. Right in the centre of the room was a magnificent desk which clearly needed to be as big as it was, judging by the number of tomes and papers on it.

I eyed the robed back of the surprisingly young-looking scholar as he closed the door to his study. A smile softened his features as he turned with a quill in his hand, his eyes cast downwards until he approached us, taking us all in.

It was when his gaze met mine that his smile fell, the atmosphere in the room changing entirely.

"It's you," he whispered.

Chapter 53

"It's you," the scholar repeated, a bit louder, the quill falling from his hands as he stared at me in amazement. Dracho's gaze narrowed dangerously; Antares took a step closer to me.

"I'm sorry," I said nervously, "I don't believe we've met."

The scholar shook his head, moving towards me. "No, no. Truthfully, I never dared to believe we would in my lifetime. But I have been waiting many years to see if *you* were real. I had no idea what the future Queen of Meridium looked like, but now you're here. It's *really* you."

I looked at him in confusion. *Waiting many years?*

"What do you mean, *real*?" Antares asked.

"Come, come." Phillipe ushered us around the edge of his cluttered desk. We followed him down a clear path through the heaps of books until we stood beside him.

Removing a key on a chain around his neck, he unlocked a drawer in the desk and removed a wrapped book. He carefully peeled back the protective wax wrapping, unveiling a large leather-bound tome. It looked like it could have been hundreds, if not thousands, of years old. Gently turning pages, I saw illustrations—great grey mountains, an immense black shadow, an explosion of unimaginable colour—and writing that was sometimes so faint I couldn't read it.

Philippe took the book from me and flicked through it, searching until a grin lit up his face. He turned it, pushing it towards us on the other side of the desk.

My mouth dried.

"What is the meaning of this?" Dracho asked, his tone alarmed. Antares stood as silent as stone beside me, gazing down at the image on the bottom half of the page.

It was an illustration of a woman. A woman with flowing dark hair tucked behind elven ears, piercing green eyes, and a glowing sword of silver clasped between her hands.

If the eyes hadn't been the exact shade of my father's—of *mine*—I would have said the image was one of my mother. But there was no denying what was drawn upon the page.

"This is me," I whispered in shock, my fingers drifting across the picture.

"Who drew this?" Antares asked, his gaze intense on Phillipe.

"I can't say for certain who did it," Phillipe replied. "This book dates back over four thousand years."

My heart twisted. How was that possible?

"Why?" was all I could say.

"There is a passage above it. I can translate, if you'd like? It's written in a combination of the two oldest languages known to Ruvalon."

"Both?" Antares asked eagerly, and Phillipe nodded.

"What?" I asked.

"The two oldest languages are draconi and elven," Antares told me.

I processed that. "What does it say?"

The scholar pulled the book back to him, looking at the passage of script above the drawing. He cleared his throat.

What came out was a deep voice that sounded nothing like his own. Awareness spread over me, pulling me in. I realised I'd taken a step forward.

"When The Elders fall, a betrayal begotten by serpents shall usher forth an age of pain. Made from the same stars, only when they can see as one shall a new power rise. A king of stars and smoke, a queen of survival and to all, a warrior of shadow and justice."

Antares stiffened beside me. The scholar continued. *"The clouds will roar with fury, and death will rain from the sky when the last divine falls. But with the true heir's blade, and the daughter of the firsts, an aeon of unity and serenity can begin. For the saviours of the people have navigated life with pain, and only through their sacrifice can all be saved."*

I turned, finding a look of heartbreak on Dracho's face. His chest rose and fell quickly. My own heart was thumping, and my chest felt constricted. I swallowed hard.

"What does that mean?" I breathed.

"It's a prophecy." Antares's voice was like thunder. "Why have I never seen this?"

"This tome stays with me at all times," Phillipe said. "It contains every prophecy ever heard. But we could never be certain of when these events would occur, so every master has kept it close, ensuring it doesn't fall into hands that may seek to use the information for the wrong means."

"Who else knows about this? Who has access to this prophecy?" Dracho asked.

"Other than the masters, only one other has ever seen the script," Phillipe replied.

"And you trust us—her—now with the words?" Antares asked. I glared at him, but he just rolled his eyes.

"Don't you see?" Phillipe took an eager step around the side of the table, pointing to the image in the book. "*She's* the one who will save us all."

"That can't be right." My palms were clammy.

"It's there on the page, Eliana," Antares said.

"I can see that," I snapped, and his dark brow rose.

Phillipe coughed, looking away from us. "I haven't been able to decipher most of it. But I deduced that—as it's your portrait holding a sword—*you* are the 'true heir'. Are you familiar with the blade?" he asked.

I leaned forward at the same time as Dracho, eyeing the silver blade. The hilt was hidden by the clasped hands. I shook my head.

"The sword of Orian?" Dracho asked, and my eyes snapped to him. "Have you ever seen it?"

"No. My mother hid it somewhere in Meridium. I've never seen it, nor would I know where to look."

"Her mother?" Phillipe asked, his brow creased.

Dracho nodded. "Eliana is the remaining heir to the Orinan family." The scholar's eyes blew wide. "All right—for now, I'm going to say true heir, check. We just need to find the sword. Daughter of the firsts? That's easy; that obviously means Roux."

The 'firsts' were the first mages—those who had blessed the draconi with their transformation magick and long life.

Antares nodded in agreement. "The beginning, when the elders fall... That could mean any elders."

"No. It couldn't," I interrupted. Three sets of eyes turned to me. "*The* Elders. There have only ever been two monarchs referred to as *the* Elders."

Realisation dawned in Antares's eyes. "The elven king and queen of Adref."

"Your grandparents?" Dracho asked.

I nodded. "Until they died... when Jandar started his campaign for revenge."

"So that essentially gives us a timeline. Betrayal begotten by serpents?" Dracho asked. Antares and I shook our heads. "The titles?" Dracho pointed to the third line Phillipe had read from. "What could that mean?"

Made from the same stars, only when they can see as one shall a new power rise. A king of stars and smoke, a queen of survival and to all, a warrior of shadow and will.

"The first was relatively easy to decipher." Phillipe smiled, pulling a scrap of note-covered paper from the desk. "And now I know you to be queen, I can decipher the other."

He nodded towards Dracho. "When you were born, as with all royalty of Tenebris, your parents marked your birth in the book of Draconis." He turned, pulling another thick, leather-bound book from the shelf and resting it on the table. He mumbled to himself as he looked for the correct page, exclaiming in delight when he found it. We all leaned closer.

On the full moon of the seventh month, Their Excellencies, Eltanin the Wise and Irena the True, rulers of Tenebris, welcomed a son. First of his name, blessed by the firsts and carrying the blood of the ancients—Dracho Celesta, a future king of stars and smoke was born.

Dracho blew out a long breath, his eyes furious. "Why didn't you ever tell me that I was part of a prophecy? Tell my father?"

Phillippe held up his hands. "Begging your forgiveness, your Excellency, but you could live for millennia." Dracho's gaze fell at that. "I couldn't be sure when you would come across the true heir. Nor did I wish to potentially ruin anything by divulging the information before I had to."

Dracho reluctantly nodded. "The second title... a queen of survival and to all."

"It's Eliana," Antares said, his voice low.

Phillipe nodded, and my spine straightened as his gaze found me. "I can't speak for what you have survived, dear, but you are a queen to many, if not all. The elves, those in Meridium... and to all those born of two races—those many would consider exiles."

"They are not exiles!" I stepped forward, baring my teeth, and Phillipe bowed his head in apology.

"I—I can't believe it," Dracho muttered, his eyes back on the drawing. "That means—"

"What? What is it, Dracho?"

"You are estellars." Antares's voice was quiet, but as far as I was concerned he might as well have shouted it from the highest mountain.

Long ago, when the stars that floated about our cosmos fell to our planet, they eventually turned to dust. We are all made from that dust. Estellars are those who have come from the same star...

Dracho was frozen, stunned; Phillipe nodded, practically dancing on the balls of his feet.

"You know what that means? The final title." Dracho was looking at Antares, who crossed his arms, nodding solemnly.

"What now?" I demanded.

"A warrior of shadow and will. It's Antares," Dracho said.

I felt like I had been dropped in a bathing tub of the coldest sea water.

"It is?" Phillipe asked in astonishment. "How do you know?"

"My father used to call me his warrior of shadow. It became a popular nickname around the training arena," Antares said.

I frowned. "But that means..."

"The *three* of you are estellars!" The scholar clapped his hands. "This is remarkable to witness. There hasn't been a pair since your parents." He pointed at Dracho. "To see *three* in my lifetime is astounding."

I suddenly felt extremely claustrophobic.

"Why?" The word burst from me. Phillipe stopped gushing for a moment, looking at me in confusion. "Why the three of us?" We came from entirely different backgrounds. How could I be celestially linked to both of them when I didn't share their faith in the stars and their ancestors? I tried to remember everything Dracho had told me about estellars. "I-I don't even share the same beliefs as they do—"

"My dear." Phillipe came around the desk, stopping short of clasping my hands. "Belief makes no difference when it comes to the truth. You have been chosen because estellars are those destined for greatness. With your estellars and the sword, you are destined to unite the elves and people together, saving Ruvalon!"

I jerked back, almost stumbling over a pile of books; Antares caught me by the crook of my elbow. I pulled myself free, my gaze never leaving the eager-looking man. "No one decides *my* destiny for me. Not fate, not some belief in the stars, not anyone. I will not be bound to a fate that I would never choose for myself. I don't want this."

Philippe recoiled in shock. "My dear, your existence means preventing Ruvalon's end—"

I held a hand up. "I don't usually worry about the end of the world. It's ended for me many times."

My chest was heaving. I was aware of Dracho's gaze on me, before it flicked to Antares, who said, "Eliana, let's get some air."

I nodded, turning to leave the stifling study. The cool air in the long corridor outside was like surfacing from suffocating waters. Moving towards the staircase, I rested my hands on the balustrade, breathing deeply. Antares stood by my side, watching carefully.

"Well?" I snapped. "Aren't you going to lecture me on what a selfish person I am?"

He leaned forward onto his elbows.

"I don't think you're selfish," he said after a moment.

I turned to see if he was joking. "You don't?"

He shook his head, reaching up to tuck his hair behind his ear. "I would despise knowing my fate was tied to a prophecy too. They're unreliable and speak in riddles."

"You *were* a part of the prophecy."

"Perhaps," he said. "But *I* wasn't declared as the saviour of the land." His eyes pinned me, and I sucked in a breath. He tilted his head, his eyes narrowing. "You know, being estellars doesn't just mean what you think it does. I thought you had discussed this with Dracho."

I swallowed hard, uncomfortable. Once again, Dracho's words floated back to me. *When it happens, it doesn't mean the people involved are destined to be together. It can mean a friendship that goes beyond blood or loyalty. Like a platonic soulmate.*

"I'm not sure how Dracho described his parents' relationship to you—"

"Like soulmates."

He nodded. "But their mating was what they *chose* it to be. A soulmate doesn't mean irrevocable love, or lust—despite the relationship between you and Dracho." I glared at him, my cheeks heating. "It is simply a life bond. Whether that means friendship"—he glanced down at his clasped hands—"or something more..." His gaze rose to mine. "It is always your *choice*. Don't trap yourself into thinking you have no free will."

I exhaled deeply in relief. His words helped resolve my questions. This explained why I felt drawn to Antares—not in a sexual way, but wanting to be close to him. We were estellars.

It explained why I always felt pulled in Dracho's direction, too. Why my chest tightened in his presence, and why our time together felt so much more meaningful than it ever had with any previous lovers.

Being estellars wasn't the end of the world. And it felt nice knowing that I still had a choice in the matter. As did they.

"Is that what you want? A friendship with me?" I dared to ask.

His surprised expression made him look younger. "I have already chosen you to be my friend."

My heart squeezed. I almost choked on my inhaled breath, rubbing a hand over my face.

"I..." I hesitated. "Until recently, I never got the impression you liked me—only found me mildly irritating. What changed?"

Antares's brows lowered in uncertainty. The expression was so childlike and unlike him that a smile pulled at my lips. Then I froze, my breath hitching, as he lifted a hand, hovering it over my face before he tucked a strand of hair behind my ear.

"You make me feel... you make me *feel*. I—despised it. But now we know why; I am drawn to you because we are the same. We are all one. I do not declare my feelings loudly, as others do. But surely you have seen that I feel more for you now and consider you a friend... rather than the disdain I felt when we first met?"

"Gee, thanks."

Antares chuckled.

"How can you be calm about this? That there are three of us—"

"I grew up with Dracho; he is and will always be more than a friend to me. A bond stronger than siblings. Which is why I wasn't shocked to discover we are estellars. Also, my decision to get closer to you over these few months wasn't just for Dracho's benefit. It was because *you* drew me in. I wanted that friendship with you too, after analysing my feelings over the whole situation.

The revelation of us being estellars just means it all makes sense."

"You wanted to kill me before," I stated.

"I didn't *want* to kill you. I wanted more than anything to protect Dracho at the time. He, whom I have spent nearly my whole life with. But you saw his reaction; his bond with you grew a lot quicker than mine... he stood in the way. I could never have hurt you."

I believed him. What shocked me more was that I *wanted* to believe him.

"Don't overthink it. We can deal with everything that comes with being star bonded as we move forward. What's more important is what the prophecy implies. What do you want to do?"

No one had ever asked me that before, besides Dracho, and I'd never considered what I truly wanted beyond fulfilling my duty. I had chosen to put off my coronation, but always known I would have to return to that.

"What if I don't want to pick up the sword?" I whispered. "If we even find it?"

"Then that is your choice to make."

"Dracho said before that I was selfish... for not taking up my birthright."

Antares breathed deeply. "That was before we knew of this prophecy. It is *your* choice to make. Whatever you decide, Dracho will of course respect it, and we will deal with it—together."

"Together," I repeated, feeling as though this was the first breath I had taken since leaving Phillipe's study.

Antares held his arm out. "Shall we?"

The corridor felt never-ending as we walked back down it, the door to the study appearing like a speck at the end of it. I wasn't sure if I was ready for more revelations.

When we entered, Dracho was leaning against one of the bookshelves, arms crossed and an intense expression on his brow that lightened when he saw us. Phillipe watched us with a remorseful eye.

I fidgeted as I approached the desk. "Thank you for giving me a moment. I know you were only helping, but it was too much to take in at once."

"Thank you, but no apology necessary, Your Highness." Phillipe nodded. "It was a lot to take in at once. I should have reined in my enthusiasm."

I gave him a small smile. My gaze returned to Dracho; that heaviness on his face was still present.

"What's on your mind?" I asked him.

He exhaled deeply. "Phillipe was just telling me about the poison."

"And?" Antares took a step forward eagerly.

Dracho's steps were silent as he stepped forward, two fingers reaching down to turn a book in our direction.

I read the words, and my head snapped up. "It's tied to the Hollow itself? Not just some corrupt magick?"

"The poison is unknown, but there are cases like my parents'—like your father's—from thousands of years ago. Bisa said it was known before, but that information had been lost to time. Phillipe says that other than the actual Hollow itself, situated in the Vildspire, nothing has been written about anyone ever infected by it. Several pages are missing—it's like the knowledge of it has been removed. Hidden. But..."

"But?" I pushed.

"The poison... apparently it's made from the Hollow *itself*."

Phillipe nodded, his face solemn.

My brain stuttered for a moment, trying to comprehend it. "How is that possible? The Hollow was nowhere near my father," I argued.

"Nor my mother. Only my father came face to face with it," Dracho added.

"The Hollow is full of corrupt magick," Ant said. "We have seen in the wyverns it possesses that this poison infects them, but doesn't kill them straight away. Perhaps that is down to the Hollow's magick and control. But perhaps..."

"What?" Dracho asked.

"It's just a theory... but perhaps someone worked out how to extract the corrupt magick from it."

A beat of silence passed as we processed that. Considered the implications. It meant that the Hollow wasn't the only weapon being wielded against us.

"That means Cirdan could have it," I whispered. Cirdan had been at the temple with the Hollow and his father. There were many natural poisons that he could use against his enemies, but most from the continent and beyond were natural, and had antidotes. What terrified me the most about this new finding was how quickly it worked, and that we hadn't yet found anything that could fight against it.

"I'm so sorry I haven't been able to help further," Philippe said, breaking the silence. "I shall get some of the others to keep looking, of course, and keep the prophecy safe."

"One other has seen the script..." Antares said, his hand rubbing across the line of his jaw. "Who was it?"

Phillipe looked confused for a second. "A prince. He carried with him a royal seal. He told me that he was on a diplomatic visit to learn more about the elves. He never said why, only gave his name."

"What was it?" I asked, my heart thundering behind my ribs. If Cirdan already knew about the prophecy, he was one step ahead.

Phillipe's eyes seemed to age before me; realisation dawned on his face. He stared at me intensely, as if reluctant to say it.

"Morgwn Cervidae."

My brother.

Chapter 54

The view over Tenebris from the palace balcony was magnificent. The deep orange-gold of the sunset stretched far and wide, the colour of fire and marigolds. My lips turned up in a small semblance of a smile, and I paused.

Our visit to the Scires had provided us with valuable information, but also more questions. We had learned of the prophecy—something I would gladly have forgotten, had Dracho not kept bringing it up. But what kept me up at night was the question of why my brother had gone looking for it, carrying my mother's family seal—how he'd even known to look for it. What did it mean? Why had my family kept secrets from me? Secrets I would never find the answer to, because they'd died before their time!

I didn't know where the Sword of Orian was, so I couldn't use it to unite anyone, even if I'd wanted that responsibility. The thought of being the person responsible for uniting the different races throughout Ruvalon was incomprehensible and terrifying. My shoulders felt burdened enough without the addition of saving the world. The threat of Cirdan, the people waiting for my coronation, my feelings for Dracho... it was so much.

Being back in Tenebris reminded me of my duties. Boone had met us on the throne room balcony, waiting as Dracho and Antares transformed back. There was correspondence from a few council members Dracho had to address—another burden for me. My very presence here was a cause of conflict for Dracho. He'd sighed in exhaustion; the day had tired us all out.

Being left alone in my room had paralysed me with a familiar fear until my room had become suffocating, reminding me of being confined in that cell. Now, standing on the balcony under the brightening stars of the twilight sky, I reminded myself that it hadn't been that long since it had all happened—since they'd found me in that castle, saved me from Jandar and Cirdan.

If I had been saved at all.

"So… you are openly and proudly elven now?"

The raspy voice caused my stomach to dip nervously as its owner came to stand beside me, leaning his arms on the edge of the balcony, though it didn't feel like a malicious question. Thuban—Dracho's uncle.

I nodded, lips pressed together, and there was a pause as I peeked at the side of his face. He must have been very handsome in his younger years; scars and a broken nose had roughened up his features. But his dark eyes were intimidating. I remembered the ferocity in them that day in the throne room when Dracho had announced we were to be released.

Thuban's gaze swung to mine. "I must say, I was surprised to see you here again."

"Believe me, I'm just as surprised as you to find myself here again," I said coolly.

"Though it seems to be working out in your favour with the emperor." I met his stare as he continued. "You know, our two kingdoms working together. It's a nice surprise. One I had not anticipated, after everything." He gave me a charming smile.

I exhaled slowly, glad I had not reacted verbally to my initial understanding of his words. "Honestly… after my last visit here, I didn't think we would ever be able to work together. But the threat of the Hollow keeps growing, and I think it will take even more than our two kingdoms to end it."

Thuban leaned forward, eyeing me. His aura was guarded, but he studied me like I was a complex equation that needed figuring out. "I believe you may be right. You know, Dracho is like a son to me. It was hard on his father when Dracho's mother, Irena, died. Eltanin's grief manifested in the distance between the two of them. It made Eltanin weaker. So Dracho started training with me instead."

His words were a reminder that Dracho and I had a shared bond when it came to the loss of our parents. It was interesting to hear how Dracho had coped after his mother's passing.

"I am sorry for your loss," I said, meaning it. It wasn't just Dracho who had lost Eltanin, but Thuban also.

The skin around his eyes creased as he smiled tightly. "Thank you," he said, his eyes sad. "I admire your views on our kingdoms working together. But it does not blind me to Dracho's actions."

I swallowed. "I'm not sure what you mean?"

"Dracho has been an unbelievable leader in his short time. He united the people and raised their spirits after Eltanin's death. He reassured them after the Hollow had breached the mountains. He strengthened the magick boundaries. And he has led our people with grace and strength surprising for his age. Yet I fear his emotions go unchecked... when it comes to you."

My heart rate kicked up. "Me?"

Thuban nodded, giving me a close-lipped smile. "Dracho put off the hunt for his father's killer for months because he knew it would bring him face to face with you."

I remembered what Althea had said back in Aion. *Our arrival was a lot more peaceful than what Thuban wanted.*

"My father wasn't invol—"

"Dracho has informed us all of such. I was hesitant to believe him at first, but I trust his judgement... and there was no debating it with him, anyway." He laughed darkly. "But still," his voice turned quiet, "the last our people saw of you was you being interrogated in our throne room, your large companion hurling insults at the emperor. Now those same people see you have returned, and after the death of your own father. Can you understand why they are wary?"

I flinched, but he kept talking without giving me a chance to respond. "Some may worry that you have returned to enact your own plan of revenge. To use your familiarity to get close to Dracho."

Every muscle in my body tensed, and my hand curled into a fist against the cold stone of the balcony. People believed me to be seducing Dracho for my own ambitions?

"Is that... what some of the court truly think?" I found my voice as disbelief rocked through me.

He looked at me with pity. "Some members of the Mortal Council and leading families believe so. But I can see that you have been through much—I have heard some of it from Dracho myself."

I tensed. *Dracho told him what happened with Cirdan? Why would he do that? To defend me?*

"I know Dracho wants you to stay here until you've recovered," Thuban said. "But should you ever change your mind, I offer my aid to help you return to where you belong. You only need tell me."

The breath I took was shaky as I processed his words. This was something that had crossed my mind already—the idea that I could potentially harm Dracho's reputation as emperor. That my presence in his kingdom could tarnish the view his people had of him, cause dissent amongst those who helped him lead. I had seen the effects myself, in Dracho's sunken eyes and the exhausted smiles he gave me. It was another reason why I felt he and I could never truly be together.

Now, not only was Thuban giving me his advice, but he was offering his help. I knew what needed to be done.

"I understand." I dragged my hands over my head, brushing my hair away.

Thuban's eyes narrowed on my ears. His features tightened for a moment before smoothing out, but I was beginning to accept that there would always be those who felt uncomfortable around me because of my lineage.

"Thank you for your counsel," I told him. "I really do appreciate it, and your offer. I need to return to my city soon—I have been away too long. I will tie up any loose ends here and take my leave."

My departure would mean that any questions surrounding Dracho's capability to rule could be quashed. We could then still work together for the good of Ruvalon, finding answers to the Hollow and everything that had happened. I knew he wanted me to remain in Tenebris until I was fully recovered, but some scars ran too deep and would take years to heal... if they ever did.

Meanwhile, the threat of Cirdan grew. I couldn't leave Meridium defenceless for long, not when he potentially had access to such a devastating poison. I had to get back and prepare. If Cirdan was going to target anywhere, it would be my city. After failing to take me as his bride, his eye would no doubt be fixed upon me and my next move. Meridium was in a vulnerable position right now, and it was the wisest decision to return, if only to prepare for a potential war with the elves. Our saving grace was that there was no clear way to attack the city other than from the east, where Lys's castle in Asaph was strategically placed, so that she could warn us of any incoming army.

"Will you need my help?" Thuban asked.

"No. Dracho won't stop me."

Thuban's eyes softened in a way that told me he didn't believe that.

"It's not his choice either way. May—may I ask you something?" When he nodded, I said, "Will you take care of him?"

His eyes held mine, and he smiled. "Of course." He raised his hand to his chest. "All I ever want is the prosperity of my kingdom."

His words tingled at something in my brain, seeming familiar, but I only smiled politely before walking away.

Chapter 55

"Hey, Eliana, how did it go—? What are you doing?" Roux's steps faltered as she entered my room, glancing quickly at Vyn and Bas.

Pausing as I packed clothes away in my rucksack, I eyed her warily, worried about this conversation. "We are returning to Meridium."

"Right now?" Her voice rose sceptically.

"As soon as I can. I've lingered too long away from Meridium, and it's time I return."

Roux's silence was deafening. Vyn and Bas glanced between us. I waited patiently for her to break the tension.

"Does Dracho know?" she asked at last.

"I... I haven't spoken to him yet," I admitted, my cheeks heating.

More silence.

Roux's eyes narrowed, then blew so wide I thought they would pop. "You—" She paused for a moment, speechless. "You slept with him?"

I stared at her blankly. *There's no possible way she can tell that... can she?*

Vyn's lips thinned; Bas's gaze turned to the wall beside him. I had already updated them on what had occurred in the Scires, and all that had happened between Dracho and me. They'd been confused as to why I wanted to leave until I'd told them of my conversation with Thuban. They didn't completely agree with my reasoning, but eventually they'd both agreed it was best.

My head was still spiralling over the revelation that Dracho, Antares and I were estellars. I thought some time away to check on Meridium and process everything would do me good.

I considered lying, but thought better of it. Roux and I had always been honest with each other. "It's more complicated than that," I said, turning to continue packing away the things I had gained in Tenebris.

"Well, of course it is," she laughed. "There's more than just physical attraction between you both for it not to be."

"We're estellars," I blurted out, throwing a shirt onto the bed and staring up at the ceiling, exhaling deeply. I focused on my breath for a moment before risking a peek at her.

"That... kind of makes sense."

I scoffed. "You sound like Antares... who, by the way, I am also estellars with." I dropped down to sit on the edge of the bed, my teeth finding the inside of my cheek.

That shocked her. "Wait, what?" Her head snapped to Vyn, who only nodded.

"To be completely honest, it's all slightly overwhelming right now... There was also a prophecy. *You* were mentioned." I winced, mentally cursing myself for casually dropping that into conversation.

"Me?" The question was wary, as if she too were already burdened by all that had come before. Too tired for the expectations of the cosmos—which was highly likely.

Guilt overwhelmed me, and my tongue felt like chalk in my mouth. "Antares has written it down. I'm sorry I sprang it on you like that. We were going to sit down and discuss it with you, but Dracho was called away by Boone. I haven't seen him since."

"It's all right," she said, her brown eyes glazed. "I... think I'll go and find Antares." She bee-lined to the door without so much as a goodbye.

"I am sorry, Roux."

She paused and looked back at me for a moment, much left unsaid behind her clamped lips. "It's all right, Eliana."

The door closed with a hollow thud. I gave up on packing, choosing instead to clamber onto my bed and sit there cross-legged.

"Well?" I asked Bas and Vyn. "Just tell me I'm a terrible person and get on with it."

"You're not a terrible person." Vyn pushed off the wall, joining me on the bed as he smoothed my hair away from my face. “You’re just under a lot of stress.”

“That’s no excuse for blurting it out like that,” I said.

They said nothing. They didn’t need to.

“I am sorry, guys. Vyn, I know you and Antares—”

Vyn scoffed, waving a hand. “Eli, you know me. That was purely a physical scratch we both needed to itch. There’s nothing lost between us.”

I nodded, my lips quirking at the edges, somewhat disturbed by the memory that flashed before my eyes of the two of them. “Bas, you and Roux—”

“Can continue to get to know each other, E. Going back home isn’t gonna change any of that. We can always return, with Dracho’s permission.”

I nodded once more. I knew that. Then why did it feel like the world was ending?

“Do you need us to do anything?” Bas asked, his warm voice like an embrace.

“No.” I shook my head and sighed. “You’d better go and pack. I don’t want to linger if I can avoid it. As soon as we’re ready and I’ve spoken to Dracho, we’ll leave.”

Their solemn expressions almost made me cry.

It wasn’t long until Dracho found me, entering my chambers shirtless with a smile and a swift kiss on my forehead. I jerked in surprise, trying to breathe through the churning in my stomach.

“I heard you pacing back and forth and wondered if I should come save the floor from being worn down,” he laughed, picking up the fresh pot of tea I’d been brought. I shook my head when he offered it to me.

“Are you all right?” he asked, a well-defined brow arching as he poured himself a cup.

“I’ll be returning to Meridium in the morning.”

Dracho barked out a laugh as he sat in a chair, bringing the cup to his mouth. His smile fell and his hand stilled as his eyes found mine and he realised I wasn’t joking. “What? What are you—”

“I’ve stayed away for too long… and it’s time for me to return.”

“All right.” The porcelain cup tinkled as he placed it on the table and rose from his chair, and for a moment I was caught off guard by the sight of his muscled chest, all his skin on display. He reached forward, touching my cheek gently. “We’ll prepare to leave—”

I stepped away. “I’ll be leaving. You should stay.”

His mouth parted, but no words came out for a moment. His gaze flickered over my expression.

“I don’t understand,” he said.

I looked down, an uncomfortable squirming blossoming in my gut. A seed of uncertainty, blooming into poisonous guilt that flooded me—a taste I was becoming far too familiar with. “You have responsibilities here. You’ve been away too long also. Once Antares has found some more information, we can discuss it at a later date—even a letter will suffice.”

Dracho’s eyes were icy blue with shock.

“In the meantime, we should stay in our respective cities,” I added.

“What is this?” he asked softly.

“We both knew this day would come.” I rushed the words out. “I must return and accept my crown. There’s little use in you coming with me.”

His face pinched as he took in my words. My blow had landed.

“I thought...” His jaw flexed as he ran a hand through his hair. “I thought we worked things out.”

I wrapped my arms around myself. “No, we did. This isn’t about all that.”

He shook his head. “Then I don’t understand where this is coming from. Only a couple of days ago you were—”

I shot him a look that made him stutter.

“I-I just... don’t understand what’s changed. I wasn’t prepared for something like this so soon after we—”

“Fucked?” I asked curtly, and he cringed. “That didn’t mean anything, Dracho.”

He turned at my harsh words, his back muscles expanding with each breath, causing his tattoos to look like a living thing under his skin. He gave a humourless laugh. “You’re unbelievable.”

“What?”

“How can you just trivialise what happened between us so easily?” he growled, running his fingers through his hair.

“We agreed that it didn’t mean anything—” I started desperately.

“It meant *everything*!” he shouted as he turned, flinging his hands out as his raven hair fell over his wild eyes.

I held my breath, feeling the unsteady beat of my hammering heart as I stood motionless. His cold, hard eyes stared at me for a moment before narrowing painfully.

"I agreed at the time that it didn't. Stupidly. Selfishly. Because I told myself that I was willing to accept whatever part you would ever be willing to give me, after all I'd done. And I would be happy with it. That it would be *enough*. But it could never mean *nothing* to me."

I exhaled roughly, but he wasn't done.

"But I thought—after—that things were improving, that you felt something too."

I took a step back, suddenly regretting the direction this conversation had gone in. I *did* feel something.

It's for the best.

"I can't understand why we've gone back to this," he whispered.

And I realised for me it had always gone back to this. That my decision had been made by the version of me who had been thrown into a dungeon in Tenebris. Who had been betrayed and hadn't got over the hurt of it. Who had been captured, abused and had nothing left to give.

"You speak as if it wasn't your own doing," I bit out as painful regret twisted at my insides.

His brows flew up.

"Everything that broke between us—the reason everything changed—is because of you! You talk to me as if you didn't have me removed from your throne room. As if you hadn't surprised me by announcing your identity to my father and threatening to destroy him if involved with your father's death." I forced myself to feel that frustration, going numb as it crept through my body like a poison.

Because I didn't truly believe what I was saying. I may not have forgiven what he had done, but I *had* moved past it. But I knew if I told him of my fears for the future, if I truly made myself that vulnerable, I was opening my world to a whole new level of pain.

So I lied.

My canines lengthened as I hissed at him. "Tell me why I should just fall back in—into anything with you? When I could never trust you implicitly!"

Dracho's chest heaved. "I apologised... and if you felt that way, why fall into my bed in the first place?"

I stared at him, my hands trembling. "It... was obviously a mistake. This was *all* a mistake. Maybe you shouldn't have come back into my life at all."

Cold hurt and rage flickered in his eyes. "And where would that have got you? *Dead,* or married to some elf prick. Ever the obedient, *broken* wife."

Nausea rose in my throat, and his eyes softened immediately.

"How dare you?" I whispered.

"Fuck, I'm sorry, I didn't—I just don't understand any of this, Eliana," he cried. "W-why won't you let me in?"

I bit my tongue, biting back the too-hurtful words I wanted to throw at him. The words I would use to push him away.

"You're so afraid that you'll let someone truly in, that they'll see inside the real you and they won't like what they'll see. Well, guess what? I've seen the real you and I'm still here!" He stretched out his arms.

And I could see it, the truth in his too-wide eyes. Looking up at the decorative ceiling, I took a deep breath as a thousand words ran through my mind.

"Tell me," he pleaded.

I swallowed hard, shaking my head. I knew if I shared my fears—about his court, about our rules and being separated from one another—that they wouldn't matter to him. But they were *real* fears. They couldn't just be waved away. "It doesn't matter."

"It matters to me."

"I don't want to talk about it," I ground out.

He stepped forward, arms still open. "Eliana, please be honest. I don't care about my own feelings over this. I care about yours. If you don't believe my words when I say I'm sorry, then I will *show* you."

"Dracho—" He dropped to his knees, and I gasped.

"Eliana, *please*. I'm already on my knees. I'm already where you want me."

"That's not what I—"

"Just wait." He spoke quickly, as if afraid this was his only chance to tell me. "It *was* a mistake."

My heart dropped to my stomach. "*What?*"

He moved forward, still on his knees, to clasp the fabric of my shirt, pressing his forehead to my stomach. "It was a mistake..." He shook his head, pulling himself to his feet and cupping my cheeks between his calloused but soft hands, placing his forehead to mine with his lips hovering inches above my own. "Because—because not a day has gone by that your scent hasn't invaded every one of my thoughts or driven me mad with longing. That I haven't thought about the taste of you on my tongue."

I couldn't breathe. Couldn't move.

"And no, it isn't just because of the physical stuff... or because we are estellars. I felt like this long before any of that. Returning to Ruvalon only made my feelings stronger. Your presence made me believe I could be something more than the numb monster I felt. Every conversation lifted me and reminded me how to smile. Thinking of every word you said, trying to figure out what it really meant. It's how your laugh makes my chest quake and knuckles tense at the thought of never hearing it again, because I don't make you do it often enough. How you purse your lips and chew on the inside of your cheek when you're thinking..."

My throat constricted. Tears sprang up behind my eyes, but I was unable to tear them away from his gaze. Because I knew it was coming. And I wasn't ready for it.

"Because—because I would *adore* you in a million ways, and there's no going back for me. There never was. Not since the moment I met you." His words were still hurried, as if he was panicking that I would interrupt at any moment. "It wasn't at first sight, not exactly. More like—an awareness. As if my heart knew, but the rest of me had to catch up. Because my heart said—it's going to be you."

A tense silence filled the air between us, becoming unbearable.

His uncle was right.

Pain ripped through me as my breath caught. I had been living in a fairie-tale, wrapped up in silk sheets and the lush scent of him. This was bigger than us, and I was a *distraction*. Had always been a distraction.

When I had met him that day in Ruvalon, after he had fallen over that damn water bucket. When he'd met my father and journeyed with us to Aion. When he'd stayed with me after the Uhane ceremony instead of looking for Antares, and helped Roux in Volente. When being at risk had made him transform, revealing his identity, and when he had shown me pleasure like I'd never felt before, first in Crystalwood, and now again in Tenebris.

Even after we had parted ways, I had been a distraction. He'd put off confronting my father about that Goddess-forsaken pin, because of *me*.

All that hurt more deeply than any betrayal of his ever could. It was the realisation I needed.

"Say something. *Anything*, please." There was desperation in his eyes as he pleaded. Pleaded like it was a prayer to any god that listened.

After a painful moment, he released my face and took a step back, as if he already knew the blow I was about to deal. I hugged myself tightly, feeling cold after his distance.

"I can't," I whispered, my voice surprisingly steady.

He nodded, resigned, and I hated the tidal wave of pain that passed across his cold, ocean eyes. Something else dawned there, like a long-forgotten fear remembered and become real. The look of a man who had just realised it was too late.

He sniffed. "I'll... I'll give you some space to think."

"You don't have to. I'm leaving in the morning." I hadn't realised my mind was truly made up until I said it.

"Eliana, please—"

"My decision is final, Dracho."

He stepped forward in a blur of speed, every mask slipping away as he clasped my hands gently between his. "Listen, I know I've fucked up. But please stay. At least until you're fully recovered."

I shook my head.

"Please, Princess."

"It's time to be queen now," I fired back louder. "And I need to return to my people. Us... us meeting was a mistake."

I stepped back, everything inside me trying to push towards him as I removed my hands from his. They remained in mid-air for a moment, until he stood straighter, running them through his raven hair.

He nodded.

"I... I will escort you back to Meridium." He sounded lost, his tone dull.

My heart skipped a beat, and I swallowed the tight ball of emotion that threatened to choke me. I had never seen him look so broken. "There's no need. I'll ask Althea."

He didn't look at me. "I... I'll leave you in peace then."

I turned, looking out the window, until the click of the door sounded behind me. I moved and dropped down onto the bed, but a sudden panic had me springing up towards the door. My hand hovered over the handle before I gently pushed down.

The door opened.

I wasn't sure why the thought had crossed my mind that he would lock me in, but a wave of emotion made me sink to the floor, cradling my knees as the tears rolled down my face.

He hadn't caged me.

I could leave right now if I wanted to, return to Meridium and leave Tenebris behind. My tears fell over my cheeks, my lips; they tasted like regret. They fell for the pain I had caused him, the pain it would continue to cause him.

I cried until the sharp, knife-like pain in my chest was a dull, continuous ache. There was nothing left in me to give there.

He *loved* me... And I had nothing to give him.

And at that moment, I felt like I would never know peace again.

Chapter 56

"Jeshwa will be close behind with Bas and Vyn. Roux is staying," Althea said quietly.

I nodded, understanding that Roux had to process what the prophecy meant for her, and that her bond with Dracho ran deep. After the hurt that I had seen on his face, I was grateful he had her to care for him.

More guilt plagued me as I thought of Bas's developing relationship with her, knowing that I was responsible for splitting them apart. I hadn't witnessed too much of their connection, but I knew that leaving Tenebris was bound to halt whatever progress they had made.

"I thought we could use the girl time," Althea said. "Plus, I wanna know if I can talk with you in my dragon form."

My teeth clenched as I dragged a heavy bag onto my back full of clothes, beauty items and shoes that Althea had demanded I take with me. She claimed that *the southerners could use some scandalous fashion to shake up their swanky balls*.

She sighed when I didn't respond. "All right, out with it." She plopped herself down onto one of the plush armchairs in her room, holding her hand up to scan her long, beautifully painted nails. I'd stayed in her room for the night, unable to stay so close to Dracho with the pull I felt towards him.

Antares had knocked on her door late the evening before, asking to speak with me. I had refused, and she'd told him I needed to be left alone.

"I'm just tired," I huffed. "Ready to go home and deal with everything going on there." Sleep had not found me the night before, my mind haunted by memories of soft lips and broken eyes.

She studied me, lips pursing.

"Have—have you spoken to him?" I asked.

She cleared her throat, shifting in her chair. "No. He hasn't left his room since yesterday."

I flinched.

Althea frowned. "It doesn't have to be this way, Eliana."

I glanced down at the soft fur that lined the top of the beautiful boots she had given me. For a second, for one moment, I wanted to take it all back—to be selfish and take everything Dracho could give me with no promise of being able to give anything in return. Part of me was doing this to protect him. To help ease the friction caused within his court at my presence. But I was also scared. Scared that if I were to take things further with Dracho, I could lose him, just like I'd lost my mother, father and brother.

Keeping him at arm's length but still in my life as a fellow ruler felt worth it when compared to letting him into my heart and potentially losing him. The risks were greater, especially with Cirdan no doubt on the war path. The thought of losing either Dracho or Antares was physically painful. I knew it was the estellar bond, but I didn't want to experience the pain that would come should that bond break. I had barely survived the loss of my own family.

The image of Thuban's grateful eyes floated across my mind, and I knew what I had to do. If I could give Dracho one thing, it was the gift of stability by removing myself from his city.

"It has to be this way, Althea." I snatched my dagger off the small side table, sheathing it on my thigh before turning to exit the room.

"Do you love him?"

I froze before the door.

"No." The word was much harder to get out than I'd thought it would be. My chest ached.

I couldn't, could I?

With a sigh, I turned to face her and almost baulked at the disbelief in her eyes. I swallowed, looking away. "All I know is, for the one I love… I'd give up everything."

That was why I believed my feelings weren't that strong. We were estellars, but that didn't mean all-consuming, breath-taking love. Surely if I loved him, I wouldn't be able to leave him?

Althea replied with a clear, unwavering voice. "That's how I know that he loves you."

I didn't respond, too scared to hear more.

"He was going to give up his rule for you."

My eyes snapped to hers. "What?" My voice broke.

"During the meeting with the whole council, Antares's mother questioned his integrity and capability to rule, considering he brought you back here."

My stomach sank. Everything I'd feared had been correct.

"She questioned whether someone else would be better qualified to rule," Althea added.

The sudden bitterness I felt was too strong to prevent me from holding my tongue. I had become fond of Antares, but his mother left a foul taste in my mouth. "And she's still alive—why?"

Althea laughed. "She *is* Antares's mother. Don't worry, Dracho put her in her place well enough. But afterwards..."

"Afterwards?" I asked tentatively.

"For just a moment, something changed in his eyes. Ant and I could tell straight away where his thoughts had gone. He's new to rule, and young by a draconi's standards, so he was questioning if he *was* right for the role. We told him he was, of course. But then Antares brought you up."

I frowned.

"I truly believe that if you asked, he would leave all this behind and join you in Meridium."

"I would never want that," I told her.

"I know. So does he. Which is why he's letting you go. But that's also how I know he loves you."

I shook my head in denial as I walked to the door. "It's just a brief infatuation. When I'm gone, he'll forget all about me—"

She laughed. "Don't think I don't know what you're doing."

My hand hovered over the doorknob.

Althea jerked her chin in the direction of the hallway. "You're running."

I gave her a lingering stare. She was right. But it didn't change anything. "I am."

"Why? I thought you were never afraid," she breathed, her frown deepening.

"Because, Althea..." I pulled the door open, facing the emptiness—not only before me, but inside me. "I don't want the world to burn... and I am *always* afraid."

I stretched my arms above my head, feeling the ache in my thighs and up my spine from sitting atop Althea for the hours it had taken to return to Meridium. Dracho and Antares had not been present when we left from the throne room balcony, and I couldn't tell if I was hurt or relieved. I wondered if Antares had been absent because I had sent him away. I felt bad, thinking he believed he wasn't welcome.

I almost laughed when Connaught raced down the palace steps into the courtyard. As Bas and Vyn climbed down from Jeshwa, Connaught stopped just before me, his hands clasping my arms gently. Then his eyes widened, and he pulled my hair from behind my ears to cover them, glancing around in fear.

I cursed myself. I was so used to walking around freely in Tenebris that I had forgotten to hide who I was. It felt sickening.

"Are you okay?" were the first words out of Connaught's mouth.

"I'm fine," I told him with a small smile.

Althea huffed through her large nostrils, her icy blue dragon eyes set on him. I hadn't heard a word from her since leaving Tenebris, so I assumed my ability to hear Dracho had to do with us being estellars. I wondered if it meant I would be able to hear Antares too.

Connaught clearly wanted to ask more, but refrained from doing so as he looked once more to the winged beasts behind me. I glanced back as Bas and Vyn joined us.

"I really want a dragon," Bas sighed as he looked up at the pair. Jeshwa's head tilted, and I almost laughed.

"They aren't pets, Bas." Vyn shook his head.

"I know," he whined.

Jeshwa seemed to purr deeply, the sound sad, but it was the look in Althea's eyes that made me want to turn away from the draconi. Instead, I came to stand before Jeshwa, his expression reminding me of a forlorn pup. I smiled lightly and patted his neck before facing Althea. My hand reached out of its own accord, sliding over the smooth lilac scales.

"I'm going to miss you," I whispered.

She moved, lowering her head slightly to rest the space between her nostrils against my forehead, careful not to knock me over. I knew what she meant, and my eyes closed tightly as I pressed my forehead to her. "Thank you for everything."

I choked down my remorse for hurting Dracho and leaving those who had become my friends. Without a second glance back I turned to ascend the stairs, ready to begin the next terrifying chapter that was my rule.

Chapter 57

Dracho

"The guard is in love with her," Althea said softly.

I remained silent. I didn't need anyone to tell me that; I'd realised it a while ago. Who wouldn't love her?

He would be better for her.

"Does she know?" Althea asked. She had arrived home a couple hours ago, having escorted Eliana back to Meridium.

"I believe she does deep down," Antares said, ever all-seeing, "but it isn't reciprocated by her."

"How do you know?" Althea asked, her brows pinching low over her bright eyes.

"She doesn't look at him like she looks at—"

"That's enough." I stood, swallowing the knot that had formed in the back of my throat. Ever since my last conversation with Eliana, I'd felt like a prisoner in my own skin. My wings begged to burst forth, to take flight and feel the cool, soothing breeze of the skies.

But I couldn't. I couldn't allow myself that freedom or relaxation. Not after taking away hers all those months ago when she'd first come to Tenebris.

Ant frowned, making his eyes look even more intense. "This is all a misunderstanding, brother. We should return to Meridi—"

"She made her feelings clear. I won't chase her. Nor shall I make myself look a fool."

Ant scoffed. "The only foolish thing here is how asinine you're both being."

"I am sorry to say I have to agree with Ant." Althea pursed her lips, and Ant looked smug. "The girl is clearly in love with you, Dracho, and we already know how *you* feel. It isn't as complicated as you're both making it."

"Isn't it?" My voice rose. "Not only do we have our own kingdoms to rule and an enemy that threatens to destroy all of Ruvalon, but she can't trust me!"

Althea's lips parted. "Dracho, you've—"

"*I* did the worst thing anyone could possibly have done! I had her thrown into a cage, with no way out until *I* said so! I've said sorry, but I don't blame her for not being able to get over that. Not after everything she's been through. No, there's no forgiveness for that. That beautiful, *good* woman has to deal with everything that's happened to her, everything she's learned... and now she's been thrown to the wolves and into a rule she's not emotionally ready for."

"And you were?" Ant drawled.

No, I hadn't been. My behaviour that day in the throne room when I'd had Eliana seized was evidence of that. But Eliana... Eliana had gone through so much, overcome so much already before this. Before Cirdan...

All I had wanted was for her to recover before she became queen. To take some time for herself before politics got in our way. I'd worried some of my council members were going to prevent that from happening.

As it turned out, it was my own actions that had done so.

I missed her so much already, and I would never finish missing her. At every pause I thought of her. Her scent still lingered in my room, in my whole being. Heartbreak felt painful, its level limitless. But what do you do when your soul breaks?

"Dracho," Ant said softly, "we should just go and speak to her—"

"I said no!" I hissed, my eyes warming as they flashed silver.

He stood suddenly, his own eyes flashing as his hand clasped the back of my neck. "Do not assume you are the only one feeling the strain of this distance, brother. You are both *mine* too, remember."

I closed my eyes and exhaled through my flared nostrils.

"This can be fixed," Ant continued. "It must be fixed."

I knew what he meant. The prophecy had all but spoon-fed us the fact that our relationship made a difference to the future of Ruvalon.

"Ant's right, Dra—"

"I won't force it on her." I pulled myself out of Ant's grip. "Nor will I encourage her to burden herself with some words written thousands of years before her birth. As if that's the *only* reason she is alive. Her only purpose!"

"That's not what we're saying, Dracho. We just want you both to be happy," Althea murmured, her eyes cast downwards.

"I can't afford to be selfish," I whispered. "I take her lead on this. If the day comes when she calls for me, then I will go with open wings. Whatever she needs of me."

"And what of your needs?" Ant asked, his tone irritated.

I shook my head. "It doesn't matter. So many choices have been taken from her already. I will not do the same again."

Chapter 58

Eliana

They say habit keeps you going, and I had to agree. Ever since my return from Tenebris three days prior, I had stuck rigidly to the same routine. Breakfast, training, bathing, followed by a walk through the city, reassuring the people of my presence. Then paperwork, meeting with visiting dignitaries and going through Meridium's finances with Sizwe...

It was a lot. My coronation had been set for three days' time, and the fast approach set my body alight with nerves.

I had briefed Connaught on everything I had found out. All I had experienced in Tenebris and the Scires—but not of the extent of my relationship with Dracho and Antares. That was an awkward conversation I hadn't felt like having. He had begun an even stricter regimen with the soldiers, so we were prepared for any news of Cirdan.

Connaught had sent a letter to Aunt Lys whilst I was away, informing her of what had happened and asking her to let us know if anything suspicious was seen. She had replied with her concern for my safety, and advised that she would be vigilant.

On the advice of Sizwe and Connaught, I had decided to also write to King

Proditor, inviting him and Jak to Meridium so that I could reveal my true lineage. In my letter I had also informed him of Jandar Morven's death, and how Cirdan now controlled Jandar's elven armies.

As soon as Jareth knew, I planned to make an announcement to my people. They deserved to know who was ruling them, no matter the consequences. The deception I had lived my whole life upon my parents' bidding suddenly made me feel like a fraud. If my people and the continent didn't know my true nature, could I even feel like a queen? Did I have the right to rule over them when I hadn't been honest with them?

The question plagued me as I undertook my daily pilgrimage through the streets of Meridium, speaking with the people and hearing their concerns, praises and stories.

It was almost funny how quickly my plans went to shit.

"Your Highness!" A young man with strawberry-blonde hair and a crooked nose ran towards me. His eyes widened when Marcus took a menacing step forward.

I held up a hand, stepping around my mountain troll of a guard to clasp the man's hand. A scrap of paper was held between his fingers. "What is it, Warwick?"

The boy was the son of local bakers. Bas, Vyn and I often frequented his parents' store to buy several of their delicious cream-stuffed pastries.

"It's—it's—"

"Speak up, boy," Marcus said impatiently.

The boy did not speak, but held out his hand, offering me the paper. I took it gently, but as I read it, discomfort and panic grew in my chest, fear seeping into my brain. Printed as if the front page of a city news sheet, a sketch of my visage was depicted—with elven ears exposed.

Below the image was a headline in bright blue. *You have been lied to*, it read.

I felt the overwhelming urge to run, to escape—to abandon all my mental faculties and succumb to my baser emotions.

"Is it true, Your Highness?" Warwick asked warily.

As my mouth opened, the palace bell rang. Marcus unsheathed his sword, hovering his free hand above the small of my back.

"We need to get you back now, Your Highness." His voice was steady, but my elven ears didn't miss the nervous undertone.

I turned once more to Warwick's worried eyes. "Thank you. All will be explained, I promise."

Marcus navigated me away, but not before I saw the uncertainty in the boy's expression.

We were too far from the underground tunnel that could be used as a secret entrance or exit to the palace. As we rushed through the trade district, people appeared in the doorways of shops, holding similar flyers to the one Warwick had given me. Their chatter grew louder, their eyes widening with shock as they watched us pass, and Marcus grew more anxious as we went.

On approach to the open gates of the palace courtyards, we found a large group of people gathered, calling out to the two guards standing before them.

"Is this true?"

"Where is the princess?"

Marcus took hold of my arm, the action jarring me as he led me forward.

"There she is!"

"Princess, is this true?"

I clenched my jaw, bracing myself for the onslaught, but Marcus ploughed through, the people parting easily.

"Make way for the princess! Guards, protect your future queen!" he called. They rushed to obey, unsheathing their swords, making my gut twist. I swallowed my uneven breaths as the crowd continued to call after us, their confusion evident. Several more guards rushed towards us from the direction of the palace, aiming to close the gates behind me.

"Princess, please!"

"What's going on?"

Their calls followed me, and a wave of overwhelming guilt halted me in my tracks.

"Your Highness, we must—"

"Wait." I turned, facing the crowd just beyond the gate. "Hold the gates!" I called.

Bewildered, the guards paused their efforts. I approached the crowd once more as they stilled, Marcus close beside me. Their muttering fell silent as they waited for me to speak.

"I understand that there is much confusion. Please spread the word; all are to be present in the palace courtyard. I shall be addressing the kingdom within the hour. If everyone could please gather, I'll be along shortly."

The people murmured their agreement, shuffling or running along to relay my message.

"Are you sure this is a good idea, Your Highness?" Marcus asked, eyeing me cautiously.

I nodded, turning and walking swiftly to the palace. "If I am to rule this city, Marcus, I will not start with more dishonesty."

It didn't take me long to change into an outfit more suited to address my city. Shedding my breeches and shirt, I chose a deep green gown with a love-heart neckline and long lace sleeves.

I had never felt more uncomfortable than I did as I approached the balcony above the courtyard, the area filled with everyone—mortal and fairie-folk—quieting below. Connaught stood close behind, his stillness belying the concern he obviously felt.

It was a life-changing moment. I realised that. I would have preferred fighting a hundred men to what I had decided to do. But for the good of Meridium, for the good of Ruvalon, I had to be honest—coronation or not.

My throat closed on itself as I stared over the silent crowd. Words failed me, and nothing would come out.

A small cough sounded behind me, and I glanced over my shoulder. Connaught was looking at me, his eyes saying a thousand things. A memory drifted through the panic-laced fog—of Dracho wearing a similar expression.

If there is no fear, there is no being brave. I had told him that once. It was time I lived up to it.

I knew why I was frightened. Speaking up was courageous, but it didn't mean everyone would be in my corner. There would be backlash, and that was something I had always been terrified of.

But I couldn't allow my fear to dictate my life anymore.

"Many of you will have seen the words that have been spread throughout the city. I come before you to address these rumours..."

In, and out.

"It is true."

Blowing out a nervous breath, I took my hair and tied it at the back of my head.

Several people towards the front of the crowd exclaimed loudly—not in anger, but in shock—as the news spread further back.

"My mother, your late queen... her real name was Lorelai Orinan." Gasps and chatter broke out; my guards' hands tightened on the hilts of their swords as they stood beside me, on the staircases and surrounding the courtyard. Bas and Vyn were here too, ever my protectors, ever my friends. "My mother was heir to the throne of Adref. She was elven."

"I am half-elf. And I cannot be sorrier than I am right now that this was kept from you. You see, my mother—your beloved queen—fled Adref and her betrothal to the King of Stillmere, Jandar Morven. She fell in love with my father. I promised to be honest with you today, and I mean that." I swallowed the knot in my throat and blinked back the tears that sprang in my eyes. My shame for the world to see. "The Tain started because of Jandar's jealousy and determination to get revenge."

The chattering grew.

"He failed," I called out loudly.

Had he? My mother and brother had died during that war. My father and I had lost almost everything. Had he truly failed in his revenge?

"More recently, Jandar and his son took me captive in a bid to claim Meridium for the elves." The revelation caused a disturbance amongst my people. "He failed again. Jandar Morven is dead. But his son, Cirdan, still poses a threat to Meridium... and *all* Ruvalon. I have no doubt it was he who arranged for these papers to be distributed amongst you all. He wishes to tear our community apart."

I swallowed hard. "Now, I understand that my lineage may concern you, because for years so many have believed that all elven kind hates mortals. I understand that it is hard to let go of the violence that tore families apart in the war. I have suffered losses too. My mother, my brother, my father. Being half-elf means I straddle two worlds. *I* believe that means as your queen I will better understand the needs of all.... and I have prided myself on being a part of a city that has accepted *all*."

My trembling hands clasped together as I prepared for the worst. "I am so sorry for the loss this city has faced in the past—a loss caused because my mother fell in love with your king. But they promised to do their best to protect you, and I shall do the same. No matter what I am, I promise to protect you, serve you... and die for you if necessary. I have no doubt that Cirdan will bring war to our doors one day—but it is a war I will face *for* you, not against you. If we can stay united, he will fail. Just like his father before him.

"Troubled times may lie ahead, but I promise as heir to the throne that I will give my life for the city, for you. If you'll have me."

It was a shock to the system. All I had feared was coming true. I might, in fact, have to one day give my life for this city. But it was a humbling feeling that blossomed inside my chest as I realised I would. For these people, for this place, I would gladly die.

For a moment the silence spoke louder than any words could, but then a voice from the back of the crowd called out. Loudly and clearly, like a bright beacon in the darkness of night.

"Long live the queen!"

My mouth parted, my lower lip trembling as I squinted in the afternoon light.

"Long live the queen!" he called out again, and I would have recognised the strawberry-blonde hair of the baker's son anywhere.

"Long live the queen!" cried out my personal maids, Beatrice and Milly, who stood towards the front of the crowd, and I sent them a grateful smile.

More called out, in sporadic pockets around the courtyard. And then more. And more. Until the chant was all I could hear, a symphony of voices united over the thunderous, rapturous applause.

I reached forward, flattening a hand on the cold stone of the balcony to hold myself up. Connaught stepped forward, but didn't touch me. There were no more words that I could say, that I could form to express my gratitude, my shock. They had broken the silence of my creeping panic. So I just bowed, shaking away the numbness that almost overwhelmed me, to those who had accepted me. Those I'd had always believed would never accept the real me.

Dracho had been right; I'd had too little faith.

I didn't realise I was crying until a teardrop splashed on my hand. A shaky laugh left me as I raised that same hand to wave to the crowd, my smiling laughter coming until I was breathless. Connaught came closer, allowing me one last bow before he escorted me back to the palace.

"I always believed in you," he said with a touch of pride.

"I know." I smiled at him brightly. "I just needed to believe in myself."

Chapter 59

Dracho

Days passed.

I stopped leaving the palace. I still hadn't taken flight; the thrum of magick and my dragon vibrated along every nerve and fibre of my body. Yet all I could feel was numb.

Ant and Althea did their best to encourage me to leave the place, even sending Jeshwa to challenge me to a sparring match, but the thought of training did nothing to lift my spirits. My uncle stopped by once, the disappointment on his face like an arrow to my stomach. Boone was much more discreet when it came to his emotions, joining me in my father's study daily as I started to devour every book that lined the shelves, trying to find some meaning or distraction in the words.

"Your Excellency," he said, holding a thick book in his hands, his tone soft, as if gently speaking to a frightened animal. "Perhaps we should head to the library, play a game—"

"I don't want to play, Boone," I snapped, fed up with his requests for the silly chess games he used to play with my father. "It's pointless."

"But—"

"Why should I let fate dictate to me how my life plays out? If it is fate, might as well get on with it. We all die anyway. And your games didn't exactly help Dad, did they?"

"They did."

"What?"

"I said they did, Your Excellency."

Only the birds outside the window disrupted the silence as I processed that. His patience only heightened the tension, the magick within causing my spine to stiffen, as if anticipating a fight. My anger and pain resurfaced, so intertwined that I almost couldn't tell which was which, as Boone's words settled and it became clear what he meant.

"I think it's time I told you the truth," he finally said, a sad smile on his face.

"He knew?" I asked, my voice breaking. "He knew he was going to die?"

Boone nodded.

I leaned back in the leather chair, rubbing my hands over my face. My eyes found the portrait of my mother, and again I was reminded that I was alone. That both my parents had been taken from me.

My father had known all along he would die. And hadn't told me.

"Your father's death could not be prevented, Your Excellency. He knew not of the manner, but only that it would come soon. He accepted it almost straight away."

"That's why he expedited my training?"

Boone nodded again. "Your father left a letter. I hadn't the heart to give it to you yet. He told me to, only when you were ready. When it was needed."

He walked forward, pulling a sealed envelope from the book he was carrying. I stared at my father's jade wax seal for a moment before opening it and removing the letter inside.

"Do you want to be alone?" Boone asked.

I exhaled shakily, shaking my head, and opened the letter.

My dear boy, Dracho,

There's a level of freedom that comes with knowing you are going to die. It is also a bittersweet thing. Bitter because of time spent apart from friends and loved ones. Bitter because of everything I wanted to teach you, and because now I realise that I did not spend enough time with you after your mother's passing.

It is sweet because you know the pain is going to end. The loneliness that hits in the late of night when I miss your mother the most will end. And I will be reunited with her in the splendour of the stars. I will be reunited with her, my father, Rastaban, and all our ancestors.

It is sweet because I have faith in you, my son. I know you are going to be an exceptional emperor. You have your mother's compassion, her strength, and a determination all your own to ensure the safety of our realm. The most beautiful gift we can give during our lives is to improve and enrich the lives of those around us. So don't live with any regrets, Dracho.

Do not allow your sorrow to linger after my passing. You have many around you who love you. Those who love you and will help you along the way—some of whom may surprise you.

Remember, wherever you are, if you should find yourself looking to the stars, your mother and I will be watching over you. We love you, and we are so proud of you.

To the stars, my son.

Grief hit me again, like a soft, slow song, building until I could no longer hold back the tears that I had suppressed whilst reading the letter. Grief... and relief.

Relief that my father wasn't in pain, missing my mother. Relief that they were now together, even if I had been left behind.

Boone allowed me the time to get through my fresh wave of anguish. I rode it, allowing the fond memories and conversations to flood my brain. The waves of anguish turned into waves of love and warmth. My heart beat strongly as I gave a final sniff, embracing, not fighting my warring emotions.

"There is one more thing, Your Excellency." Boone gave me a small smile.

More? I wasn't sure if I could take another emotional onslaught.

Boone removed a small golden key from his pocket as he joined me round the front of the desk. I pushed my chair back as he knelt, ducking his head under the desk and unlocking a drawer I hadn't known was there. He removed a book—the book that contained the history of Ruvalon, of all its families.

Opening it, he turned the book in his hands, placing it before me.

There were letters. Many of them, placed carefully between the pages, written by someone I did not know to 'Eli'. Pain lanced through me at the memory of her, before I remembered it was the nickname my mother used to call Father.

"Why would he hide these here?" I asked, my brow furrowing.

"Well, he knew it would be a while before you opened the book of histories, even if you had found the drawer. You've never been one to enjoy reading non-fiction."

I rolled my eyes. "But why these? What's the significance of these letters?"

"Read them," Boone answered seriously.

My hesitation only lasted a second. I skimmed the first letter, determining nothing from its contents. I read on, letter after letter…

After a few I looked up, finding Boone's eyes fixed on me. "Is this genuine?"

He said nothing, but nodded.

"How long, Boone?"

Again, he did not answer. I stood, placing my hand on the desk, on top of the letters. "Boone, please… How long?"

He paused for one moment, as if knowing his words would tear apart everything I'd thought I knew.

"For always."

I sucked in a breath. The pain in my chest was no longer from my grief, and had everything to do with regret.

Chapter 60

Eliana

"Your Majesty." Marcus entered the tea room breathing heavily, his hand on the hilt of his sword.

The city had been relatively peaceful since my speech; I had even ventured out with my ears on show, despite my fears, finding that I was treated with no less respect than I had been before. The people embraced me still as one of their own, and I started to feel a peace that I could live with what I was. Be accepted by those around me.

Marcus bowed as I rolled my eyes. "I told you, Marcus. You don't have to call me that. I am not queen yet—" I paused, pushing to my feet when I noticed his nervous expression. "What is it?"

"Th-there is a *dragon* approaching the city, Your Majesty. A black dragon."

There couldn't be. He couldn't be here. Foreboding tightened my stomach; breathless panic came over me.

"Shall I fetch the captain, Your Majesty? He is training recruits in the arena."

I took a deep, focused breath before shaking my head.

"No need, Marcus. I shall deal with this myself."

He followed as I hurried to the palace courtyard, passing people staring out the windows at what was no doubt a colossal dragon flying towards us.

"Theon," I called to one of the guards by the main palace doors. "With me." The guard immediately stepped up beside Marcus to follow.

Outside, a bitter taste filled my mouth as my teeth clamped down on the inside of my cheek. I watched as Dracho landed—so gently, for a beast so large—his silver eyes finding me immediately. Marcus and Theon stepped beside me despite their obvious nerves.

I didn't even look away as Dracho transformed. I stormed down the steps, watching him dress himself with a simple click as I remained a respectable distance away.

"What are you doing here?" I asked, wrapping my arms around myself.

He didn't answer me as he rushed up the stairs barefoot to stand directly in front of me, where he took my arms firmly in his hands. Steel rang in my ears as my guards unsheathed their swords, but I raised a hand.

"Why *Eli*?" Dracho asked with a shaky breath. His eyes were glassy and red-rimmed.

"Excuse me?" I asked, incredulous.

He shook his head, breathing hard. "Why did you choose the name Eli?"

Shock rendered me silent for a moment. "It's short for my name," I said vaguely.

"Then why not Ellie? Or Ana? Why *specifically* did you choose Eli?" he urged.

"What's this about, Dra—"

"Please, Eliana. If you've *ever* trusted me, please. It's important."

This was clearly extremely important to him, though I had no idea why. "Fine. I saw the name once on some letters my father had. They seemed to be good friends, and when I had to change my name, for some reason it popped into my head. Why?"

His head dropped between his arms, a rough, emotional laugh leaving him.

"Did your mother ever call your father by a different name? A nickname perhaps?"

My mouth popped open. There was no way he could know that. I had never told a soul. "I don't understand—"

"Please, Eliana!"

"She called him Ryon." It burst from me in response to his desperation. "A play on his name, as if it were some private joke. She called him Ryon."

He inhaled sharply, face pinching as if in pain, tears springing in his eyes.

My hands lifted, trembling as they hovered over his. "Dracho, you're scaring me. What is it?"

"Eli... *Eli* is what my mother used to call my father."

My brow furrowed in confusion, wondering for a moment what that had to do with my name. But then it hit me as I thought back to those letters. I sucked in a sharp breath, my eyes flicking back and forth, before pulling out of his arms.

"Come!" I called as I sprinted towards the palace, through the double doors. I could hear Dracho's steps behind me as he kept up easily, following me through the palace halls and up the staircase, past the bewildered staff, until we reached my father's study.

I stormed to his desk, wrenching open the long drawer, my hand pausing for a moment before pulling out a stack of letters. Carefully, I placed them on the desk as Dracho walked forward, placing down some of his own from the sack he carried.

Before I could read them, Connaught burst through the door in his training gear, panting and his sword unsheathed.

"Some..." He watched Dracho cautiously. "Some of the staff said they saw you running."

"We are fine, thank you, Connaught. Please, wait outside."

"But—"

"Connaught. I promise you I am fine. Please. This is important."

His eyes skipped between us until he nodded, his mouth set in a thin line. Sheathing his weapon, he bowed, before leaving the room and closing the door behind him.

I blew out a breath, my gaze returning to a letter in Dracho's hand. I took it, my own hand shaking, and placed it between two addressed to my father.

My old friend,

I trust this letter finds you well. I know I've been putting this gathering off, but I am afraid I shall have to postpone it until further notice. There is still no sign at the moment; I have even resorted to placing a bounty, just so I know she is safe.

I am so sorry, Eli, I know we were both eager for them to meet. To discuss plans for all our futures. I hope we'll be able to rearrange soon.

Yours faithfully,

Ryon

Ryon,

I am sorry to hear of your troubles, my friend. I do hope you are able to resolve the matter soon. I can't imagine what you are going through. If you need any assistance, please don't hesitate to let me know. I, too, was looking forward to introductions. Based on D's temperament and your description of E, I think there definitely would have been much amusement to be had by them meeting. I hope I am there to see what they can accomplish together.

Let me know if you ever need me, Ryon.

My advisor sends his regards, as always.

Eli

My dear Eli,

I write you today with the best news. She has come home. My oldest friend, I cannot put down in words the elation I feel. I only wish you were here to share it with me. Hopefully, now, our plans can go ahead—and perhaps sooner than hoped, because... I met your son today.

I must admit, it was a bit of a shock to see his mother's eyes staring back at me. The poor boy looked so frightened, I had to stop myself from laughing at his expression. From our meeting, I gathered you have not told him anything of our friendship, and so I kept this ruse up. For now, I am happy in the knowledge that I have finally got to see D again. He obviously doesn't remember me from when he was a small boy, and doesn't seem to remember E either.

He is a credit to you, Eli. So smart, articulate... and I think my E has grown fond of him.

I have hope for where this is heading, and I hope I get to see you soon, old friend.

Your friend for always,

Ryon

My dearest Ryon,

My heart swells with happiness at this fantastic news. I think our plans shall most certainly move ahead at haste. I laughed at your last letter; I wondered how long it would take him to break the 'rules' I gave him to avoid mortals. But I'm glad he found his way to E, and you, even if he has no idea who you really are.

Thank you for not informing him of our friendship. I think I shall have some explaining to do once he returns home. As soon as he does, we shall make

arrangements, my dear friend.
For always,
Eli

Dracho handed me one more letter, this one addressed to himself. For a moment I wanted to refuse to read something which would obviously be personal. Instead my shaky hands unfolded the paper, eyes quickly scanning the words written in a handwriting that now looked familiar.

My lips parted in shock, my chest tightening as I struggled to take in a breath. A single tear fell from my eyes, trailing down my cheek.

"He knew he was going to die?" I finally whispered. Dracho nodded with a heavy expression. "They knew each other?"

They were planning for us to meet. Excited about it.

"They were best friends." Dracho swallowed.

"How do you know this?"

"Boone told me."

"*We*... knew each other?"

His icy blue eyes looked sad. "We must have been very young. I would definitely remember you." He whispered the last part.

"We were going to meet either way. It didn't matter when you arrived," I told him. "We were *always* going to meet."

Dracho gave me a soft smile; guilt kicked me in the stomach.

"Until I ran away," I finished.

Dracho shook his head, coming around and reaching out for me. "It's not your fault."

I jerked away. "Isn't it? I ran away. My father didn't get to see his best friend again before he... before he..."

"Before he died."

I collapsed into the chair, burying my head in my hands. I was trembling. I had taken away something my father had longed for. His opportunity to see his friend; to possibly unite two kingdoms.

Dracho knelt before me, his hands soft upon mine, pulling them away from my face. "Don't, Eliana. Don't do this to yourself. You carry so much already."

"But it's all my fault! If I hadn't run away, we would have met years ago. None of this would have happened, and our kingdoms could have worked together sooner. Our fathers, after all they'd lost, could have been there for each other!"

I slipped off the chair onto my knees as Dracho wrapped his arms around me. Like a torrent of water smashing through a dam, my tears flowed freely. I sobbed into his chest, my fingers clasping his back in desperation. Desperate to rid myself of this guilt I knew I would always feel. *More* guilt to bear.

I felt broken, worse than anything else that had happened to me—because I'd done it to my father. I'd taken it away from him. And I couldn't stop the tears that fell.

At some point I ended up sitting in Dracho's lap, his legs outstretched before him as he silently allowed me to grieve. Allowed my tears to soak his chest. His hands brushed up and down my back, comforting me, as I unleashed it all.

We stayed in that position for a while after my tears had ended, and I absorbed all the warmth I could radiating from him. With a final sniff I pulled away, Dracho's arms loosening. I stood, swiping the errant tears on my face away as I turned to stare out the window.

"Is it too late?" Dracho whispered. "For both our kingdoms to work together? For *us* to work together. For the dream that we had?"

That conversation besides the waters of Gwdhŵ rapids felt like an age ago. The memory was almost bittersweet now. Could we go back? Could I ease the guilt I felt after all I'd said in Tenebris? After all I held on to within?

"I'm not sure," I said honestly. "What *we* want doesn't matter anymore. I have to do whatever I can to make my kingdom happy."

He lowered his eyes. "Happiness hasn't got to be something found in big gestures, Eliana. It isn't this huge, elaborate thing. It's not a kingdom's power or glory. You can find it in the smallest things. A smile from a friend, dancing freely, the sound of the rain... you've forgotten that, haven't you?"

Unrelenting sorrow filled his face. I nodded. "Yes, I think I have."

I could feel his burning gaze all over my skin.

"Dracho—"

I felt a slight breeze kiss the skin at my back as he was suddenly behind me, his warm breath tickling the back of my neck. My shoulders tightened as his fingers ran up my arm, leaving a trail of goosebumps in their wake.

I sighed deeply. "We shouldn't—"

"Don't... don't give me a thousand reasons why we shouldn't." His voice sounded desperate. "Just give me one reason why we should."

I didn't acknowledge out loud that actually, I didn't have those thousand reasons. But what he really wanted I couldn't give him. I couldn't risk it. I turned, inhaling his hypnotising scent as I looked into his eyes, his intense gaze threatening to unravel all of me.

"And what's the reason why we should?" My voice was barely a whisper.

His head tipped down, his lips ghosting inches above mine, every nerve ending in my body tingling in hopeful anticipation.

"Because you want to." His breath tangled with mine.

I placed a hand over his mouth. "We wouldn't work, Dracho," I whispered.

"Why?" he asked desperately, pulling my hand down, his ice-blue eyes shining.

"Because we have our own kingdoms to rule." My voice rose. "Because of the treaty. Because of Cirdan. It would take time. Time we'll never get because of our duties. I..." I trailed off. *I can't offer you anything.*

"Well, then, maybe we could *try*," he suggested.

"Try?" I asked. His expression was hopeful, even though I'd just prevented his lips from claiming mine.

"Try. We could try being *friends*," he offered. "Start from there, and see where we go."

"I don't think I could be your friend, Dracho," I laughed.

Could I?

But perhaps, if I couldn't have him in the way I truly wanted, at least I could have him in my life in another way, and not just as my ally. Friendship was a step back from where we had been... but to keep him in my life, it was worth it.

"I think we could try."

He looked stunned.

"For our kingdoms, *anything* is worth a try."

Several emotions flashed across his face, and I knew there was more he wanted to say. "What is it?" I dared to ask.

His hand drifted down my arm until his fingers intertwined with mine. "I want to be your friend, Eliana... I really do. But more than that, I want to *know* you. When I found out I'd made your nightmares worse... I didn't think I'd be able to live with myself." I shifted, facing him fully. "You've been through too much, and I contributed to that—"

"Dracho, I—"

"I'm sorry, Eliana. I know I've already told you, but truly I am. For any pain or hurt I have ever caused you. It was not my intention, nor will it ever be. I just want to see you happy. If I ever get the blessing to be a part of that... I'll consider my purpose fulfilled."

It was difficult to allow myself to feel anything other than the guilt and shame that riddled my gut over the revelation of our fathers' friendship. But there was a flicker of hope that perhaps we could move forward together, and the smouldering ember within sparked.

His apology was contrite and delivered with such honesty. He was sharing his shame with me. I couldn't utter the words to forgive him, but perhaps I could share some of my own shame.

"Sometimes..." I exhaled. "As you know... I'm taken back to that night when I was attacked. And... I feel like those *men* are tethered to me. Like they'll always be a part of who I am. No matter how strong I become, or how much I think I'm over it... it'll always be there."

His arms fell, hanging limply at his side as his eyes lowered. As he realised this was one of the reasons I found it so hard to forgive what he had done.

I licked my lips. "You never get over a trauma like that. You just adapt to life with it. You recover from it. But it's still hard, you know? Especially with everything that happened with Cirdan and Jandar. And..." I trailed off, chewing my cheek as I looked to my feet.

And with you.

I knew that in comparison to everything else, his actions the day his father had died were trivial. But it had been incredibly hard for me to get past it. To fix the broken looks he gave me and to stop him from hurting by just forgiving him. They said what didn't kill you made you stronger. Maybe I was tired of being stronger.

He suddenly stood before me, tipping my chin up with his hand. "Eliana," he said, and I craved more of his soft tone. "Those monsters... they are *not* tethered to you in any way at all. What happened doesn't define you. You didn't deserve it. *Any* of it. And I wish I could take away that pain. I wish I had been there to protect you."

I wanted to reach out, remove his own pain. Bringing my hand up, I clasped his wrist. "You didn't know me back then. You were just a boy."

His words were soft, his eyes capturing mine. "And you were just a girl." A muscle in his jaw flexed. "I hate the men that did that to you. I hate every man that has ever hurt you."

I wondered if he included himself in that, and looking into his eyes, I knew he did.

A flash of silver showed in his gaze. "There is *hate* in my heart for them. And I hate that they are not around for me to personally torture and slowly bring to their knees."

My breath hitched, and I couldn't tear my face from his.

His tongue darted out to moisten his lips. "But what I hate more is that they didn't look at you and see someone beautiful. The daughter of a king, a queen, and someone worth protecting. But do you know what I love?" A small smile appeared on his lips. "I love that you did not let hate grow in *your* heart over what happened. You did not let it turn you into a hateful person. Especially since..." The unspoken words hung in the air between us.

My mother and brother died the next day.

"There's something I've always wanted to ask you."

I nodded.

"What happened the night Engel found you?"

My fight-or-flight response hammered at my senses, scraping along my nerves like rose thorns. I had never shared that night with anyone but Connaught. Never shared my greatest shame. My weakness. My heart skipped a beat as panic seized me.

"You don't have to tell—"

"It wasn't long after I had been attacked," I blurted out, and his icy gaze shot to me. "My father hadn't long returned from finalising the treaty. He was... distant. Because of everything that happened, I don't think he knew how to deal with what had happened to me whilst he was gone. I think he blamed himself. I..." I paused, looking once at my father's sword upon the wall. "I couldn't live with the loneliness."

Dracho's mouth fell open in shock.

"One night, I sneaked out of my room and headed to the bay. I didn't think twice as I walked off the dock. I just wanted the pain and loneliness to end. It was only when the water started to fill my lungs that I realised I wanted to live."

A kind of horrified awareness I'd never seen settled upon his expression. "Engel saved you."

I nodded. "I don't know how he knew or how he found me. But he did. He carried me to shore, where Connaught was searching for me. He'd seen me leave the grounds and followed."

"Did your father know?"

"No. Connaught kept my secret, but he hardly let me out of his sight from then on. Until he was sure I wasn't going to do it again."

There was silence, so acute it was jarring, as I allowed Dracho to process everything. His expression was unreadable as he stared at me. My gaze dropped to the floor, my cheeks heating.

His finger brushed against the skin of my jawline, and he tipped my chin up. "You're the bravest person I've ever met," he said, his eyes alive with light.

"No I'm not," I whispered. "I was a coward."

He shook his head. "No. You were courageous. You had to go through that to realise you wanted life—you wanted to be here. That takes bravery. You were a twelve-year-old girl! I can't even imagine the thoughts running through your head back then, the pain you went through. But after Engel saved you, you decided to fight. You've been fighting ever since. Despite the nightmares, despite all your trials. You continue to fight every day. I always thought you were fearless. Now I know better." My skin tingled as he tucked a strand of hair behind my ear. "You feel fear, and you face it head on, with courage. Fear hasn't beaten you, Eliana. It never will."

It was difficult to swallow the lump of emotion in my throat. I couldn't get rid of it to form the words I wanted to say. To thank him for seeing me beyond what I saw in myself.

But my chest also swelled at the truth I felt inside. That fear *had* beaten me. That every day was a struggle as I recovered from what had happened in Fallstone. As I still denied what was clearly between us, hoping it would benefit his city and his rule. Hoping it would stem the conflict it caused in his court. His father's letters gave me hope that we could, together, ease that tension.

Fear prevented me from really choosing what I wanted. From diving in head-first. But I couldn't admit that. Instead, I was a coward once more.

"Where do we go from here?" I asked tentatively.

He smiled. "I'm going back to Tenebris, but I'll be back. With Roux. I left in such a hurry I'm not sure if any of them have even realised I am missing." Red bloomed on his face as he ran a hand through his hair.

"My coronation is in two days," I told him.

He nodded. "I have some things I need to sort out back home, but I promise we'll try and make it. Fine-tune and celebrate our new partnership." He squeezed my hand comfortingly, and I couldn't help but smile in return as I resisted the urge to embrace him. I didn't think he'd mind, but I wanted to do it right this time. No rush—even if my body and soul called out to take him in my arms.

"Then let's eat before you go." I looked up at him.

A faint smile appeared on his face. My chest swelled with hope and another emotion I couldn't decipher. After everything that had happened, it felt unusual to hope, but I welcomed it gladly.

Chapter 61

Dracho left after a late dinner with a promise to return, hopefully before my coronation began. I knew he had a lot to deal with back in Tenebris, but I prayed he would be able to make it. Nervous energy was all I knew as my coronation approached. Connaught, with Sizwe and Vyn's assistance, made all the arrangements.

He was distant the day after Dracho left, quiet for most of the day until lunch, when I finally braved confronting him about it.

"I merely have my concerns, Eliana."

"And I would rather you discuss those with me than burden me with your silence."

His jaw clenched. "I just... I don't want to see you hurt again."

I rubbed my temple, from the countless papers I had been reading through since that morning. "I understand, Connaught. However, Dracho is my friend. We have agreed to work together for the benefit of both our kingdoms. I would appreciate it if you can support me in this while we navigate the details."

"I'm sure that's not all he wishes to navigate," he said under his breath.

I stood suddenly, my chair scraping along the floor as I pushed it back. Connaught took in my furious expression with chagrin, his cheeks and the tops of his ears turning the same colour as his hair.

"I. Will. *Not* have such insolent words. Not from you."

"I'm sorry, Eliana—"

I held up a hand. "I appreciate your concern. I am grateful, more than you could ever know, for all you have done for me. You are my *friend*." A muscle twitched in his temple as he looked away, his brows lowered. "But don't fight me on this. I can't deal with the conflict. Not now."

"Because you'd choose him?" he blurted out.

This was the closest we had ever come to addressing what he had always felt for me. I would not venture down this road with him. I couldn't.

"With him around... there'll never be another choice."

A sharp jolt lanced through my chest at the pained expression on his face. As he saw behind the veil of my words to the true feelings that lay underneath.

The silence chipped away at me as he stared at the wall, and panic blossomed in my chest that I might lose him. A selfish thought.

"Connaught, I am so—"

"No." He sniffed, shaking his head before stepping closer to me. "You are my queen. I shouldn't have spoken with such boldness." He reached forward, taking my hand to rub it soothingly with his thumb. "You will always be my queen, Eliana. You will always have me."

"Thank you," I whispered, grateful for how selfless he was being. Besides Vyn and Bas, Connaught was one of my oldest companions. The thought of losing his friendship caused me heartache. I appreciated the sacrifice he was making by respecting my feelings.

"I think..." I exhaled roughly. "I think I'm going to visit Mammy before the big day."

He nodded in understanding. "She'd be so proud of you, Eliana. They all would."

"Would they?" I asked without thinking, that feeling of weakness causing my shoulders to sag.

His hands found my shoulders. "I don't know exactly what they'd say. But I know they wouldn't want you to live like you're made of glass. I think they'd want you to live as if you didn't have forever. To love unashamedly. Fight ferociously, especially for those you love. They'd want you to be free, Eliana."

I blinked back tears.

"You don't need a crown to be a queen. You wear your courage instead. *That* makes you a queen. And I couldn't be prouder to be a part of your life, in whatever capacity you'll have me."

I sniffed loudly, then gave a wobbly laugh, and he winced as I punched his arm.

"Prick." I felt as though all I did was cry lately.

He beamed, rubbing his arm. "Glad I could help."

They weren't here.

It was all I could think of the morning of my coronation. Dracho and Roux weren't here. Aunt Lys hadn't responded since my last letter, so I had no idea if she was attending. King Jareth had accepted my invitation for a visit, but advised he wouldn't be able to make it for at least a month. I wondered what business the king had to delay it that long, but news of my lineage would no doubt reach him soon, if it already hadn't.

Vyn and Bas had done all they could to calm my nerves as the palace began to fill with visitors.

My hands smoothed down the skirts of my dress, and I felt calmer. I had rummaged through my mother's old things in storage the day before, finding her own coronation dress. I had cried for a good half-an-hour after finding it, my fingers gripping the fabric tightly, and I'd decided to wear it as my own.

The green was so dark it was almost black. The skirts were a fine silk, with layers of lace laid over the top. The sleeves were long, ending in a small loop slipped over my centre finger. The sweetheart neckline was slightly tight on my bust, but not indecently so.

Beneath the skirt, my dagger from Morgwn was strapped to my thigh, and when I accepted the crown, I would hold my father's sword—Antur. It would become mine. It felt like I had my family with me.

And finally, proudly, my hair was fashioned into a braided bun at the back of my head, a few tendrils loose around my face: my ears on show for all to see. I would be sworn in as who I was. A queen of both mortal and elven blood.

Horns sounded out for my entrance to the throne room, but I hesitated. I needed a moment.

My brain seemed to flash through all the memories of what had come before this, what had led to this, and I smiled. This had always been Morgwn's destiny, to become king—but I felt ready. I felt ready to make them proud.

Two guards opened the double doors, and my eyes did not waver as I walked down the red carpet. The sides of the throne room were filled with people. From the corner of my eye, I could see them all smiling and nodding.

The master of the city's temples stood beside the throne, a robe of pure white covering him from neck to toe. He beamed as I approached, indicating that I took my seat on the throne. Connaught stood on the other side in full regalia, trying to look serious, suppressing a grin.

My skirt swirled as I turned and face the room, inhaling deeply before sitting upon the cold throne. I focused on my breathing, spotting Vyn and Bas to the left. Bas winked, holding two thumbs up; Vyn rolled his eyes. I choked down my laugh, a twinge of sadness hitting me as I thought of Dracho missing this, then jumped in surprise as the master's voice rang out, clear as a bell.

"Welcome all, on this auspicious day! The Goddess herself smiles down upon our heir as she embarks on this new journey. To the people: today, I present unto you Eliana Cervidae, first of her name, your undoubted queen. Here is your wisdom, your royal law, your defender in all things. Will you accept her?"

A booming acceptance shook the throne room. Connaught raised my father's sword, bowing to me before placing it upon my open palms. The master came to stand before me, blocking out the room behind him as he held a magnificent silver crown of antlers above my head.

"Eliana Cervidae, will you promise to defend Meridium for all your days? Use law, justice and mercy in all your judgements? And do your utmost to bring prosperity and peace to the kingdom? All this do you promise to do?"

"This I promise," I called out, surprised at the lack of nerves in my voice.

"Goddess bless thee, Eliana Cervidae, and today anoint you with a crown of glory and righteousness. May you lead your people in the way wherein they should go. I now crown you Queen."

The cold metal of the crown pressed upon my head, and a moment of silence fell before the master took a step back. I stood.

There was applause. Rapturous, happy applause. People threw flower petals, the bells of Meridium sounding throughout the city.

But another sound rumbled through the room. A steady thunder that seemed to roll closer to the city—only the roar of each wave was too close together to be natural.

"What is that?" Connaught demanded as he came to my side. The crowd's applause spluttered; muttered chatter broke out.

Connaught rushed out of the double doors, no doubt heading to the upper balcony which overlooked the grounds and city beyond. I placed my sword against the throne and followed. Stepping out onto the balcony over the main courtyard, I saw nothing amiss within the city walls. But the people had felt the shift, and I could feel the tremor from what felt like an impending stampede as they rushed into their respective homes. The royal army lined the courtyard below me, looking around in confusion.

"Your Majesty!" Connaught wrenched my attention to the east.

A wide, black smudge sat on the horizon, coming closer and closer to the city walls. There must have been thousands of them. No banners or colours were visible from this far, but I knew.

"It's Cirdan."

"What?" Connaught's head twisted in my direction. "How were we not warned?"

My gut clenched. "Something must have happened to Lys."

One of the men came running onto the balcony. "Captain!"

"What is it, Tomas?"

"It's an elven army, sir. From the east. There are too many!"

Thousands approaching the city. With no warning and no time to contact our allies, nor to recall our hundreds of patrolling soldiers back.

We were on our own.

Pain shone in Connaught's face as his eyes found mine.

"Ring the bells," I told Tomas, who sprinted off. "You need to go—warn the soldiers. Prepare," I added to Connaught.

As he stepped forward into my space, I felt his heat across my skin like a warm embrace. "I *need* to be by your side. Protect you."

I cupped his cheek, the lace of my sleeves rubbing roughly against the fine stubble there. "They all know what I am now. Let them come, if they have the courage. You must go."

He scoffed. "Is that an order from my queen? Or a request from my friend?"

"Yes." I tried to hold back my grin.

Connaught growled, before bending and sweeping his lips across my cheek in a soft kiss, hesitating only slightly as he pulled away. My breath hitched in shock.

"Be safe, Eliana. Don't take any stupid risks."

That was why I loved him unconditionally. Not as anything more than my friend, but because through it all, he had remained loyally by my side and would not prevent me from fighting, despite how much he wished to. He knew with certainty that I would not shy from the fight—do what many other rulers would and stay safe behind the walls of my city.

His rough gloves were scratchy against the skin of my arms. "You don't have to hide anymore," he said. "Use all the gifts that your mother gave you. If... if the situation turns bad, you get out. Take Engel and run; run as if the world's on fire. Flee to Tenebris and Dracho, or Aion. But you leave. Do you understand?"

"Connaught—"

"*Promise me,* Eliana."

I surveyed him from underneath lowered brows before nodding once, hoping I wouldn't have to break it.

"I'll await your signal below. Later, find me at the front lines." His cape swished behind him as he turned.

"Connaught," I called, and he stopped without turning. "Cirdan had wolves. Warn the soldiers."

He huffed without humour. "I'm still not sure they believe me, but I'll remind them."

He left and I turned, startled to find Vyn standing by the balcony doors beside my other guards. He stepped forward, holding a sword in his hands. "I thought you would need this."

I reached out to take my father's sword in my hands once again. Antur, the sword of Meridium. A smirk made its way onto my face. "Really shouldn't have just left this lying around," I joked.

Vyn's teeth flashed in a smile, though his yellow eyes were sad. He shrugged. "I thought I'd grab it for you... knew that we were in a bit of a rush."

I laughed before blowing out a long breath, returning to the edge of the balcony. Running my free hand along the cold white stone, I looked out over the royal soldiers amassing below, suppressing the feeling of dread that tried to overwhelm me. Our full army may not be in the city, but one soldier of Meridium was worth three of any other. The elves that had come with Cirdan would have to rely on their abilities of enhanced strength and speed to overcome our people. It would be no easy battle for them. We might lose... but we would fight.

Cirdan had brought his army to the gates of Meridium as a declaration of war. My heart was saddened; the people had seen enough of war. But I would defend them, and so would my army.

Citizens who had congregated at the palace were being evacuated from the grounds and told to return to their homes and protect themselves.

Connaught and one of the commanders of the army oversaw the gathering of soldiers in the courtyard, and I waited until he caught my eye and gave him a nod. He commanded them to attention.

My nerves thrashed as I addressed them.

"Today... today is a difficult day for Meridium. For us all. Cirdan Morven would see you all banished from this land in favour of the elves. But his path we shall never choose, and that is the path of surrender. Cirdan may seem invincible now, but the past has shown us that, despite the bloodshed and tyranny, those with evil intentions will always fall!"

Encouraged by several shouts of agreement, I continued. "Join me in the fight to unite our peoples. For whilst the blood of mortals and elves runs through my very veins, I promise I will always fight for you! For Meridium! And for all who wish for peace throughout Ruvalon!"

More called out.

"You are my brothers, you are my sisters—"

A deep battle cry sounded out from all the soldiers in unison.

"I am proud to have trained with you. Together we raise our swords against tyranny. For Meridium, and for all!"

I thrust my arm up, holding Antur above my head. The battle cries that erupted as the soldiers followed suit drowned out the sound of the approaching army. Together, they turned and started marching towards the gates. Towards battle.

The breeze coldly kissed my cheeks as I watched, collecting myself. When I turned, skirts flaring around my ankles, I realised that Bas had come to join Vyn, dressed from head to toe in plated armour, his battle axe held at his side.

"I think you'd better get changed," he chuckled.

Looking down, I laughed in return.

"Better had." My gaze passed between my two best friends. "Don't go running into the fight without me."

"Never." Vyn's voice broke. Both tipped their heads forward in a bow, placing their hands on their chest.

A choked laugh broke free as my throat constricted.

"You guys are pricks," I told them, pushing past in a run, ready to join the fight. "Get the people out of here!"

In my chambers, Milly and her mother, Beatrice, helped me put on my armour. Armour I had never worn before, because it had belonged to my mother.

The breastplate was made from several layers of rounded metal sheets which perfectly sat under the shoulder plates, a small gap between them allowing me more freedom to move my arms. It covered almost everything from the neck down, ending at my hips. My forearms were protected by vambraces, and my thighs were covered by pointed, half-covering cuisses. My shins bore greaves with metal leaves adorning the outer sides. The best part was a finely engraved stag on the overlapping sheets of my breastplate.

The armour was heavier than the leathers I was used to, though bearable. It would slow me down slightly; I stretched, adapting to the reduced movement. If I needed to, the leather straps made it easy to shed.

A choking sensation filled my throat as I looked into the mirror, my hair braided and resting over one shoulder, my ears visible. I had started the day in my mother's dress, and I would end it in her armour.

Beatrice sniffed, and I turned to take her hand. Milly stood beside her, her hands wringing a handkerchief.

"You look just like her." Beatrice's voice broke. "The last time I saw her, she was wearing the matching set to this armour. I pray to the Goddess it is not the last time I see *you* in it too, Your Majesty."

I blinked back tears, placing my free hand upon Milly's, staying their movement. "I cannot thank you enough for everything you have done for my family. For keeping my secret." Beatrice shook her head. "If things go bad, take the south gate and flee to Aion. They will protect you there."

Beatrice nodded, clasping her hand desperately on top of mine. "Come with us, Your Majesty! Run and survive another day."

I shook my head, giving her a small smile. "I cannot stand back and allow Cirdan's evil to prevail. If I must fight him with my dying breath, I will."

A sob broke from Milly's mouth, and my hand tightened on hers.

A tear tracked down Beatrice's cheek. "She would be so proud of you, Eliana. They all would."

Pulling them into a tight hug, I looked to the ceiling in a futile attempt to stop the tears from falling. Then I released the women, turning away. "I must go."

The sound of the armour broke the silence as I reached for my father's—*my*—sword from my bed, catching sight of my dagger beside it. I had planned to leave it, but I suddenly felt incomplete without it. On a whim, I picked it up and strapped it to my thigh. It wouldn't do much against better weapons in the thick of battle, but I felt whole having it with me.

Now all that was left was the set of throwing knives Dracho had gifted me on my birthday. His absence worried me for a moment. This battle would likely go much smoother if he was here with me—even if I would have the added worry of him coming to harm, I still would have felt better with him by my side. I only hoped I would survive to see him again.

With one last glance in Beatrice and Milly's direction, I nodded, too overwhelmed to speak again. I walked out, hoping they would be saved.

That we all would.

Chapter 62

Even with the bells of Meridium ringing behind me, the silence surrounding thousands of soldiers on the battlefield was eerie. Both armies were poised, waiting.

To protect the city, and the people within, Connaught and I had decided to face Cirdan's army head-on. It would give a small number of our soldiers time to prepare the citizens for evacuation, should the battle go in Cirdan's favour. The people could escape through the southern or western gates, and hopefully we could save as many as possible.

It would take Cirdan's army hours to get through the rises, potentially longer as they tried to bring down the walls, but the people were my priority. Meridium was the people, not the walls we had built.

I knew that the first step would not be made by us. I had never seen so many people in one place—so many people willing to die. The sight made me feel slightly claustrophobic.

I had found Connaught at the front line, with Engel at his side. His eyes scanned over the sigil of my city sitting proudly over my chest as I mounted my steed. My legs tightened stiffly around Engel, the beast a picture of calm, even as hot breath steamed from his nostrils and his ears twitched at every sound.

"Suits you," Connaught said, his tone low.

I laughed, feeling strange. "Trust you."

His smile fell, jaw clenching as if there were a hundred things he wanted to say, but no time to say them. "Are you frightened?" he said instead.

Looking out over Cirdan's army, I smiled.

"No," I told him, feeling that wicked stretch of darkness coil in my soul as my fangs lengthened. "The most terrifying thing here is *me*."

Connaught's teeth flashed in a wide smile, and it was blinding. "You have my life, till the very end." He bowed his head, hand flattening over his chest.

"And you mine," I said quietly.

Bas and Vyn stood at Engel's side. They shared a glance before giving me a nod in solidarity.

"To the end of all things," Vyn promised, echoing Connaught's gesture.

"Always," Bas said, and smiled tightly.

Swallowing my emotion, I looked out over the battlefield, scanning our enemy. A sheet of black hair drifting on the wind caught my eye. Cirdan sat atop his horse at the back of his army, on a grassy knoll. Beside him was Vyn's father, Adven. I didn't need to be close to tell he was smirking. Gloating over their triumph at sneaking up on Meridium. I bared my teeth as a horn sounded out in the distance.

And so it began.

Catapults creaked as Cirdan's army launched projectiles at our ranks, soldiers going down with them. Despair and rage went through me as our soldiers fell, but I needed Cirdan's army closer for our quickly-made plan to have a chance. Small numbers of archers at our flanks volleyed at those controlling the catapults as the first lines of Cirdan's army started to march forward.

Scanning the trees to our left, on the edge of the battlefield, my eyes travelled until they met white. The white-painted bark of an old oak—a marker of our archers' range. Gaze back on the approaching army, I nodded at Connaught.

His longsword reached into the air. "Archers!"

A straight line of yellow flags was held up behind me, one by one, until they could be seen by our longbow soldiers. The sound of bow strings being drawn tight reached my sensitive ears; I stared, waiting for Cirdan's men to pass that line.

"Steady," I called.

Closer.

"Steady!" I repeated.

The first lines passed the tree.

"FIRE!" I screamed at the top of my lungs, my generals following my lead, a string of red flags shooting up. The first lines of our archers let loose, an arcing volley of arrows flying over our heads, whistling through the air until they rained down upon Cirdan's men.

Many stumbled. Some went down. Too many still marched.

The rear lines of our longbow soldiers drew their bows, releasing another volley. Gaps started to appear in Cirdan's lines, but not enough to slow their advance.

I took a shaky breath before unsheathing Antur and raising it into the air, my knuckles white beneath my gauntlets. The soldiers drew their weapons, awaiting my command.

Once several lines of Cirdan's forces made it past the white oak, I tipped the sword forward, nudging Engel forward.

I rode between Vyn and Bas, on foot, and Connaught on horseback, the sound of steel from the marching men and women ringing out behind me. I could barely hear it all. My stomach roiled—even if we didn't lose, it was likely that not all of us would make it through this.

Our pace quickened, the lines of both armies breaking into a light run; Engel was cantering, his dark blonde mane turning a luminous white as it rose as if caught on a gentle breeze.

"Engel," I called, panting. "Once we breach the lines, I want you to run. Back to the water. To your kingdom."

He shook his head and whinnied loudly in response, as if refusing to leave my side for even a moment.

"Do as I say!" I snapped, as if I could ever command the lord of all horses. "I can't lose you too."

I heard his breathless huff in response. I could only pray to the Goddess he would do as I asked; I wouldn't make it if he didn't—not after everything he had done for me.

I inhaled harshly through my nose, swinging my sword as the armies came together. The sound of armour clashing was deafening. I cleaved through Cirdan's soldiers, the sword heavy in my grip but uncompromising. It sliced easily through flesh and bone as berry-red blood spurted from their wounds. Men wailed; the ground became sodden with gore.

An hour passed. Soldiers slipped in the sludge. The groans of the wounded surrounded me. I could only be grateful that there seemed to be no wolves in the fight.

Connaught's steed had been brought down, and he now fought on foot, his cape gone. His longsword slashed across the abdomen of an approaching soldier, his innards escaping the hole Connaught had made.

The battle was becoming difficult to navigate on horseback. Slipping off Engel, I smacked his hind leg. He turned, his eyes staying on me as he reared.

"Please, Engel!" I spun to shove my sword through a man's chest before yanking it out, the blade stained red with his blood.

Engel only hesitated for a moment. My relief was instant as he galloped back towards the castle. Now I could turn my mind to the battle on foot.

It was carnage.

It was the Notherworld brought to life—chaos, bloodlust; it made it difficult to remind myself that we fought for the light. To quell the rage of that darker part of me inside that wanted to see them all suffer.

My friends fought hard around me. Vyn's hands were furious as he used his powers to suffocate those around him, sweat dripping from his brow. Bas stood close by, swinging his great battle axe, cleaving a man's head free from his shoulders. I clung to the strength of my friends. That kind of inner strength, that light, reminded me of who I fought for. What I fought for.

Time didn't exist on the battlefield. Only the butchery. The sun, now almost disappearing behind the city walls, was the only indication of how many hours we had spent battling.

Despite my burning muscles and the sweat, my sword felled any enemy who came close enough—and many tried. As soon as Cirdan's soldiers noticed my elven ears, they realised my identity. There was no attempt at capture now, only a desire to take my life.

They all went down upon my blade.

"Eliana!" Connaught roared, pointing. I saw that Cirdan and Adven had left the grassy knoll and were making their way into the fray. That dark piece inside of me rejoiced. Wanted to taste Cirdan's blood upon my sword.

Connaught bellowed at the soldiers to advance, sweat trickling down his brow. The men cried out as our longbows fired volley after volley past the white oak, continuing their onslaught. For a moment, I wondered why Cirdan's archers hadn't fired anything.

Connaught sliced his way through all who dared come close, advancing further into Cirdan's lines. A flash of silver caught my eye, and horror gripped me as I caught the hesitation in Vyn's movements. He was face to face with his own father, Adven. Bas was nearby; I prayed to the Goddess that Vyn would beat him and moved on, scanning for that sheet of black hair. I followed the path Connaught had cut, calling his name as I caught a glimpse of black just before one of my own men ran across my view.

The soldier passed and Connaught's eyes caught mine, a silent gasp etched on his face.

For a moment, everything stopped. There was no sound, no chance I could look away. Connaught's gaze dropped to his chest, where a slim steel blade protruded. An elven blade that could cut through mortal steel and flesh.

Cirdan stood behind him, teeth flashing wide in a sadistic smile.

I heard nothing as my scream pierced the land around us. My elven strength blazed in my legs as I launched forward without thought, killing all who dared come between him and me.

Connaught's eyes returned to my face, pain etched on his own. Cirdan ripped his sword out and my friend fell to his knees, clutching his chest over his armour. He gave me a smile; I shook my head as I continued my path, swinging my sword. *Just hold on.* If I could just get to him—

His lids lowered slightly, and he mouthed three words he knew I could never return.

"NO!" I screamed.

His eyes closed, and his body fell forward into the dirt.

Chapter 63

It no longer mattered that there were hundreds around who wanted me dead. Who fought for that very thing. All I saw was Cirdan.

I sliced and clawed my way towards him as he cut down more of my soldiers. The scream of his name tore at my throat even though he was only several feet away, his gloating smile taunting me. A small circle of space formed between us, soldiers on both sides eyeing us with cautious anticipation, but fearful to step in. Both of us were poised, ready to kill the other.

I stabbed Antur through the air to point at him, feeling my fangs brush against my tongue as I snarled, fully embracing that long-hidden side of me. "I won't even offer you the decency of a pyre. The crows will feast on your rotting corpse before this day is done," I spat in a voice that didn't sound like my own. I vowed to him, the Goddess, and anyone who could hear me.

He laughed darkly. "Such strong words for a *half-breed*."

The west wind keened through the field as I screeched at him, dashing forward, my weapon raised with both hands. My arms shook as he blocked my blow, our swords sounding out. We each exchanged a couple of swipes, neither enough to cause a fatal wound. My heart pounded against my ribs as we fought, and a cut along my upper arm stung. We continued.

Cirdan shouted angrily as the tip of Antur sliced across his cheek, leaving a thin line of red. I huffed out a laugh as he seethed, coming for me again. He didn't tire.

But part of me was human. And *my* arms grew tired.

I will not stop.

His eyes widened in surprise as I went for him with a ferocity that burned through my very soul, that darkness trying to claw its way out of my throat with every scream—screams which were suddenly drowned out by a roar, causing my steps to falter.

Adrenaline shot through me. The sound was so full of rage and the promise of death that soldiers lowered their arms against each other to look. Cirdan's head snapped up, brow knitted.

It came from the north. *It came from Tenebris.*

And through the morose clouds, shadows formed in the shape of large wings.

A second roar sounded. Not *one* shadow, but two.

A relieved sob escaped as I observed the obsidian scales of the larger beast, his razor-sharp teeth gleaming, tendrils of smoke leaving his nostrils. Sat atop him was a familiar form, the remaining sunlight kissing her beautiful brown skin. But it was the high-pitched call of the second beast that made my blood run cold. Its hunter-green wings folded as it dived towards the battle.

I watched as Antares pulled out of the dive above Cirdan's rear lines, the latter turning to bear witness. The draconi's mouth widened, inhaling deeply before breathing a line of what looked like black fire, trapping screaming soldiers between the flames and Meridium. He swung his tail, destroying the ration wagons around him.

Terror gripped my stomach. It wasn't fire, but a line of thick, living shadows that enveloped its victims, leaving nothing but bones that fell to the ground.

Cirdan snarled as his men perished. Dracho landed behind my soldiers, allowing Roux and Cubra to climb down before taking off again, releasing brilliant, blinding white fire upon the enemy. Roux burst into the battle, using her magick to soar over my men and land in a circle of her own black and gold fire amongst the elves. Her flames whipped at Cirdan's men, whose skin bubbled and burst at the contact. She threw out her arm; a flaming vine circled a man's neck, burning through to the bone, separating his head from his body. Cubra's tail rose behind him like the head of a serpent, whipping forward and slicing through skin and muscle.

Bas cheered as he noticed the mage. I gasped in relief as I saw that Vyn still stood across from him, one of his short swords drawn, sparks flying as it clashed against Adven's sword. The two looked exhausted, sweat sheening on both their brows. Vyn lifted one of Cirdan's men up into the air with a gust of wind, throwing him in Adven's direction. Adven dived out of the way in time. Bas swung his axe, catching the unnamed soldier in the chest and slamming him into the ground already dead.

Vyn dived in, using his power to wrap an invisible rope of wind around his father's throat. On his knees, Adven grasped at nothing, unable to free himself. His eyes widened up at his son, an odd expression of approval passing over his face as he came to terms with his imminent death. Bas battled around Vyn, keeping any who would try to rescue Adven from reaching them. I saw Vyn's lips move, but before his father could reply, a flick of his blade drew a red line across his father's throat.

I sighed with relief and turned back to Cirdan's surprised gaze. The smell of burning flesh permeated the air; I laughed.

"The fight isn't over, Princess," he threatened.

"That's *queen* to you." I lunged forward, and he met my blade. Dracho's appearance had rallied my troops and the last remains of my stamina.

Cirdan laughed cruelly. "Then allow me to present your coronation gift, *Your Majesty*."

He thrust his sword into the air, and a horn sounded. I followed Cirdan's glance over his shoulder; a small number of his men stepped forward onto the grassy knoll he had stood upon earlier. They drew back the strings of enormous longbows of the blackest night, and my eyes narrowed in confusion. Arrows would not reach me or penetrate a dragon's scales. *What is this?*

As Dracho and Antares rained fire upon the soldiers below, the men released their arrows. They whistled as they flew, and I was sure I heard Dracho huff, as if in amusement.

Most of the arrows missed. One hit his front leg.

His horrifying scream of pain threatened to deafen me. As his wings seemed to fail, he dropped, the impact of his large body causing the ground to tremble and dirt to fly up into the air.

It's not possible. My feet took an unconscious step in his direction as an almost unbearable pain sliced through the centre of my chest.

The most terrifying sound I had ever heard burst from Antares. Goosebumps erupted over my entire body as he landed before Cirdan's men, who scrambled to arm themselves again. Most he engulfed in shadow, but he also tore at them with claws and teeth, his anger a raging volcano on the battlefield.

I couldn't speak. Something inside me seemed to have cracked.

Cirdan took advantage of it. With a solid strike, he knocked my sword to the ground. I cried out as his sword embedded itself into my right shoulder and his foot caught behind my ankle, tripping me; I landed on my back, the impact winding me.

"Did you really think it was *just* the might of Cirdan Morven who stood against you? Who used the Hollow?"

His dark laugh grated my nerves as his foot pressed down on my chest, putting his elven strength behind it, and I gasped for air. I tried to reach over to stem the agony in my shoulder, but my armour prevented me.

"You're a fool. Even if you did defeat me, more will follow. You've been so blind that you've failed to notice what's been right under your nose."

I gasped out as he removed his foot, his hand gripping the top of my chest plate to pull me off the ground. I let my hands fall limp to my sides.

"And even though your dragon lover has come to save your city, he's too late to save you. To think, you could have played along nicely. Joined us and saved your people. Not that these mortals are of any importance; I shall break them, just like I broke you." He raised his sword, placing the tip against the skin of my throat, and I closed my eyes as he pulled his arm back. "After all, death will come to *all* men."

No.

I didn't need Dracho to save me. I never had. I didn't need anyone.

I could only save myself. I didn't truly realise it until that moment. It had been a trial bitterly overcome, from the attack when I was younger to all the loss and pain of the recent past. It was suffering that only I could pull myself out of, but if anything had been worth winning in my life then it was certainly that.

I was *worth* saving. Even if I had to save myself.

I will not break.

My eyes shot open as Cirdan's widened. Blood dripped from the corner of his mouth; a choking sound came from his throat, and his sword fell to the ground.

My hand tightened around the oak handle of my dagger in his neck, taken from its sheath along my thigh, hidden by my armour. His hand released me, flying up to claw at his neck as the blade slipped free, and I fell back to the ground.

Cirdan slumped to his knees, blood pouring from the wound at his throat. I climbed to my feet, kicking him onto his back as I picked up my father's sword, limping over to stand above him.

"You do not look upon a *man*," I spat in his face. "And you did not break *me*!"

With a loud cry, I thrust Antur down through his chest, just as he had done to Connaught. I watched as he choked on his own blood. Watched as he fell back and the light left his frightened eyes until they stared up lifelessly at the early evening sky.

And so the line of Morven ended.

Chapter 64

My hands sank into the mud as I crawled over to Connaught, grasping his body with all my might and pulling him out of the dirt and onto my lap. As small pockets of fighting continued around me, though the tide had turned since the draconi's arrival, I smoothed his wine-red hair off his muddy face, memorising his features.

The sound of Antares landing on the field some way behind me reached my ears. Even as my heart pulled me in another direction, I took the time to lay Connaught down, placing his hands to rest upon his sword.

An erratic rhythm pounded in my chest as I stood, looking towards the small crater caused by Dracho's fall. Turning, I caught Bas's eye. Good, he was still alive. He nodded to me and continued to vent his rage through the soldiers that remained.

Unclipping the straps of my chest plate, I dropped it and removed my gauntlets and the armour on my legs. Then I *ran.*

There's a moment when your exhaustion is so overwhelming that you start to feel mad. That was how my body and mind felt as I sprinted across the battlefield, which now resembled a graveyard for the unburied. The battle had been won, but some of Cirdan's braver men still fought, despite being outnumbered and facing certain death. Many fled, morale lost with the death of their king and the onslaught of Roux and Antares. Those who came for me whilst I ran fell on the edge of my sword.

I slowed as I neared the edge and leaned over. Dracho was in his mortal form, no sign of wings or tail in sight. Roux and Antares were now with him.

I stumbled and slid down into the crater, crawling the last few feet towards them. I scanned Dracho quickly, seeing that the arrow had wounded his left forearm, though it must have fallen out when he'd transformed back. His free hand was squeezing his arm tightly just above the wound, the pain clearly radiating up through his body. He was mumbling incoherently, seemingly unaware of those around him.

Antares knelt by his side, so oblivious in his naked form as his trembling hands hovered over Dracho, eyes wild and questioning. Roux removed her cloak, placing it over Dracho's lower half, then grabbed his arm to inspect it, her hand—alive with magick—hovering inches above the skin.

I got a glimpse of the wound as she did, and it felt like my stomach went into free-fall. Thin black tendrils spread from the edges of the open gash, just a few inches above his wrist. Twisting and writhing, as if trying to spread through his body.

No.

"This can't happen," Antares kept saying, watching every movement Dracho made, wincing at every noise of pain.

Slowly, I reached a hand out towards his shoulder. "Antares."

"What?" he snarled, head swinging towards me, eyes molten gold with the vertical slits of his dragon, warning. *Daring.* My breathing came faster, and his eyes softened.

"W-we need to get him to the castle."

His eyes returned to normal; he nodded a few times. "You're right."

Without another word, he turned, jumped up the side of the ditch with ease, and disappeared from view. A moment later, a high-pitched cry reached my ears; Antares had returned in his dragon form, hovering above the crater. I realised his cry was a warning. Clasping Roux's arm, which still trembled over Dracho's form, I started to pull her away.

"Roux, we need to move!"

She looked up at the dark green beast above us and got to her feet. When we'd given him enough space, Antares lowered himself down slowly so that Dracho lay between his two front legs. I clasped Roux's face in my hands.

"I'm so glad you're okay," I cried, and she pulled me into a quick hug.

Antares's huge wing spread out to lie flat upon the ground before us. I glanced up at his magnificent face. His golden eyes skipped to the outstretched wing with a tip of his head.

I gasped as a smooth voice brushed against my mind. *Climb on.*

"Eliana, he wants us to ride him," Roux said, obviously having received the same message.

I nodded, still shocked that I had been able to hear him, holding Roux's hand as we made our way to the edge of his wing. Carefully manoeuvring up, I avoided treading along any of the bones before reaching the top of his back. Sitting behind Roux between his shoulders, I wrapped my arms around her waist, then turned at the sound of my name. Bas and Vyn stood on the edge of the ditch.

"Dracho's hurt! Will you be all right?" I shouted down.

They wore twin looks of concern at the sight before them. Bas cupped his hands around his mouth. "Yes, we'll be fine! We'll meet you back at the palace!"

I nodded, turning back to Roux. She leaned forward, asking, "Ready?"

Antares turned his head, catching my gaze before nodding. We jolted forward slightly with his take-off. Peering around Roux, I saw that he had gently picked up Dracho, carrying him across the Meridium sky as we made our way to the castle.

The evening sky dipped under the horizon in the west, the sky a captivating blend of orange, pink and red. Cries of battle still sounded out from below; nausea swirled in my stomach as I thought about Connaught down there. So many had been lost, but mostly from Cirdan's side. The arrival of the draconi and Roux had tipped the odds heavily in our favour, and I sent a silent thank-you to the Goddess for my friends.

Antares headed towards the balcony beneath the palace's stained-glass window. Hovering, he rested a wing on the railing of the balcony. Roux and I climbed down carefully, and I watched with bated breath as he carefully lowered Dracho to the balcony floor. Two royal guards ran onto the balcony, but I ran to Dracho's side. My fingers caressed the silky strands of his raven hair as I protected his head, my other hand finding his shoulder.

His skin was cold—too cold. His eyes were clenched shut, teeth chattering, and he kept wincing in pain.

Antares transformed in mid-air, dropping and landing gracefully on his feet. Whether his nakedness bothered him I wasn't sure, but he didn't show it. He stepped forward, taking a cloak from a guard but waving away my command for the guards to carry Dracho to my chambers. "There will be no need."

The guards took off in the direction of my room as Antares picked Dracho's body up with ease, cringing when Dracho let out a cry of pain.

"I'm sorry, brother," he murmured.

Roux and I followed, the walk silent besides Dracho's groans. At one point I opened my mouth to direct Antares to my room, but he seemed to know where he was going. He'd probably had the whole castle mapped out the first time he'd stepped into it last year.

The guards opened the double doors to my room. Antares stormed past them like he owned the place. Putting Dracho gently down on top of my bed, he turned, his eyes scanning every inch of my room as he pointed towards Dracho.

"Fix him," he commanded Roux, who flew to Dracho's side with no complaint.

Ant walked over to the mirror hanging on my wall and pulled open the secret passageway. He walked the path to Bas's room, coming back in a pair of trousers a couple of sizes too big for him and closing the doorway.

I stared at him in astonishment. "H-how did you—"

At his tense gaze, I trailed off; a brow arched on his smooth forehead. "I could sense the air."

I just nodded. "All right." Dragging the chair from my window, I placed it next to my bed and took a seat. I found Dracho's hand and grasped it tightly. "What's happening to him?"

Roux responded with a growl of frustration. Her hand continued to glow as it hovered over Dracho's arm, but she seemed unhappy. "It's the same thing that was under that loscura's skin. But I have no idea how to stop it."

She was right—it looked almost identical to what had crept under the skin of the Hollow's creature.

"It's what killed Dracho's mother," Antares said from where he stood by the window, his back to us.

"He can't die. He *won't* die," I swore.

Roux's face crumpled. "If we can't stop the spread of this—"

"He. *Won't*. Die!" Antares said between his teeth. "Fix him!"

She had tears in her eyes. "I wouldn't even know where to start! We don't even know what this really is!"

A rough voice interrupted us from the doorway. "I do."

Chapter 65

Bas and Vyn walked into the room still in their armour, caked in mud and blood. And walking between them...

Malzan, the lupera who had cared for me in Fallstone. Shirt ripped to shreds and blood splattered on his face, he had obviously taken part in the battle. For whom, I wasn't sure.

"Malzan?" I asked, but before he could speak, Antares had appeared before him, bending down and snarling in his face.

Thick, black claws burst from Malzan's fingertips, a growl rumbling deep in his chest. His burgundy eyes flashed, his head lifting to meet Antares's golden glare with dragon pupils visible—and then lowering, breaking eye contact as a whine sounded out.

Antares bared his teeth once more, then stalked back to his place at the window.

Vyn blinked. "That was kind of..."

"Scary?" Bas put in. "What the hell was that about?"

Malzan ignored him, giving Antares a sidelong glance before approaching the bed. My stomach dipped at his approach, though I was sure he meant no harm.

His cheeks flushed slightly as he caught my eye. "Hey, Eliana."

I nodded. "Were you at the battle?"

"I was."

"He was fighting for us, E. We saw his wolf form and almost shat ourselves, but he turned on Cirdan's men!"

"You fought for us?"

Malzan nodded. "I fought for *you*, against Cirdan. Saw as you struck him down."

"Why didn't the other wolves fight?"

"After Erix was killed, they turned on Cirdan. Fled before he could kill them, as they refused to fight for him. They're scattered."

"Then why did you come?"

"I felt like I owed it to you. After what they did. After you spared my life."

I swallowed hard at that.

"Life isn't worth very much when you take everything else away. So why has she inspired your loyalty?" Antares quizzed him, his tone dark with veiled threats.

Malzan glared at Antares, for which I had to commend his bravery. "Erix may have been our alpha, but only because of the butchery he carried out to get there—on many, my parents included. My father was the last alpha."

"Then why did this Erix keep you around?"

"To keep in line those still loyal to my family," Malzan told him. His gaze turned back to me. "Your Majesty—"

"You killed Cirdan?" Antares asked me, his voice calmer.

I tried not to be offended as I confirmed that I had. He looked impressed.

"What is it?" I asked Malzan, desperate to get back to the situation at hand as Dracho's groan of pain sounded from the bed. The sigh that left his mouth didn't fill me with confidence.

"Cirdan created this poison, with the help of others. It's made using the essence of that *thing*... the thing that's been attacking villages."

"The Hollow?" Vyn asked, and he nodded.

"How... how is that possible?" I asked.

"The creature... he—he used its blood, if you can call it that, to create the toxin. They call it hollowshade."

"Wait, wait." Bas held his hands up. "You're telling me that thing let Cirdan take its *blood*?"

Mal winced. "No. He had a mage that would take it as they watched. I'm not exactly sure how the mage syphoned the blood from it. But the sounds that came from that room... Well, I won't forget them anytime soon."

"What did the mage look like?" Roux asked, eyes still on Dracho as she held his other hand.

"Um, dark-skinned, brown eyes. And scars all over his head."

Roux looked at me, and I grimaced. *Kanu.* It seemed that Cirdan had not lied, and Roux's uncle was behind it too. Roux had discovered plenty of new powers, such as her ability to prevent a draconi from transforming, so perhaps Kanu had used his corrupt magick to hide any trace of the Hollow on himself. But it didn't explain why Kanu had gone on to become Jareth's dignitary. Had he been trying to get close to the king? But for what? To help Cirdan take back Stillmere?

Unless…

"Who were the others involved, Malzan?" I asked, trying to make everything make sense.

"There was a redhead."

I felt sick. "Pale? Long red hair, with a slight build?"

"No." Malzan shook his head. "Muscled, with shoulder-length hair. Bit nasty-looking. I never got his name."

I felt both disappointment and relief that Jareth wasn't involved. We needed to speak to him as soon as possible regarding Kanu—but first we needed to figure out how to help Dracho. "Malzan, tell me everything."

We sat in silence as he told us how Kanu, Cirdan and the unknown male would summon the Hollow, using a dark ritual. Malzan said that everyone would avoid being around Cirdan during those times—that the wolves could sense the evil of the creature that would visit.

"It was what finally turned the lupera away," he explained. "Their use of that thing, and Erix's death… it turned them against Cirdan. A fight broke out, but most of the lupera fled before the battle. Many have returned to Eshmnor."

It was hard to keep my focus on his words while Dracho tossed and turned, groaning in pain. I wanted to snap at Malzan to get to the point and tell us how to save Dracho, but I knew this was information we needed to prevent us from making him worse.

As soon as I thought it, Dracho's back arched unnaturally and a sharp gasp left his mouth. He thrashed in the bed; Antares joined me as I tried to hold him down, protect him from hurting himself. His chest was heaving, and he was clearly oblivious to all going on around him.

"It's all right, brother. It's all right," Antares repeated, but the panic in his eyes was evident.

Dracho finally calmed when I climbed onto the bed to cradle his head in my lap. I hadn't even realised I was crying.

Roux's hands were still outstretched as she watched him in shock. I reached over Dracho, clasping her hand. "Roux, there must be something we can do?"

"I—I..."

I had never seen her so speechless or scared. Fresh tears ran down my cheeks as I looked down at Dracho's face. "Malzan, there must be an antidote. Did you ever hear them mention one?"

The sorrowful shake of his head tore a sob from my throat.

"There is something you could *try*," Sizwe announced as she entered the room, her own tunic covered in soil and blood.

"Auntie?" Roux gasped.

"You joined the battle too?" I asked, and Sizwe nodded as she walked around the bed to place a hand on Dracho's forehead, smoothing the stray hairs away.

"How has he lasted longer than Eliana's father?" Antares asked her bluntly.

"Bisa would know more," Sizwe replied. "But perhaps it has to do with the wound. It's spreading up towards his heart, whereas Teyrnon drank a form of it. But there's no time to wait and figure out why this is different. We have potentially minutes before it reaches his heart."

My eyes found the black veins spreading to his upper arm.

"The creature, and this poison, is made from corrupt magick. Perhaps our pure celestral magick can reverse it?" Sizwe went on to Roux.

"Perhaps pure magick is the answer," Ant murmured under his breath, raising his eyes to meet mine.

Roux inhaled quickly, looking hopeful. "Do you think it would work?"

Sizwe frowned. "I can't be certain, but with both of us it just might."

"Do it!" Antares commanded, his amber eyes ablaze.

Roux looked at me, and I nodded. "If it's our only chance, you have to." My voice cracked.

She blew out a breath. "All right. Antares, I'm gonna need you to hold his legs down."

Antares and Bas moved forward at the same time. Each of them took a leg, whilst Vyn and Malzan moved around us to take one of Dracho's arms. I held his head steady, swallowing hard.

"I don't know how much this will hurt him," Sizwe said. "So hold on tight." She had moved around the bed to stand by Roux's side. "I need you to focus your magick onto the wound. Tell your magick to heal, to pull the corruption from his body. Ready?"

Roux nodded, albeit a little hesitantly. They held their hands inches above the wound in Dracho's arm.

"One, two…" Roux began.

"Three," Sizwe finished, and a blast of magick was emitted from their hands, blinding us momentarily as we held on to Dracho for dear life. I noted the beautiful waves of their magick as it attempted to burrow deep within Dracho's skin—the black and gold of Roux's intertwined with Sizwe's blue magick.

I couldn't look at it for long.

A gut-wrenching cry burst from Dracho's mouth as his head tipped back, knocking my hands away. His fangs were visible as his upper lip peeled back, his body straining against us, and black claws ripped from his hand. Vyn just narrowly avoided being cut.

I knew Dracho's screams of pain would forever be etched on my very soul. Tears trailed down my face as I secured his head again and turned to watch the mages work. A bead of sweat ran down Roux's temple; her teeth were gritted with effort. Sizwe had dropped to one knee beside the bed, her breathing heavy, though she still held her hand out towards Dracho. The mages' free hands clutched each other, sharing the burden.

I glanced down, watching as thin strands of their combined magick wove through his very veins, along each tendril of black that was poisoning him. My breath held as the pure celestral magick travelled up his arm. The tendrils looked as if they were fighting the pure energy that sought to remove them.

"No," I gasped.

With a shaky exhalation, Dracho's body went still, his head limp in my lap. His chest wasn't moving.

"N-n-no!" I cried, my hands caressing his face and moving his hair from his eyes. "You can't leave! You can't leave me too! *Wake up!*" I looked up frantically.

Sizwe's eyes were soft as she gave me a sad smile. "He'll be all right," she promised.

Releasing Roux's hand, she grasped her own wrist tightly and gritted her teeth. The wave of blue light intensified as it twisted along his arm in spirals with Roux's own bright magick.

I glanced down at the black lines up Dracho's arm... and the furthest one retracted. Burning up underneath his skin, slowly but surely, the black vein-like magick was retreating.

"It's working!" I blurted out, hope warming my insides.

Sizwe huffed with humour, looking up at Roux. "You can do it, Roux. You've always had the power. I believe in you." Her eyes found mine once more, and she nodded, giving her magick one last push.

A wave of blue pulsed from her hands and into Dracho. As the combined magick made its way into the veins closest to his heart, Dracho sucked in a sharp breath and roared in pain, his eyes flashing open. Not blue, but silver.

He tried to pull himself free from us. Bas grunted in effort, and Malzan's lupera eyes shone as he used his advanced strength to hold one of Dracho's arms down. Vyn held on as hard as he could, freeing a hand to create a cuff of wind around Dracho's arm, pulling it down. I could tell the effort was taking its toll on him.

"Almost—almost there!" Roux called out, her voice breathless.

I saw Dracho's eyes flash to me, open but unseeing. I leaned in close, whispering in his ear. "Fight it, Dracho. Come back to us." My voice shook.

His screams of pain calmed as the magick removed the deep block of corruption. Only a few small tendrils remained. The magick worked its way backwards as it finally reached the wound, its black edges disappearing before my very eyes.

With a final wave of combined magick, the light from both Roux and Sizwe's hands was extinguished, Roux stumbling back. Dracho stilled on the bed, no black veins visible in his arm, though he did not wake.

And Roux's scream was eerily familiar as she dropped to her knees, where Sizwe now lay dead.

Chapter 66

Four long days had passed since Roux and Sizwe had removed the magick from Dracho's body. Four days since Sizwe had given her life.

Pain cut through me like a sharp blade whenever I thought about her. Goddess, I missed her. It was clear to me now that in that room, Sizwe had known she was going to die. She had used every bit of her magick, her lifeforce, to ensure that Dracho lived.

Guilt ate away at me, for I knew why she had done it. She had been unable to save my mother and father—so she'd brought Dracho back to me, knowing it would cost her own life. It was a gift I could never repay.

What made it worse was that Dracho still hadn't woken. Antares and I took shifts sitting at his bedside, hoping he would wake. On the second day, Roux had left Meridium for Aion; the Aioni's custom was for their funeral ceremony to be performed within three days. Roux had sent word ahead to her mother, though she'd confessed her guilt to me about imparting the news via letter. An exception had been granted for her to escort her aunt's body and see her put to rest there.

I had no idea how to act around her. My grief and guilt escalated, along with shame for feeling such a way about my friend. It was why I felt relieved she was going to leave Meridium for a short while. I had offered to travel with her—despite the pull to remain with Dracho—wanting to honour her family for Sizwe's sacrifice, but Roux was adamant I was needed here. She had kissed

Dracho's forehead, promising to curse him if he didn't wake, before clasping my hand and embracing me tightly.

When I wasn't sitting with Dracho, I helped my people recover the bodies of our fallen. They were placed upon pyres made by our craftsmen just outside the walls of the city, where they'd given their lives for it. We'd noted each individual's name, and I had declared that a memorial would be made for them.

A singular, large pyre had been made for Cirdan's men, their bodies put to rest. I had promised Cirdan that his body would be left for the crows, and I had meant it, but that didn't mean I would disgrace his soldiers. He remained where he had fallen, his features almost unrecognisable from the birds that had eaten his body.

Connaught I had retrieved myself, helping two soldiers lift him onto a stretcher. My wonderful friend, my captain, my protector... his pyre was the greatest, set before all of his soldiers. Survivors who lived all came to give their prayers—injured or not. Marcus had stood by my side, promoted to captain, as he grieved the loss of Connaught with me.

Bas had recovered my mother's armour, returning it to the palace, where Beatrice had cleaned it thoroughly, her face covered in tears as she praised the Goddess for my survival.

I found myself back in my chambers after the burning of the pyres, watching over Dracho as he continued to sleep. He looked peaceful—serene, almost. He uttered no words, did not move an inch. He looked to be in a deep sleep, but with every hour that passed, I wished more desperately to see the icy blue of his eyes, or the silver of his dragon's.

I lay down onto the bed next to him, gazing at his face. There wasn't one single feature that made Dracho so beautiful, but his eyes came close. I missed them. Missed the twinkle in his eye as he did everything he could to get on my nerves. They were always intense, but also genuine and honest.

Honest.

From a deep chasm in my chest, where I had hidden so much emotion, came a wave of despair so powerful, I had no hope of stopping it. It tore me apart in its jaws. My arm wrapped over Dracho's waist as I buried my head into his chest, muffling my sobs.

I missed his honest eyes, which had always shone with the truths he knew I was not ready to hear. *I'll take care of you. I'm here for you. I'll protect you. I love you.*

I had been wrong. Wrong to have allowed my anger to overrule my rational thinking, when my feelings for him could have created something beautiful. Wrong when I had left Tenebris, believing it was for the best because I felt I had nothing left to give him. I had been stubborn. And being stubborn was *so* easy, because it was all that I had ever known. Letting go was harder because it was a risk.

My chest felt warm as my heart pounded an erratic rhythm against my ribcage. I raised my head, my eyes greedily taking in every feature of his peaceful face. A strangled laugh left me as my hand pressed against his chest.

I had *everything* to give him, but I hadn't told him. I hadn't been honest. I had walked away, believing my actions were right for him and his kingdom, hurting us both in the process. Despite us overcoming most of our differences, I had not expressed the words that would finally give us some closure. Give *me* some closure, and finally heal my heart.

I may never get the chance to tell him again.

I'd believed that if I loved him, I wouldn't have been able to let him go. Letting him go, for the sake of his rule and kingdom, was probably the most selfless thing I had ever done. I had created a false narrative in my own mind by pushing all my feelings aside, trusting that us being separated would be the best thing for both our kingdoms.

I decided to change my mind. To be selfish.

"Dracho, if you can hear me... I'm so sorry," I whispered. "I'm sorry for punishing you for all that time. I was afraid. Afraid that, if I let you in completely... you would hurt me, or leave me."

I listened to his steady heartbeat.

"Or that something like *this* would happen. That I would fall completely, but like so many others I've loved... I would lose you." I raised a hand to furiously wipe the tears from my cheek. "But I n-need to be selfish. I c-can't lose you now!" I sobbed. "I haven't had the chance to tell you."

My heart raced, fearful of what I was about to admit aloud, but more terrified that he would never hear the words.

"You're so irritating. I can't believe you'd do this to me." I thumped his chest lightly, hearing a slight stutter of his heartbeat. "I need you to wake up so I can tell you. That I do forgive you. I think I forgave you a long time ago. I was scared. Because it's me who needs *your* forgiveness. I said awful things to you. Things I could never mean. But I..."

My teeth pressed down on my lower lip as I gathered my courage to voice my secret truth. I loved him.

I had been in love with him for a long time. Perhaps my heart had never been broken by his betrayal at all. I had kept falling in love with him even when he'd returned to Meridium. Especially after he had learned the truth about my elven heritage and accepted it without question. I'd already been in love with him when he had rescued me from my cell, his appearance granting me relief that if those were my final moments, at least I had seen the image of him one more time.

He accepted *all* of me. The stubborn and dark parts alike—even the part that wanted to strangle him sometimes. I loved him when he accepted whatever I could give him as if I had presented him with the rarest treasure. Even when his uncle advised against staying in Tenebris, I had loved him. And I had tried to let him go, believing I had nothing to give him—when I had *everything*.

But our love was a painful one. The pain came from fear. Fear that after everything we had already lost, we could lose more. And the thought of losing Dracho, wishing I had said something to him before, was like taking a knife to my own heart. My love for him had become part of the very oxygen I breathed… and the possibility that I would have to say goodbye without telling him wasn't something I could face.

"I *love* you, Dracho Celesta," I whispered. "I love who *I* am when I'm with you. And I'll love you until all your stars in the sky have gone out." I released a shaky breath, my bleary eyes focusing on the window. "So I need you to wake up, and love me back."

"Well, with a command like that, how can I refuse?"

The low, croaky voice startled me. My head snapped around, finding his eyes. Luminous eyes that were *open*.

Eyes that looked straight through me, as if finding the truth in what I had said.

My lips parted, no words able to escape as I tried to comprehend that he was awake. It was when his hand rose and brushed my cheek gently that it became real.

I punched him in the stomach.

"Ow! What was that for?" he laughed weakly, the sound bringing something to life within my chest.

I sat up out of his embrace. "You arse! Were you awake, listening the whole time?!" I covered my face to hide the fresh tears of relief that fell.

"Well, it was a bit hard to sleep after you punched me the first time. I just enjoyed the monologue after that," he chuckled.

"You cruel, cruel monster," I cried, the sound muffled behind my hands.

"Um, *dragon,* thank you," he pointed out. The bed shifted, and a calloused finger traced the top of my ear, before he pulled my hands away from my face and cupped my cheek. "My Eliana. *Mia estra.*"

A sob broke out from me, and he used his thumbs to wipe away my tears, then leaned forward to press his forehead gently to mine.

"I wanted to remain quiet for longer," he said. "To hear what other sweetness would leave your lips. But when I heard you whisper the words I thought you'd never say, I had to see your eyes when I said them back." He pulled back, his chest lifting with a deep breath. "Say it again."

"I love you," I said with unwavering truth.

His exhalation was shaky; his eyes closed before opening, glassy. "I love *you*. And I don't deserve it."

My breath snagged. "You're wrong," I told him. "I don't deserve your love. I've loved you for so long and denied it, pushed you away, lied to myself and you about my feelings."

"How long?" he asked, as if the answer would be the answer to everything he had ever known.

I shook my head. "I can't be sure. But I knew I wanted you long before Tenebris happened. During our journey together, you made me laugh. Made me feel alive. Even after you learned about my scar, you made me feel seen. Like I was more than the princess who had lost her mother and brother... more than the trauma I live with. You didn't smother me, but you still protected me." I placed my hand on his chest. "I always wanted you, but I think it started to become more once I awoke in Aion, after the Uhane ceremony. When I realised you'd stayed with me."

He nodded, remembering.

"It was why it didn't matter once I found out who you really were. Once your dragon had been revealed and you told me all about Tenebris. Because it gave me more hope. Hope that, together, we could make a change to better the lives of all in Ruvalon. A hope that we could be partners through that."

"You still felt all that after what I did?" he whispered.

"Even when you dismissed me from Tenebris... I now accept that you were doing that to protect me. I understand, and even though some pain caused can't be forgotten, I know that your feelings for me didn't factor into your decision."

He nodded a few times quickly, and my lips twitched.

"But this all terrifies me. It's an intensity I've never felt, and…" I swallowed hard. "My biggest fear was that I could give you my heart, and you could hurt me. Hurt a heart that is already tired—that perhaps wasn't healed enough to give in the first place. But you smashed through all my walls with no expectations, taking the scraps I could give you and always giving yourself fully. And I pushed you away. It's me who doesn't deserve your love."

Tears burned at the back of my eyes as he shook his head again, pressing his lips forward in the whisper of a kiss.

He breathed deeply. "You deserve the love you give to everyone else. To your friends, to your people… I can only hope to live up to the love you share with others. Because no star that lights up the sky across the cosmos could ever burn as brightly as you do in my eyes. They're but a shadow, when compared to your light." He laughed shakily. "I think I've loved you since the moment I fell over that water bucket."

We both laughed, but before I could reply, his lips were pressed hard against mine, and I was floating. The passion behind his kiss made my mind empty, a thousand thoughts condensed into one single moment. It ignited the blood running through my veins, turning my body into a raging inferno as I pulled him closer. I kept kissing him, almost overwhelmed with emotion as I realised that within his arms, I felt safe. I felt loved.

His kiss was *home*. We weren't two stars colliding in destruction. We were *creation.*

With a few more small kisses, I pulled away, brushing the tip of my finger under the skin of his eye, smiling as shining silver stared back at me—the vertical pupils of his dragon visible.

I clasped his hand in mine, turning his arm over as I traced my fingers over his skin where the wound had been.

"I love you," I whispered as I stared at the creamy skin, my heart twisting at the reminder that I had almost lost him. "You stopped breathing," I choked.

His firm finger tipped my chin up to look at him. "I'm here. I don't know what's in store for us, and I don't know what I've done to deserve you. But I promise I will live each day showing you how much I love you." He looked at me as if I were the moon, the stars and the sun combined.

"You know, I have a half a mind to let you," I joked.

"You have no idea how happy that makes me. How can I prove it to you?"

I smiled slyly, moving my hand up his arm. "I can think of a number of ways." His grin in response was positively devilish, and I sighed. "But *that* will have to wait for later. You should call Antares; we have a lot to discuss."

"Already called for him."

"What? When I *just* suggested that we—"

"Ant wouldn't have cared." Dracho waggled his brows. "We could have invited him to join us."

Scoffing, I pushed him away. "You're intolerable."

"Ooh, big words," he said, pulling so close his whispered words tickled my ear. "But don't pretend the thought of that doesn't excite you." I buried my head in my hands as loud steps sounded outside the room.

The doors flung open so fast they smacked against the wall. The guards outside stared in horror at Antares, who stood shirtless and panting, his hair and eyes wild. He clearly couldn't believe what he was seeing. His breath hitched as he stared at Dracho, not even acknowledging my presence, and I smiled.

"Y-you..." Antares started.

"Hello, brother." Dracho smiled.

A draft brushed against my skin as the bed dipped. Antares suddenly knelt beside me, clutching Dracho in his arms as he touched his forehead to Dracho's affectionately.

"I thought—I thought I was going to lose you," he breathed.

I had never witnessed such vulnerability from Antares. I had always known they were close—more than best friends—but I had not truly appreciated the depths of their feelings for one another until now. My heart swelled at their embrace, the pull in my chest warming.

"It'll take a lot more than that to be rid of me," Dracho laughed, and Antares pulled him into a tight embrace. His chin rested on Dracho's shoulder, and his eyes opened to gaze at me.

I stilled as, releasing Dracho, his hands came to grasp my shoulders tightly but gently. Gratitude and awe shone in his eyes.

"I don't know what you did, or how you did it," he said. "But thank you, for bringing him back."

I laughed awkwardly. "I didn't do anything, Antares, he just woke up."

"No, you're right, Ant. She wouldn't stop talking about how unbelievably attractive I am, so I woke up to tell her to stop objectifying me." Dracho looked at me with an exaggerated scandalised expression.

"You're such a prick sometimes," I told him.

"I can show you a pri—"

"All right, that's enough," I laughed, unable to hold it in.

Antares huffed, his head dropping between his arms. Raising a hand, I cupped his cheek, raising his head. "He's all right."

Something crumpled in his expression. He lurched forward, wrapping his arms around me in a tight hug. My eyes found Dracho's over Antares's shoulder; he covered his mouth to suppress his laugh at my shocked expression.

I hesitated only for a second before placing my arms on Antares's back, his scent relaxing me as my chest tugged. Then, pulling back, I gave him a pointed look. "We need to update Dracho on a few things."

Antares's eyes narrowed, and he nodded.

"Why?" Dracho asked. "What's happened?"

I blew out a breath, dreading this conversation. From now on, everything would change.

And we were in much deeper water than we'd thought.

Chapter 67

Dracho didn't take the news of Connaught and Sizwe's deaths very well. His first reaction was to burst out of the confinement of the castle walls, transforming into a creature as black as night as he took to the skies. Antares had gently squeezed my shoulder before joining him—presumably to ensure he didn't do anything stupid.

I was in bed that night, unable to sleep, when he returned to my room. He climbed into my bed, completely naked, resting his head on my stomach as he clung to me like his life depended on it. The slight shaking of his back told me he was crying, and I ran my hand soothingly over his skin, understanding the guilt he felt.

Everything with the celestral ancestors was a balance, and Sizwe had given her life for his. It was a huge debt, and payment would be to use the extra time he'd been given wisely. The beautiful thing about Dracho was that he didn't believe he was more important than anyone else, despite his station and upbringing. He would gladly lay down his life for anyone. But I also knew he still carried guilt about our own situation. About his reaction in Tenebris all those months ago, when his father had been murdered.

No matter how many times I would tell him I forgave him, I knew deep down, he would feel undeserving—of forgiveness, of my love, and of Sizwe's sacrifice. But I promised myself that we would honour her gift, every day. Together.

Eventually, Dracho stilled and I pressed a kiss to his raven hair. Tilting his head up, he looked at me, sliding up the bed by my side.

"I'm sorry about the captain," he whispered.

My throat tightened, my lips pursing as I nodded.

"He loved you." There was no question, no doubt.

"I..." I hesitated, guilt riddling me. "They were his final words, but I..." I cleared my throat. "I think I always knew. I just never acknowledged it out loud, or even for too long in my mind." A man who had saved my life, paying for it with his own. There had been no one with greater loyalty.

"Because he was your guard?"

"Because I could never feel the same. And he knew that. Didn't treat me differently because of it. He was a great guard. A great friend."

"He was a great man," Dracho agreed, and I smiled softly. A moment's silence fell between us.

"I thought *you* were going to die," I whispered, still reeling from everything.

His head lifted, and moonlit silver eyes held mine. "Do you really think a small thing such as death could keep me away from you? If so, you haven't been paying attention, *mia estra.* Because there is nothing I wouldn't do, nothing I wouldn't face, to be by your side."

I stilled against him, the warm tears springing to my eyes. His own eyes glinted with a sheen as his fingers mapped a journey over my face—tracing underneath my eyes, across my cheek and over my lips. His expression was full of wonder. As if I were a rarity he had never seen before in his lifetime.

"Can I keep you?" he whispered, tucking a strand of my hair behind my ear.

My heart gave an unsteady leap as I wriggled closer. "Until my last breath," I vowed.

He sighed, his hand moving to clasp the back of my neck. "And even after." He laughed. "I knew you were dangerous from the moment we danced in Stillmere."

"Why?" I grinned.

All his features softened. "Because of the way you laughed."

"The way I laughed?"

He nodded, resting his forehead against mine. "Yes. My mother always told me, if I wanted to make a woman fall in love with me, make her laugh. But when I heard you laugh as we danced, I knew *I* had already fallen."

My heart began to pound. "Kiss me," I whispered.

I didn't need to ask him twice. He pulled me closer still, as if we could become one. The kiss deepened, and a surge of heat went through me as his tongue met mine. I committed the feeling of it all to memory, aching for him.

I always ached for him.

We pulled apart, Dracho leaning forward until our foreheads were touching once more.

"Yours," he whispered.

"Mine," I breathed.

Neither of us spoke for a few moments, and I pondered how much had changed in such a short amount of time. There were still many things we needed to discuss, but I was done denying my feelings for him. After Sizwe's sacrifice and the battle with Cirdan, I would accept graciously what could no longer be denied, and deal with the consequences later. That included his court.

It was a calming feeling, to have one's secrets all laid bare and be given love freely by those you'd thought might reject you. Dracho's unquestioning acceptance of my lineage and his actions to free me and protect me had proved his love repeatedly. The same way my friends had come to my aid and fought by my side. Vyn, Bas, Roux, Antares... Connaught. Sizwe. At that moment I felt very lucky to have those around me.

But...

"Dracho... there's something else I need to tell you. Somewhere we need to go."

He stilled, his shoulders going rigid.

"We need to visit Aunt Lys."

Scouts I'd sent ahead returned before they were due, informing me of bodies along the road that led to Asaph. Cirdan's own scouts had killed travellers along the way, preventing anyone from warning us in Meridium about Cirdan's force.

Concerned that Cirdan might have left men behind in Asaph, Marcus had gathered a small force to escort us to Aunt Lys's manor, two days away to the east. Dracho had demanded he be present, despite my protestations that he should rest. So, naturally, Antares accompanied us.

The journey was quiet, the road to Asaph slick with mud from the army Cirdan had marched to Meridium. The closer we got to Aunt Lys's manor, the more my gut twisted in anxiety. Lys would never betray us and allow Cirdan to march upon Meridium with no warning. Which meant she'd either locked the gates and doors to the manor, shut herself away in safety after seeing Cirdan's forces—which wasn't like her at all.... or something terrible had happened.

As soon as we arrived in Asaph, we knew something was wrong. The gates to the castle were open; the courtyard was a mess of debris and overturned carts. Those who had lived within its walls had fled, or worse.

A bitter anger grew in me as I climbed from Engel's back and we entered the main building, the stench hitting my nose. The smell of rot and decay. It took everything not to gag at it, and I covered my nose as we walked silently through the castle's halls. It didn't take long to come across the bodies. Many of Aunt Lys's guards had been butchered, their remains decomposing on the castle's floors.

My stomach twisted, a sickening feeling overwhelming me as we neared Lys's wing.

Her room was completely silent and devoid of all life. My steps were deafening. An open door to the left caught my eye, and I cautiously approached.

"Lys?" I called, pushing the door into a private study. It seemed empty, and I almost left until something caught my eye. The back of a chair faced me, the lower half hidden behind a large wooden desk; hanging over the arm of that chair was a hand.

My chest heaved, and the hairs on the back of my neck stood on end. I stepped forward, coming around to the front of the chair.

Aunt Lys sat lifeless, her head resting on one shoulder, not a hair out of place. My hand flew to my mouth, smothering a sob. There was so much blood covering her dress, the acrid smell of death pungent. Her throat had been cut.

My gaze drifted to her crimson-covered hand, next to her desk, and spotted smudged drops of blood on the wood where a word had been crudely written. My brow furrowed. Tears trailing down my cheeks, I took a step closer.

Confusion overwhelmed me as Antares made his entrance into the room, silent as a ghost. His face became a mask of horror as he saw Aunt Lys.

"I'm sorry," he whispered, wrapping an arm around my shoulder.

His harsh gasp was loud in the otherwise silent room as he glanced at the desk. I saw disbelief and shock flash across his face.

"It's not possible," he mumbled.

"What?" I asked, placing a comforting hand on his arm. "What is it, Antares?"

Dracho anxiously entered the room, his steps hurried as he pushed into the space beside us.

"We... we need to go," he said, his body suddenly tense. "Now." He was shaking, his claws escaping the confines of his skin as an escalating rage filled his eyes. As he stared down at the word on the mahogany desk.

And I realised it wasn't a word. It was a *name*. Not Cirdan's; not one I knew. But Aunt Lys had named her killer...

And Dracho knew who it was.

Now for a sneak peek at the epic finale: Truth of the Hollow

Eliana

"You brought a blade?" Ant chuckled, although apparently not surprised. "Are you trying to flirt with me, Eliana?" he asked, lowering slightly.

"I'm beginning to think this was a bad idea," Dracho muttered, leaning against the outer wooden posts of the training arena. Several Meridium soldiers stood along the platform around the outside, chattering amongst themselves as they watched with rapt attention.

Ant's golden gaze flickered in response to Dracho's words, causing the hue of his eyes to darken.

"And why is that?" he asked, never taking his eyes off me as we circled each other.

I levelled my sword at his throat. "Maybe Dracho's worried about my men seeing his big, bad draconi advisor getting knocked on his arse?"

Dracho laughed deeply as the corner of Ant's lips pulled up.

"I don't think that's it," Jeshwa laughed conspiratorially, ignoring how Dracho rolled his eyes at him. Jeshwa had arrived from Tenebris the day prior, seeking an update to deliver back to Althea.

"*Now* that's a concern," Dracho said. "But watching you is distracting and I'm worried that I'll have to rip out all of your men's eyes after my big, bad dragon advisor has his way with you."

I stiffened, my cheeks flaming as I processed his words. Jeshwa chuckled and Ant's teeth flashed in a satisfied grin as he used my distracted moment to his advantage. A grunt left me as I found myself on my back, Ant straddling my thighs and holding his dagger slightly away from the skin of my throat.

I growled at the use of his draconi speed. "Cheater."

Ant's brow lifted as he reached up to remove one of my soldier's daggers from my hand. Considering my own emerald dagger—crafted by my elven ancestors—was able to harm them, I had wisely decided to leave it behind.

"I never said I played fair," Ant arched a brow. "Perhaps you should concentrate on training and not allow your filthy thoughts to distract you." He smirked in Dracho's direction.

Using my foot I twisted it around his calf and flipped him, switching our positions. He looked up at me in surprise whilst Dracho laughed loudly.

"Now who isn't concentrating?" I smiled and he scoffed whilst a few of the soldiers above clapped.

"All right, all right," Dracho said as he walked over to us, offering me a hand. I took it, standing before Dracho pulled me up against his chest.

"Let's end this session, so I can *distract* you in other ways," he breathed quietly against the shell of my ear.

My *elf* ears.

Since my admittance to my people, and the battle of Meridium, I hadn't once felt the need to hide my true heritage. The people had surprised me by accepting me fully. Even after the battle against Cirdan outside the walls of the city, as I visited those who had lost children, fathers, family in the fight, not one single person had shunned or turned me away. An elf, like he who had tried to destroy our city—yet they accepted me with open arms.

Dracho had held me close those few nights after the battle—after losing Sizwe—telling me that it was so easy for the people to accept me because of who I was. Who I had always been. A benevolent princess who had taken the time to get to know her subjects. Never one to hide behind her palace walls and treat them as lesser.

"Ah, ah, brother," Ant chuckled, getting to his feet and tapping Dracho's shoulder with the flat side of his blade. "You know she needs to train."

Dracho groaned, his eyes darkening with a different emotion now, but nodded in agreement as he stepped away, and I felt the absence of him immediately. I pouted.

Ant pointed at me with the sword now. "No."

I bared my teeth at him playfully as I collected my training sword from the ground and he grinned.

"Fine," I ceded, "Let's go."

I shot forward.

Acknowledgements

How is it almost the first anniversary of *Prince of the Ancients* release date, and now book two is out in the world!?

Queen of the Exiled was infinitely easier to write than *Prince of the Ancients*. It is an ode to women and women's mental health, which we continue to work hard on today.

It's a story of guilt, survival and how we bear so much, we crack, but we hardly ever fall apart. And even when we do… we get back up. I cried so many times while writing this book. Eliana's journey is one which reflects my own, in its unique way, and I genuinely felt emotionally drained after finishing it. It was a form of therapy to write this book. I hope there are people who read this and can relate, on some level, and who know that I *see* you.

There are some people, who without, this book would probably not have existed.

Emma, my amazing editor. Never have I seen someone work harder, in the face of adversity. You emulate Eliana's strength—both physical and mental—in several ways, and I hope you know that you inspire me greatly. It takes a great strength to be gentle, and you are one of the most kind and gentle people I have ever had the pleasure of meeting.

Brit, Beth, Erin and Kelly, who have been with me since *Prince of the Ancients*, once again your feedback and advice have helped mould this story into what it was meant to be. I couldn't ask for better hype women and I am so grateful you have been on this journey with me.

My little piece of the Bookstagram community—I have met so many talented indie authors, published or not, and I genuinely love the connections I have made with you all. You have made me laugh, cry, scream with excitement—never change!

My mam and dad, for always encouraging and supporting me to follow my dreams. My mammy for once again being the best alpha reader—

even if you did ring me from abroad to demand book three! My little sis and bro, for continually pointing out my Hermione moments and granting me much needed comedic relief when I'm feeling crappy. I love you all, and I know I'm so lucky to have you all.

My nan & grandad, who have always been some of my biggest supporters—I love you.

My two demon-spawn, once again this book would have been completed much quicker without your fighting, distractions and weird questions. Keep asking those questions my beautiful girls. Be tenacious, clever and strong. And never let anyone tell you, you can't do it.

To Cae, my best friend and soulmate. From checking my page reads daily, to reading the story (when I know you're not much of a fiction reader), your support and love for this series has been second-to-none. Even when I'm asking you for advice on plot points, and you haven't got a clue, I appreciate you taking such a big interest in my stories and excitement at me chasing my dreams. I love you infinitely more every day. Together forever.

Finally, to you. The reader. Out of all the amazing books released today, I cannot say how thankful I am that you have picked up mine. Know that your love and support for these stories is what keeps indie authors going, and it means more than you can ever know. Whether it's the excited messages on social media (which I love by the way) or the beautiful reviews left, those are the little things that matter.

And as always, if I can inspire just one person, and make them feel like they can escape into my world... it will all be worth it. For the stories we read, and the dreams that follow, never forget them.

Photo by Jack Harper

Amazon bestselling author of fantasy, Gem L Preston, comes from a small town in South Wales. It was there that she was influenced by the mythology and legends of her country and that, along with her love of video games, led to the creation of her debut series: The Stag & Hollow Chronicles.

Her characters are brave and outgoing, but in real life, Gem is scared of moths and loves nothing more than relaxing with a cup of tea. She wouldn't last one night without being able to charge her kindle!

When she is not writing (or trying to write whilst her two demon daughters run wild), Gem spends most of her time reading, gaming or spending time with her family and friends. A passionate member of perhaps too many fandoms, Gem loves nothing more than indulging in Marvel/Harry Potter/Star Wars theories—a passionate discussion is probably one of her favourite things.

Gem has been living with an incurable disease known as IIH for over a decade, something which she tries to raise awareness of often. She also has a heart condition and, knowing how these types of conditions can affect not just the physical health but mental health of a person, she loves speaking to others who deal with chronic illnesses.

www.ingramcontent.com/pod-product-compliance
Lightning Source LLC
Chambersburg PA
CBHW072035190726
48294CB00005B/1268